PRAISE FOR `

'In *White Butterfly*, Saoirse Prendergast has walked that fine line between darkness and light. She has created a book that is written with a lightness of touch while, at the same time, dealing with coercive control, a darkness that has long been a weapon used by some men in their relationships with women. The thing that is most disturbing, most frightening and ultimately, most powerfully dealt with in *White Butterfly* is the banality with which that control is exercised. The author brings us ordinary, credible people who find themselves in very dark circumstances, people whose lives and losses are unforgettable.'

John MacKenna
Author, Broadcaster, Playwright & Poet

'An incredible, insightful portrayal of the solitary and self-loathing world of a victim of coercive control, and the power of evil to destroy lives. Yet despite the evident challenge to be understood, Saoirse crafts a meaningful pathway to hope, spotlighting the critical role of those heroes who provide support and refuge to women in need. A brilliant and much needed insight into the reverting crime of coercive control.'

Louise Crowley – Professor of Family Law, UCC

'A powerful debut by a powerful presence. This compelling book holds important insight. It tells the truth of what it means to suffer daily, incremental incidents that amount to abuse which can't always be determined. It is a powerful and present novel, true to the reality of what can't be seen and must be named. The chief achievement is that it is free of typecasting. It offers acute insight of how abuse can creep around the strongest growth and strangle it.'

Suzanne Power – Author, Mentor and Editor

‘A white butterfly, a symbol of purity and hope, representing comfort for those left behind. In *White Butterfly*, the author portrays the distressing torment of Sakura’s life, lived as a victim of coercive control. A story that draws you in, where you find yourself willing Sakura’s family and friends to listen, to hear, to see, whilst knowing that they can’t truly understand. A powerful insight – *White Butterfly* is a heart wrenching story that must be told.’

Lisa Kavanagh

‘*White Butterfly* shows what real love is through friendship and family and what unhealthy abusive relationships are and how this “can happen to anyone”. Coercive control is extremely hard to explain and hard for those around us to understand but Saoirse did an excellent job of showing the complexities of it and how it manifests itself. *White Butterfly* shows how ultimately it can ruin someone’s sense of self and their whole meaning of life. The story so eloquently shows the insidious nature of coercive control and the devastating consequences of it. The message is clear – with the right support and self-love, there is life after abuse, but it takes a lot of work.’

Lisa Morris – Manager, Amber Women's Refuge

‘*White Butterfly* takes the reader into Sakura’s world as a young girl dealing with a traumatic loss growing into womanhood. We see her excitement at falling in love accompanied by a sense of unease slowly creeping in to weave layers of confusion and self-doubt. We get to see how a relationship can present as loving and caring whilst Sakura navigates “invisible landmines under her feet.” We see the obliviousness of her family and friends to her being in a relationship where incremental woundings are obscured and concealed. This story illustrates the deep chasm that often exists between family and friends seeing and understanding when their loved one is in a coercive control relationship.’

Geraldine Kennedy – Psychotherapist MIAHIP

Therese
Enjoy reading
Saoirse

WHITE BUTTERFLY

SAOIRSE PRENDERGAST

Paperback edition
First published 2024 by Marble City Publishing
ISBN-10 1-908943-46-7
ISBN-13 978-1-908943-46-0

 Canadian English spelling is used throughout.

Let her sleep, for when she wakes, she will move mountains.

Napoleon Bonaparte

For Amélie and Freya

FALL

The white butterfly will never fly away from this moment.
Its wings folded, stuck to the board with a knife.
Watching it try to use the last of its life.
She disappears into a time when butterflies were free.
That was before him.

She was four then and followed the white butterfly's flight.
Its diving into the nectar, sucking its juices.
Her dad calling. His voice warm.
She smiled.

She smiles now, full of the memory.
But Sakura is a woman now. Not all butterflies live freely.
She has to leave the white butterfly of that time, to be in this one.

CHAPTER 1

A warm arm lays across her chest. There is hair stuck to her face.

Sakura moves the arm off, but not before her stomach realizes and hits her heart with a force that expels a scream. Who is making this sound?

Her mom grabs her, and their sobs melt into each other.

'I don't understand. Where is he? Where's Dad?'

'He's gone, he's gone, he… he… died.' Mom's words stumble out and fall into a whisper.

'But how did he die? Why did he die? He was fine, I don't understand.'

'I don't understand either. I'm sorry, I'm sorry.'

Tears find homes on the sheets, soaking through to the duvet. They pool behind their necks. Funeral's over, silly sorry-looking faces, standing too close, gripping her hands, hurting.

Later, through swollen eyes, she's nibbling toast, every mouthful a betrayal.

She sees her dad's mug on the counter, big fat mug, silly picture of a cat with pink whiskers.

'He's everywhere and nowhere.' Sakura runs out through the screen door, the outside big enough for her grief.

Mom is on the phone, talking low and slow. Her hair is matted and pulled into a low ponytail at the back, her eyes are red and she lowers her head into the phone. Sakura wouldn't want to listen anyway. Where is Eli? Where is Dad? Where is everyone?

Eli her brother, only a month ago he shared his hockey try out stories. He hoped to get selected. Sakura doesn't know if Eli is any good as far as others are concerned. But, in her mind, he's the best. Four years older, tall, and sporty.

He doesn't know how to do Dad not being there. No one knows what to do.

The McCleans. Now they are a family of only three. Pizza night needs the four of them.

Sakura can't go back inside. Jack. She needs Jack. They're sisters who don't live in the same house.

Without telling Mom, she walks out down their road, Cedar Lane. The panelled houses are dressed in flowers at the base. Wraparound porches hold baskets, and parched flowers droop their heads. Worn-out blankets are flung over swinging chairs, holding onto the last of summer. The winters here are harsh and long.

On schooldays, she'll meet Jack on the corner of her road, Rose Avenue, with its sight of the North Strait. Today is not a school day. The North Strait looks like a big, shining snake when it is calm. Sakura has walked this way alone since she turned ten. Dad wasn't sure of this at the time, but Mom convinced him.

This was her safe place, her South Acres Island. Filled with houses with no fences, and mowed lawns lining the invisible boundaries. During the hot summer months, you can see who mows weekly. The grass blades barely lifting above an inch. Her neighbour is one of them. He tends to give a gruff look at their house's longer grass blowing in the wind. Since it happened, he doesn't complain.

The locals call it Acres Island. The Island is small. They are protected. When the day is done most of the visitors leave. Islanders can pretend the bridge isn't there. Feeling no need to lock doors until late into the night.

The bridge joins the Island to the rest of Canada.

Sakura's house is less than a kilometre from the main town of Fort Cape.

The town leads down towards the harbour. Some houses with decorative bargeboards and creative shingle patterns, others have steep gables, intersecting roofs with dormers, turrets, and towers. Downtown Cape, the hub of Island life. People gather during festivals, and smells and colours change, depending on the season. Sakura's favourite, before all this, was the Harvest Festival. Pumpkins, bigger than hands can hold, are turned into pies, and decorations filled with lights and scary faces.

The Bridge reaches over eighteen kilometres, crosses ice-covered water. Islanders love telling visitors that it is the longest bridge in the world. Before, people had to fly or take boats to get here. Most welcomed the change. But a few begrudged it, citing too many visitors as a reason, wanting to keep it to themselves. Her family's neighbour is one of them. Dad welcomed the visitors.

Jack, on school days, will be waiting by the fence, same as always. One of them this year has no father. Jack's not at the fence, they haven't arranged anything. Sakura keeps walking.

Sakura can and does push open the screen and porch door at Jack's. Only once she found it locked and banged her nose right off the newly painted timber panel. She forgot they had left early for spring break that year.

Jack's mom opens the door and immediately her friend appears behind her. Jack's face changes from surprise to worry, her silk, even forehead scrunches over her eyes. No one knows what to do.

Suddenly she can't go in.

'Come in, Sakura.' Jack's mom stands aside to let her pass.

'Mina will leave us alone, won't she?' Jack asks her mom for reassurance. Her mom agrees. 'Come on, Sakura. We can go to my room.' Normally Mina, Jack's older sister, would shout from somewhere, '*Our* room!' Jack's sisters normally annoy her, mostly Mina, who she shares the biggest bedroom with. Now Mina leaves them alone. Ever since.

'No.' Sakura wants the days back when she had to comfort Jack over Mina's slow takeover of her space. 'I want to go back. I want to go back home.' Now she is the one who everyone feels sorry for.

'I'll drive you home.' Jack's mom Christine reaches for her keys. She keeps daily schedules for everyone on the refrigerator. The house is busy with fall returns. Vacation has ended. She helps in any way she can. Sakura likes Jack's parents, they're polite and always kind to her. Never make her feel like she has come through their door too many times in any one day.

Christine works in the local university and sometimes travels for her job. Then Dan, her dad, takes over. This annoys Jack as he doesn't do things the same way as her mom. Sakura feels differently. She loved being around her dad, especially when it was just the two of them. Now she can't look at Jack's parents. They're here.

'I want to walk home.' No one behaves the same around her.

'Then I'll walk with you and Jack.' Jack's mom, so kind and organized. Mom isn't anymore. Mom can't help or notice much anymore.

'I only want Jack!' Sakura was always polite to Jack's parents, even now it feels weird being so direct. But she can't help herself.

'Okay,' Christine says softly, 'we'll figure it.' The agreement is Jack's parents will come and get her as soon as Jack is ready.

Jack walks along and takes Sakura's limp arm. Sakura has always felt for both of them. She knows Jack feels awkward in the silence. She has never seen her so sad, even when her dog Sam died. This is different. Her whole world, their whole world, is forever changed. Jack wants to make her sadness disappear. She wants things to go back to the way they were.

'Maybe it's my fault, maybe it's my fault that Dad.... If I had got back on the boat, he wouldn't have...' her voice trails into nothing.

'It's not your fault,' Jack jumps in, 'you can't think that. Remember what you said about people going somewhere nice when they die?' Jack pulls her arm closer. She's normally excited, she's trying to sound like her mom. Talking about the time they found a dead mouse on the ground, on the way to school. Sakura had helped that day.

'We're not talking about mice! I don't want him to go somewhere nice. I want him here with me.' Sakura can't help it. She has to say what she really wants. Jack is the only one she can really say what she wants to.

The agreement is they'll just walk home. But Jack pulls her arm even closer. It's uncomfortable, but Sakura doesn't say anything.

'Come on, let's go to Tim's and get hot chocolate.'

Tim's, two streets over from theirs, is the perfect place to go for candy and everything else. The entrance door is small, and the inside is crowded by the stock overflowing on shelves that greet you on either side when you walk in.

Everyone is here in summer. Bikes are carelessly thrown on the ground by eager kids running in for their ice lollies. In winter, the snow is piled so high it's hard to use the kickstand for boots with any effect. Sakura wondered what was in all those jars high up. Her dad used to say it was cans, to stockpile, in case they needed to batten down the hatches.

'Before the bridge we could be cut off for weeks. Months in the old days.'

Sakura couldn't ever imagine such a scenario. Even on the worst snow day she could remember there had always been some store open, and even a place for her mom to get coffee. Tim's is not the best in town for hot chocolate, but it's their place. Chocolate lines Jack's upper lip. This would have been funny, now she wipes if off before Sakura notices.

'Hot chocolate is always nice.' Jack is the only one trying to make things as they've always been. Everything that dies goes somewhere nice. Sakura doesn't argue but wonders if anything will taste the same. 'Maybe after this we might buy a couple of Timbars?' Tim's own brand of candy. Another special thing about Acres Island. You don't get it anywhere else. She has five dollars in her pocket, but Mom says she can use their Tim's account, in case of emergency. Jack feels like this is an emergency. The account will rack up seventy-six dollars by Thanksgiving.

Fishponds, pizza on a Friday, Christmas, and Thanksgiving supper, Timbars, nothing will ever be the same. Sakura cries there in Tim's where she has always been happy.

Again the look of Jack's forehead. The smooth is scrunched up. When Jack looked like this before, Sakura could help her. Now she is the cause.

Jack goes to get her parents to take them back home.

CHAPTER 2

'That's everything then,' Dad says as he unties the boat.

'All aboard.' Sakura giggles. She loves saying that even though it's just the two of them.

'I thought you wouldn't be as keen now you have your horses,' Dad admits. She went to the riding school for last birthday and then had had the lessons after.

Her dad smiles, guiding the boat off into the near-perfect waters. Mid-August is the time to go. Before fall, before school's back, before everything.

'You see things differently from the ocean.' Sakura smiles, using his phrase. She doesn't really know what he means, even after he's tried to explain himself it just leaves her even more confused. But she knows he'd like to hear it now.

This day on the boat, it shows she still needs him and loves these times together in the same way she has done every summer since she can remember.

'The ocean is the other side of life,' he finishes off his own sentence. It's something he's said almost every time they run along to Barley Cove, past Heather's Cave. Sea erosion gives the appearance of a cave because of the jutting rocks overhead. His hand on the tiller and her watching the waves as they leave the harbour behind them.

Dad speaks about seeing things differently, here, where they are.

'Fishing soon, Sakura,' he says to her, but more to himself.

This simple act of casting. It's beautiful, an almost invisible sound. A few miles out, they drop anchor and start fishing.

'The line hits the water, then you wait and hope.' Dad gives another of his phrases. He shoulders into Sakura.

She's thinking of the gleams of a horse's eyes as the sun catches the water. Looking forward to riding out tomorrow. The horses are fast becoming her passion, but she still loves this side-by-side time.

Chat coming easy as they focus on something else. Her dad has this time with Eli too. A lot less now, since he turned sixteen. His room is also his kitchen and dining space. He likes to eat with his friends, or in front of his own screen. Sakura can't remember the last time they all watched a movie together. Dad and he don't banter anymore like they used to. It's not fighting, but it's not the same.

Last night she heard Dad saying to Mom in the kitchen,

'I dread the time when they'll no longer join me.' He was sorting tackle at the table.

'They may stop for a while, but they'll come back to it, and the memories are forever.' Mom would normally prevent him from putting hooks and barbs and cleaning the fishing rods at the kitchen table. But lately, because Eli is out of the house so much, at practice or at parties, or is in his house, his room, a life they know nothing about now, it's time they are counting down on.

Sakura walked in on them. 'I can't wait for tomorrow.' And she still meant it.

She still means it. She knows she's lucky. Dad has always been nearby. Other fathers' passions take them away from their children. Dad has shared his with them and been passionate about what they love too.

This day, Sakura's here, and he's delighted. Once or twice he's even gone out alone this summer because she and Eli haven't been free to join him. She's delighted too. The closeness is even stronger out on the water. It has never been her mom's thing. She joined them when Dad first got the boat over ten years ago. Painting is her thing.

'Ooh, I think I caught something,' Sakura shouts out, feeling tension and a pull on the line.

'Yes! Easy. Firm but gentle.' Her Dad shouts instructions with the same excitement. His eyes light up. He's never calm when there's a fish on the line.

'That doesn't make sense, Dad!' Her elbows clench close to her body. She turns the reel as fast as she dares, trying not to give the fish too much to fight against.

'You know what I mean. You've done this before.' He half laughs and leans over and helps steer the rod, his hand on hers, guiding. 'That's it. Oh wow!' he shouts at the first flash of silver. 'What a beauty! That will make for an awesome supper! Well done, Sakura.'

They pull the line up together. Sakura isn't grossed out by fish, she loves knowing that what they catch wild will directly go onto their plate later. Jack can't understand this. She will only eat fish sticks, so covered in breadcrumbs you can barely taste what's underneath.

The fish gasps on the deck, it's given up the fight for life. It lies flapping on the board.

At this end, Dad moves to the side to let Sakura get away. She still doesn't like this part, happy for him to take over. But she hears him do it as he did with his father and his grandfather, on different boats, at different times in the same waters. There's a crunch and a sudden stillness.

'It's okay. It's done.' She hears the sound of the catch landing in the icebox and the lid closing down. 'You caught a beauty. A beauty, Sakura.'

Sakura is chuffed. She likes bass, but seeing her father's pride and joy makes her feel great. She knows he loves her completely. This is just extra. Moments only they remember. Only they have.

They recount the catching several times. The pull, the gleam of the fish, and the help he gave her guiding it in. And she thinks of the talk between Mom and Dad she heard in the kitchen. The things she thought he and Mom did just because they were good parents, well, her dad loves them as much as she does.

'I wonder what the feast is in the cool bag?' Dad asks. Sakura already knows.

Mom has packed tuna sandwiches and homemade pie for lunch.

He takes out his thermos and then they sip tea and dangle their legs off the edge of the boat. Getting warm before the ocean dive.

'Time for a swim,' Sakura shouts, suddenly younger than twelve, forgetting she is growing up.

'Maybe in a while. Let lunch settle,' Dad responds with a yawn. She knows soon he will be resting his eyes, work cares lost, feeling a different side of life.

When they get home Eli will look a little funny, and shrug, and say, 'Wish I was there too.' But then, as soon as supper is eaten, he'll go out. Mom and Dad will be busy having a Saturday night together. Sakura may go and see Jack. It's all changing. But now is now.

Sakura takes herself off and suns herself on deck with her book. She borrowed it from Jack, who borrowed it from her older sister, Nina. It's all about Addison who has a superpower. Sakura loves reading about her adventures, bit like her own but wilder. She doesn't need a superpower right now. She's enough as she is.

Later she will think of Addison and would wish for a tenth of her magic.

Later again, she will realize that she has all of it, a hundred percent.

*

Afternoon arrives and she and Dad jump into the cool blue. It always takes a minute, and then she begins to feel like the fish do, weightless and free. Dad is splashing her and laughing.

They climb up the ladder onto the deck, it's hard to do when your limbs are cold. But he pushes her ahead of him.

'Looks like I caught another!' He laughs. They throw on clothes, drink the rest of the thermos and warmth comes back into them.

'Time to make landfall.' He opens the throttle and pushes the boat into gear, nosing back towards home. 'Time to ride the white horses, just like your friend at Tye's Stables, Sakura.'

She knows Dad is saying it's ok, Sakura. Eli has his hockey, you have your stables. Somehow it all feels okay. They will always have boat trips and they can change and still come out on the water together. He's heard from Mom that she loves a horse at the stables that most find difficult. But she and Snowy have a connection, that's what Tye says. She's coming on so well that they will buy her riding boots. For now, she's borrowing some from the stables. Her mom always talks about committing to something before investing. She will be able to go riding every week. She can come out here too. There's time for both.

They bounce across the ocean on the way back. Sakura watches Heather's Cave appear and disappear. She looks back out to the horizon, where they have just been.

She looks at her dad as he loves to be, outside, on water, with her, and the only thing that would make it even more perfect is if Mom and Eli came too. But then she wouldn't get him all to herself. There's still a part of her that loves that. She thinks about what she overheard. She wants to say to him, when she was ten, she didn't want anything to change either. Now she's twelve coming up for thirteen, she can see Dad feels that way too. His life has been doing things for his kids. That's how he shows his love. But he looks so happy, right now. She wants to say,

'Dad, stop working so hard. You should go out fishing more, you love it.'

The journey back is always shorter, and the jetty comes into view too soon. There's still light left in the sky. The sun is setting fast.

'You hop off first Sakura, I want to secure this.' Grabbing the rope, her dad ties the boat to the pier.

'I'll take stuff off too,' she offers.

'No, I've got this.' He hops back aboard to retrieve the satchels and their beauty catch. 'You've had a long day. I'll pass things up to you.'

Sakura stands waiting.

Notices her dad wobbling.

This sets the lunch bag free.

It's landing in the water.

'Oh no!' she shouts out.

CHAPTER 3

Jack and Sakura don't take so long to walk home from school now. She has to get back to see how Mom is. Sometimes she just doesn't know what to do. The one person to help her with Mom has gone. Dad always seemed to be grown up. He wasn't as distracted when she told him things.

Sakura felt his complete eye gaze when she wanted his attention, last fall it was all about the pond. She can still remember trying to talk to Jack about it. It was to be a science project. Jack wanted to talk about boys more than she did. 'I'm going to ask him when I get home.' Jack had already forgotten what.

The time of waiting for Dad to come home from work was always so long. She knew he'd get excited more than anyone else about this. He'd plan it and build it. Mom was busy. Meals were her way of showing love. There are few meals now.

The fridge was new last year, always full and it made ice. It was a Friday, the day Sakura asked. The day of the week Mom made pizzas, they tried out different toppings but always reverted to pepperoni and peppers.

When she walked through the door the pizzas were done. Mom put them straight in the oven as soon as she heard Sakura come in.

'Dad's home early today, and Eli too.'

Sakura's heart lifted, taking it as a sign.

'We'll have supper soon. Can you fill the big water jug and put ice into it?' Her mom threw her eyes up high to the top shelf, home of the larger things that didn't fit anywhere else.

'Hey, my job!' Eli shouted out on the way up from his bedroom. He had turned icemaking into a craft. Dad would craft the pond with his spade. Sakura knew.

He came up out of the shower. Clean and smiling. His big arm reached around and pretended to tickle her. Sakura ran away, then ran back. How thick his hair is and how dark its colour. Jack's dad was balding. He had started to shave it all off.

'Dad, I have something to ask,' she began before they even sat down, needing an ally.

By the end of supper Dad was on her side, and took Mom on.

'Marie, honey, I think Sakura needs this pond. It's the biggest school project. We all need to help.'

'Not near my hydrangeas, Mike, please.' Mom rose her eyes to heaven.

Eli sighed, but he didn't say no.

That Saturday she woke earlier than anyone. After much discussion, the smell of soil, budding chanterelles and hard work danced with the golden leaves and encircled their urban yard. Hours later, after much digging, a hole resembling a small pond emerged.

Sakura hovered around, offering iced tea, encouraging the work to continue.

Her dark brown hair trails over her shoulder, kept in place with a hairband. She doesn't know there are ways you can look. She just looks the way she is. Brown eyes eager to see everything. That's the way she was that day.

By nightfall, Dad covered the hole and they all headed inside.

Several days later, it was filled with all things gathered by Sakura and Jack. She spent hours checking the fish and making sure they had enough food and places to hide. Everyone needs a place to hide.

She can't go down there now, his work, his hands, everywhere.

She couldn't even imagine Dad as a baby. He was smart and always knew what to do, even when she was fighting with Jack. Sakura and Jack aren't fighting but they can't have fun right now. It won't happen inside her. She wondered where Dad got his answers.

All these thoughts bring her right up to her front door. Her heart sinks further.

'Mom,' Sakura half shouts. Nothing. She follows the quietness towards a faint mumble in the bedroom.

'Ah, Sakura, you're home. There are leftovers in the fridge. I didn't get around to supper.'

Sakura can see the puffy eyes even with the curtains half-pulled. Mom sits up in the bed and shuffles the pillows to help her stay propped. She doesn't look like her mom. Mom was organized, always had her school things ready before Summer even ended, had her favourite breakfast ready for her birthday. Her love was busy, especially around meals and festive seasons. Sakura often wished she wouldn't notice if she missed practice or hadn't completed a school assignment.

Now she doesn't notice anything. It scares her.

'Are you ok, Blossom?' Mom sounds bleary and like she's been asleep all day. 'I…' She pulls Sakura's hand into hers, and tears fall.

'It's ok, Mom, I'm ok.' Sakura doesn't feel there's enough room for both their tears. So, her eyes stay dry. It's almost a month since it happened. She missed the start of this year's term. Never wanting to go back. But her mom insisted after three weeks.

Friday used to be the day for pizza and anything possible. Today the only smell in the kitchen is gone-off flowers and cooked food. Uneaten Pyrex dishes of lasagne and pasta bakes, wrapped in cling film, stack on top of each other. Some don't fit in the fridge, the fridge that did everything, but no one expected this, so they just lie on the countertop.

Seeing anyone walk towards their door, Sakura has taken to hiding.

When no one answers, she'll hear the clink of the dish gently placed at their front step outside their screen door. Hunger pangs are replaced with an ache that never leaves. Sakura has been at school all week and all she wants now is her own mother's food and warmth.

'Are you getting up?' She pulls her hand out of Mom's hold.

'In a while.' She turns to lay lower on the pillow. Mom doesn't even ask about Eli.

Eli is with his friends. Eli is always with his friends. They used to meet them all the time and Mom cooked for them. Now he never brings them here. Sakura is often asleep when he comes home, and he's gone before she gets up to make herself breakfast.

'Will I open the window a bit?' Sakura feels she has to be more grown up, and care about things that she shouldn't have to because her mom can't. The room smells funny. Her dad's smell was now mixed with something new, pain. She didn't know it could smell. But it does, a bit like Eli's hockey bag and the room she has for math class, things that she doesn't like.

'No.' Mom's now lying down fully again. She doesn't look tidy and neat anymore. Effortlessly pretty. That's how she always thought of her mom. No, she smells stale. Dad was tall, clean, and smelled fresh. She loved his hugs; her head reached his ribs. He was affectionate, and she never got to reach the age to mind. She wonders if it's easier for Eli since they didn't hug any more. Making her way to the kitchen, she sees Dad walking towards her in his robe and flip flops, out of the shower, towards the bedroom, towelling his thick hair.

'I never got to not want his hugs,' Sakura cries. Then she realizes she is alone and talking to herself. 'I would have in a while.' The while never came.

Sakura roughly cuts a square of a pasta dish onto a plate and puts it into the microwave. She's not sure how long for, sets the timer for three minutes. She doesn't put a lid on. Spitting food sounds are made with every heated rotation. It's not like anyone will care.

She leaves the kitchen for the small room that leads outside towards their yard, passing one of Mom's paintings on the way, near the double door. The small room is used for different things. At times Mom used it for painting, but then the canvases became too big. So she moved down to the spare room to paint and just dried them or put works in progress here. It was where Sakura's hair was cut every season. Sakura wishes for the haircuts she used to loathe. Before, she could never see why hair had to be trimmed. It's dead anyway. She remembers her last cut, just before she went out on the boat.

'Stay still.' Her mother brushed her hair and decided how much to take off. Each time Buddy Holly played. Canvases, stopped and started, surrounded them. Kana and the Ikigai book she gave Mom remembered.

'I am.' Sakura's resigned voice. She has dark eyes and brows, like her mother. A half-hour later, inches of hair scattered on the floor. What remained was beautiful, thick, and healthier looking. Her mother shaped this then.

'Do you remember why I named you?' she asked at that moment, one of few where she was alone with Sakura. Just like the boat with Dad. Except Sakura never wanted those trips to end and never was sure of why haircuts had to begin. To keep her amused and still, Mom often told her stories of her childhood.

Sakura was a natural name fit for her daughter when she burst into life in late April. Her mom loves the blossom tree, its pale pink flowers peaking in spring.

Mom planned to visit Mount Yoshino. Sakura believed her. She didn't know Mount Yoshino would disappear from the conversation and lie lost along with her mom's hardened brushes, no longer in use. Mom's love of Japanese culture started when she met Kana, new to the Island, right before meeting her Mike, Sakura's dad. These two events made her adult life. The love of painting was always with Mom. Even before Kana. But for some reason she had stopped.

That last haircut before the boat trip, she cut Sakura's hair surrounded by half-finished canvases, brought up from the spare room studio to make more room for the project in focus, bringing her artist's attention with scissors and comb.

'Kana and I became close quickly. Just like your father and me, I knew we were something for life together.' This story often came up. Sakura heard again how Kana just pushed a book into Mom's hands one day. It explained a Japanese concept; reason for being. Mom had followed it naturally to find her Ikigai.

'She had delicate small hands; she always had her head slightly bowed.' Mom snipped the fringe and smiled, inclining her own head to the memory. Paused, lost in a previous moment. Sakura shifted, jolting her back.

'You know, Kana brought painting back to me, Sakura. One day you'll find what you'll love most, and you'll have me reminding you not to let it go. You may not always be able to practice it, but you can't let it go forever, or you let yourself go.' Mom pulled Sakura's hair between finger and thumb to even out the layer she was cutting in. Neither one knew then what they would have to let go. These are the luxurious conversations where love of painting can be discussed because all other loves exist, unquestioned.

'Stay still, nearly done.' She steps further behind her, pressing Sakura's hair down with her spare hand, ready to nip any uneven bits.

Kana encouraged her mom to start painting again. She did and not long after she brought her work to the local art festival every fall. Kana helped her put them up, her biggest supporter. Many of her mom's paintings filled Kana's small home outside of town. But then she moved back to Japan, to care for her aging mother. They lost touch. But Kana had stayed in Mom's heart, the way only a true friend can.

Sakura would see Mom take out that book, touch its cover and carefully put it back safe again. Mom had stopped and started painting over the years. Later Sakura would realise its importance. The core of her existence. Before and beyond her arrival into the world.

'Passionate, ethereal, determined, wilful and gentle.' Mom, standing back to look at the daughter she and Mike have made. Dark features with a few freckles on the side of her nose. She is of her but not her. Sakura is Sakura.

The hair fallen to the ground, a part of what she was. They swept it up together and Sakura forgot she never liked it being done.

'A haircut for each season,' Mom advised. When will the next one happen? There, the painting that caught her eye, completed at the beginning of August, just before the boat trip. Mom was in one of her creative moods. A world of lupins, multicoloured, only darkened by the red soil below, near the frame's edge. Sakura stops and looks. She never really noticed it before. Now it stands a reminder of that time.

The room has become a landing ground for lost things, some of Eli's hockey gear, her dad's books, and his work folders. Picking up her dad's latest book, he was only starting to read it, judging by the bookmark. She can't open it, and puts it down, and opens one of the double doors to step outside. 'I'm alone,' she whispers to herself. A lump forms in her throat. She can't swallow. The pasta seems silly and pointless now.

Sakura doesn't want to go back inside, so she sits, staring. She used to think that her father's purpose was to be there for her. She was so sure of it. Whose decision was it to take him away? Who will look after her if Eli stops coming home altogether? What if Mom never gets out of bed again? What if she goes too? What if she dies too?

'My mom.' Sakura races down the hall. Her mother is asleep. 'Wake up,' Sakura whispers, but not too loud, so anyone will hear. A pain holds her heart in a clench. She stares at her mother. Her arm falls over her body, used tissues half held in her half-closed hand. She seems almost inhuman. Not her mother. Since the doctor called a while ago, she is less here. Sleeping more. Her mother used to make pizza and would want to know where Eli was all the time. This mother doesn't wake up and doesn't care to ask.

'Please.' Sakura tries again. Mom mumbles and stirs. Sakura lays on the ground, resting her back against the door and sobs all the sobs she has. None of them wake Mom. The tablets. She has taken too many to be roused.

Sakura wails, wiping snotty tears away on the back of her sleeve.

Eli is out with friends. The pasta will be eaten by wildlife on the deck.

Sakura crawls onto the bed, places her mother's heavy arm around her, and prays for sleep.

'No, no, Dad! Stop! No, no!' Sakura wakes up screaming,

Her mom runs in, grabs her midsleep and holds her till she stops gulping for air.

'It's ok, it's ok. I've got you. I've got you, Blossom.' Mom's voice is rushed. Holding her too tightly. Sakura doesn't mind. Pain is everywhere. Mom must have got up after she fell asleep with her. She's lying on the side of the bed where Dad used to be. The curtains are now fully closed, she doesn't know whether it's night or day.

She never thought you could hurt so much on the inside. That time when Cara in Grade Two laughed at her. Her wet pants, the juice exploded. The whole grade joined in. Sakura cried so much. She thought she'd never be the same again. After the pant wetting, Mom reassured that everything passes. Mom was always right then. Two weeks later it had.

'It will pass for us, Sakura, it will pass.' Mom is holding less tightly and speaking slower, softer. Sakura knows this is different. It will never pass,

'But I miss him. I miss him,' she cries out.

'I know, I miss him too, shush now.' Mom has slipped in beside her, holding her across her body now.

'My heart is sore. What if you die too?' Sakura burrows into her side.

'I'm not going anywhere.' She shushes her back to sleep and gently lays her down on the pillow. Putting her head beside her, stroking the hair she used to cut, and telling her the story of her friend who gave her back painting, who gave a love of all things Japanese, and the name of Sakura.

But Sakura already feels bits of her mom gone, down there, bits of them all down there, in the cold water. That day, she plays over and over in her head in a loop. If she retraces with enough details and force of mind, she can change the story, change the ending, change her now.

CHAPTER 4

She saw her dad keel, one foot on the jetty, one on the boat.

His body lurched, his landed foot drifted and banged against the side of the boat.

Losing the jetty, landing right beside the lunch bag bobbing in the water.

'Dad! Dad!' she screamed.

Jumping back on the boat, leaning over, trying to reach him.

The press of the rail against her belly, not enough, she has to lean out further.

His safety drills with her on land and on water. She has no time to grab the ring buoy.

His lifejacket is keeping him afloat. Hers stopping her from grabbing him. She strains more and falls in.

Gasping with the cold, she grips him with her fingers already turning white. She tries to pull him in, but she can't. Screaming against her lack of strength and his water-heavy body.

'The life jackets are life,' he warned constantly, and everyone complained. Now they are all that is keeping them afloat. She has a hand through the arm of his, grabbing his shirt, tugging.

'Don't jump in after anyone, throw them a line, secure the line.' He issued the advice.

There was no time to take it.

Hearing the commotion, a local fisherman, just docked for the day, runs over, jumps right in, and drags Dad away from Sakura. His hand under Dad's chin, he said to her sharply,

'Get to the pier.'

Sakura climbed out first, hauling herself up, no one to help her.

Just before summer ended Sakura began to feel afraid of change. She didn't mind the seasons once she was in them, but never liked to leave one. She was getting taller, and her thoughts seemed to be different. Her mom had spoken to her about things that would happen to her, explained that things were changing and would continue to change for Eli too, just in a different way.

But she didn't want to know, she didn't want changes. She wanted her world as it was. That's why she asked Dad for one more boat trip.

'Can I just pretend it's the start of summer again, please?' She was so surprised when he said yes, instantly.

'You can never say no to her, Mike,' Mom complained. 'There's so much to do before school!'

Later that night, when she heard them in the kitchen, when he was getting the tackle ready, having said to Mom how he felt, Sakura heard her say, just as she crept away to close her bedroom door,

'Mike, you always made time for them.'

The fisherman is already pulling Dad up over the side of the pier, onto the cold concrete. Breathing fast, racing back to help the man. But he doesn't need her. Dad's lying too still. A new scream ripples across the bay. Sakura's. But it doesn't feel like hers.

She crawls to where Dad is. Others have come now. Others are now helping. The last of the summer sailors arriving in for the day, some doing jobs before taking their boats out of the water for winter. She lies there beside Dad.

'What's wrong with him? You've got to help him. Help him!' Lifting her flailing arms and legs. Someone tries to take her away. She fights until they let her go.

'Dad, Dad!' She rolls over to put a hand on his face. But it's knocked away.

Someone is trying CPR.

She just needs to talk to him. He will wake up. They are doing it all wrong.

Even as the sun is beginning to set, she can see his face is a funny colour. She has seen him sleep; his arms normally thrown over, hair messed, followed by a snore. Just like today on the deck, while she was reading, when she cast glances over to him.

Here he is like a snow angel – arms and legs spread, his hair wet and flat, his face looks no colour she can think of.

'Get off him, get off him. You're hurting him.'

A big arm scoops her up, and she kicks in vain, sobbing big sobs.

'I want my dad. I want my dad.' She can see the man push down hard on her father's chest and counting. 'He's going to hurt him.'

The man trying to take away the sight of her father from her is not listening. She has seen this lots on TV and even in her own school's first aid course. But this is her dad. The arms carrying Sakura break their hold for a moment. Her tears fall. She tries to run back along to the place where Dad's lying. But the hands are pulling her away. This man just continues walking, pulling her by the wrist. Her cries fill the air. She just wants her dad.

There are people shouting and people running to help. Instructions fly through the air. An ambulance arrives. Another flashing vehicle. Uniforms and a stretcher.

They have formed a circle around her father.

Someone calls Mom.

She sits watching the boat. The icebox still on deck. Someone needs to go and get it.

Her mother's wailing at the pier. Eli has come with her. Eli screams.

Sakura is in the middle of them.

The beauty of a fish.

The fabulous supper he won't have.

CHAPTER 5

The smell of bacon greets her halfway up the hallway. Eight weeks since that day in mid-August. August will never just be August anymore. It will be the month of before and after the thirteenth. This is a new kind of Saturday.

'Good morning, Sakura. Sit down for a minute.' Squatting down in front of her, Mom places her hands on Sakura's knees. A small gesture but this causes Sakura to wobble. Even though she often holds her hand, this way means Mom can see her eyes and she can see hers. The crying has changed them.

'I'm sorry I haven't been there for you since…' Her voice not able at times to say those words. 'I guess I wasn't coping very well and shut you all out. When you needed me most, I wasn't there for you.' She's wearing her white sweater and light blue pants, trying hard to make this different. Her voice sounds calmer but still panicked. Like if she says it clearly enough it will stick.

But Sakura has heard this before. Four weeks after Dad died, Mom had a burst of energy, then by early evening, she was back in bed fully dressed.

'I'm so sorry. But I am here for you now, if you'll let me.' Her face seems smaller, her hair pulled back. She hasn't been eating.

'I missed you.' That's all Sakura can get out. Tears spill and drop from a height onto her mom's hands. Sakura hopes this time is different.

'Come here.' She pulls Sakura into her arms.

'I don't want to lose you too,' Sakura cries. At night, when the nightmares come, she goes to check if Mom is still asleep, or if she's died.

'You won't. I'm here now and always.' Her mom's knees still on the floor, she's moving her weight from one to the other, trying not to let her see the discomfort, keeping eye contact. Sakura looks away.

'Gosh these tiles, your dad was right!' The uneven floor tiles, a purchase from *House and Home*, were Mom's choice.

Sakura smiles at that. Dad wanted the lighter-coloured ones. Mom wanted these. Sakura remembers coming home from school and hopping from one to another. Playing hopscotch on the samples that took up space near the window, and more near the dining table.

'The lighting will make all of the difference,' she remembers Mom saying.

'We won't need the light it if we lay the other ones!' Dad responding.

One waiting for the other to give in.

Now, bits of the mosaic pattern dig into Mom. Sakura rises up from her chair, and Mom rises too. Here they hug big, still smaller than Dad's. She will never feel his hug again.

'Let's have breakfast. I've made your favourite.' Her mom breaks off and turns to stir the large jug of batter, white-grey clusters of flour forming on top. Pancakes piled high, drizzled with maple syrup. Sakura grabs a plate and tucks in.

Just over two months ago Dad was here, teasing, grabbing the last of the bacon, then sneaking it back onto Sakura's plate when she wasn't looking.

The pancake sticks in her throat, the maple syrup suddenly turning to bile in her mouth. Pushing her plate away, momentarily, and then pulling it back without her mom seeing.

The screen door squeaks, Eli joins them. He talks much less than he used to, which wasn't very much anyways. Sakura can read between his silences and see his softness. Never rebuking her when she looked for a hug. His feel more like Dad's. For the first few weeks they never saw Eli. Mom never saw anyone. It was Sakura who missed him.

'Up and out this early, already?' Mom looks at him. But Sakura knows Eli has only just come home. If Mom sees, she's pretending not to notice. 'Are you around later?'

He gives one of his still frequent hair flips in answer. He used to do this when they were out together before all this. Especially if they passed his friends. She also knew that was a time he found her annoying. Then she kept her distance. But she felt his protection. Like that time when they were on vacation during spring break, four years back. Tripping on the edge of a deck chair, she went straight in. The deep end. She felt his arm lift her right out. Sakura remembers feeling bad. Eli was dripping wet in his good clothes. They were all dressed to go out for supper. Now she feels his arm release and slip away and will again in years ahead. She will wish for that arm to hold her and save her again.

Pain hides behind his manner. It looks like indifference, almost angry, but Sakura sees it. She saw it before, the day he realized he didn't make it onto the AA hockey team. His brown eyes seem to fill his whole face. His lashes flapping trying to hold in the tears that just need to be released.

Sakura splits in two. Her pain and witnessing the pain of others. Wanting it to stop for Eli and Mom. Wanting it to stop for herself. The child in her leaping forward, pulling her into ignorant adulthood, without the years to back up her knowing how things are.

Eli disappears into hockey and his friends, and the rest of his time is spent in his room. When Mom isn't trying to be a mom, she's crying or painting, or both, in the spare room. Confused and broken right now, Eli not answering might send her crashing to the floor in sobbing fits.

'Come on, Eli, can you just give me an answer?' Mom pleads, but she isn't crying or falling down.

'Yes, think so, earlier on, why?'

'Hockey isn't on this afternoon?' Mom continues preparing extra pancakes that no one will eat. She's thinking measurements of four.

'No. Hmm, just the guys are meeting up later.' Eli slinks into the chair.

'Lucas?' Mom plates up the pancakes in front of him.

'Yeah.' Eli flicks his hair again. 'Think so, maybe.'

'As long as it's not too late, you have that big assignment for Monday.'

This is the first time she has even mentioned school. She's afraid either Sakura or Eli could ask what does she care? Either one of them could say it to her, how they had to get started this year without her. Mom had neighbours and friends bring food over. Some helped her with paperwork and organized the things they needed for school. But Eli and Sakura were on their own with being the McClean kids, who lost their dad over the summer. This year's Science Project, Sakura couldn't have cared less about.

Her mom fills the silence with extra chatter. But the number of three is so odd. Dad's chair is casually filled with clothes. It looks accidental, but Sakura sees through the half-fallen socks. Its emptiness is permanent. Her mother interrupts her grief.

'Let's go to the market after breakfast. We haven't been there in ages.'

'Sure,' Sakura responds.

Eli shakes his head.

Mom knows not to push. A wounded lion. She doesn't know how to reach him without getting clawed.

Later, Dad's clothing will disappear from the common areas. Sakura will look through bits of rags, hoping to find her dad's old clothes squared and used to clean. She'll find bits of herself, things she's grown out of, too worn to donate, scissored for new use.

The fall leaves colour the dashboard. Sakura puts on her favourite radio station.

Her mother lets the music sit between them.

It feels almost normal. Dad could be just at work. He often worked Saturday mornings. They park just outside and head into the market. The wooden rail leads to the opened door. A gust of unexpected wind blows the crowded noticeboard over. The blue paint on the external panels is starting to chip close to the ground. The smells travel out to greet them.

Looking over at her mom, she's trying to read her face and wonders if she is ok. She never wondered this before.

Inside, the natural oil scent entices them over to a stall, and her mom buys lavender soap. Next, they discuss how many mussels they will need for supper. She is trying hard. Sakura likes being a part of the decision.

'Let's have coffee, I'll get you a hot chocolate,' Mom shouts over the noise of the grinder.

Sakura is swirling the marshmallows around with her finger. They break and melt. She's sitting down, waiting for Mom who is at the counter. Mom comes with a cappuccino and they both for a moment sit at a table, and it feels almost normal. They're not speaking. But it's okay. Their silence and comfort interrupted by a voice calling her mother's name.

'I'm sorry to hear about Mike.' It's their neighbour, Nancy, standing over them. Nancy's husband is the guy who gets grumpy if the lawn is not mowed to his standards. Now the grass is high, and he doesn't say a word. He has offered to mow theirs. Mom said no, leave it. She liked things neat, now everything is everywhere, and order is gone. Unsafe.

She reaches down and covers her mother's hand. Sakura wants her to leave. She managed to park it, the death, just for a moment. She wants not to really know death. Her Nana May died when she was a baby, her mom's mom. She was old, it didn't seem to be a big thing. And then there was Jack's neighbour, he was hit by a car. She remembered someone saying he was drunk. It was whispered, like a secret. He was kind of old, at least over fifty and no one was that shocked. But she couldn't understand, being too young.

In her head it was just old people that died. And they never come back. Nancy is bringing it up. Making them remember. She and Mom did this kind of Saturday together and it might be possible to pretend Dad is back at the house. His being gone isn't taking up huge space, like it normally does. Now it is. Mom stands up to take Nancy a little further away. They are almost whispering. Like they are saying something wrong.

Sakura can hear everything. Nancy's apologizing for not coming near them at the funeral, wanting to give them space. All faces merged into one that day. Big, embarrassed, pitying, scattered eyes. It's the same things she hears every time Mom and she bump into someone.

At school kids never mention it. But they give her that look, eyes down and take a step back. Like Mina does when she walks into the room while she's at Jack's. She just wishes Mina would go back to her mean old self.

Nancy finishes with offers of help if needed, while she holds Mom's hand too tightly.

'Thank you,' her mother responds. Her eyes look up then back down.

Sakura wonders why everyone is sorry. It's not their fault. She still feels it's partly hers. If she had managed to get him out quicker, maybe he could have been saved. Sakura repeatedly imagines water going into his nose before the life jacket self-corrected his position, mostly a part of her nightmares, no one to stop it. Even though she heard it was his heart, Sakura doesn't believe this.

Nancy looks awkwardly across to Sakura and then back to her mother,

'Call to the house whenever suits.'

'Sure. Thanks, Nancy.' They'll never call up.

Sakura looks at her marshmallows. They seem to mock her. She hates them. Now she hates Nancy. Why couldn't she just leave them alone? She has to pin her eyes wider. She isn't going to cry in here. People pushing past. Cotton bags swing and lie on the floor close to their feet. They don't know her dad. They don't know he died. Chatting like everything is normal. Vegetable stalks stick their heads out. Steaming coffees in hand. Sausage rolls with mustard sauce sliding down the side. One man licks his up. Grief, it follows you everywhere. The comfort is gone.

'Let's go home.' Her mom leaves her still hot, half-drunk cappuccino on the table. Sakura follows her through the market to the outside.

Sitting in the car, heaviness fills the space where music was. Sakura can feel her tears bubble from her heart, looking straight ahead. She dare not look across to the driver's seat.

In that moment, her mother pulls her over. She has seen Sakura's unseen eyes. Her body half over the console, and her head rests on her mother's lap. She wails, the bubble is released.

'This is tough, this will be very tough, but we will be ok.' Her mother's words are almost unheard. 'It will be ok, we'll be ok.' Her mom doesn't sound convincing, like the time Sakura decided to layer her hair, copying a magazine Jack took from Mina. Her mom wasn't annoyed, more panicked.

'It's fine,' she kept saying, ruffling her hands through Sakura's zig-zagged strands. 'We just need to even them out.' Grabbing her phone, she scrolled down, looking for her hairdresser's number. She didn't believe her then. she doesn't believe her now. That was minor. Sakura didn't really care what way her hair looked.

Chapter 6

'Are you not waiting for Jack to walk to school?' her mother shouts from the kitchen.

'I need to go in early, ahead of her, for my project,' Sakura shouts back, continuing to walk. The Science Project was done last week.

'Oh yes.' Mom trying to pretend that she hasn't forgotten. But it's never been said. 'Best of luck, it will be great.' She planting a kiss on her forehead.

Sakura doesn't need to go in early for anything. She's finding it hard to be with people, including her best friend. Since Dad died, she feels misplaced, like she shouldn't be here. She's the one who lost her father, that's how everyone thinks of her now. They started off wanting to know what happened. But when she wouldn't or couldn't tell them, they started to feel awkward.

'I was there, I was the *only* one who was there,' she says to herself as she walks the road, past Rose Avenue, past the spot where Jack used to dump her backpack. Now all Sakura walks with is what she's lost. She was there with Dad, and now she remains among the living. Later the lines will become blurred between what living is and what dying is. She curses the leaves on the ground, kicking them away.

'Why don't you go and die!' she shouts to herself. 'Just get this over with.' Angry tears appear, roughly wiping them away. Forgetting she can be heard. Then she composes herself, pushing her pain away into the crack now formed in her bitten bottom lip.

This road brought her and Jack to so many places. They were happy safe legs then, that could walk for ages, and mouths that never stopped talking, or Jack's didn't.

Now silent, heavy, and feeling misunderstood, she trudges alone.

'Sakura, Sakura!'

She hears a faint call of her name. Turning around, she sees Jack running to try and catch up.

'Why didn't you call for me? I would have gone in early with you,' Jack pleads with sad, abandoned eyes.

'I didn't think of it.'

'Never mind.' Jack links her arm. 'We're together now, aren't we?'

Sakura allows Jack to chat about their plans for the weekend. Avril is having a party, and Jack is planning to buy a new outfit. It almost feels normal, then she remembers she couldn't tell Dad about this year's Science Project. It was still good even though it was done without his help. She can't tell him about the party, how she doesn't like them, and pain fills her heart.

'It's just a stupid party,' Sakura utters.

'Why do you have to be so mean?' Jack responds sadly. 'I'm trying to help you.'

'Well, you can't help me. No one can.' Sakura runs off and takes a road right down to the stream and covers her eyes, but the tears still come and come.

Later, her mom is cooking supper as Sakura walks into the kitchen.

'How did it go?' she asks.

'Okay, I guess.' Sakura gulps orange juice from the carton. How will she say she didn't make it to school today? What will she say if Mom asks about the project? Mom walks over to the fridge and gently takes the carton from her while pointing to the glass cabinet in this kitchen where she looked forward to Friday nights. To the side, under the table, Sakura sees the footstool. The one she used to reach things. The sink when she was three. The top shelf now. Three is a time of wishes. Three wishes. She wants them now.

Sakura wants to push through the screen door, to be here, before.

Her mom making homemade pizza. Balancing freshly rolled dough, kicking the cupboard closed with her free foot. Waiting for Dad to come home. Waiting for Eli to come home. Sakura watching her at work. Her hair dark like Sakura's, just above her shoulder. Tied back, low ponytail. Cut straight, sharp. Always looks neat, smart. She's beautiful. Sakura remembers holding her face when she was younger and telling her this often. Mom always responded,

'Most important you're beautiful here,' putting her hand to Sakura's beating heart.

Sakura fetching things with the footstool she used on her littler legs, lifting one at a time, stepped up to reach the sink. Washing her hands took forever. Her mom repeated, 'I think they're clean,' trying not to get impatient and to encourage her daughter's newly found independence. The stool is faded, the blue colour gone, now a dirty off-white, but still there. Her second wish – that her life is still here. That her dad comes early, through the screen door.

'Hey, let me take that from you.' Him grabbing the full jug like it's a glass of water.

'I thought I was going to drop it.' Sakura could breathe. One day it will tumble and crash because he's not there. Little bits of broken glass will pierce her delicate skin, land close to her heart. Too close. But she is wishing now. And Mom turning around to see Dad catching hold. She and Dad smiling at her and then each other.

Her third wish. Her world to be perfect again. To not know any different. Eli arriving, flicking his hair. The four of them to tuck in, swatting away the last of the summer flies.

'I'll get the citronella.' Dad pushing back his deck chair and heading into the garage. Always anticipating the next thing, watching her mom tap the food, unbalancing a mosquito. The side door a few steps down from their backyard. Her dad repainted the door azure blue. Her mom's favourite colour.

'I'll come with, and get the lights.' Eli jumping up. They're all holding onto summer.

Dad still taller than Eli, but not for much longer. His hair dark, darker than Mom's. They all wonder where Eli got his sandy hair. Dad's arms tanned, lightening at the top of his polo shirt. He works as an engineer with a local construction company. Sakura doesn't really know what this means. She sees his hard hat and high vis jacket on the floor beside his laptop bag. This is when he's really hungry and doesn't want to move it out of the kitchen. He does later before he fills the dishwasher every evening.

He has his everything with them. When you wish....

Mom's voice pulls Sakura back, just the two of them. Sakura meets her gaze and immediately looks away. She can't bear it. But her mother gently puts her arms around her, and she doesn't resist. It's the first time she has felt real all day, and safe.

The screen door bangs. It's Eli.

'Supper must be ready.' He talks low, dropping all his gear in the kitchen, like Dad.

Her mother breaks the hug.

'How was your day?'

Eli responds with almost inaudible words and few of them.

They sit around the table, and her mom's constant talking means she and Eli don't have to. Her attempt to normalize things pushes Sakura's grief into the corner of her plate.

Eli always eats quickly. Within a few minutes, he's gone. A different bag swings from his shoulder. Someone is giving him a ride. Her mother doesn't take him anymore. It has something to do with Dad once being in the crowd, being tall and seen, and Mom just can't fill that space. So, they aren't trying.

Lately, there are only two chairs filled at the table.

After, her mother suggests,

'Let's get watching a movie, a comedy. Something Eli will object to!'

'I'm ok with that.' Sakura smiles.

'No homework?'

'No.' None that she knows of anyway.

Part of her had hoped Jack would tell her parents. But then this part of her doesn't, not now they are sitting on the sofa. In between moments of escaped laughter, Sakura glances at her father's empty place on the couch.

The image of him lying there cold and wet on the concrete becomes her whole vision even when she tries to blink it away. If she leaned in and let her hand brush against the cool water in the jug that didn't break, she might sense the ripples of what's to come. When she is quiet, so quiet. The world reveals its everything. Past, present, and future become miscible.

Later, Sakura will think back to this time and try dissecting it. Did she distort the reality, glossing over the rough edges? No, she hadn't. Dad was happy. His face warm and kind. Content, he wasn't looking for something else.

Shaking her head to move the sight of him on the pier, she snuggles into her mom, an attempt to move towards the living, away from the dead.

'Why don't you bunk in with me this evening?' Her mother yawns, on her way to bed. Eli is still not back. Later she gets a message from Lucas' mom, he's with them. She'll drop him back in the morning.

That night, she sleeps beside her mother, snuggled in darkness.

CHAPTER 7

Late October, leaves hanging on by a thread, knowing it's time to fall. Change colour, change form, disappear into the earth. Become again. She overhears her mother on the phone. It seems like she's onto someone important, talking in that voice.

'Who was that?' she asks after Mom hangs up.

'Oh, just the bank.'

'What did they want?' Sakura knows it's where the money is kept. She has seen them use what she calls the magic card. 'It's not a magic card,' she heard Mom saying last year when Eli wanted a new hockey jersey. But it was, they got everything they needed and mostly what they wanted.

'Nothing for you to worry about.'

But Sakura does worry.

'See you later.' Sakura pulls her hat down over her ears. She leaves for Jack's house. That day she skipped school Jack told no one and made an excuse to the teachers when Sakura didn't show. No one bothers them at the moment if she and Eli go missing without proper absence notes. It made Sakura realize that Jack was trying really hard to keep being her best friend and that should count for something.

'Okay, don't be late for supper.' The meals are regular again, but Mom about everything else, all the time, is distracted.

She knocks her secret knock, two quick, followed by one big. Jack comes running.

'Hiya,' she says, beaming. 'Come in. I have a new game. Do you want to see it?' Placing stray hair behind her ear, revealing her ladybird earrings. They picked them out together on their trip during the summer to Merlin. Sakura chose hummingbirds. They're on the locker beside her bed. Safe in a trinket box.

'Yes, great, which game did you get?' Sakura asks, following her inside. The last time she didn't want to come in to see Jack's dad's bald head in a chair, reading or watching TV. She didn't want to see two parents. Some days she can, today is one of those days. Jack's parents are always nice. Even Jack's sisters are nicer now.

Later, she and Jack are sipping juice. Cards, dice and figures scattered on the table.

'I'm sorry about the other day,' Sakura says while pushing her drink around. 'Thanks for covering for me.'

'It's ok, where did you go?' Jack never asked before. But she was waiting, earlier the next day, in case Sakura tried going to school on her own again.

Sakura can't answer. It was just anywhere at all. Sometimes back to the pier, watching it all happen again in slow motion. If she could just stop the reel. It would all change.

'Come on, let's go get some treats.' Jack playfully grabs her arm and walks her into the kitchen. 'Are you ok, you seem a bit quieter?' She has started to read her new moods in between the old. Jack pulls a chair over to the high larder press, where the best treats are kept.

'Yeah, just, you know.' Sakura doesn't want to talk about the call she heard and her worries. 'Hey, what do you have?' she distracts Jack.

'Catch!' Jack drops her bags of Lays chips, and they head to the fridge to restock on juice.

This moment feels good, but a small part of Sakura remains behind, trying not to think of her own half-empty kitchen, her own half-empty family, and phone calls she can't follow.

She wants to get back to the game, to being best friends in Jack's room. Mina never bursts in now.

'We won't get away with this forever.' Jack sighs. 'She keeps complaining, but Mom and Dad keep telling her to leave us alone.'

That's the thing Sakura wants to change, she wants Mina to be bursting in, annoying them. Jack goes quiet a moment, realizing what she's said, then they start to play another round of the game again.

December first. Sakura wants to change the date back to yesterday when it's still November, back to four months ago, when her dad was still here.

She goes over to the calendar on the wall and puts it back to August, and she sees the writing on the August thirteenth square –

Boat trip with Dad.

She didn't recognize her writing and then she remembers, she had wanted to have something she wrote on the calendar too, not just school starting, or extracurricular things. She wanted to write something special as the summer ebbed away.

She reads it and re-reads it, wishing it to be now or in the future, to rewrite it. She is jolted by the screen door opening.

Mom arrives with groceries under her arms. She helps her unpack, and the calendar remains open in August. Brochures for a Christmas getaway lie on the countertop,

'I thought we could do something different this year and go away. We'll chat about it when Eli comes home.'

'Where would we go?' Sakura's heart fills with small hope. She won't have to stand watching the town tree light up. She won't have to put the red and gold-themed decorations up and pretend. But she will still have to be somewhere.

'It will be weird without... you know, but it might be better than staying here.' Her mother is putting things away, she spots the mozzarella. Maybe pizza can happen again. They haven't made it since....

Then it occurs to Sakura. This will be the first trip without him. The first time new memories are not made for four. Really neither option seems good. She glances back at the calendar where the August lupins stand out in full colour. That's where Mom got the painting idea from. Suddenly she feels her heart will burst. She can't talk. She needs to leave.

'I'm just going to Jack's.' Already pulling on one of her boots.

'It's too late, you'll see her tomorrow.' Mom opens the fridge.

'Just need to drop a book over. She needs it for her homework.' If she doesn't get out, she will scream. Her mother is doing her best. Where is Eli? Why can't he hear this too? It's always her around. It's never him listening to Mom's phone call, dealing with her ideas.

'Okay, come right back, it's getting late.' Mom sounds confused but isn't quick enough to catch up on her.

She runs all the way and arrives panting at Jack's door.

'What are you doing here?' Jack looks surprised.

'Just needed to get out, can I come in?' Sakura hovers, what if Mina is in the room? This isn't planned.

'Yeah sure, Mina's at practice, head to my room?' Jack stands back as the cool rushes in past her.

'I just don't know how she can talk about vacations.' Sakura is pacing up and down Jack's bedroom. Mina arrives home but hasn't barged in. In fact, most people don't come near her. They don't know what to say. Like she'll explode. Most days Sakura feels as though she will.

'And how will we afford this? I heard her talking to the bank a few weeks back. I want Christmas here like it used to be with Dad.' Sakura stops pacing and sits down on Jack's bed, holding her hands up, catching her tears as they fall.

'Come here.' Jack pulls her onto the bed. 'I'm sorry, I know how much you miss him.'

They sit for a while longer, then Sakura suddenly jumps up.

'Mom will be worried, I told her I was just dropping off a book, better go.'

'I heard her on the phone to my mom before you arrived,' Jack admits. 'I didn't think it would be that you were coming over. They sometimes talk to each other.'

'Do they?' Another thing to dread. How is Sakura? How is Jack coping with Sakura?

'We all love you.' Jack has a way of putting things right. Sakura feels relief. This can't be done without her best friend. If she is leaning too heavily, Jack might be taken away from her too.

Walking Sakura out, Jack waits until she has her boots back on.

'See you in the morning, talk then.' Jack hugs her.

'You are great. I…' Sakura can't say any more. Closing the little gate behind her, Sakura walks under the streetlights as snowflakes begin to fall, catching one, seeing all the ice crystals.

She imagines one of them is her dad. Completely unique, completely gone. The snow is on time this year. Last year it fell early. She went outside with Dad to clear their drive.

'A bit earlier than expected, it wasn't due till next week, the mini-storm that was forecast.' Dad sounds muffled beneath his neck warmer, pulled up just under his nose.

'Kind of like it though. It's like a blanket.' Sakura shovels deeper without much success. 'And love the snowball fights!'

'Snowballs eh?' Dad turns, grabs a fistful before Sakura has time to move. It lands and little ice crystals sneak under the top of her coat, coldness causes her to yelp.

'I'm going to get you.' Sakura makes a bigger one and takes after him.

Shovels remain on the ground where they were thrown. The snowball fight lasts until they both can't feel their feet.

The Christmas conversation continues the next day. Someone has changed the month on the calendar back to December. Their lives are transformed in winter, icecaps, hills, frozen lakes, inches of snow. They adapt. They learn to. The place where white Christmases are expected and mostly delivered on.

It's all Sakura's known. When she was five of her dad's hands high. Building snowmen, where mounds looked like mountains. The fun sleighing down Taylor's hill with friends at the weekend. She misses the moving rivers and sea but loves its quietness. Sakura and Jack feel they should whisper on their early morning walk to school. They were always told to respect the winter. It, too, has its promises.

Sakura drifts back to this time last year. Ice skating with everyone at the local arena. Dad, with his new winter jacket and ridiculous yellow hat. Sakura laughs at him, watching him spend most of the session holding the side of the rink. Jack looping around him with elegance. His face beaming and not caring if he looks clumsy.

'You make it look so easy,' Dad shouts over. One time he braved it into the middle.

'Come on, I'll show you.' Sakura skates up alongside him, and takes his big, gloved hand.

Sakura moves her left hand over her right, imagines it's Dad's. She's pulled back by voices. She doesn't want to be here. Rubbing her own hands is empty.

'I don't mind, either way,' Eli says in a voice that means he does not care.

Sakura has thoughts overnight of watching all the other dads at the tree lighting, and nods. Nothing will make them feel better. They might as well hurt somewhere else.

Mom looks relieved and presses on, telling them a short time later,

'Okay, two weeks in Florida. We leave December eighteenth.'

For once, Eli is still around to hear.

For ten days. All the main Christmas memories with her dad took place during that time. But no matter how hard Sakura tries to move them away, they travel thousands of miles west.

CHAPTER 8

The ocean can be seen from their beach house windows. It is beautiful, but a heaviness sits where joy should be. Outside, instead of sunshine, she can see the snowstorms of last year.

The snowstorm passed and it was time for Christmas to begin. Most wait until ten days before taking this step. But not the McLean family. 'M&M's,' Sakura joked. Marie and Mike. To her, always, Mom and Dad. They have their own timings, their own traditions.

Sakura hearing the sound of the pickup. Dad's pulled it up to the front. Making space. The trunk is finally empty.

'That should do it.' Banging it closed, Dad hops in and starts the engine again with a roar.

'Come on. The best ones will be gone!' he shouts out.

'We're coming,' Sakura shouts back, running out and bagging shotgun.

'Hey, you.' Dad looks over and does his playful wink. He smells fresh, woody. On Saturday mornings, he always smells different. Mom says it's the aftershave she bought for his birthday. He keeps it for weekends and special occasions.

Mom opens the front passenger door, and after arguing, Sakura jumps in the back with Eli.

'I wanted to sit up front!' Mom is playing *Santa Baby* and singing along badly.

'Stop, Mom,' Eli mumbles, mortified. He pulls down his hat over his eyes.

They arrive outside the wooden house, the half fallen *Cedar Cove* sign swings above their head and the smell of hot apple juice and cinnamon meets their noses on the way in.

Cups in hand, they head to the forest, and after surprisingly little arguing, they pick their tree. They all love real and big. Wrapped up. It's loaded up and ready for decorating.

The last real tree they were to have.

In this out of season sunshine, in the bedroom next door, Eli is whistling and changing into his shorts. This annoys Sakura. How can he be happy?

'Come on, Sakura, let's go down to the beach,' Mom shouts down to the bedroom Sakura's sharing with her in their little beach house. Eli has one on his own. Mom is in the living area.

'Maybe later,' she responds, curling into her pillow.

'Ah, come on, it looks lovely,' Mom persists. She knows Sakura can see the sea too.

'Yeah.' Eli bangs on her door and lets out a bright shout. 'Come on.'

'No, how can you both act like he's not here?' she shouts, leaps out of bed and wrenches open the door.

'I'm just trying to make the best of it,' Mom says quietly. She's standing in the corridor in her beach dress, like everything is okay. Behind her, Eli is in his neon pink shorts, and has resuscitated his lime green trainers. He shrivels his eyes so they can't be seen. The red tell-tale rims, half hidden, his head down, in the darkness of the little passage.

'Stop wearing all this bright stuff.'

The two of them are looking in at her. She can't stand being with them, being without Dad, being somewhere where they should be happy.

'We need to make the best of this, Sakura.' Mom comes towards her. Eli shrinks back.

'What's the point?' Sakura runs past them to the washroom and slams the door.

Sitting on the floor, crying into the freshly cleaned tiles, Sakura whispers in sobs,

'Where are you, Dad? I need your help,' she whimpers. She doesn't want to swim in the sea he died in. The sea she tried to pull him out of. She turns on the tap to shroud the noise of her crying.

When the tears are all gone, Sakura lifts herself off the floor and returns to the kitchen-dining space. It looks onto the ocean. Its beauty is painful. Sakura turns away, holding onto the counter. Eli sits on one of the little blue and white striped couches, playing on his phone. Twirling his hair with his free hand. Mom arrives beside her.

'Sit down,' Mom instructs, bringing her to the sofa Eli's on, gently patting Eli's leg. He shuffles himself up and looks lost. 'I thought it would be good to get away. Just to…' Mom's voice trails off. 'I'm sorry. There are so many reminders everywhere at home, with everyone asking. I just thought this would be easier.' Brushing her hand against her lip, holding her grief in. She looks away to the window.

Sakura holds her own hands, afraid to look at either of them.

'It's fine, we're here now,' Eli mumbles. Sakura is surprised and confused by his addition. It might be something Dad would have said. The words don't seem to fit with his changing voice. He's sixteen now. He never knows what voice he is going to wake up with or use. Why can't anything be the same?

At least at home, Sakura would have Dad closer. Here he seems lost, as though he always was and never was. At home, his things are there, his smell still lingers at a certain time, certain parts, especially when she walks into their room, near the side of the bed where he slept. Her mom keeps it empty.

'Okay,' Sakura agrees. 'I'll come.' They hug her from both sides. She wants to say how awful it is, what she's thinking of. Burying her words.

Falling in slow motion over the next few days. The water providing occasional relief from her constant ache. On the last night, they are packed and eating their last meal. The next year has begun. The first one without Dad. No one knows what to do, or to say.

They return home, the sun behind them, becoming the harsh winter.

CHAPTER 9

Seven months pass in the first year her father won't live in.

School happens. Jack waits for her. Mom busying herself. She has a part-time job in the local tax office. And Eli is just Eli. But everything is different.

There are some days when she wakes up and knows she can't take it. She pushes this down. Until it escapes in Math, at the sight of a white butterfly nestled in the corner of the class window.

She can remember, she was four, Dad was telling her all about the miracle of the butterfly, as a white one fluttered above their heads. This one is desperate to get out. Summer is coming, the first one she doesn't want to be a part of. Sakura doesn't even grab her books. She just runs out. She can hear Ms. MacLeod, her Grade Seven teacher's trailing voice, 'Sakura!'

Running home, all the way, hoping someone lets the butterfly out.

She finds her mother crying, sitting with the door of the fridge to her back.

'What are you doing home?' Quickly trying to wipe away her tears, they are already seen by Sakura.

'I just can't do it, Mom,' she sobs. 'He's everywhere and nowhere.'

Her mother stretches her arms up and beckons her to sit beside her. Sakura's tired, grieving body falls into her and, like the first night after it happened, their tears mingle. After a few minutes, her mother straightens and pulls Sakura's face towards her own.

'We need to let go, get on with our lives. He would want that.'

Sakura stops crying. I don't want to let it go. I don't want to let Dad go, she thinks.

She pulls away from her mother's arms and wonders where her tears will feel safe now.

She doesn't know there is a time limit to grief. From where she is, from twelve years old, crying will never cease, joy will always be just out of reach.

CHAPTER 10

'Here.' Mom slaps the leaflet down on the table. 'I have booked you in for Saturday morning.'

Sakura picks it up. It's the riding school she went to for her birthday and then had the lessons afterwards. She hasn't been since.

Remembering waking up and feeling lovely niggles on her last birthday. The time of beautiful blossoms. She can hear her mom's feet stepping the certain boards that creak, and Sakura is shuffling herself into an upright position. Smiling, she anticipates the warmth of the day, snuggling into her duvet.

'Happy birthday, my beautiful blossom.' Her mom places the tray on her lap and sits at her feet.

Sakura drenches the pancakes and bacon with local maple syrup.

'Thank you, Mom. I love you.'

Her mom rubs her foot. 'I love you too.'

'Is that my present?' Sakura asks.

'Well, part of it,' Mom responds.

She opens the small box. Inside is a dainty silver chain with a beautiful locket. Inside it displays a picture of herself and Jack. She throws her arms around her mom. Love's visible moments.

Every birthday, Sakura and Mom spend the day together. She loves the freedom it brings, everything is her choice. First stop, a visit to a coffee shop on the far side of the island beside the red soil sea. It has the most amazing cinnamon rolls and hot chocolate. Together they sit and chat. Her mom tells her about the day she was born.

Sakura never tires of hearing the story.

Being born through her mother's birth canal amazes her. She can't imagine it, but somehow she does.

When they leave the coffee shop, it feels like that's going to be it. Instead Mom drives on, past their turning. Love's surprises. Her mother has something planned besides treats. They travel across rough roads to River Farm.

'Oh, you're kidding! That's why you told me to dress casual, comfortable!' She has always wanted to horseback ride.

Tye, the owner of the ranch, arrives with two horses. He walks with purpose, with his head slightly bent as though his passion pushes him into the public, away from his preferred place, alone with horses. Mom laughs.

'I'm not getting on a horse,' she says nervously. 'Only one learner here.'

'Yes, you are,' shouts Tye, his face a practiced smile with nervous new customers. He looks younger than her mom, but his unkempt hair flattened by a hat makes it hard to guess an age. His eyes are soft, like it's a privilege to see them when he does look up and straight at you.

'But I'm not wearing the right clothes.' Mom isn't sure.

'What you've on is fine, we have boots inside.' Tye talks quietly but is not giving up.

Mom gives in and minutes later they are trekking across farmland. Sakura loves the height and the sound of the horse's movements. Powerful.

She and Mom smile and share something new, something truly unexpected. In time she will remember this moment and forgive what happens when nothing can be the same again. The horses know where they're going. She and Mom just have to hold their reins for balance. What is so new to them the animals know inside out and Tye, upfront, keeps the sense that everything is under control. Mom starts to enjoy herself. Sakura feel like she does out on the boat with Dad. This is an adventure.

'Thanks again.' The car door slams shut, and they wave to Tye.

He raises his hand like he's done this a lot and turns back to his horses.

'That was the best, can I go again, please? Can I go for lessons?' Sakura clutches her fingers together, her body twisting her safety belt, trying to face Mom.

'Well, we have to find out the cost, and the times, remember you have your other after-school commitments.' She's referring to her violin lessons and soccer practice. Matches every other weekend. Sakura can take or leave the violin, but her mom insisted she had to choose the instrument. 'It's a gift to learn music,' she hears her say.

'I know I can manage! I can think about giving up soccer!' Knowing to suggest ditching music would set this whole bargaining conversation in the wrong direction.

'You'd have to commit to a few lessons to start with. That's if I agree, and the drive in and out. We will have to figure all that out, with Eli's hockey and everything, let me think about it.' Mom goes quiet. Sakura can see her mind running the math and loops of time.

Sakura knows she has already won, relaxes her body a little, and turns face forward, her safety belt no longer strangling her. Their quiet journey is eventually broken outside Ridge Creek by Mom's question. 'When does your soccer finish?'

'School's training finishes next month, but I can leave summer practice this year.' Sakura turns her body again.

'Okay, then you can do a few lessons starting next month. I'll ring Tye and figure out the times.' Mom glances over to Sakura and gives her a loving wink.

'Thank you, thank you, wait till I tell Jack!' Sakura is doing little jumps on the passenger seat.

'You're welcome, now remember...'

'I know, I know, the rule,' Sakura interrupts Mom. Sakura moves her fingers up in air quotes. They both start laughing. Her birthday ends with a trip to the shopping mall, hands heavy with bags, Sakura smiling, a perfect end to a perfect day.

Dad is on the doorstep waiting.

'Where did you get to?' He smiles. 'I thought I'd have to blow out candles alone.'

'We just rode into the sunset,' Mom tells him.

'She liked it?'

'I love it.' Just like that, turning twelve, she thought the best part of her future had arrived.

She loved horse riding and meant to book more in the fall but then everything changed. She had a sense she shouldn't too, after Dad saying that day on the boat that he knew she preferred horses now. It was true then, but not now. She would give horses up to have her father here.

'I just don't feel like it, Mom.'

'I know your father never brought you and it feels like you are hurting him by going on with your life. But I took you, Sakura! You loved horses. You'll enjoy it. Do you remember how desperate you were to go?'

'Yes.' She doesn't enjoy anything, or she may not now as much as she once did. There's too much that could go wrong here.

'Let's go and buy you some boots.' The boots she wanted to buy after they agreed the lessons. Mom said she would have to wait and see if she continued. If she kept it up six months then yes, she'd get a real, proper pair, not just rubber wellingtons. That had been May to September. But August thirteenth put anything else out of their minds.

Then she sees Mom needs this, to feel that Sakura can let go, as she's trying also to do.

Sakura doesn't even have to try pleading today, Mom wants to buy the boots for her now. These small things made up the highs and lows of her days and filled most of her chats with Jack. What Mom would or wouldn't let her do or buy. Now the big thing hangs like a black dragon covering the whole sky and travels with her, traversing her whole being.

Sakura doesn't bother protesting again and just nods her head. Some part of her likes the idea of being on a horse. Dad had seen how much. Maybe he would understand. For the second time in her life, the white butterfly has produced a miracle.

She searched for the trapped white butterfly when she got back to school. Someone told her in passing it had been let out by her teacher just after she ran out of class.

Ms. MacLeod never asks her why she ran away that day.

Saturday morning. They turn down the bumpy road towards the stables. Sakura feels in her body the excitement of that first time. Her first birthday without a father has come and gone. Mom wanted her to bring friends over.

'You're a teenager.'

'I just want to do something with Jack for a day.'

They went out, and for a while, they forgot. But then it hit her. Dad wouldn't be here for any more of them, to light candles on her cake.

She knows it now. Her mother interrupts her thoughts.

'There's Tye. I told him we were coming and to pick you a nice horse.'

Sakura's heavy new boots and heavy heart stumble from her mom's car.

'Hi, glad you're back.' Tye pulls straw off his jacket. Sakura doesn't understand why. It's already coated with bits of everything horse.

'We're happy to be here.' Mom puts her arm around Sakura, gently pulling her from where she's half-hidden behind her back.

Tye is right into chatting about what they'll do this morning. He's casual and relaxed, and something in her is the same around him. Tye doesn't treat her like a grieving daughter, a lost child. He looks at her and he doesn't have to look away or say something deep or dumb. He doesn't ask why she hasn't been there in almost a year or make stupid comments about her growth spurt height. He likes horses and horses like him because he takes them and everyone else as they are.

'We have someone who missed you.' Tye looks behind and throws his eyes in the direction of a snorting sound inside the stable. The sound is also kicking the door. Snowy. Sakura had forgotten the white horse up until that moment. Her white butterfly with a mane.

'Your Pegasus,' Mom called him once when Sakura found it hard to leave him after ring class.

'You can go over and brush him down if you like, I'll be right there,' Tye gently encourages.

'But he hasn't seen me. He won't remember me.' Sakura pulls away from Mom and her face opens up.

'He never forgets anyone who rides him like you do. He knows you for life.' Tye pulls his cap down over his eyes, he doesn't like to talk too deep when you can do everything straight up. He is a man of actions.

Sakura grabs the worn wooden brush and moves her hand to open the stable door. Snowy shudders at the first touch of the bristles. He's white with flecks on his feet. 15.5 hands tall. Sakura likes him and he likes her. Rubbing his forehead, he snorts back.

'She's been through a tough time.' Mom is talking to Tye.

'We'll take care of her, horses are great therapy.'

Sakura feels a bit sick, please don't treat me like the grieving kid.

Sakura sneaks a look out the half door. Tye has just moved on from what Mom said, is already giving a nod to a student looking for his advice to come over to him.

'Okay, I'll leave you to it, I'll be back later,' Mom calls over.

'Leave time for her lesson, and then she can groom some more and stable Snowy and feed him.' His looks says it's time to go. He's all about the horse and Sakura now.

Mom flashes a big smile, and Sakura can see her relief. She is leaving Sakura safe.

Sakura and Snowy know it too.

'See you later, have fun,' Mom shouts over the noise of hooves and stable goings on.

Sakura lifts her hand and waves, a little bit happy now that she's here. The smell of Snowy makes her feel safe. Heavy, horsey, immovable smell.

'Can you get him tacked up?' Tye has opened the door, handing her the bridle.

'It's been a while.' Sakura is nervous.

'If he lets you brush him some more, he'll be good to have you ride him.'

Her new left boot fits into the stirrup, and she lifts herself up over the saddle and fits her right boot in. Snowy responds with an approving head toss, knowing he's going outside. Her favourite place and his.

'Are we heading to the arena?' she asks.

'No, trek today. I'll be with you.' Tye falls in with his bay mare beside her. 'Snowy and she get along.' Three other riders, mounted up ahead, follow his instructions to walk on to the trek start.

Sakura is last. She likes it. She feels so tall on Snowy, his heavy body walking in rhythm, his hooves balancing the stepping on stones and gravel. She was amazed they seemed to know where to go. He pulls off right and tries to eat the long grass.

'Hey, Sakura, you know he's going to eat his way around if you let him.' She's reminded by Tye to walk on.

'Later, I promise, a carrot,' she whispers.

Sakura gathers her reins up as they trot, up to one-two, up to one-two. She can hear Tye near the front. She had learned this easily before but is reminded of the coordination required. Bobbing up and down until she gets it, and then with concentrated ease, she does the rising and falling.

'Nice job, Sakura,' she can hear Tye shout back. 'You're a natural.'

Sakura smiles. At this moment, she feels ok.

They trot back towards the stables, and at the last paddock Snowy returns to walk.

He knows what to do. Sakura can feel his warm body underneath her stirrups and a hint of the steam rising off his back.

'Good boy.' She pats his neck. She dismounts, and suddenly feels so small on the ground beside him. Leading him by the reins into the stable, Sakura loosens the girth under his belly, steam rises, and she goes in search of a carrot. She returns with an apple, and Snowy gladly accepts.

'Thanks for making my day, Snowy.' She unbuckles his tack, rubs him down. Tye doesn't even check on her, even though she's only helped him or one of the stable guys do this before.

When she comes out, she can see Tye has been working in the next stable block. He hasn't made her talk or anything. But has stayed close by.

Sakura sees her mother's car, hops in, and tells her everything in one long burst of chat.

'Wow.' Mom's face is clouded but Sakura is shining. For the first time she doesn't think about what Mom is feeling. She is fully alive.

'See you next week!' Sakura leans out the window as they pull away.

Tye waves as they take off, leaving the sound of neighing horses and hooves behind.

Mom listens but Sakura speaks faster, hoping that will catch her attention more. It doesn't. She nods and says, 'That's great you like it.' She looks straight ahead. Sakura understands now, her mom was getting her over the line, but has no idea herself of what to do next or how to do it. She's just clutching at straws, like the ones Tye was pulling out of his jacket.

The stables are the first place Sakura can go and not talk about her father. Maybe that is why he never took her to a lesson. Maybe it was because it was meant to be this way. A place she feels Mom brings her because she doesn't have to talk about her dad.

Sakura senses Mom knows she's grieving herself and the grief is hurting her children. So it's best to let Sakura have the sense of it being somewhere she can go without her family at all. And to talk about that place would mean something might be lost.

The place, her sanctuary, her place with Snowy, and Tye who lets her be.

Gradually, she talks less on the car journey home. Elbow on the window, riding boots mucking up the mat, jodhpurs imprinting Snowy's scent on the clean car seat.

Just like Dad's fishing tackle on the table, that last night, Mom will look but not say anything.

This first time all Sakura says is, 'From now on I'm taking a carrot.'

Eli is at home, the door to his room closed.

For the next six months, they trail the road to the stables where Sakura tells Snowy how heavy or light her heart is. Snowy listens in silence, digging his hoof into the earth and always accepting Sakura's carrot at the end.

CHAPTER 11

If her mom and Eli notice the new month, they haven't drawn attention to the fact.

It's the beginning of August. Sakura feels her step should be more delicate, as if to be heavy might hurt her dad. She still feels guilty for having horses, and for feeling a sense of freedom in some days. She and Jack laugh a lot more now and talk about Dad without Sakura feeling the need to cry or to run.

'Where do you think he is?' Sakura asks Jack. Her friend is taller now. Still taller than Sakura. Her hair's getting longer. She manages to make a small plait. A few freckles like painted dots on her nose.

'Who?' she responds. Jack even forgets sometimes.

'My dad,' she says, almost annoyed, but nothing like she was before. 'I know he was buried in the ground. But is there any of him left?'

Jack is relieved that Sakura keeps talking. She has done that a lot lately. Asking a question and answering it herself.

'Does he remember me? Can he see me or Eli or Mom?' Sakura goes quiet. Then she says what's really in her heart. 'Sometimes, when I go to the harbour, I can almost smell him. For a second, it's like he's here.'

She doesn't know what else to do. She has never known what to do since Dad died. Except when she's at the stables, there she doesn't have to think, just does what she knows is right for Snowy and learns what to do to be a better rider, the best she can be. Jack has never been riding. She has no interest.

Jack responds with a side hug after a small silence.

'I think he's everywhere with you, Sakura.'
'Yes,' Sakura agrees. 'And nowhere.'

The morning of the thirteenth of August arrives. Sakura thinks she will feel different, like her dad might just come back to visit for today. He didn't last year for his first anniversary service.

Her mom bustles into her room.

'It's time to get up. We have lots to do before the service.'

Sakura turns over in her bed. She at least expected her mom to be different today. She isn't sure what she needs, but it isn't this. Since Mom got her into the stables she's becoming less patient, as if she has to hurry the business of being a one-parent family along.

Now cross, Sakura huffs as she pulls herself out of the covers. Her mom interprets this as defiance. A row ensues.

'Come on,' Eli shouts from the kitchen. Mom looks guilty all of a sudden, no wonder he is never home. Sakura wishes she hadn't said anything in the first place. But they weren't there when it happened. They came when it was over.

It's the second time doing this, the first anniversary a few people came. Now it's just going to be them and Jack's family. The three of them sit silently in the car on the way to the church. Eli had been slipping out of their lives before Dad died, but now it feels like he's gone completely. Huddled up in his room, only coming out for food and grunting a few inaudible short words.

They all had a place. Now the jigsaw is broken and doesn't fit. She starts to cry but buries the sneaky tears down. The last thing she wants is her mother's pity when she still feels so angry.

Later. Gathering dishes in the kitchen, Jack's family just left, the bang of the screen door. Her mother catches her eye. Sakura turns away.

The wall is still up but Mom hugs her from behind, and the wall crumbles in an instant. Bits of plaster scatter all over the floor. Sakura turning to her, tears already filling her eyes.

'I'm sorry,' Mom says, as she wipes away tears, not sure whose she's wiping.

Just like those first horrible weeks and months, Sakura feels her warm, safe body. She got what she needed from Mom hours later.

Mom is back, almost, to being Mom. The first birthdays come, which don't hurt as bad as the first ones without Dad. Sakura is fourteen, Eli is eighteen. But the wall bricks are never far away for Sakura. The wall will be built and knocked time and time again. Until one day it will have cause to stay up. Years pass before this happens. In the meantime, things are better. Two years pass in this manner where everything is just about okay.

CHAPTER 12

Sakura grabs Jack's arm as they walk into town. Normally it's the other way around. But Jack has been dragged up and out for this trip. Both she and Jack turn eighteen this year. Each walk has an air of finality about it. Jack has other things on.

The familiar steps of big wooden boards, creaking and aching in parts.

The last of the snow long gone into the landscape. It's almost impossible to imagine it. Lupins are planning their big arrival.

They pass the harbour and see the boats setting out to sea at dawn, the fishermen's first day of the season to set their traps. The boats line the ocean as they make their way out to deep waters in search of spring lobster.

'I've never seen that before,' Jack says pulling Sakura closer.

'Aren't you glad I got you up early now?' Sakura responds, smiling.

'No,' Jack says, pretending to push her away, while still linking arms. 'Seriously, you know I am always here for you.'

'Thanks.' Sakura looking straight ahead. While she knows Jack meant that with all her heart, the apartness she feels from everyone else is a chasm getting so big, soon she won't be able to cross.

'I always wanted to see fishermen leave on the first day. I feel like they're bringing Dad with them.' Sakura still standing, still looking out at the departing boats. 'While he wasn't a fisherman like them, he's always a fisherman to me.' He was happiest on the water. He was happiest with his family. His job was just a thing he did to keep them all going. He did it well, but his passions were different from his working life.

Jack responds by squeezing her closer. Taller now, Sakura's dark hair is longer and straighter. She keeps it in place with a hat. Rust-coloured eye shadow covers the lids of her big brown eyes. Mascara layers her lashes.

Turning eighteen this year, coming of age. They're wearing jogging pants and trainers, with tops that loop over their thumbs. They're holding their neck warmers by now, the downhill nature journey lessening their need.

Arriving at the harbour, Sakura feels that ache fill the entire space of her heart and spread all over her body. Her mother didn't want to go.

Mom is always busy. When she's not working, she's preparing meals that no one eats. Now and again Sakura will walk into their house and smell her grief, it unleashes itself on a blank canvas made manifest.

Mom kept on at Sakura to let go that first Christmas. But it was too soon for any of them. It seems that Mom is the one who hurts most openly now. He has been gone for almost six years. For Sakura that's almost a third of her life without him. Mom lived half her life with him, Sakura tries to remind herself. She's answering her pain with activity. It's rare to get her standing still now.

The house is noisier, but Sakura doesn't like the sounds as much, or at all sometimes. Her mom's music is on and the windows open. A new painting lies waiting to be hung up. That was her dad's job. It sits near the edge of the spilled paint and blank canvases. A single lupin.

Eli is away, having gone to the local University for a year after high school, and then left for Toronto. Just her at home now.

At the jetty, holding the little candle, she whispers,

'I miss you, Dad,' and then blows it out.

Jack is with her, as she always has been. Mina's gone to University too. No more cramped sharing. Jack talks of University and not much else. Even after they leave the harbour, she starts in. The future is an important place for Jack. Sakura doesn't want to leave but doesn't want to be here either.

She continues horse riding and helping out in the yard. This is the one place her pain doesn't follow. It's contained amongst the straw-filled manure and swishing horses' tails.

'You're not just a natural now, Sakura, you're a trained one.' Tye doesn't say much at all but everything he says is important to Sakura. She takes out his bay when he isn't riding out, for the harder treks. Snowy has since retired from the main riding school but she still loves to brush his body free of all the dirt and flies after their ride out together. Tye allows them this.

'Old friend.' She hands him his carrot and tries not to look in his stable when she is taking a younger horse out for a trek she would love to do with him. They're both getting older. Her final year has arrived, and she's applied to do equine science, the only thing she can think of doing. Snowy and the other horses are the only things she loves, well, apart from Jack and her mother at times.

Sakura has no interest in the parties and the life Jack has outside of their friendship now. The room Mina used to share is all hers most of the time. But she doesn't want it and is looking forward to sharing dorms at University.

'Will you be coming?' At the turn to Rose Avenue Jack asks her about tonight's party, frequently off to parties, so rarely at home.

'No, I have a ride out tomorrow.' Sakura is using this as an excuse. She has no interest. She breaks off and walks on towards Cedar Lane, to a house of blaring music, played by a mother and not by her. 'Thanks for coming to mark it with me.'

'Anytime.' Their linking arms are loosening and breaking free. Jack waves and smiles as she leaves. No Jack waiting anymore, at the corner of Rose Avenue.

Sakura doesn't walk that way much now.

CHAPTER 13

There is an ease between herself and Tye, now that she's eighteen this year. She guesses he's not the old guy she thought him when she was first coming here.

He seems to be in his early thirties. Sakura couldn't be sure though. His hat and permanent dust layer look could add a few years. And everyone looks a lot older when you first become an adult. It's easy with him, non-intrusive.

One day, when clearing out a new arrival stable, she told him about Dad. Tye had mentioned he was due to go sea fishing with his friend that weekend.

It just came out of her. She told him about the last day and didn't regret saying it.

'I'm sorry, Sakura, I didn't know all of it,' she remembers him saying. 'You being there. That must be the worst that can happen to someone, and you were only a kid.'

Their sharing was brief, but somehow she felt he heard her completely. He arrived out an hour later with a coffee. He knew she liked it black with a drop of milk. Just a drop. It didn't make sense, but Tye didn't question it.

He brings her a coffee with really no milk at all, today.

'What are you planning on?' It's the question everyone else asks.

'I don't want to go to University.' Sakura has a warning in her voice. Don't start on me, Tye. 'I've picked something, Equine Science but I don't want to do it..'

'All about horses. We've got plenty of them here,' Tye says softly, sipping his own coffee.

'I know, I just can't see myself learning about them in a classroom when I can learn more here.' Sakura looks into hers.

'Good.' Tye raises his shoulders. 'I didn't want to say anything until you had made your choice. Do you want to work here full-time? I could use you. It's not a job that pays well but it pays enough.'

'Yes. I would work here for nothing.' The focus of this makes her stand tall, take notice, and think.

'Now, I don't want your mother scolding me.'

'I'll defer for a year. I'll do University when I'm ready for it.'

Her mom isn't that happy but knows Sakura's mind is made up and lets it be.

'You want more than stable work eventually, Sakura.'

'And I'll figure that out. But right now, I love it there. You're doing what you love too.'

'True.' Mom had done a lot since the thirteenth of August that year. She has lost her husband. Her son had practically emigrated to the city with very few visits to Acres Island. Now Sakura is leaving, but not far away at least.

Sakura knows there are times her mom regrets taking her out to the stables. They lost each other partly on August thirteenth, then the stables took the rest of Sakura.

'It's not like I haven't been heading in this direction. I got my Instruction Permit when I was sixteen.' Sakura knows to be gentle, like she is with all frightened horses.

Mom gave in. 'You can borrow my car. At least you're nearby.'

But they both know Sakura is far away.

CHAPTER 14

Arriving for her first day, Sakura has her mom's car as promised. She wears her weathered ankle boots and her new jodhpurs.

Tye has pinned a list of jobs to the notice board, beside all the stacked hard hats and boots. Sakura starts straight into them. They don't have to say too much to each other to do what needs to be done around here. Sakura doesn't have to be asked twice.

Tye is quiet. Sakura likes that. She doesn't need to be around anyone loud.

He isn't like the guys they hang out with in the local when Jack drags her down. Those guys don't interest her, they make her stressed out, like she has to find some way of talking she doesn't have.

He gets jobs done without much fuss. Always wearing a baseball hat. Sakura wonders if he ever washes them. Sakura likes that he doesn't pry about her life, but listens when Sakura is in a burst to talk.

'Not one of my schoolfriends know anything about horses for me to talk to them.' She says schoolfriends but she means Jack. The stables are the first thing Sakura did without Jack. 'It's like we're on different planets. And the guys at the bar are all about sports and gaming. I can't talk about that stuff. I've never even played.' She finds herself telling him the things she might have told Mom at one time.

'I was pretty much the same, back then when I was young.' Tye has a habit of lifting the side of his mouth to smile when he answers her about these things. 'I only wanted to do one thing with my life. When you find that, Sakura, the rest won't matter.'

Sakura smiles. She feels at home here, but can't help feeling like she's hiding, hiding with her pain, safely surrounded by horses and people who only want to talk about horses. She never feels afraid of them; big, broad, four-legged animals, whose gallop is the only place where, even if only for a minute, she forgets the ache in her heart. As if they, horse and rider, have outsmarted it.

'Hey, Sakura.' Tye rubs his belly to show it's lunchtime. They've worked at opposite ends of the yard all day.

Her body has the ache of work and the hunger to match it. They can eat what they like here in the yard. Since morning she has mucked out ten stables, filled hay nets and filled freshwater buckets. She doesn't mind this work, it's physical and she feels her feet on the earth and the smells around confirm that.

In the kitchen, which is little more than a room with a primus stove, bits of tack, and a couple of hard seats, they eat their packed lunches until the food energy metabolizes. This is the time she might find a rush of talk. Her first full-time day she's quiet. It's everything she was doing before here, all the same. But this is where she'll be more from now on.

'Time to meet the general public.' Tye stands up with a groan at the sound of the first car. 'See you later. Can you ride out the ones not scheduled for lessons?'

Sakura smiles. He's good with the riding students, but he's better with horses.

People start to arrive for their lessons. Tye pulls down his cap over his eyes against the afternoon sun and instructs them all. Which student leads out which horse. Tye likes them to collect the horse from their stable, so they are in a relationship before they even mount up, unless they're beginners. He finds it increases confidence. Just like he did hers when she began.

After lunch, Sakura slips to the back paddock and brings in a horse, saddles up, and off they go to exercise, just the two of them.

She begins to sense each horse's mood, when they want to go slow, when they are giddy and need to canter or want to break out. She lets them lead.

One mare leads her down a windy path through the forest, onto a paddock. They canter, then gallop, the horse snorting and raising its head in enjoyment. Sakura smiles, she feels free. After, Sakura relaxes the rein a little, giving time for both of them to recover.

Back onto the path, they head towards home. Sakura lifts her right leg forward over the saddle, releases the girth and steam rises up. Back at the stables the horse lowers her head and offers her bit and bridle. Sakura slips on a head collar and lifts the half-filled bucket of water over, sets it down at her front hoof and begins to wash her down. After a drink, Sakura turns the horse out to the paddock. Her favourite part.

On the road home, she thinks about how lucky she is to get paid for that experience she just had, a chance to unite with a proud animal and watch a landscape they can both be free in.

That feeling lasts until the turn into Cedars Lane.

Jack calls in, no need for knocking anymore, the screen door banging behind her. She hasn't left for University just yet. But it will be days. Jack hugs her before speaking. She's carrying books collected for University.

'Hey, just wanted to call in, to see how it went.' She sees Sakura drinking iced water from the fridge. That trick still works on the appliance and even though it's September, Sakura is thirsty like a heatwave.

'Is this your new wardrobe now?' Jack gently taps Sakura's chaps with her leg.

'Don't be such a keener, look at you, all University prep-like.' Sakura tries to brush off the dirt on her jodhpurs.

They laugh, but the difference is huge.

'Come on, let's go to Tim's,' she says, grabbing Jack's arm.

Her favourite year since Dad died passes. Horses become her everything. Jack leaves. When she's home she loves parties as much as Sakura hates them.

Tye, he's a bit like her, solitary. Works more than he should to care for the animals who don't answer back.

'Don't know where I would be without you, Sakura,' he sometimes says.

Sakura doesn't mind staying on at the yard to fill in time and to keep her from arriving home. Mom, busy often, sad often. Everything is a strain. Thankfully, when she gets back late, Mom is often out again already.

CHAPTER 15

Jack steams through the screen door again. It's another early September, and another August thirteenth has passed. Eli doesn't even come home for them now. Mom and she get through it. Sometimes days go by where Dad isn't even mentioned. She is remembering for them all, it seems, but doesn't want to make Mom cry, so only speaks of him when it comes up.

Here is Jack, carrying a new set of books. Sakura's a year into working at the stables. One more birthday and they turn twenty. They're nineteen and they're trying to stay best friends.

They don't see each other so much. But then when Jack is home it feels the same, in moments where everything has changed.

'Come on, let's go to Tim's.' Sakura grabs Jack's arm, just as she did last year. Together they sit and Jack relays stories of campus, the study groups, the parties, the pranks, the fun.

'And you?' Jack smiles. 'What about you?'

'Still horse mad.' It's her shorthand. What can she say? Jack never sat on a horse in her life. Sakura is the listener.

While she listens, Sakura feels that familiar ache rise up in her chest. The things that give her comfort, the yard, Tye's easy authority and relaxed approach, and the horses, are all keeping her exactly where she was. The only place she can be.

Jack has moved on, and here she is, shovelling mud and manure. Walking into town alone along the boardwalk. Staring at the Strait, too afraid to live.

'Come visit me on campus. You can stay with me,' Jack begs while holding her hands, knowing she won't.

They hug and Sakura turns and walks away in the dark of her own shadow, wondering where change can find her when she won't let it.

CHAPTER 16

'There you go.' Sakura pats the horse into the stable.

She hears a loud pickup truck enter the yard. She turns to see Tye greeting a man and showing him into the office. She takes the brush and combs before clipping the stable rug under the mare, then enters the next stall to continue to muck out. She hears voices. It's a busy place, always people coming and going. Maybe a lesson she didn't know about? Hopefully she won't have to lead it. There's a lot to do. No. It's Tye and the guy.

They pass her stall, and for a second she thinks they'll pass by.

They're discussing the amount of bedding needed.

'Sakura, this is Chris. He'll be providing us with the bedding.' Tye backs up and opens the stable door.

'Six bags per stall per week…' The voice is immersed in figuring out.

'That's for sure, sometimes more. We're clearing seventy pounds a day. Sakura and I do most of the honours. Best hand I have.' Tye indicates to Chris to come and meet his right-hand woman. A shadow falls over the stable. Sakura looks up and immediately wishes she had wiped away the muck she can feel on her cheek.

The guy with the pen and clipboard, Chris, smiles at her, his mouth half turned up, a cheeky smile. His hair floppy ash, he flicks it, like he knows how this will land. He's handsome, strong features, big brown eyes that know their impact. A cheeky smile that used to be on Dad's face. Her gone dad. The only man in her life who knew her. Eli, the one who used to be a hero without much words, has none at all for her now. He was left in his own lost world.

After University, he stayed in the city working. A tech job with a big company.

Chris is different to Tye. Taller, confident. The stables put Tye's finances under strain and his love of horses makes him take more care of them than he does himself.

'Sakura.' Chris states her name. It's like he's put it in lights. He seems so sure. She will learn later this to be egotistical. Confidence is different, it's quiet, humble. Right now, Sakura is stuck. Everyone is leaving, everyone is moving on. She's made a living out of one of her last moments of joy before Dad died. The horses came for her before they took Dad. But nothing else has come for her since. She needed something big to shake her out of her life. Chris shakes big.

From the first moment, she knows that he is change.

Her heart beating fast. She doesn't know what's happening. She's used to the ache. Her face blushes pink.

'It's the Japanese word for cherry blossom,' she finds herself saying.

'Ah. A spring baby.' Chris grins.

'I didn't know that about you.' Tye smiles too. 'But I know you're an April child. She came for a riding lesson and from the day she got in the saddle she was a natural.'

Sakura blushes deeply. Attention doesn't rest well with her. That day on the boat was the last time any man paid her attention. She's relieved when Tye suggests moving on. Chris glances back and gives a cheeky smile. Sakura raises her hand to her cheek to contain the blush she feels is spreading.

They talk about the delivery days, the totals, and they seem to be at ease with each other. It's like they haven't noticed her embarrassment. But Chris did. Sakura continues with her jobs but keeps replaying the meeting over and over in her head.

His pickup truck is long gone.

*

She hasn't had any interest in boys, dating a few here and there, instigated by Jack on her visits home. Boys is what they are. Booze-fuelled boys.

But this man, she guesses his age, maybe mid-twenties. He isn't a University kid. He has his own pickup.

'Well, I think we found our supplier. I think he took a liking to us, Sakura. We get a discount on the first quarter.' Tye grabs a pitchfork and seems happy.

'Where did you find him?'

'His name is good in the equine supply world. Turns out I've met him at a few events. We know a bunch of people in common.'

She wants to ask Tye more, but resists, worried she might give something away. This new occupation fills her mind until she sees him again. Tye doesn't mention him, and Sakura watches the old stock run down, wondering how long before delivery, and will he deliver?

Two weeks later, he arrives. She realizes she's been listening out for the sound of his truck. Tye and he offload in the far-off stable, so she won't get to see him. Sakura heads for Snowy's stall. She just wants to be around Snowy, to set off this horrible tension she feels. Feelings she doesn't want.

As if he hears her thoughts, Chris walks through the yard after and stops at the stable she's in, tacking up Snowy.

'Hey, Sakura, isn't it?' Leaning his arms over the door, his over six-foot frame holding his elbows in a v shape.

'Yes,' she responds, looking away.

'Lovely horse,' he says, reaching in to rub him.

Horses she can talk about, safety in their warm coats and height.

'Getting old, but my favourite. His hooves know where to go,' Sakura continues while tightening the girth underneath his belly, aware Chris is looking at her throughout.

Snowy snorts, indifferent to the flirting going on by his bed.

'You know a lot about horses, eh?'

'I guess,' responds Sakura. 'I've been here a while. So, you're providing the bedding from now on?' Asking her first question. She would like to know much more.

'Yes, I have an equine business and farmland in Brightwood.' He stretches up from the stall door, extending his height. He shuffles his feet and straightens his back. His head jerks upwards. Too high, he quickly corrects this and levels with her again.

Snowy is shifting.

'I better go.' Sakura turns towards the stable door as Chris grabs it and holds it open. Seamlessly, Sakura puts her foot in the stirrup and swings her leg over and she is up and away. Smiling. She knows Chris is watching.

'See ya,' she hears in the distance. She thinks she may hear the words, 'Next week, eh?'

That scene keeps Sakura company until the next time she sees him.

His weekly trips to the stables set her heart thundering like hooves on a gallop. But he always appears not to notice. He makes his way to her, and always concludes with a short chat, just enough to get to know her.

'Well, he certainly finds time to get to talk to you,' Tye remarks softly.

'I don't know why.'

'You should.' Tye doesn't say more but she knows he means she's attractive.

She's too buried in her bruised heart to know it. Jack has said it.

'You're beautiful. You just won't try.'

Her mom has said it. Back in the days of haircuts. But somehow, with Chris coming close to her, she is willing to think there may be something in her to see. Something worth seeing.

Chapter 17

She becomes familiar with the sound of his truck, fixing her hair, waiting for him to come over, she'll be busy working whenever he does.

'Oh hi, Chris,' she says, turning around. The usual talk of the stables fills the first five minutes. She tries not to get lost in the height, the smile, the hair. She tries not to get lost in everything.

On the days after he leaves, she wonders if he will ever make a move. If he does this with all the female staff at the stables. Sakura tries to keep a distance from any potential disappointment. Something tells her this could be one of the biggest of her life. But nothing like losing Dad. Nothing like losing her whole life after that.

One day, it just comes.

'So there's a place downtown that does good food if you'd like to go, maybe Saturday night?'

Sakura hears the words, the sentence, she's been dreading and waiting for.

Her voice suddenly sounds giddy, calming it, she says a simple, 'Eh, sure.'

She continues lowering the shovel under the wet, steaming straw and emptying it into the wheelbarrow. Some of the newer stables haven't changed to the bedding yet.

'Great, pick you up at eight? Cedar Lane on the Island wasn't it? What number?'

'Cool, you have the address.' She looks up, and their half-formed smiles meet to create one.

'I made sure not to forget.' He turns to leave.

She calls out the number after him.

*

For the first time in her life, she is looking forward to a future day. The stables are her comfort. But this, this is the confetti feeling of excited joy. At the house she doesn't think it's Friday, there used to be pizza, she doesn't wish her mom would stop painting just to truly notice her or stop working just to truly spend time with her. Sakura doesn't feel left, she feels like something is happening.

Immediately after supper, she goes to her room, the way she used to when she was hatching plans with Jack or eating Timbars, or having dreams. There is someone to share tomorrow with.

Her mom, snoozing on the sofa, tired from a day not just life, notices her good mood later. She doesn't need to know why. She's just happy to see a change and guesses it might be a boy. But it's not a boy. It's a man.

Sakura can sense her come down the hall and catch the contents of her wardrobe upturned on the floor, through the crack of her bedroom door. But Sakura won't turn.

She knows her mother is smiling to herself, as she eases her own door closed.

When Sakura comes out the following morning she sees a fifty dollar note on the kitchen table, with a message on top.

Buy yourself something nice.

Mom x

While her mother has drifted off into the ocean along with the boats that day, she loves her little touches. This is one of them. Sakura takes the money and skips out the door.

She feels happy and catches herself, an unusual feeling. She feels alive.

*

What is this sense? Then she remembers, it's the Christmas feeling. The last one. A feeling of magic ahead and magic happening.

Her mom pulling down the decoration box from the attic. Sakura loves this part; choosing what should go where. All trees are unique, and they show you how they should wear their jewels. Their theme is red and gold, started by her mom and loved by Sakura. Soft white lights are the last dressing. Dad helps thread them around the tree and then the little angel on top. She watches over everyone. Complete. Eli is out, with friends. It's just the three of them. Dad has gently pulled her mom into an embrace and is dancing.

Sakura embarrassed, but delighted, when Dad coaxes her up. They dance under the arms of their beautiful Christmas tree.

'Time to take you shopping.' Their tree is the first one up. This is always followed by a trip to the stores, for presents and her clothes. Christmas, the one day Sakura likes to wear a dress. Mom and she decide to walk into town, up their road, Cedar Lane, and just past Jack's on Rose Avenue and peer in and watch trees on display.

All the little and big houses, most glittering and magical. A few in darkness. Sakura is confused. She thought everyone celebrated Christmas. Her mom speculates as to why.

Then the following year, theirs is the house in darkness.

'This one, this is it!' Sakura twirling the light golden fabric in the changing room, the curtain open, shouts over to Mom on the other side of the store. Her new Christmas dress. She imagines wearing it with her flat pumps.

'Oh, that's lovely, and you love that colour.' Her mom laughs.

'Come on.' Mom brings it to the cashier to pay when Sakura has taken it off, not wanting to. 'We have lots more shopping to do.' Linking arms, they move through the mall. Each store front has splashes of red and white.

Sakura buys Mom a beautiful book about Ikigai. Her mom talks about it still, at haircut time and other times when she's lost in thought, taking it down, flipping through the pages. The lady at the store, when Sakura asked if there was more than one, said,

'Oh yes. It's a whole philosophy, the Japanese reason for being. Yes, we have a few different ones, come over here, I'll show you.' The woman moves from behind the counter and continues talking while glancing at the shelf to the right. 'You're very kind. I hope my kids think of something as thoughtful as this.'

'My mom's friend taught her,' Sakura confides. 'She's trying to teach me what my reason for being is.'

'And you're reminding her of hers?' The woman has found a book and they both agree it's perfect. Moving back to the counter, she wraps the package for Sakura.

'Yes. My mom wants to visit Okinawa, to see her best friend. This will remind her to.'

'Maybe you will go with her?'

'Maybe, but my best friend is here, her name is Jack.' She wonders what her mom's reason for being is. Is it her and Eli? What if she didn't have them? What would her reason be then? Later she would realise her reason is nothing to do with them. It's to do with herself. Her alone.

She thinks her own reason for being is to have fun. Thanks the woman and leaves the bookstore. Her mom is waiting for her outside.

The Island is small, but it has some good stores for clothes. Brushing her hands through the rails, holding the dresses, and stretching the fabric. Her eyes zoom in on a black dress with small, coloured flowers, little sleeves and buttons down the front. Holding it up in front of her, imagining the first fitting.

It's perfect. The girl who only liked dresses at Christmas time, who twirled in gold, is sophisticated in black. There is no one with her to ask. The cashier looks over and smiles. But for once she doesn't need reassurance.

I like this, Sakura thinks to herself. Thirty-five dollars, the cashier drops the receipt in the bag. Sakura heads for lunch with the change. She misses Jack, she would like to tell her about the date with Chris. It's not the Christmas feeling anymore, as there's no one to share it with.

Then she thinks of Chris and the new dress and puts the outfit together in her mind. Older butterflies are still butterflies.

Saturday arrives, and Sakura is ready and nervous.

'Are you off out?' Her mom notices her pacing the kitchen.

'Yeah, kind of,' says Sakura.

'Oh. What's his name?'

The pickup truck roars into the drive. The other cars seem tiny alongside.

'Chris, ah there he is.'

'Have a lovely time.' Her mom goes to hug her.

'See ya.' Sakura is gone before it can happen.

Chris opens the door, and she hops in. It's high. She's used to this working at the stables, but tonight she's wearing heeled boots, trying to look elegant.

Glancing over nervously, she thinks he looks gorgeous, his sleeves rolled up on his crisp shirt, revealing a summer tan. A smell of musty cologne fills the pickup, and she can see the glimmer of the gel setting his hair.

'You look lovely,' he says, giving a cheeky wink. 'Different from the horse gear.'

'Thanks.' For the first time, it's important to say more. She can't find the words. But she never could. He's the kind who will do the talking, thankfully. With Tye at the stables, she doesn't have to try and that's why other things come to her, in bursts. But this, this is pressure. She wonders if Dad was alive if she would have asked him guy-type questions.

They sit down, and the waiter hands them the menu. Something about this, the fact they are going to eat out, like she used to do with her family before it got smashed, makes her smile. The initial awkwardness melts into giggles and stories.

His hand brushes off hers while reaching for the water. She looks up. He feels it too.

He drops her home, and before she opens the door, Chris says,

'What are you doing Wednesday?'

Smiling, she thinks to herself, nothing, absolutely nothing and responds, 'Eh, not sure, why?'

'They're playing a movie in the drive-in theatre, thought you might like to go?'

'Yeah sure, that would be nice.'

He drives off, she dances inside.

'Did you have a nice time?' her mom asks the next morning.

'Yeah, it was fine.'

'Lovely, I'm delighted, Sakura.' Mom kisses her on the forehead. Sensing she isn't going to get any more details.

Wednesday arrives, and she decides to wear jeans and a top, more casual, and her long chocolate brown hair, straight over her shoulders, smelling of fresh shampoo. They pull up outside and get the popcorn and sodas. The movie begins. It's romantic. Chris and she carefully take their turns sharing the popcorn, watching for accidental brushes. No wonder Jack got so obsessed about boys.

Sakura is excited and terrified in equal measure. She's used to her pain. It forms an edging around her being, not letting anything in or out. But now, there's a gap, and anything could sneak in. Maybe she should shut it closed for fear her heart might burst right open.

Then, Chris reaches into the back of the pickup, grabs a blanket and places it over her lap. Sakura raises her hands, unsure what to do. He gently tucks it in, her hand lowers, and he takes it fully in his, encircling fingers, this thumb rubbing her palm. She raises her head and meets his gaze, and that moment emerges where the space between them evaporates as they pull closer. Her eyes seeing his, heads naturally tilting, his lips on hers, eyes naturally closing.

CHAPTER 18

She will never not hurt, her dad will always fall into the water in front of her at some point in any day, but being with Chris brings something that takes the sight of that away. The horses gave her peace, Chris gives her a chance to love as a woman, not a lost child.

People told her mom, ‘She will suffer the most, having seen it.’ Her mom, trying to live, couldn’t get Sakura the help she herself was unable to give. She is still powerless to face the memories sometimes. Mom keeps the roof over their head, the meals. They talk. They don’t relate. But they watch movies Eli would hate even though Eli is not there. They try to get past the thing that never leaves the house, that’s always there. It’s a house where things break and, unless they’re big, repairs don’t happen.

Sometimes Mom is pretending so she can make it through the day. Sakura, quiet by nature, always having known who she was, can’t pretend like others can.

‘How are things?’ Mom asks about the dates.

‘Good.’ Sakura can’t share this. Not until she has felt it all for herself. All her feelings and Mom’s have been tied up in Dad. She is not being cruel. She is just keeping a needed distance. Like when a horse is skittish. Let them know you are there, but don’t crowd. The horses, this one in particular, like it when you are honest. You can’t have a relationship with a horse without honesty.

She is honestly more alive now with Chris. It scatters excited confetti over her emotions. One minute she is thrilled. The next terrified. The stables keep her steady, keep her calm between dates. Like visitors crossing to the

Island, Chris has been let into an island in her. She's trying to keep the bridge open.

Snowy notices the flurry of thoughts and nuzzles her arm, looking for more treats. Sakura hands him an extra apple. Closing the stable door, she feels another shower of excited confetti fall on her.

Let it in, Sakura. You're young. Be happy. She knows Dad would have wanted this and vetted Chris and they'd have things in common – hard-working, cheeky smiling. But even at this stage, she knows Chris is something more. Maybe this is what makes her so intensely absorbed by him. The first man she has wanted.

'Mom says you met someone?' Eli asks Sakura from a distance he keeps, over the phone.

'Maybe.' Sakura would like to tell him.

'Do I have to give him the once over like, eh?' Eli tries to show concern. But a once a year visit doesn't make a man about this house.

'No, I'll get Mom.'

Jack is home later, and she wants to tell her everything. She has something to share for once. They meet in their new favourite place, Truffles Café. Tim's closed last year. Sakura felt her tummy drop when she saw the sign pinned to the door. Jack shrugged. 'We'll have to find somewhere else.' But Sakura stood, lost, staring through the window, through to their table.

Ten years old, the first time they were allowed to walk downtown on their own. Only to here and straight back. Giggling. Then when giggles turned to silent, unrelenting sad face. Even Jack couldn't cheer her up. The rest of the Island was moving with the times, upgrading, renovating. They didn't and shut.

'You're getting through quicker today.' Tye comes over, having seen how many wheelbarrows of manure she has shifted.

'I've got a friend home.' Sakura smiles.

'Not a date then?'

'That comes later.'

'Look at you, love your hair.' Jack reaches in for a big hug. Jack's hair is shorter. Smarter, neater. If they had still been seeing each other every day, Sakura might have said, don't cut it all, I love your hair. The hug reaches Sakura. Jack is walking differently now, not leaning in, as they used to, walking straighter, and not looking as much as she used to into Sakura's eyes. But then, it's been so long.

Sakura has no idea that she too has changed. She doesn't notice the way her hair has gone down past her shoulders and travels on, seemingly taking a life of its own.

Sakura blushes, pushing her hair back behind her ear, trying to hide her beauty she wants no one to see. Except Chris, at times when he flirts and pulls her in close. When he comments on her features, she becomes bashful. She tries to look away.

'You know you've beautiful eyes.' Chris holds her face with his two large hands. Sakura, embarrassed by the direct attention, takes her eyes from his and tries to move her head away.

But he won't let her pull away. Instead, he stares longer.

'Let me look at you and your beautiful eyes, Sakura.'

So she does, because her whole heart wants that, but her hurting heart is so scared. He wins.

Then, just when she can't take it anymore, he pulls her head in, looks in the eyes he calls beautiful, and kisses the lips he calls his. Bites the lower, not enough to make a bruise. Just enough to hurt a little.

She feels a sense of something in the air from the beginning. It exists, but not knowing its shape lingers and gets caught on the lost branches of Sakura's heart and confuses it with grief. There is something. But for now, there is everything she has lost, in one man, in the hope he has brought for a different life.

Jack's hug is still around her, and through it, she knows Jack is still there, and she is still there too, so she says,

'I met someone.'

'I knew it.' Jack punches the air. 'You're so beautiful, they find you.'

'Stop it,' Sakura says, but she smiles. She pulls out her phone.

'He looks lovely. Cute,' Jack says, nudging Sakura. 'When do I get to meet him?'

Sakura wants to keep this to herself for now. She has never introduced Jack to anyone. Not wanting to get this wrong. Her dragging sad self is happier, she doesn't want this to change. Her mood leaves room for their friendship to expand. Things seem exciting again.

'Soon, maybe next time you're home?' Sakura responds.

'Sure. Have you?' Jack looks at her hard.

'Not yet. Maybe soon.'

'Wait until that happens. You'll feel things you never thought you would.'

Sakura answers with a smile. For some reason, it feels like old times. They link arms on the way out. They may be both adults now. A part of them will always remain children. Instead of turning up Rose Avenue, Jack says she's going to walk Sakura to Cedars Lane. They talk like it's yesterday. Arms linked. Ease restored.

'See you tomorrow then before you head back?' Jack smiles.

'Yes, great.' And it is. The small gate closes, and Sakura heads inside.

Chris is calling to the stables more than once a week on some pretext. Tye senses it isn't only to provide bedding for the horses,

'I've never known the boss guy drive the delivery himself. And calling out twice a week when he has the whole territory of the Island to cover. That's service.'

But Sakura won't say anything. Tye lets her alone, lets her be who she is, and only talk when she needs to. So he makes sure not to mention it. Sakura is so grateful for this.

Chris sneaks into the stable, grabs Sakura by the waist and she inhales that lovely smell of faded cologne and hard work. His eyes wide open, peering into hers. She doesn't pull away now. She is getting used to it. She loves it. He sees her and wants her.

'Pick you up later?' He seems to fill the stable. His height, his rhetorical question. Tilting his hat down, he turns to leave. He seems busy and important but has enough time for her.

'Yeh,' she says, grinning. She never thought she could grin. She knows he could have anyone. He seems perfect, tall, kind, real handsome, hardworking, a gentleman. She knows he wants her. She turns to look back, but he has already gone. All day long she imagines the next time.

Sakura's glad she didn't go to University. She might have missed this. Her mom didn't push when she didn't take her deferred place. There are times when she feels so much freer than the people who go to school. Fresh air. Horses. Chris.

He's packed a picnic and included her favourite foods: peanut butter ice cream, brioche bread, and sodas. Sitting on a blanket, he spreads it out under her feet.

'You are so beautiful.' Chris reaches her face with his hand, kissing her softly, then intensely, then all at once. Similar adrenaline that Sakura felt on her first gallop rushes through her. Excitement and fear. Then she goes all in, wanting to please him, matching his intensity. The moment Jack has talked about.

'Ah, it's just different, intense, not like you imagine,' Jack shared after her first time. They were both seventeen. Sakura hadn't dared go there. Until now. Running from grief into passion.

With Chris, grief has less of a pull, passion winning her away from memory. Later they will merge, all out of kilter. Sakura will stand, dripping in the lost bits of herself.

He looks at her, smiling. He has brought her back to life. Pulled her from the cusp of death.

Each day at some stage, she travels back to the pier in her mind, watching Dad gasp, watching her life disappear amongst the foaming dancing white horses, seeing her mom and brother, hearing the wails. Chris intervenes and takes away all of that.

'Think I'm falling in love with you.' He's pretending to look away for the briefest second. Sometimes he mimics her bashfulness. She wishes he wouldn't because she wishes she weren't. For a second, she's not sure but then he looks at her. Sakura's whole face changes. She used to try and make it look different, happy, for the sake of other people. Now it does. The joy spreads across her face and she tries to catch it. Maybe it's too different. Sakura sucks in her cheeks, making the smile smaller.

Pulling him closer, she feels his weight heavy on top of her. Contained. Nowhere to go. Their noses almost touch.

Sakura's heart, all of her, down to her knees, is on fire. He opens the buttons of her jeans, pulls them down along with her underwear, down just enough and does the same. Pulling out a condom, he rips it open with his mouth and quickly puts it on. Lowers himself, moves her legs apart and pushes himself into her.

At the stables, driving home, at home, over supper, in town, everywhere she used to feel the pain of loss, the sense of promise grows. If she could see him all day she would. The stables are a focus. At home, she only really wants to be alone, in her room.

Mom, who used to know her thoughts, or could read them, is just a visitor to this life Sakura has now, under the same roof and in the same house. Chris and Mom have yet to meet. She appreciates Mom isn't asking for it. She loves that Chris doesn't push for this. They just date in a world of their own and there are no other people. It's what keeps it safe for her.

Suppers, picnics, and walks holding hands. The simple things she prefers to parties and events, to booze and noise. They are alone to be together, in quiet places, matching the quiet in her. The same things fill and follow in the weeks and months ahead.

The times when it feels something is not right. He knows those times, and so he brings in something new, or a diversion. And she wants to feel this shudder of joy, to be alive to herself, so she ignores it too. One of the diversions, after a walk where she wasn't certain, where the kisses were wonderful, but the holding wasn't right.

'Hey, Sakura, isn't it time I met your mom?'

Sakura knows she can't wait any longer. Afraid to bring to light her deep vague sense. She pushes it away and they agree to call over for supper later that week. He is polite and brings a cake.

*

Opening the door before they arrive, her mom greets them. The smell of cooking travels out and Sakura is momentarily distracted from her nerves.

'Mom, this is Chris.' Sakura glances at both of them and stands back while Chris reaches out his hand.

'Very nice to meet you.' Mom smiles over at Sakura. The worst is part over.

Sakura doesn't like doing introductions. Afraid the words will be mixed up. She doesn't like introducing her new life to her old one. The joy may be diluted. But she can tell Mom is relieved to set eyes on the mystery man of some months now. The table shows she has been cooking all day long.

'Come in, supper is almost ready.' Mom leads the way and offers drinks.

'Thanks.' Chris accepts a beer. She hopes he doesn't have another. She's not insured to drive his pickup. He seems casual about having a drink or two and driving.

'It's just one drink really,' he says when he has two beers. 'Sure, they're tiny.'

'So, Chris,' Mom, still leading the way, 'tell me about your work. You met my daughter that way?'

'I did, I've got a horse bedding business and some land. That takes up most of my time, before I met Sakura that is.'

Mom smiles. He smiles. Sakura tries to. Mom asks more questions about his work. The conversation flows.

He brings his plates to the sink and Sakura knows her mom will love this. While over at the sink, Chris comments on the drip.

'That's an easy fix.'

'Really, are you sure?' Mom sounds too grateful.

'If you have the right tools. I think I have some in the pickup.'

'We should have some out in the shed. Mostly these days we get workmen in,' Mom says. No one mentions that they belong to her dad. 'Sakura, can you go and get them please?' Mom is smiling, not fake, real smiling.

Sakura runs out and grabs the toolbox. She stands back, watching Chris squat down, reach in, twisting and turning. God, he looks good, like he knows what he's doing and he's here with me. Hoping her mom can't hear her thoughts.

'That sink needed fixing for the longest time.' Mom's just behind her, watching.

She and Chris leave shortly after supper for another walk, and another chance for her to realize her fantasy while he fixed the sink.

Later, when she comes back, it's late but Mom is still up, wanting to bond, to give her stamp of approval.

'He's lovely. You seem happy.'

'I suppose.' Her body is happy. Her heart is full. Things might be okay. Please, just let them be okay.

'You seem happy,' not, 'you are happy.' Her Mom's words will play loops in her fogged brain. The brain of later. She was happy. She is happy.

Sakura will try to convince her tired self. Today, Chris is an intense lover, a win with her mom, and a fixer of sinks. She must be grateful.

His town, just south of hers, is on a peninsula surrounded by magic water views, bounded by Lawrence's Marsh and East River. Smaller than hers. Here, people gaze longer, wondering who she is, but won't ask. Maple Bakery on Main Street opens its doors early and the fresh smell of cinnamon rolls trickles onto the sidewalk. Always a queue. They join it to pick some up.

'They're the best around,' Chris says, more than once. They head out to his land.

Trips to Brightwood, his land, and business, she feels how much he has succeeded already in life. 'You did all this, and you're only in your twenties.' She looks out over his land, his business, and the equine logo above the lower barn. It's an amazing achievement.

'You could move in here and make it more special.' Shuffling on one foot, the words are coming out but almost being pulled back in. She won't notice this until later. Much later. He asks like it's a joke. The experience she needs at this point, she won't have until after him.

His business is working because the owner is dedicated to his life. But he has said, aloud, he wishes to share it. She is smiling at the thought. Maybe Tye will let her buy Snowy to come and live here. They could get more horses. He's standing beside her, leaving enough space for her to wiggle but not enough to leave. They're standing on his front patio, looking out over all he surveys.

'I fixed up this cladding.' Chris thumps the new white boards behind her head.

'Good job.' Sakura doesn't really notice his handiwork. She is still swimming in his earlier words, 'Move in.' She could stay here. In a house where everything is fixed, with a man to love. This is not the town. This is not where it all happened. She won't have to look at the pier each time. She won't have to walk the road along the North Strait and see the spot at Rose Avenue where Jack used to wait. She won't have to note Eli's absence. She won't look at the drained pond and a mom the same. The black canvases and single flowers won't feature in this house. There can be life.

'I lost my parents too, you know,' he reminds her, knowing she's lost in thought and how to leave her childhood home, ever. The house where she once had a loving father.

She remembers, from the covering history conversation they had in the first weeks. She remembers Chris saying about this house,

'It's mine now, I have to make sure everything is kept right.' He's a man of his word.

He never mentions his parents and doesn't expect her to mention Dad. She feels they both understand that loss doesn't have to be spoken of. It's just lived. But that doesn't mean that the pain is not there. The way the house is tells her that he is not going to let his legacy go to waste.

'Both of them died four years ago. Just months apart.' He tells her a little more than before. It's what she suspected. This is how he inherited the family home. Keeping it right is what makes it right. 'It would be nice to have someone here again.' He says it so flatly. But she puts this down to being like her. It's hard to ask for things.

Sakura answers his question by resting her back against the newly painted cladding.

Chris holding her in place with an arm around her shoulder. Reaching down, he kisses her. He doesn't need a verbal response to his question. Her whole-body reaction is response enough. The sense that things can be different is what pulls her along. But also, Sakura likes the idea that she could still walk away if she wanted to. This is not marriage. This is something new.

Only Chris already knows she can't leave.

Stories of stables and horses and their love of nature carry them into the spring. He holds her in that space she thought no light could get in.

She is happy.

CHAPTER 19

Something is changing but she can't even say what. When Jack comes home for Spring break they go to Truffles. For once Sakura is doing the talking. Her new life is coming. Her time with Chris is time she is alive.

Jack and she talk about her for a change, and they talk so much, even on the way home, Jack says she'll walk on to Cedar Lane. She has planned to go home and change, but there's still so much to talk about before Chris arrives, they need more alone time.

'What about your life?' Sakura breaks her own bursts of talk to ask.

'Oh, same old. Assignments. Parties. Some new friends. I'll have them visit the Island sometime to meet my best friend! Guys. But none like yours. I can't wait to meet him.' Jack pulls Sakura's arm closer as they arrive at her gate.

'He'll be here at seven sharp,' Sakura responds, pulling her into the hook of her arm. Sakura tries to downplay this meeting's importance, and that it's important Jack, who is only an average timekeeper, is here. She is so nervous again, of letting her old world and her new one connect. Sometimes Chris can get impatient with insignificant things she doesn't realise. It's because she is younger. She's playing catch-up, learning how to be a girlfriend, having never been one. He has a lot more experience.

It's everything right now. Chris's invisible thoughts already landing in Sakura's head.

The pickup doors slam closed. Supper at her house has gone well. But she's not staying home. Jack and Mom wave them off from the gate. It feels a bit strange.

'I told you, she's lovely.' Sakura glances over at Chris.

'Yes, she's chatty alright, a lot about University stuff.' Chris doesn't look back at her friend and mom standing at her old gate, waving still.

'We spent all afternoon talking about me, and you,' Sakura adds. 'Mom made supper while we were out. Jack was supposed to go home, but she stayed on.'

'Nice.' Chris uses one hand on the wheel, the other he places on Sakura's leg.

'Let's stop and get some ice cream.' He leans over, moves his hand further between her legs and kisses her on the cheek.

'You said you weren't hungry for dessert.' Sakura thinks of Mom's pie.

'I am now.' He pulls in, applies the brake. 'Let's get your favourite.'

Her line of thought is broken. Her doubt is dispersed by cold peanut butter flavours.

He pretends to push the ice cream in her face, leaving them both in giggles.

'Let's head to the lighthouse and look at the sunset.'

The right suggestion. Sakura lights up again.

Holding hands, they walk out along the headland. The sea is to their left; gently lapping, the lighthouse in the distance, the setting sun framing its silhouette. Perfect.

The rest of the vacation weekend is bliss.

'When are you going to move in with me, Sakura? I'm driving all the time, you know it makes sense.' Chris turns and stops in front of her, taking both of her hands. His eyes narrow, his face impatient. Like she is doing something wrong.

'Maybe.' She wants the moments they've had to be all she thinks of.

Pulling her hands to his chest, he asks, 'What are you afraid of?'

Sakura shrugs, then kisses him on the cheek. Feeling this is not going to go away.

He drops her off at the gate, to an empty house. Mom must be out.

She's cold. He doesn't come in.

The pickup roars away and she's back to feeling alone.

'Move in with me,' he says, going down on one knee in a mock proposal.

'You're distracting me,' Sakura responds, smiling and trying to shovel the last of the manure out of the stables while Chris keeps moving the wheelbarrow.

'Come on, why don't you?'

'You're serious,' she says, her face bursting with blushes.

'Well?' he pushes.

'Ok. Yes. I will. Get up!' She could never have imagined feeling anything close to perfect, but this feels perfect. Everything is going to be ok. Everything is ok.

Suddenly Sakura feels as though all those things she sees other people doing are within reach. Are possible. Everything is possible.

He pulls her down to him.

'No, Chris, not here. Tye, and Snowy!'

This is the beginning. She watches his face... she knows she is happy, she knows Mom has taken to him, she knows that the things in the house that got broken over so long will be fixed. Since Eli does not come home much, and when he does it's as if he is not there. Chris will do things a house needs a man for.

Snowy's tail swishes their kisses away.

'Okay.' He releases the pull he has on her. 'Once you agree to move in with me!'

'Why not?' Her grin is real. He is gorgeous. He is a working guy. He loves horses. Jack thought he was great. Well, the text Jack sent after their meal together said,

I like him, take it slow, eh xx

It's all so good. Okay. It's early. But it's the best she has felt in years.

'Yes!' Chris punches the air.

'I have to tell Mom.' She jumps up, giddy with excitement. 'She'll be worried about University. I'll tell her I'll go next fall.'

'That's a great idea. I'll be dating a University grad.' Chris grabs her by the waist. His voice gives way. 'Okay, I gotta go now, see you later.'

Sakura doesn't know what it is exactly. It might have been nice to have more moments savouring the decision. But that's him. He's a busy man. The kind women want. Running his own life. Making his own way. He could have anyone. He wants Sakura.

His pickup truck kicks dust in its trail.

Sakura picks up the shovel and drops it again. She sees Tye leave the office and runs over.

'Hey guess what!' Sakura joins Tye in walking to the far stables. He is checking in on some of the new arrivals.

Tye looks over and sees her face.

'Whatever it is, you're happy. It must be good.' Tye half smiles

'Chris has asked me to move in.' Silence. Sakura fills in the pause. 'And I said yes.'

'Wow. That's big.' Tye keeps walking.

'I know, it's massive, I can't believe it. I said yes. That's ok, right?'

Sakura doesn't know why she's asking for Tye's approval. He has been here, quietly after Dad died, helping her with her riding skills, partnering her with Snowy, knowing they have a special connection. Knowing how much she needed something to care about and for someone to care about her. And when she came after high school to work full time, he became this constant figure. Their little chats. Sakura always wants to tell him big stuff. He always has a knack of just saying the right things, which is always extraordinarily little. Just the way she likes it. Now this is the biggest thing she has ever said. Please, let it be ok with this man she trusts.

'It's right, if it's right with you, Sakura,' Tye says and disappears quickly.

Sakura stands, going through his words. She can't leave and waits for him to return.

'I'm happy for you, gotta go check in on Hunter.' The new horse arrived last week. Tall, handsome. 'He looks like he needs re-shoeing,' Tye shouts back from out the far gate. He's left the stable through the other door. He could have come out the same way. Maybe he didn't know she had been waiting. He's gone.

'It's right with me,' Sakura convinces herself aloud. Repeating this, expecting this to enter her being. Become the truth of every fibre. Mom likes Chris. Jack took to Chris. Tye never complained about his passing visits when there was no bedding to drop.

Filling in the hollow created by Tye's few words, she's slightly annoyed but can't say why. On the drive home, she realizes – it's Tye who's taken the place of Dad and Eli. But in the end, he's the guy who pays her wages. She's attached too much importance to him.

So she can let it go, and see he's like her, not confident outside a horse arena. But she has Chris. Tye is on his own, as she has always been. She doesn't wish to be this anymore. So it's time to talk to Mom and make the commitment he's been asking for, for months.

Later, she would think of Tye's reaction.

CHAPTER 20

After work, she's so hungry she doesn't want to lose her appetite. She waits until after supper to give Mom the news.

'Are you sure? Sakura, it's a bit soon, you don't know him that well. What about University?' Mom presses her palms together, elbows on the table, looking straight at Sakura, asks all the questions she knew she would. The fear of something going wrong never leaves Mom these days. They both have it. It's time they had space from each other.

'It's okay. We talked about University. I'm going next year. I love him, Mom. He makes me happy.' Sakura throws her arms around her, hoping the hug will quiet the worried look in her eyes.

Mom releases her hug and puts on the kettle. Sakura knows she does this when she hasn't asked for coffee, to buy some time.

'I'm just worried, you know, with everything you've been through.' Her voice trails. Mom won't go there. The there that she wasn't there for. 'It's just you don't know him that well and you've already deferred Uni, you'll have to apply again.' She opens the cupboard and lifts down two mugs. 'Coffee?'

'Yeah sure, thanks, I do know him. I know it's not been for long, but he makes me feel…' Sakura is looking for the right word, '…he makes me feel happy and I said I'll go to Uni, I will.' Trying to convince both of them.

She thinks of heading for the shower, to break the chain of talking. So many days she wished for the talking, the insight that would come with it. But Mom just became so absorbed, her confidence gone, her intuition clouded, this kindness was the mom she remembered.

'You're barely twenty. I think University would be good for you. You got good grades despite…' Mom pauses, then says, '…me. You're clever, Sakura. You're smart. There's an entire world.'

'Mom.' Sakura puts her hand over her mom's. 'You married Dad young. You stayed on the Island. You were happy.'

'Sakura.' Her mom looks deep into her eyes. 'I just got really lucky. It doesn't happen so often. You have a whole future ahead of you.'

'Chris is motivated, Mom, hardworking, just like Dad. He's a fixer.'

'I know, but you haven't seen the future you might have without a relationship yet.'

After more than an hour of more of this, Mom resigns her protests.

'So, when is it happening?'

'This weekend.'

Her mom's face forms an O.

'Why wait? It's not like I'm getting married.' Just like that, Sakura flips it to talk of the move. 'I need to get a few things for the house. Do you want to come with me to the store this weekend?'

'Yes, sure,' Mom says quietly. Then reaches over and kisses the top of Sakura's head.

'Thanks, Mom.' Sakura rises, lifts one of Mom's cookies off the worktop, and skips off.

Only in the shower does she let her face fall into the worry and tension she's feeling. Everything Mom has said to her is right. But Chris is insistent. He's so busy with work, it's not fair to expect him to do the driving to see her and to call in on her.

Now she just has to tell Jack. Her anticipated quiet disapproval will be harder to shrug off. It will meet the pushed-down doubts of her own. Jack knows the Sakura who doesn't say a word. She will sense the thing she can hide from a mom she drifted away from in the years of grief. Jack knows how afraid Sakura has become of anywhere but here. Chris is the closest to change and staying the same she can get.

She picks up the phone. Jack is distracted, so the call is short.

'I'm moving in with him,' she says, looking at herself in the mirror, just to check it's her speaking.

'Thought so.' Jack is not challenging her. 'You're crazy about him. I knew you'd never go to University this year. But don't rule it out, okay? Promise me you won't get tied down.'

Immediately Sakura has an image of the pier, the boats at anchor, the netting folded to catch fish. She has in many ways tied herself to the harbour, but it's not a safe one, it's where Dad died. She can be close to the worst that's ever happened and maybe nothing as bad will ever happen again if she just stays right where she is.

Sakura knows this is safe. Stay here, don't leave, delay/defer University, don't change.

Her dad is still here. His spirit and memories of him lingering around the harbour, amongst the bobbing boats and coarse fishnets. Sometimes she has dreams of joining him in the water, being unable to surface.

Someday her tangled body will be wrapped in the nets, struggling to break free. No longer safe. Never was. Not since he died. The child of then, the woman of now. Both of them are united in the fear of a future where they know everything can be lost, in just a moment.

*

'They're lovely.' Her mom is rubbing the cotton material, patting down the pleats.

'Think they're the right size, and they'll match the tiles.' Sakura reaches up and lifts down the wrapped linen.

'I'll get these, and the bowls you like, a housewarming present.' Mom is warming to the idea of all of this, or trying to show she is.

Sakura sighs inward relief. She doesn't have a great deal of money. What Tye gives her for full-time work mostly goes on the loan to repay the small second-hand car she bought and the insurance and tax costs. Going out with Chris and some new clothes disappears the rest of her salary quickly. She has handed Mom money towards groceries but can't pay rent. Another reason life with Chris is helping them all move on.

Chris never asks her what she earns. She doesn't know what he earns. He seems comfortable. But what he has he works really hard on. He doesn't talk much about his past.

The parents he lost never come up. She understands this clamp down on painful subjects. It's her own way too. When she told him everyone was wondering about University for her, and if she was moving in with him, he just smiled.

'I went. A University locally, two years of a business course. You can find things to study on the Island.' She's not clear if he finished. But then he doesn't say much about anything.

She goes over the things he told her in her mind now, as Mom's paying for the material.

He always gets animated talking about how he built up something from nothing. University research had shown him an opportunity,

'That's how I found the opening. I was scouting around for a project subject. Bedding for horses was coming from way too far away for cost-effective distribution. If I could bring in a big shipment, and then distribute myself with a couple of part-timers, I could still supply under the cost. So I went to some agricultural and equine marketing and distribution events and that's where I met Tye, and you.' He smiled like she was one of the opportunities that had come with the sideline which had become a full thriving enterprise.

Chris found a niche and now provided the bedding to almost all the larger stables on the Island. Then he fixed up the house. She remembered him saying,

'It's mine now, I have to make sure everything is kept right.'

Could it be the same with her? Now he's securing Sakura. Sakura doesn't know what he means by 'kept right'. She has never crossed the bridge and lived on the other side. She's always lived at home. Her hobby becoming her job. Her family and her friend Jack. That's all she has known or needed.

Her lack of experience in life is obvious in their conversations about money, and futures. She keeps quiet with Chris. She's never paid an electric bill or had to budget for household things. But she admires his grown-up sense, dedication, and responsibility to duty.

She doesn't see yet duty can be an excuse to stay fixed, to never change, just feels maybe his efficiency and eye for chances might give her some too.

Mom has finished paying. Sakura takes the heaviest bags and then notices the heaviness around her mom's eyes.

'I'm going to be living alone for the first time since I was your age. And you're going to be living away for the first time. I'm sorry I was so remiss, Sakura. I wanted you to feel no pressure until you were ready to feel it.' Her eyes are full of tears. 'You've missed so many things. Don't miss out on your youth.'

'Come on, Mom. Chris has shown me what you build, and what you can do, and he'll help me find my move on from the stables. You wait and see. Why don't we go to Truffles?'

Over coffee, Mom opens up to Sakura. It feels like she has to get things out and find things out, and even though she doesn't have to, doesn't want to. She's afraid of her own doubts, but knows she has to be understanding of this decision.

'Can you tell me any more about him?' Mom tracing the top of the cup, looking dead straight across the table into Sakura's eyes. 'I don't know where the line is anymore. I want to respect your privacy, but I just need to know something, about his family. I know his parents are gone. Has he any other family?'

Sakura smiles outwardly, and inwardly sighs with relief. Chris told her when they first met that he had a sister, Zoey. If that conversation hadn't happened, she wouldn't have been able to tell Mom anything at all. He's rarely mentioned her again. She doesn't think it's wrong. They share a sense of disconnection from older siblings. Another thing they have in common.

'Zoey's his only sibling, like Eli to me. She's eight years older than Chris, left home when his parents died. He doesn't talk much about her and when he does, it's mostly short. She wanted out of Brightwood and off the Island, South Acres. It was too small for her.'

Mom nods, then asks, 'Do you know any more about her? Will you meet her now you're moving into the family home?'

Chris's always reluctant to talk about exactly where Zoey is and what she's doing. Sakura doesn't want to put across his dismissive approach, so she feeds the line like it's all that needs to be known.

'She's in Montreal, working with a design company. I won't meet her for a long time, most likely.' Thinking of Chris's response when asked. *No, Sakura she's doesn't come home. You won't be buddying up.* His annoyance obvious in his tone. 'I don't think I'll have a friend in her,' she confesses.

She doesn't say that she doesn't push Chris for personal information anymore. She knows from her own family how things can be difficult.

'She bailed out and he had to take on the work of the farm. I admire his decision to stay. Like my own. We're showing you can make a go of things here when you're young. It doesn't all have to be tourism. The Island gives you other chances.'

'I agree.' Mom smiles. 'He's learned the value of money and work young.'

They get to the car and Mom drives home. Sakura looks out the window. Why does every talk she has about Chris make her feel defensive? She's young, but she grew up when she was 12 on August thirteenth.

If people weren't so cautious about this move, she might even open up more instead of talking it up. Like how she notices he's careful with his money. He suggested that they go to a cheaper restaurant down the road when they were away for her birthday weekend last year. That was instead of dining at the hotel where they were staying.

She didn't have much and felt in no position to object, plus he had planned and booked the whole trip.

Her birthday is no longer this gaping reminder of another year without her father but of flowers, of love, of Chris. Perfect. But still, her first one with him. Another niggle. She wants to confess her fears, that she's doing all of this for the first time.

So many firsts.
Tomorrow a new one.

Chris would have come in with the pickup but there was a last-minute delivery.

Mom and she pack up Mom's car and travel the red road to Brightwood. Mom hasn't been here before. Sakura left her little car at the stables on Friday. Chris will drop her to work first thing Tuesday. She has Monday off, to settle in.

'See, Mom?' She hugs her mom's shoulder. 'It's not far.'

Ten kilometres between her home and work. Mom's house is twelve kilometres further in towards town. Not too far away from anywhere.

'As long as you're ok and know you can come back at any time you need to.'

When they get to the house, Chris isn't back.

Sakura knows where the spare key is.

'He's done a wonderful job. An excellent job.' Mom looks around, impressed. Relieved. After the bags and boxes are out, she just helps to take them to the porch. Sakura's glad, because she doesn't want to show how little she knows of where she lives now.

'I won't come in. Tonight's your first night. I'll visit soon.' Her car leaves dust. Just like Chris's pickup does when he leaves the stables.

Sakura leaves the unpacked bags and boxes in the hallway, unsure of where to put her things, waiting for Chris to come back.

Sakura wakes in their new bed linen, pressing her hand against its bright white. Smiling, she feels grown-up. So, this is what adults do, she thinks, resting her head on the soft pillow, yet to be moulded to the shape of her head.

Chris has already left to drop off supplies at the farms. Sakura walks around every room with a new eye, whereas before it was just a passing glance, rushing to work, having stayed over. Being the visitor. Now she is living here with Chris. This is their home.

Smiling at the kitchen, she's already thinking of colours to paint.

Chris's house has the old look of traditional farmhouses on the Island: two-storey, pitch windows with white exterior board cladding. The overhang on the ground level is supported by two wooden beams, providing a seating area protected from the glaring sun and harsh winter.

Empty flower baskets hang nailed to the beams, remnants of his mom's time. Sakura will fill them with flowers and make them her own.

Last night he told her that, actually, it was his parents who had upgraded the property some years back, with a new downstairs washroom, back porch, and fitted kitchen. He's just done the painting outside and a few interior jobs.

Sakura steps over her bags and boxes to fill the coffee pot and takes a cup outside.

Sitting on one of the chairs, leaning out over the countryside, she can at a stretch see the inlet to the right. The red road highlights its place and straight ahead a forest of sorts; green, swooping birds breaking the colour. Now that she's crossed the threshold, and no longer has to anticipate, she is happy, here with Chris.

Later that day, chopping vegetables, and making supper, Thai coconut curry. She hears the pickup and smiles.

'This looks lovely.' He wraps his arms around her waist, and she inhales his familiar smell. 'I couldn't wait to get home to you.'

She casts a downward slightly embarrassed gaze, she feels noticed and loved.

Bellies full and plates with traces of red curry lie carelessly piled in the kitchen sink. They will be done later.

'I'd love to walk, if you have the energy.' Sakura moves to get her mac.

'Sure. Let's show you the homestead.' He sounds proud. He should be.

They walk across the worn path through the forest's edge, towards the red road, and down to the water.

'I'm so happy you are here.' Chris puts his arm around Sakura and kisses her.

Tingles fill up her heart space and spread. She nuzzles into his shirt.

They step in unison along the bay, feeling the evening sun on their backs, talk about their day, the fisherman they see on a boat, and make up a story of his life. They laugh and head back home, hand in hand, making new shapes on their pillows.

CHAPTER 21

'Morning, I've made you lunch.' She gently throws the bag at him.

'Thanks, you're the best,' he says, kissing her goodbye.

It's like they have been doing it all their lives. She thinks of Mom and Dad in the kitchen, long ago, sharing love and chores.

The following few weeks form their own rhythm. Shared meals with Chris, long kisses, spontaneous, gentle pulls of Sakura's arm by Chris back into bed, dancing, and giggling. A feeling of safety and belonging prises open her bruised heart.

Working with Tye is just the same as always. She doesn't have to feel awkward because they've only ever spoken about things when she was ready to speak. She can keep the happiness wrapped up, away from doubt. And Tye will never intrude. So it's like it always was between them and at work. They work so well together there's no room for argument.

She never brings Chris up. When the thrill of it all gets too much for her, she runs to see her oldest equine friend and confidant.

'Here you go, you love the pink ones.'

Snowy grabs the last quarter of the apple.

Sakura grabs the saddle and lifts it high up onto Snowy's back.

'Let's go to the far paddock.'

Snowy concurs with a snort.

The last of the clouds clear, revealing the full warmth of June. Pressing in gently, Snowy responds and leans into a canter. Sitting deep in the saddle, Sakura smiles. The place she came running to, to get away from her grief, becomes the place of joy.

They both go for a gallop. The sounds of rhythmic hooves and flaring nostrils fill the quiet space of the north paddock. Sakura feels close to flying.

You fancy going to The Lobster? Her favourite restaurant. Sakura reads the text illuminating her phone. Warmth spreads through her body. *Yes, great*, Sakura texts back. She loves his spontaneity. How could she have doubted anything at all? It was nerves. This is the best she has felt in years.

'You see, Snowy? I just had to believe.' She presses her heels into his sides, and he takes off like she wants him to. Back toward the stables and on toward home, her new home.

'How was your day?' Chris asks, reaching for the menu.

'Yeah, great. Snowy's in great form. We went to the far paddock.' She feels the warmth of the afternoon ride again.

'You seem to love that old horse. Aren't you supposed to be working with the newer horses?' Chris knits his brow. 'Don't get too attached. He's an old guy.'

'I did earlier, this was our treat.' Sakura smiles and takes the menu out of Chris's hand in jest. 'I know what you're going to order. You don't need to look. It's the same thing every time.'

'Yes, but it doesn't hurt to look, you never know. That's how I found you. Covered in stable muck.' Chris winks at her, grabbing the menu back.

An hour later, sticky hands, napkins, and bowls full of crab claw shells. The smell of fresh fish and garlic trickles over the wooden seats onto the promenade, and the passers-by look up. They finish the evening with shared desserts and coffee.

'Life is one long date at the moment.' Sakura smiles.

'DIY this weekend then.' He puts his arm around her. 'Let's go home.'

Just to hear that last word, when it had come to mean nothing but sorrow, makes her day one of the best.

They spend the weekend testing sample colours on the wall, various shades of green.

'We could paint the kitchen units too. What about grey?' Sakura flips through until she lands on a shade she likes. 'What do you think?' She looks up to get Chris's attention.

'No, we're not changing them.' He is trying out a green on the wall. The one he picked.

'What do you mean? Why can't we?' Sakura's face changes.

'Why can't we?' He stops painting. 'Because they're solid oak.' His stony face, no space for movement. His eyes twitch a little, like when he's stressed going over his books. The silence seems to say, 'You are stupid.' The way he last spoke indicates discussion closed. Then he picks up his keys.

'Are you going out for long?' She had hoped they could sit down and share a bottle of wine, and a movie. Sakura knows they can't go for seafood every day.

'Work.' His given answer more than once.

The pickup drives away. Sakura goes back to the green colours, her excitement replaced by disappointment and something else she can't identify.

Chris comes back too late for a movie. He switches on the light and points to the wall.

'I like the sage. Come on, let's go to bed.'

'I thought so too.' Sakura nods. But it doesn't feel like they made a choice together.

They start painting the next morning. Brushes, masking tape, and paint trays fill the table. The preparation takes a long time.

'Come on, let's start,' Sakura says teasing. She wants to splash paint on his nose.

'We have to do it right.' He is serious, taking tape. Showing her how to seal all the edges.

So she takes it seriously. They hardly speak at all. Just concentrate on doing the job. Sakura thinks of building the pond. The laughter and passing out tea. Here it feels like she just has to give it all her energy. To get it right. This is what being an adult is.

Later that evening, the first coat is done, and they sink into the couch with a bottle of wine, limbs linking and folding into each other.

'We did good.' Chris kisses the top of her head. Just like Mom did last week when she told her she was moving out, that weekend, that she wanted her life to begin.

It feels like home.

CHAPTER 22

The phone in the kitchen goes.

'Don't stay on all night,' Chris warns. 'That's a line for suppliers too.'

'Ok.' Sakura hasn't seen Jack since she moved in with Chris. After the phone conversation before she moved out of home, there was a little silence. But then that was to be expected. They're both moving on.

The next vacation weekend Jack went off with other friends to another city, off the Island. Sakura wondered had Jack continued to come home just to connect with her. A loyal best friend. A true one. When Jack invited her to visit her in the university, Sakura always said no. She didn't fit in here. How would she fit in there?

'You want to visit?' Jack throws in her usual invitation. 'I'm staying near campus all summer for vacation work.'

'Yes, how does July suit?' But now, her life has changed, and purpose and place have sneaked in where there was none. 'You always talk about how fabulous the summer is.'

'I just can't believe it!' Jack responds.

'I told you I would someday.' Sakura smiles down the line.

When she comes off the phone, she's a little nervous. But Chris is in the doorway, smiling.

'Is that okay?' She knows he's heard.

'Sure.' He seems to have no issue at all.

Chris drops her off at the airport.

'Have a good time.' He leans over and kisses Sakura goodbye.

'Don't miss me too much.' She winks.

Things the past few weeks have made her feel wanted again. Pulling her back into bed. 'Come on, Tye won't mind if you're late,' Chris teases. His faded black t-shirt. It looks good on her. His eyes have that flirty, persistent look, the same one she saw the first day at the stables. They've been out again for supper. Maybe he wasn't used to having to cater for someone else at home. It's all a lot to get used to.

'Maybe next time I could go with you?'

Suddenly, Sakura feels like a girlfriend again. One he's interested in. Smiling, she walks into Departures, pulling her bag behind. *How lucky am I?* she thinks to herself.

An excited Jack runs over to greet her. Jack's hugs are the best. Even better than Chris's. She's surprised to notice herself feeling that.

I can't believe you're here.' Hugging her tightly.

They walk into a weekend of fun, dancing, and closeness.

'You all loved up now? Jack nudges her and pouts her lips.

Sakura squints her eyes and turns up her nose.

'Ah no, seriously, I'm happy for you, how's it going?' Jack's eyes change.

'Yeah. It's going great, I've done a few things, painting, you know.' Sakura looks away. 'It's lovely, he's lovely. I just can't believe it.' She drifts, for a moment gone.

'What can't you believe? You are amazing, anyone would be lucky to have you.' Jack snaps her back out of rumination, but Sakura doesn't quite believe her.

Sakura can't believe she is in her life, living with Chris. Sometimes perfect, sometimes shrieking, and stuck. Here with Jack, in the big city of big chances. Jack makes it smaller, taking her to all the places she knows. She looks on with pride and slight envy that Jack can navigate all this. Sakura wonders if she was brave enough to leave would she be happy in the hustle too? But then she thinks of her own life, and the value of nature. It would have been nice to have a slice of this high life though. You can't have it all. She never wanted it when they were growing up. Parties and boys were not her things. Maybe now? She'll never know.

By the time they bus it to the airport, Sakura is jaded but sure. Being with Jack and her friends and university makes Sakura's life expand. Things are possible now. She decides she's going to go for this and pretend that she is everything Jack sees in her. Going to University next year seems almost desirable. How will she tell Chris? She'll start by reminding him, she will always come home.

CHAPTER 23

The night she got back from her visit to Jack, he was at the airport with flowers. Then supper, then bed. Anytime she tried to bring up the trip he just smiled and said,

'Back to your reality now.'

Their lives develop their own rhythm, work, sharing meals and bed, walks, and occasional supper. It's small. Not many call to the house. When this niggles Sakura, she pushes it down and decides she likes it this way,

'Mom's calling over later for lunch. I'm going to buy some things for it first.'

'Oh nice.' Chris's heading out the door. 'Are you not working, eh?'

'Not till later. Tye has new horses arriving this afternoon and needs help later rather than earlier. I'll be gone most of tonight too.'

'See ya. I won't be back today. It's a pit stop for me.' He kisses her on the cheek, and she can hear the rev of his pickup. She knows where it is on the lane from that sound.

Sakura walks around the store picking pleasant things. Things she wouldn't normally buy. Later, back at home, she adds the finishing touches to the table. Flowers in a small vase. Some of the lavender growing wild in the corner of his yard.

Chris said his mom planted it years ago. 'It's beautiful,' she remembers saying. 'Did she like gardening?' 'Yeah, I guess so.' The vagueness of his answer and his gruff tone. Sakura didn't ask anymore. She tried to fill in the gaps of this nothingness. No family around. Just his word for his whole life up till now. Her family was perfect until the day on the pier ripped it apart.

Smelling the fresh lavender, Sakura repeatedly inhales its scent. It's never enough. Seeing Mom pull up.

She walks over. 'It's so good to have you here.'

'Good to finally be here!' Mom seems relieved to arrive.

'I know, we're so busy decorating. Sorry, you had to wait.' She leans in through the rolled-down window to kiss her.

'No Chris?' Mom reaches over and grabs fresh rolls before jumping out of the car to give Sakura a full embrace. 'Hi there, Blossom.'

Suddenly it feels like the old days.

'Ah Sakura, it's lovely, they're lovely.' Pointing to the purple bundle in Sakura's hand.

'Come on, everything's ready.' Sakura's delighted to have her here, to show her all she has done. To show someone.

'Ah, it's lovely, Sakura, you've made it homely. The cupboards might look nice painted,' she points out, then slowly half puts her hand over her mouth.

'No, don't worry, I said the same thing. But it's old oak.' Sakura smiles because her taste is confirmed by her mom, who has artistic flair.

'Yes. Colour tastes change and oak ages so beautifully.' Her mom inclines her head.

This eases Sakura's anxiety about Chris's insistence. No change. Her mom understands the quality like he does, where she fails to. Then, after everything new has been shown, and the excitement subsides, it's just the two of them. The first silence falls.

'How are you doing alone? At home?' Sakura asks.

'I'm keeping myself busy. And there are canvases everywhere.'

There's a gleam of something else. Sakura realizes her mom is probably under less pressure now she has a chance to be alone with what she lost. It's an empty nest. But it's hers.

They sit and eat and chat about everything and nothing. Failing to bridge that gap. There will always be before and after Dad died. The chasm is huge now, the passing time making it more difficult and easier not to try.

Bringing the dishes over to the sink, Mom places a hand on her shoulder. 'Are you ok?'

Sakura shrugs to shake her hand away.

'I'm fine. I'm happy.'

The words taste sour on Sakura's tongue. This was supposed to be a happy reunion. One full of life. Why does death always have to come into it? It lingers close to her own niggles about Chris. Turning around.

'I just want you to be happy.' Mom's hand drops. The gulf widens.

Sakura can hear the tears in her voice. It's this that makes her so angry. At some stage in every encounter, Sakura will end up reassuring Mom. She pushes moming away, but it's what she needs. She ends up giving it and resents this. This is why she had to leave.

'I am, come on, I made dessert, let's bring it out to the yard. I want to show you what I've planted.' Sakura pushes down any doubt about her life with Chris. He rescued her from herself, her crippling grief. This has to be ok.

'Ah, that smells wonderful.' Smelling the rich French lavender, Mom rubs her hands together, infusing her palms with the sweet aroma. She picks some more to take home. They take their time walking around, looking at each new plant.

'Bye, love you.' Kissing her goodbye, reassured, again. Sakura waves from the door.

'How did the lunch go?' Chris grabs the wrapped-up leftovers from the table.

'Good.' Her eyes are strained. But she knows it went well, as well as it could have. Someone else has seen her happy home, and witnessed her happy life with Chris. It's just all going to take more time.

'Let's have our own social gathering,' he suggests so casually.

'I'd like that.' Her reply is casual. But her heart leaps in her chest.

CHAPTER 24

It's the weekend they have Jack coming, and Chris's friend's coming over too. Sakura has met Mark a few times, mostly in passing. He's also a supplier but of horse blankets. No competition. He lives off the Island but comes now and then to visit stables. She's seen him out in the yard at home and always feels like she's interrupting a business conversation. She doesn't know anything about projections or sales. She just knows horses.

Sakura feels excited, bringing in the bags of groceries and placing them on the counter. Chris passes her and puts the two-four of beer in the fridge, turns and kisses her.

'You look beautiful.'

Smiling, she kisses him back, he tugs her hand, and she playfully pats it away. 'We can't. I have to get the food ready.'

He pulls her hand again, and this time she follows him.

Later she prepares the marinated chicken and seafood for the barbeque. Jack arrives and greets her with a warm hug.

'You look gorgeous, that new?'

'You like it? Picked it up during the week,' Sakura responds, giving a twirl. 'You seem so happy.' Gives her an extra squeezy hug back. The safe ones since August thirteenth. The ones she trusts. Jack loves her because she wants to, and she's loved Sakura all her life.

'I am.' Jack glances out towards the line of smoke in Chris's direction.

Sitting around the fire pit, plates scattered, the last of the barbeque smoke drifting away with the wind. Sakura is laughing, sitting beside Chris, half on his lap. His hand behind her back pulls her closer. Sharing the story of how they met.

Chris's friend, Mark, comments, 'I knew you must be special because it's not everyone he brings home to Brightwood.'

'In fact, I'm the only person he's brought home!' Sakura laughs.

'She's certainly brought the bachelor pad to life,' Mark agrees.

'Now.' Chris points his beer at his friend. 'I kept this place before Sakura.'

'A house proud man. Worth kidnapping.' Jack smiles at Sakura. 'Where do I get one?'

Her heart leaps, the flames of the pit giving extra warmth. There are friends here. There is a feeling that life might happen and spread out in all directions. Her best friend is sleeping over. There may be University in the fall. She and Chris will get through that. Sakura is the only woman he has allowed into the centre of things, into the home of his mother. He has let her plant up the hanging baskets. He has done all he can, without letting her take over. She wouldn't want that.

Everyone gets up to go to their rooms at the same time.

'Night, hostess.' Jack hugs her. Mark does the same.

She is being what Mom was all those years at the barbecues. She may even start making pizza every Friday. The perfect end to the evening.

CHAPTER 25

Sitting out back on the newly renovated porch, on her favourite chair. It is angled, so she just reaches her feet up on the rail. Fluffy socks, an old cardigan pulled over her hands, and steaming coffee in her hand, breathing in the last of the summer air.

Below, the forest fills the whole frame, various shades of green, red, and some brown. She loves this place. Having thought her home was gone forever, there was another here waiting. Grabbing her notebook, she writes. When finished, she places the band around the middle and holds it to her chest.

Suddenly without warning, she misses her dad, longing to tell him about this life, about Chris. Like the river behind the trees, the awareness of what life would have been like, if he had lived, is obscured from view. She knows the river is there, and she knows that a different life was there. Tears fall and land on her notebook, pulling her feet off the rail, her head falls into her hands, and she sobs big angry sobs, and it's too late when she hears the screen door bang.

'What's wrong, Sakura? What happened?'

But seeing him just makes her cry more. Chris, the person who cares, her person. What did she do to deserve him?

He drops to his knees and places his hand on her lap and holds her head.

'I miss Dad. I want him to meet you. He never can.'

Holding her head and meeting her puffy gaze, Chris replies,

'I love you. I know you miss him so much. I'm here, I'm here for you.'

He pulls her in closer and hugs Sakura completely. The first hug she fully trusts. The others made her feel safe at times and aroused her other times. This is a hug of coming home. She melts, initially embarrassed for Chris to see her like this, now relieved, grief shared. No longer alone.

They sit and talk till darkness comes, meals missed, but no one is hungry. Sakura tells him everything about that day. She has recounted it briefly before. But never the details that pull at her heart to this day, when she feels an alive joy her father will never feel again. The hidden guilt and irrational shame that cause her stomach to lurch.

'I can still remember the colour of his face.' Sakura sees that little girl at the pier. 'Grey, white, blue, nondescript colour. I didn't know then death had a colour.' And she wants to scoop that girl up, carry her away from everything then, and that came after. The years before Chris.

'Come here, that must've been awful.' Chris pulls her closer and Sakura cries harder.

'But I still think it was my fault if only I had…' Her voice stops. The tears block her vocal cords. Gulping sounds emerge instead of words.

'It wasn't your fault,' Chris reassures her.

She believes him. A new intimacy arises and is felt in the cool air, where bats fly too close, not knowing something special is happening. The day when he finally has all of her trust.

CHAPTER 26

Pulling her car onto the main road, leaving the red dust rise in its rear, Sakura heads towards the local town, Redbridge. Having worked over the weekend – Tye had new horses arriving and needed help preparing the stables and exercise – Sakura's enjoying being off mid-week. It feels different and free, and the ever-present loneliness is at bay. Walking the streets narrow and wide, Sakura feels herself melt into the pavement and become part of the town.

She loves its character, smaller than where she grew up with Jack, but equal in its charm, dotted with local gourmet stores full of fresh local produce where candles and small boats canvas the windows.

Sitting down in the local coffee shop, she orders lunch and finds a spot at the window. The tea warms her as she chats to the owner, a lady in her forties. Sakura likes her. She is calm and gentle, even in the busy little café. Afterwards, Sakura wanders into the bookstore next door, smelling old books, inhaling their stories.

Then passing a local theatre, she sees a flyer for a musician she likes. He's playing later in the month. She gets two tickets and pins them to the noticeboard at home.

The night of the show arrives, and she's excited. The evening starts out well. Food before the show, chats with Chris, they hold hands walking to the venue. Inside, they get drinks and sit down. Sakura's smiling and travelling with the songs. She glances at Chris and doesn't notice his mood at first. Then, her favourite song comes on, and she's beaming and reaches over and whispers in his ear. He doesn't respond.

She puts it down to the loud venue.

Outside afterwards, Chris has walked on a few steps ahead, hands in pockets, shoulders slightly hunched. Sakura calls out, again he doesn't respond. Almost catching up to him, she says slightly loud,

'What's wrong? Why are you walking ahead of me?'

'Nothing wrong. I'm just walking, I'm cold.' He's not attempting to wait.

'Can you wait? I can't walk that fast!' She half runs to keep up. He doesn't slow down.

Sakura doesn't understand what's happening. She just had an amazing evening, now she realizes she was alone in the experience.

'What's wrong with you? Why wouldn't you wait for me?' Sakura says angrily when they reach the car.

'Nothing wrong with me. You're overreacting and shouting.'

'You know how much I loved this guy, his music, how much this meant to me, and you're storming off after. What's wrong with you?'

'For the hundredth time. Nothing is wrong with me. I'm acting normal. You're out of control.'

He's so quiet in saying this. She's so unreasonable. She realizes people are listening to them. It looks like she's the one losing it. That's when she thinks of the classroom and Ms. McCleod. Running out because the teacher was ignoring the pitiful flutters of the white butterfly.

Her anger is pitiful flutters. Chris is driving as if nothing at all has happened. Sakura sits in the car and fumes in silence, all the way home.

That night, she tosses and turns, upset by what happened, and when she turns to talk to Chris, he is fast asleep.

The next morning, he acts like nothing has happened. Sakura wonders if she maybe overreacted last night.

'Last night?' She brings it up with Chris over breakfast.

'It's no big deal. It was cold. I had a sore shoulder.'

And that's really why he was quiet. Sakura reaches over, hugs, and kisses him.

'Sorry for being cross with you last night. I didn't realize you were in pain.'

Chris gets up and places his empty coffee cup beside the sink. Sakura walks over to where he stands and leans in, pulling his arm over her shoulder and around her waist.

'Gonna let me breathe?' Chris half laughs and lifts her arms off and back. He kisses her forehead, smells of toothpaste and coffee. 'Gotta go, chat later.' His shoulder seems fine as he reaches for his jacket. Chris turns and leaves. Then, as an afterthought.

'I'll be back for lunch today. Why don't you come home too?'

Lulled into intimacy over lunch, Sakura talks about her favourite parts of last night.

He still doesn't seem to want to talk about it. She tells him anyway.

'Are you going to eat that?' He reaches for half her sandwich.

'No.' She doesn't feel hungry.

The music is still in her, but twelve hours later, it loses some of its magic. She hums it alone on the drive back to the stables.

CHAPTER 27

Seasons play catch up on South Acres Island. Snow often layers the ground in May while lupins simultaneously try to push up from beneath the earth.

And almost overnight they arrive, white gone, a burst of pink and purple replaces the winter silence.

Summer runs into fall, and Thanksgiving arrives on a mild October day.

Early in the week, Sakura and Chris travel to the local grocery store and walk the aisles, filling their shopping cart with things festive and extra things they don't need.

The closeness is back. She can feel it between aisles of veg and canned tomatoes. He suggests getting some more snacks and treats. Sakura is delighted. The day itself is wonderful. Early morning cuddles, delicious breakfast, and food treats all day, following into the late evening. Then they meet with Jack and some other friends for drinks beside the fire pit. Chris and Sakura cuddle under a blanket and wait for the stars to come out.

It's as if the concert night never happened.

You can, on nights like this, believe in the stars again.

It's mid-December. Sakura feels the steam rise from Snowy. It creates magical shapes in the early frosty morning. They make their way along the woody track. Birds dare to branch out, poking out what food they can from where the snow is thinnest.

Winter song is heard in hushed tones. Grateful to be out here away from the mood she left behind, but Sakura goes through it in her head on a loop, trying to make sense of it.

All week long the latest tension has hung in the air. During the week, Chris came home late from work. Hearing the door bang, she smiled. But his head was down, and he made some inaudible noise and didn't look at her.

'There's some food left over. It's in the fridge if you want it.' She was looking forward to catching up.

'Yeah, maybe later, not that hungry.' He walked away. Sakura didn't think much of it.

Chris arrived in later, suggesting they watch a movie, they did, and he fell asleep. Nudging him to go to bed 'What?' He got cross. She left him. Sakura hopped into bed alone. In the middle of the night, she noticed that he was far over the other side of the bed. She moved over to wrap her arm around him, but even in his sleep, he didn't welcome her.

She thinks of this and says into Snowy's ear, leaning across his neck to do so,

'What am I doing wrong?'

The question stays with her on the drive home to Brightwood. She's relieved to find the house in darkness and saddened not to know where Chris is tonight. A text arrives later: *working late.*

Sakura wakes early the next morning with a knot in her stomach. It feels like grief, but no one has died. Getting up, throwing on her boots and long chunky cardigan, she heads outside, furious and confused. Why is he like this? What's wrong with me? Why is he annoyed at me?

These questions fill her head, and the impact makes for stern walking.

Back inside, Chris is up, making coffee.

'What's wrong with you? Why are you treating me like this? You didn't speak to me last night, and you pretty much fell out of bed trying to get away from me.' Sakura is furious now, her words stumbling out fast pace, tears in her eyes.

'Nothing's wrong.' He carefully pours his coffee and sits down. 'I was just tired. You're making a big deal out of nothing.'

Sakura expects him to say something else but nothing comes.

'No!' she shouts. 'This is not ok. You come home late, don't speak to me, you're in a mood all night, and all week, and don't come near me in bed. It's not ok.'

They had planned to go somewhere. It's a Sunday. Sakura gets her coat and bag, and her actions make it clear she is heading out without him. Going upstairs to get something, she catches sight of herself in the washroom mirror and shouts out a cry, then whispers, 'Fuck, fuck,' banging her hand on the sink.

Walking back downstairs, Chris is standing there.

'Come on, sit down.' He sounds so reasonable.

Reluctantly she does and says everything again. This time he looks at her and responds.

'I feel you're trying to control me, telling me there is food in the fridge. I didn't want food.' He says his mother was always like that. Telling him when to eat, what to do.

Sakura, sitting at the corner of the table, kicking her foot off the wooden leg.

'I wasn't trying to control you. I was just trying to do something nice. I was trying to wake you up for a proper night's sleep. Cooking your supper is not controlling. It's loving.' Sakura looks away, annoyed that she has to explain her kindness. 'My dad loved that my mom cooked for us and so did I.'

'I know, it just seemed like that.' Chris avoids her gaze, looking everywhere but at her. Later she would wonder does he ever see her.

'Well. It wasn't.' Sakura becomes defensive and is about to get up. Chris pulls her chair towards him. A little surprised by the gesture but she likes his decisiveness.

'I'm sorry, let's go to that place, you know where you wanted to go.' Chris reaches in and kisses her roughly before she has time to answer.

She puts her hands to her bruised lip and shakes her head.

'I know that your mom maybe made you feel that. It's not what I'm doing here.'

She wants him to feel secure. She isn't trying to control him.

'I know where we need to go first.'

After. Picking up her underwear off the floor, Chris slaps her bum. Then laughs, his smell of horses and coffee on her neck, his breath dampens her skin. The slap pushes her against the table. She can see the scum line forming in her cold coffee cup.

It's a Saturday morning, Sakura slinks out of bed, careful not to wake Chris, but he wakes and takes her hand and pulls her back in. She doesn't resist, him pulling at her cami, teasing it off, smiling in jest, trying to keep it on. He succeeds.

Looking into his eyes, she wants to feel every bit of him. This is as close as she gets. Always something missing. Holding him close, so close.

He finishes and pulls her into a half hug.

The bit that was there for her has already gone.

Looking at her diary later, she notices she has passed her date with no period. She wonders if she should take something to prevent anything else. Chatting with Chris.

'No. I'm careful,' he reassures her. There's nothing to worry about, not a chance of anything happening. Not wanting him to feel undermined, she believes him and does nothing.

Then, a tug on her lower right side, not painful but enough to catch her attention. Breasts feel fuller. Her period must be due. The tug continues over the next few days until it passes. She drives to another town and pulls up outside the drugstore. Hands sweating, she can't believe she's doing this. Maybe she's being silly and almost turns the car to go. Maybe she's not.

'I'll get some peace of mind and then no more taking chances,' she says to herself in the rearview mirror.

Sliding the slim package into her hand, Sakura hands it to the girl, and what seems like the longest transaction in the world ensues.

Almost running into her car, shutting the door, holding the test. At home, she reads the instructions, does what is asked, and then waits. Pacing the hallway, leaving the plastic strip to tell her everything she fears and yet desires.

Sakura recalls her mom talking about being pregnant with her. And that she just knew she would be a girl.

'Being pregnant with you was different,' Mom would remind her, kissing her head. They had always wanted two children. Dad was so excited. Mom would say, 'You were perfect, small. All you.'

This feels different, unsure, alone. Beep, her phone reminds her it's time.

Picking it up so slowly, Sakura sees two pink lines, then drops it as if a baby might pop right out of the plastic decider. Panic, gulping air, she rushes outside, and the half cries and wails can be heard by the nearby horses in the stables, who momentarily look up and snort and then look down and continue eating their hay.

Thoughts race, confused and out of control, tripping over each other:

Will my drinking last weekend hurt the baby? I'm too young. What about University?

Chris will go mad. I'm supposed to be at work later. I'll have to ring Tye.

Eventually, she sits and rocks herself, tucks her legs up to her chin. Tears form bubbles at the corner of her eyes and then roll aimlessly into her winter sweater.

Having told Tye she won't be in, Sakura finds the full-length mirror in their bedroom and pulls up her sweater, standing to one side, to see if she can notice anything. Placing her hand on her stomach, she instinctively pats it gently. Switching to both sides, nothing looks different. What if the test was wrong?

Chris has been texting her, but she hasn't answered, not knowing what to say.

The afternoon slides into the evening, and he finds her in the same spot, her knees lowered, placed on a chair.

'Hey, what are you doing out here? It's dark.' He heads back inside, and she follows. Noticing her puffy eyes. 'What's wrong? What happened?'

Tears well up again. This time he reaches for Sakura.

'What's wrong? Tell me.'

'Let's sit down,' Sakura says. Pulling out the narrow plastic strip, she hands it to him and looks away.

'What's this? Is this a pregnancy test? Are you pregnant?'

She just nods, yes. Waiting for the shout of anger, the blame. She feels she wants to blame him herself. You said you were careful.

'We'll figure it out.' His warm embrace. Not what she expects.

A comment which replays in her head while Chris tries to feel the baby under his large hand placed snugly on her belly. She feels the warmth of this. The anger dissolves.

She believes him. *Why do I keep getting it wrong?* Sakura wonders to herself. I thought he'd be mad. He's not. If anything, he is delighted.

The weekend is spent thinking about whether it's a boy or a girl, looking at the size of what the baby would be now, a speck, small but massive. Sakura's bubble of love expands and fills over the coming weeks.

CHAPTER 28

It's a Sunday. Chris has to do a delivery at the last minute so couldn't come. She drives the road and then onto the highway to home. Cedar Lane.

'No Chris?' Mom is in the kitchen putting the finishing touches to lunch.

'No.' Sakura puts on her smile. The look on her face makes Mom sit down.

Sakura's mom is still hugging her.

'Are you ok?' Her first question.

'I didn't plan it, but I think so.' She glosses over a rising doubt. But it's written in Mom's face, so it hits her in the face too. She is delighted but worried. Chris being so positive was a relief. But she didn't want to trigger anything by being unsure herself.

'What about your studies? You had thought of University again after visiting Jack.' Again she plays the reassuring parent.

'Chris and I talked about it. I can apply again next year and maybe start later in the term, and he'll support studies and the baby.' But the wisdom, hidden and growing in Sakura, knows that later will never come.

'Oh!' Mom can let the joy in now.

There, the confetti of excitement again. Life in the house after the terrible death. Beginning again. Live in the moment, Sakura, drive away doubt. By the end of lunch, Mom's pulling out old baby grows, so small, a little frayed, still perfect.

'What about your job, surely you can't continue working?' Mom places the little clothes on the side of her bed in her old room.

'It's fine. The doctor says I can continue so long as I feel comfortable and able. I've been doing it all this time. I'll be careful, promise.' Sakura feels this is going to be an ongoing conversation but is secretly relieved Mom cares so much. She's in the parental role. Not just offering her fears, and regrets, helping her to see the eventualities, to plan. She says out straight,

'I'm not so sure, Sakura, it could be very risky, some of the horses are wild, you said so yourself.'

'I know but I won't ride them. I promise just Snowy and the quieter ones. Trust me, I know what I'm doing, you gotta trust me.' The conversations have to end there for now. It's like when Dad died. One thing at a time.

'Come on, I'll make tea.' Mom opens the door that leads to the kitchen. 'I've a lot to tell you! You remember I told you I carried you differently to Eli, that it felt different? Tell me how you're feeling, and we may be able to guess!' She's smiling.

'It's early days.' Sakura sits as Mom fusses over her, offering her endless snacks and advice on vitamins.

'Promise me you'll talk to Tye first thing.' Mom presses this last point.

Sakura notices Chris didn't mention her job. Why? He knows the danger of what she does more than anyone. She convinces herself that it's her mom's job to worry. Chris is just being a guy.

'I'll practice by telling Snowy first.' Suddenly Sakura is nervous. This is real.

'Tye'll have a hard job replacing his right-hand woman.' Mom puts a hand on Sakura's shoulder. Chris never said anything like this. He just assumes she will carry on, as she always has and always does.

*

Monday. She decides to get in at first light and saddle Snowy up. Start the day right. Snowy snorts indifference when she tells him the news. Sakura has decided to keep riding until she can't, staying away from the newer, unpredictable horses, sticking to Snowy and others she knows. Limiting danger.

'Come on, let's take Baby for a canter.' Pressing her heels in, a gentle squeeze, not much is needed, Snowy knows her deeply. They go, feeling a perfect rhythm. Sakura smiles and raises her head to the sky.

'Hey look, we're flying. I'm going to show you everything.' Baby has been seeing everything for some weeks. Alive before Sakura even knew.

Horses know linear time to be nonsense. Snowy gives his all, and Sakura offers hers. This will be the ride out she will remember in the days ahead. A woman growing a life force, an old, trusted friend feeling it, both of them united in something new.

After, she calls into Tye. 'Knock knock, hey, Tye.' She is nervous, but sure.

'Oh, hi.' Tye looks up, preoccupied. Paperwork for a horseman is a puzzle. 'How are you? Didn't hear you arrive.'

'I was in early, couldn't sleep.' Sakura pulls up a chair and sits down. 'So, I wanted to talk to you about something.' Sakura is slow to say the words and doesn't know why. She eventually tells him.

He doesn't say a word. A man of few words he just rises out of the chair and comes around to her.

'You'll be a wonderful mom. I know it. The way you are with the horses tells me that.' Putting a hand on the shoulder of his right-hand woman.

She has tears in her eyes. For some time she felt something like a disapproval, certainly a distance since Chris. But it's clear. Tye cares. And after the congratulations he moves the conversation quickly to how to keep her safe. They agree what Sakura has already decided. Sticking to reliable horses, no riding new, just-broken horses.

'And you talk to me, Sakura, if anything is too much.' He takes his hand away.

She's so grateful to know he is not thinking of himself, of the shortfall in the stables. He's not just a boss. This man is a proven friend. Like Snowy. An old and trusted friend. For almost ten years she has felt alone. Now she knows she never was. The grief isolated her. This new life will be the beginning of so much more.

Sakura feels it already, the air turning dirty grey, filling with invisible putrid toxins. She tries to push it out.

'You ready to go?' she shouts down into the kitchen.

'Yeah,' Chris responds.

It's in her head. *Everything is fine.* She's just nervous.

'You look handsome.' Reaching up to kiss him. His being handsome is something she never has a doubt about.

'Thanks.' He turns away, reaching for the keys to his pickup. 'We better go. Traffic could be bad.' He hasn't looked at her once.

Sakura's arm drops back down, her tears spill out and leak, dripping all over the place. *Today is supposed to be a really special day. Why do I feel like crap, like I've done something wrong*? Wiping them up quickly. If Chris notices he doesn't say anything. But he does notice she's not moving fast enough.

'Come on! Let's go.' Chris has already left, and the screen door slams behind him.

Sitting in his pickup, she slips into silence. Chris doesn't react. Slipping out of silence into annoyance. There are two choices now. Mention it and cause more harm. Keep quiet and feel terrible. What is Baby feeling now?

'What's wrong? Do you not want to go?' Sakura sits up, trying to get Chris to engage.

'What are you talking about?' He shakes his head. 'Of course I do. I'm here, aren't I?'

Sakura checks herself. Maybe it's the hormones that come with pregnancy. Chris mentions it enough. She goes with how she wanted it to be first.

'Can you believe it? We're going to see our baby,' Sakura says, forcing the excitement to mask her fear. 'I wonder if we'll see their features?'

'You won't see much. It will look like a blob,' Chris adds, pulling on his experience of scanning animals in foal. 'I'll probably be able to see if it's a boy or a girl.' A sneaky smile fills his face.

'Don't tell me if you do. I don't want to know.' Sakura wants to know the day she gives birth. She feels happy at his smile, even though what he says worries her. He seems to be coming around. When he comes around it's always so much easier.

They pull up outside. A queue to get into the lot sets him off.

'I'm glad we're not dying. They need twice the spaces they've got.' They wait and wait. She doesn't know what to say so she lets him sit there.

When they get to the unit they're faced with more queuing. They're not the only couples. Most of them look as if they're ok to wait. Chris seems to be fuming now. Sakura can't help feeling that she is pulling him away from something more important.

She can hear others talking to each other in whispers and exchanging with other couples. Two women are there alone. She wouldn't have looked out of place. But it would have been wrong. She has a partner.

'Your first?' One woman smiles at her.

'Yes,' Sakura answers with a smile of her own. She could kiss the woman for asking.

Chris says nothing. It's their turn. He jumps up and walks ahead.

Sakura wants to cry, watching his straight-backed gait, rising above her queasiness to follow him.

The sonographer's glasses are held by a long nose. She pulls up the machine closer to the bed and pats the side for Sakura to sit down.

'Is this your first?' She smiles.

'Yes.' Sakura can't smile this time. Chris nods too.

The sonographer is full of chat from then on. So normal. This talk. Sakura wonders if she notices Chris's mood. She doesn't say anything if she does. Her head is spinning. Chris slinks on a chair further back, his hand under his chin, foot tapping on the floor.

'Everything's fine.'

'Really!' Sakura beams.

'You're a healthy young woman and this is a healthy pregnancy.' The sonographer nods.

Sakura looks at Chris. You see? I'm not doing anything wrong. Chris looks at the screen hard.

'I don't want to know the sex,' Sakura blurts out in case he says it and sees it.

'Understood, now the audio.' The sonographer flicks the switch.

Sakura hears the baby's heartbeat. It's almost masked by her beating fear. But then she realizes. This is the sound of my child.

The machine beeps and the phone rings. The next appointment is due.

'You can collect the pictures on the way out.' The sonographer, matter of fact at this point, wipes away the ultrasound gel, leaving some blobs behind.

Chris leaves first. She hurries to get to the desk before him, to take the pictures, in case he leaves without her. The scans won't show the sex, the sonographer assured her.

Doors closed, back in the pickup.

'What's wrong with you? Did you not want to be there? Today was supposed to be a really special day, and you seem so angry! What's wrong with you?' Sakura shouts in between tears. She wishes she could rein it in, not let so much out at once.

'Nothing's wrong. I'm here. We saw the baby.' Chris fumbles around for the parking ticket. Looking anywhere but at her. Even his side face looks set in anger. 'You're angry. You're out of control.' His words spitting at her. In this small space, they seem to physically pierce her.

'I'm out of control?' Sakura places a protective hand on her bump. 'You need to calm down.' How much of this is her baby hearing? Their baby.

'What do you want from me? I'm here, aren't I?' Chris shouts back, roughly pushing the ticket into the machine.

'How dare you tell me to calm down!' Sakura wonders why he's here. He acts like he wants to be anywhere else. 'You barely speak to me at all. You looked so angry throughout the scan. You ruined this for me.' Sakura's breathing rapidly, biting tears back, wondering what this is doing to the baby.

The journey home is quick and full of pain. They don't even say one word. He brakes abruptly when they arrive home, she gets out and runs to the house. He follows with words.

'You're all over the place. Imagining things.'

On the porch, the one he asked her to move in with him on, Sakura sits in her favourite chair, trying to get her breathing back under control, her heart rate, her baby. Chris looks over at her, before turning on his heel.

'I'm going to work. I've had enough of this.' Chris slams the pickup door shut.

Sakura jumps with a bang, she looks down. Three little pictures of Baby have fallen from her lap. She was clutching them all the way home, not looking at them once.

'How could I forget you?' The tears she shed earlier this morning fall freely now.

CHAPTER 29

Sakura pulls up in her mom's drive, waiting for a moment to see if she can release all that she couldn't for the last three hours. She's been driving around and walked the length of the boardwalk twice. She could almost hear the laughter and feel their steps under her feet, hers, and Jack's, often shared on the planks.

Her mom sees her before she gets out. Her smile is big against the window. Sakura has a second to bury it all. The last six horrible hours. She reaches for any level of excitement.

'How did it go? Do you have pictures?' It's easy to feel it again, looking at Mom's beaming face. This woman is ready to embrace being a nana. Making up for the past. Helping the future.

Sakura recounts the morning but glosses over the dark parts that cause her gut to lurch and twist.

The giant sense decreases slightly as they look at the baby's features in the small pictures, guessing what each is.

'Is it ok if I stay here tonight?' Sakura packed a bag as soon as she went into the house. 'Jack's in town tomorrow, for the weekend. We thought we could catch up.'

'Of course! Your room is always made up for you. You know that.' Mom kisses her on the cheek. 'Everything ok?'

'Yeah. Just so tired.' Sakura averts her eyes and pats her belly.

She hasn't seen Jack since she told her the news. Sakura was surprised by her reaction.

'Ah Sakura, that's amazing, I can't believe it.' Jack's voice was soft, almost tearful, over the phone. She didn't ask about University.

'Really? You're not shocked, disappointed?' Sakura reaching to her friend for the approval she's missing.

'Of course not, it doesn't have to be like things were, you know, University, job, marriage, things are different, you are different, you create your own life. And Chris, how is he about it?'

Sakura paused for a minute, all the loving and wretched moments mixed into one. Confusion.

'He's delighted, so happy, being extra caring about me.' Sakura was not sure why she said this, it's not true. Maybe she wanted to make believe it true.

'That's great, I want to see you, I'll be back in a few weeks.'

'That'll be close to our first scan, I'd love to see you, I miss you.' Sakura surprised herself with her own words. Tears bulged behind her eyes and she was relieved Jack couldn't see her.

'Love you too, oh my God, can't believe it, Mama Sakura!'

'Bye.' Sakura held the phone in one hand and pressed the other to her mouth. Her tears fell.

For the first time since she left, Sakura wants to be here in Cedar Lane, wants to be in the house that once felt so like heaven, so much a home. Sakura wants to be alone, away from Chris.

Slipping under the warm duvet and pillow that smells of Mom, of home, she burrows into the safety of her bed. It's early, but pregnancy provides the perfect excuse for almost anything. Turning on her phone, it beeps and beeps… she feels sick waiting for the messages to appear.

She worries about hearing from Chris, and also not hearing from Chris.

Two missed calls and a few messages. All from him.

Where are you?

I'm worried about you.

The scales tip. She feels more in control and then angrier at his behaviour. Maybe she should have stood up for herself more at the scan. Sending a brief text. She is with Mom staying here for the night. Talk tomorrow. He rings. She doesn't answer. Then a text arrives.

I'm sorry about today x

No explanation. Apologies are easy. Reasons are more important. But at least she has shown him. That has to count for something. Tomorrow, she won't have to be a girlfriend/partner. She won't have to be needy.

March is the forgotten spring, old snow piled under fresh white. The town feels tired, too cold for too long.

'Ah, look at you and wee little baby bump.' Jack runs to Sakura on the boardwalk the following morning. They embrace for longer than normal.

'It's not that big, the bump.' Sakura pats to show barely a rise off her normally flat belly.

'But I see it, your little, tiny baby.' Jack reaches her head down to her belly and whispers something.

'What are you saying about me?' Sakura laughs.

'That's between me and baby.' Jack winks at her and takes her arm, the familiar link. She takes them to *Bean's*. 'I can't believe you're going to be a mama.'

Sakura's eyes fill with tears. So relieved to see Jack, her best friend. Even though she can't tell her. Being with her pulls her from the often despair of her confusion, into a more even line.

'Come on.' Jack looks at her. 'Spill the Beans.'

They both laugh at the terrible joke.

And it all comes out.

Sakura shares with Jack what she couldn't do with Chris. All her imaginings, her fears and hopes.

'I'll be here for you, you know,' says Jack over steaming hot chocolate. They might have become adults, and live in separate places now, but some things will always remain.

'I know.' Sakura looks away. 'Tell me how the work placement is going. Are you able to let go of being a student for the moment?'

Jack relays stories of University and her plans for the future. A postgraduate diploma. Sakura can see that she is happy being away. No one mentions Sakura's permanent University deferral.

'I just wish you could live in the city too.'

'I'm a country girl.' Sakura shrugs. Nature is her justification. Why does she need one? This should be the happiest time of her life. Ok, pregnancy wasn't chosen, but this baby is wanted. This baby means the past can't go on in front of her forever.

They leave and walk aimlessly, arms linked.

'So, do I get to be godmother?' Jack leans into Sakura's little belly. 'Hey little one. I'm going to be your person.'

'Ok, ok, maybe. But maybe not godmother in the old sense.' Sakura pretends to slap away Jack's head from her bump. Sakura doesn't want to have a traditional christening. They took part in church for the big events growing up, but her parents didn't push it. Mom used to say, 'How you act around your loved one's what counts.' Sakura knows Jack will be the baby's person.

She doesn't feel Chris really likes Jack, since that first time after they had supper with her mom. The nondescript put down of her best friend on their way to get peanut butter ice cream.

Chris tells her she's the problem. Sakura feels she doesn't act that well at times and feels like he could be right. It gets all confused. Self-doubt riddles her once innate sense of knowing. She heard Dad that day before the boat trip, talking to Mom in the kitchen, and she knew what adults knew about how he was feeling. She understood Eli, and still does. He sent her a congratulations text, with very little else to go on. When he was her hero, he wasn't an in-your-face hero. She's always known how people really feel and react to the truth of situations.

'Told my mom, she said if you need anything, just ask, you know she always had a soft spot for you.' Jack points at the window with the kids' wooden toys. 'Look, how cute.'

Jack's life is only starting, and Sakura is growing another life. It's not the way either of them saw this going. But it's still so much better than thinking of your father gasping for air on a jetty and losing his life.

'Thanks, how is your mom? I haven't seen her in ages.'

'She's great, big into walking now, part of the new women's group.'

'Ah, that's great. I always liked your mom. Come on, let's go in here.' Sakura takes Jack's arm and leads her into a side store.

The rest of the day is spent ducking and diving in and out of stores, mostly looking at things they can't afford. This is followed by movie time. The same movie theatre they skipped up the steps as kids, they will take her child to one day. They had their own way of making it to the top: one- then three- and then two-steps. Popcorn bellies, soda filled. Now Sakura will be mom. It seems surreal to both of them. For now, they pretend to be still kids.

'Why don't you stay over another night?' Jack says afterward. 'Come back to my house?'

'What about Mina? Don't you need to get permission?' Sakura smiles.

They both laugh. Mina is long gone.

'Sure. I know Mom will be glad.' Their friendship is still here, the foundation for Sakura that she lost in her family.

'What about Chris?' Jack asks.

'He's fine. He'll be fine. Busy. He'll have more time without me.'

She texts Chris to say she's staying another night with her mom, will be back tomorrow. He responds eagerly, almost needy. Sakura feels uncomfortable, unease is becoming more familiar.

Yet the sinking feeling has gone. She never got what she needed that scan day, but she no longer feels dismissed by Chris. For now, he seems to be missing her.

The weekend is all she needs, and driving home she opens the top button of her jeans. It's good food and the baby. She feels peaceful. She feels ready.

Arriving home, keys scatter across the worktop, her eye catches something glittering.

Looking up, she sees candles lit. Chris walks in with a broad smile, reaching out. He hugs her and says, 'Hello' to the baby, dropping to his knees to press his face into her belly.

'I've cooked you supper. Come on, sit down.' He pulls a seat out.

Sakura melts into the sauces and flavours. Her heart reaches out to Chris and accepts his gesture fully. That night, his arm is all around her. All is forgiven.

CHAPTER 30

Since she told Tye the news, he throws worrying glances her way. She's mucking out Snowy's stable when he hands her a schedule.

'You need to take it easier. Here, take this, and head into the office.'

'I'm fine, you don't need to worry.' Sakura lifts the shavings fork and leaves it to one side.

'I know you are, but take it anyway.' Tye waits until she stops.

Initially annoyed, then relieved, sitting down, giving rest to her now more noticeable baby bump. Parts of her body aching she hadn't previously noticed.

Later Chris collects her, having insisted on dropping her in this morning, this wave of kindness showing little sign of abating. He is lovely, Sakura insists to herself, he was just having an off day.

'See you later, I'm off,' Sakura shouts over to Tye.

'Okay, see you tomorrow.' Tye continues walking some of the horses back to the stables.

Chris hops out of his pickup,

'Hey Tye, do you have a minute?'

Tye takes his time and closes the last stable door. He doesn't turn to face Chris. Sakura witnesses this. Chris has to go right up to him.

'There's a new company providing horse bedding, you interested in trying some samples?'

'Yeah maybe.' Tye continues walking. 'Send me the details, and cost, etc.' He sounds level, nothing wrong, but nothing right.

'Okay, great.' Chris doesn't notice. 'I'll send some over.' He walks to Sakura. 'Let's go.' Chris takes Sakura's hand and walks away.

Sakura turns back to Tye. 'See you.'

'Bye.' Sakura can't explain the look on Tye's face. It was nothing and something.

'I found a little baby store we could check out,' Chris says as he hops into his pickup.

Delighted with his enthusiasm, Sakura's tiredness suddenly fades.

'Great, where is it? Maybe we can stop for food on the way. I'm starving.'

At the baby store, they walk, giddy, picking up and looking at all the things you can't possibly need for one little person.

'Your first?' The young woman picks up on the excitement. Sakura wonders does she know that this is a good day.

'Yes.' Chris moves his body close to Sakura and pats her tummy.

Sakura isn't sure if he's being extra-loving with her or flirting with the young woman. These confusing, conflicting thoughts cause her to lurch. *Something's wrong with you, stop it, you're ruining this lovely moment.* Chris might be right. Maybe she is a bit unhinged.

'Do you have this with the Isofix base?' Chris walks over to an array of strollers and prams.

'Yes, this one comes with all the fixtures for cars, easily transferrable to stroller or car.' The woman talks brochure speak and stands at Chris's side.

Sakura steps forward, this seems to be happening without her.

'I'll probably be doing all the lifting and pushing, I should have an input.'

Chris shoots her a look and the assistant nods. Sakura feels a bolt of fear. She doesn't want to dampen his good mood. She asks a few questions. The assistant keeps her eyes on Chris. The wallet.

They walk out. Chris pushing the first stroller he saw ahead of him. Filled with the extra gadgets, delighted he insisted on them.

She consoles herself that a few weeks beforehand she thought she might have had to do this part alone. Sakura only had enough money for a basic model. Things have changed so much for the better. She loves him in this state, smiling, happy.

They are in this together. Sakura confuses the baby butterflies with her own butterflies of contentment. Holding hands, they pick up a few things, deciding to wait until closer to the time for the big things. Better not jinx it.

Winter eventually gives way to spring, and the restless lupins burst through with the eagerness of a day-old lamb intent on walking.

Opening the door, the back porch, finally allowing the house to air, Sakura throws out the watery grey paint bucket.

'It's looking good, even after the first coat.' Chris smiles and stands back. Hands-on hips, his brush tips towards the ground. Sakura wonders if it will drip. It doesn't. Proud of his work in the back kitchen. 'Oh shit.' He notices the paint about to drop off the brush onto the floor. One splatter falls.

Sakura quickly arrives back in with a wet cloth and wipes it clean. She reaches up and kisses him on the cheek. Chris then drops the brush on the floor, the paint blobs splatter in indiscreet patterns.

Kissing her deeply, she knows what he wants. Gently he guides her to the floor, where the paint had missed.

Grabbing a cushion, Chris places it under her head. Layers are removed, the clutter becomes a distraction.

'No, let's go.' He carries Sakura in his arms, upstairs to their room, pretending to drop her, joking, 'You're real heavy now.'

Her giggles, and his smiles. Minding the bump, they move in unison, and all is given and then released. Sakura feels loved, so loved.

CHAPTER 31

Picking the dress up off her bed, Sakura wonders if it will fit around her expanding bump. It's Jack's birthday and she's looking forward to a night out. Every time Jack comes home, Sakura's bigger. Chris is going. Things can change.

Doing a quick think over the past twenty-four hours. No. Nothing to suggest he doesn't want to go. Just this morning. It was nothing. Dismissing any unease, she puts on her makeup and gets ready. She and Chris have agreed to meet at the restaurant, and Sakura will drive them home after.

Seeing Jack outside the bar, waiting for her, lifts her spirits.

'I wanted to wait out here for you. The others are inside, and we won't get to speak.'

They hug, still the safest ones in the world for her. Jack seems more protective now that her bump is more visible.

'You ok?' Jack cocks her head to one side. 'I'll make sure you get a seat.'

Sakura hesitates. In that moment the sound she knows so well rises.

'Ah, there's Chris's pickup.'

'Okay fine, I'll see you inside.' Jack heads in.

Sakura, trying to read the pickup sounds. Will they indicate any mood?

'Hey, you got here.' Kissing him on the cheek.

'Yeah, parking was a pain.' Chris is edgy, the traffic, the business, the need to get here. The fact he'll have a hangover tomorrow. They'll have to come back and collect the truck. 'I hope it's safe.'

'It is. They lock up the restaurant car park. You like my dress?' Sakura adds, giving a twirl to distract him, bring his mood up, make him nice. 'I got into it.'

'It's nice.' He nods. 'You look nice, let's go in.' His eyes don't say the same as his nod or his mouth. Something's wrong.

She knew from the moment she laid her dress out on the bed this morning, but dismissed her knowing. Paranoia, she thought. And she feels the unease growing and spreading. Like the sidewalk has turned to quicksand.

A dry swallow, it's Jack's birthday. God the panic, he appears ok, be ok.

'Look at you, soon you won't be able to fit into anything.' Chris's comment from this morning flashes back into her mind. He said it when Sakura was trying to fit into sweatpants. Then, when she laid tonight's dress out on the bed.

'That'll be a miracle. And the last time you'll get to wear it.' He raised an eyebrow, then walked away.

'Until after the baby is born,' she called after him. She patted the creases out of her dress and spent the rest of the day shaking thoughts away.

Jack is floating, happily chatting. Sakura envies her freedom, her confidence. She wonders if Jack notices. Sakura feels like her pain is obvious, like a massive sore on her face.

'Hey, do you want a drink?' Chris turns to Sakura. They're still standing, they haven't joined the table Jack is at. When Jack sees her, she'll make sure she gets a seat.

'Mmmm, not sure, maybe I'm ok for the moment.' Before she can think any more about what might suit her growing list of things she doesn't like the taste of, he is gone, buying himself a drink.

Her face feels sad, and her eyes follow him. When he arrives back, Sakura can't help herself. She's waiting to go to the table with him.

'Why didn't you wait? I hadn't decided if I wanted a drink.'

'What are you talking about? I asked you.' He raises his shoulder and drops it in an aggressive shrug. 'You said no. Are you going be like this all night?'

Sakura puts her head down. Blushing with shame, trying not to provoke, and knowing any answer will.

'I knew by the look of you, you're in that mood.'

'What are you talking about? I kissed you, tried to get you to notice me in my nice dress.'

'I said you looked nice. You need to get a grip.' He storms off to the bar again.

Sakura is left standing, shaking, music and people laughing seem to be circling her. Squeezing her hand harshly, trying to knock something into or out of her. Leave, and then you create a scene, Jack will wonder what's wrong. Stay, and you might burst into tears and create a scene.

She sees Jack again, effortlessly linking the arms of her date, a handsome man. Her family is around her too. Other friends. Sakura feels so left behind in this moment.

Is there something wrong with her? Maybe Chris is right. Going to the washroom, she fixes herself and comes back and finds Chris. He is chatting to some of the guys from town. He knows them a little. She feels a bit awkward. He does nothing to bring her into the conversation.

'Hello,' she feels the need to say to them. He turns.

'Did you get your drink?' He puts his free hand deep into his pocket.

'No, I'm fine thanks, maybe in a while.' Not wanting to upset him, she feels a slight thaw.

At the small group chat, Chris adds jokes at Sakura's expense about her pregnancy.

'She's so big now, I can hardly get my arms all the way round.' He pulls her over to demonstrate. 'Imagine what she'll be like at nine months!' He seems happier, but she can't explain why she feels exposed.

She laughs along, joining in her own humiliation. Jack hears the laughter and looks over. She gets up as soon as she sees Sakura.

'Chris seems to get on with the lads.' Jack is not stupid. She knows when Sakura is pretending to laugh. This is her birthday. Sakura so doesn't want to spoil it. She distracts.

'Your date. You guys look so cute together.' Nudging her friend, giving her a warm side hug. 'Hope you're having a nice birthday,' she says, handing her a present she knows Jack will love.

'The biggest thing is having you here. Next birthday I'll be an aunty!' It's exactly the kind of thoughtfulness she knows of Jack, to turn it back on her. 'I love you so much.'

That is the button for tears. They fall, and Sakura tries to force them back in.

'Ah, Sakura, are you ok? What's wrong?' Jack looks over her shoulder, to make sure no one disturbs them. Her date is getting up to come and be introduced to Sakura.

Quick. Make something up.

'Ah, nothing, just being pregnant. Think I'm worried about how I will manage it all.' Sakura shadows the truth for herself and Jack.

'Hey! You're going to be a great mom. You are amazing, you hear me?'

Jack's date comes, Chris just behind him. The guys he was drinking with have left the bar.

*

The drive home is quiet. 'It was a lovely evening. Jack looked great, and seems to like her date.' She tries to say it hopefully.

'It was fine. I thought he was a bit full of himself.' Chris grips the wheel extra tight, face fixed ahead. He insisted on driving his pickup, saying he only had one full beer.

Sakura, struggling to buckle up, can't turn easily now. She cranes her neck, looking over to her left to try and engage and talk with him. She wished he could look at her even once.

There is no coming back from this.

Arriving home, she goes straight to bed. No more talking. Let her roll over, holding her nauseous tummy, and growing baby, and lull herself to fretful sleep. Sakura retracts like a snail into its shell.

Holding her shoulders in, making tea the following morning, protecting this space. It was everything and nothing last night. Her head is sore with confusion. She decides to give him the silent treatment and do her own thing this Sunday.

Her only card. Go inwards, go quiet. She gets up because she knows he lies in on Sunday.

'Hey, you're up early.' Chris surprises her coping strategies. Coming up behind her. She nearly drops the steaming cup in her hand.

'Yeah,' she responds and walks off. Like a game, he senses she is off with him.

Sakura knows talking about how she feels will go nowhere and leave her feeling more confused. Sitting out on the porch, thinking maybe she will go see a movie alone and maybe call into her mom beforehand.

Having a plan makes her feel a little lighter, more in control. She goes into the bedroom to shower and to dress. Heading into the shower, Chris stops her, and gives her a kiss. She pulls away before it's over.

'Hey, thinking, will we go check out that place you have been talking about? Maybe we could have some lunch and see a movie after?' Chris shouts in over the steaming water.

'I'm not sure, have other plans,' she responds.

'Come on, it'll be lovely. What else are you doing?' He grabs her on her way out of the shower, and she can't help smiling, and her own plans lay down alongside her crumpled towel on the washroom floor.

CHAPTER 32

The summer heat is hard to handle. The fan in Tye's office mocks the distribution of cooler air.

Six months of baby growing inside her makes it a little challenging to muck out stables and pull wheelbarrows, ignoring Tye's insistence that she slow down. Never one to want her sex to define her role, Sakura aches all over and wonders if she keeps going will the baby come early. Too early? Later she talks about it with Chris.

'But sure, you're able for it, aren't you?' He raises that eyebrow and puts his lower lip out.

'Yeah, but I don't think I will be for much longer. I'm exhausted, and wondering if it's good for the baby.' Sakura rubs her belly and rolls her shoulders. Her lower back aches all the time.

'So what are you saying? You want to stop working?' Chris's eyes widen.

'I'm not saying that, I just want to talk to you about it… there is other work I could do. Tye has been suggesting it for ages.'

'Talk to Tye… you need to work. I don't have enough money for both of us and a baby.' He squares his shoulders and stands, as he did once when he was leaning over the stall, asking her to move in with him. Too tall for comfort. Her neck objects to being pushed back to look.

Fear fills every inch of her not filled with aches. What the fuck? I won't be able to work when I have the baby. When does he think I'm going back to work? The day after?

They have never talked about money. Chris has no mortgage and the business. He often objects that she doesn't do more to help him, at home and with the business. But she can't, after a full week working, and wonders why keeping the home is suddenly up to her. She doesn't know what money he has. But she knows it's more than her. She never considered this.

'I'll be off after the baby is born. How will we manage then? Chris?'

'That's different.' He sounds like he's being generous. 'We will have to figure it out. It'll be tight. No more fancy weekends away.'

'We don't have those anymore.'

'Sure, you don't have any money, do you? I was always the one paying.'

Suddenly feeling like Oliver Twist with her begging bowl. So far away from the initial reassuring hugs and kisses, when she told him she was pregnant and before that begging her to move in with him.

'Are you serious? This is not just my baby. It's our baby. You're making me sound like a burden, like I've done this on purpose. I can't fucking believe it!' Sakura storms off, slamming the door, tears running down her face.

She can hear him roaring down after her,

'That's it. Run away. I am just trying to have a normal conversation, and you can't even manage that. There's something wrong with you.'

Sitting on her bed, her head hurts. All she wanted was some reassurance from Chris that he wants her to take care of herself and the baby, be concerned she's pushing herself too much. She wants Chris to hug her and say,

'We're in this together, we are a family, we'll manage this. What matters is that you are taking care of yourself. I am here for you.'

She collapses back under the weight of herself and her sorrow. Lying sideways, with a cushion between her legs, Sakura feels her baby kick, and she smiles and then cries.

It never seems like anything in particular with Chris's words, but it's everything. Maybe he's right. She doesn't have any money, really. She's never been in a serious relationship before. Maybe this is normal? Her gut competes with pregnancy sickness, leaving her heaving.

Shushing herself, she closes her eyes. With the sound of the floorboards creaking lightly in parts, Sakura can hear Chris come down the hallway. Pushing the door open.

'Do you want some supper?' He holds the door with his hand.

Sakura just cries, moving away from the open door. Chris sits on the bed.

'Come on. I was just trying to talk to you. They're just the facts. We'll just have to figure it out. Do you want a hug?'

Sakura cries harder.

'But I don't even know what you have. I've told you everything I have, which isn't very much.' This conflict lays beside her previous grief, a volcano, dormant, but stirring.

'I don't have anything really,' Chris insists. 'It's all tied up with the business and stuff.'

'But when will we talk about this? We're having a baby! We should get a joint bank account. It would help me when I'm not working.'

'Hmm, not sure about that, no need for that, just charge you extra.' He rises from the bed, towards the door.

'But when then? I thought we were a family?' Sakura feels her eyes erupting again.

'We will, when we're married,' he says with a smile.

'What? Married. What do you mean?'

'I mean when we are married,' Chris responds, smiling broadly like he has just revealed his hidden trump card.

'You want to get married? To me?' Sakura, suddenly sitting up in the bed.

'Not now, when the time is right.' He's in the doorframe again. 'I'll sort supper. Come on.'

Suddenly Sakura feels foolish. He loves her, he wants to get married to her, they're having a baby together. She needs to stop worrying about silly things.

Maybe there is something wrong with me.

'On second thoughts, come on, you need to eat. Let's go to that place you like, *The Lobster*.' He comes into the room, right to her, helping her off the bed. He likes *The Lobster*, but that doesn't matter. He wants to marry her.

Tenderly he puts his arms around her bump, and they look into the mirror together at the end of their room.

'Look at you, getting massive.'

Sakura pretends to elbow him. 'Massive,' she says.

'Beautifully massive,' he responds. 'Come on, I'm starving.'

Linking arms, they head out into the evening sun. Calm has been restored.

CHAPTER 33

Jack is visiting for the weekend. Preparing the room, Sakura wants her to feel welcome. She arranges towels and bedding, has prepared nice food.

'Eh, look at you!' Jack hugs her, holds her back, and hugs her again and again, feeling all baby under the hug.

Sakura wells up. The occasion masks the real reason.

'Don't get upset, you look amazing, look at you, you are going to be a mama.'

Jack's hugs make the truth come up in her. From four years old, when they first met at kindergarten, they bonded over toys and colours, and then over high school, boys, grief, and now joy. Now the road splits with Jack almost done with University working, and dating. Sakura with Chris, about to become a mom. Each on divergent paths, their shared bond and love travels so deep it is a constant.

'So, where is Chris?' Jack asks, nibbling at the snacks left out.

'Working, he'll be home later. Come on, I'm making supper. Then I want to show you the baby's room.' They know when there is something wrong with the other.

They chat while chopping vegetables. Jack tries to help but only ends up in the way. Sakura shuffles around. They end up laughing.

'Go on, sit down. I'll finish here, and you can tell me all about your love life. Are you still seeing Mark, the guy you brought to your birthday?'

'No Mark on the scene anymore.' Jack fills her in.

Sakura listens as she tells her stories of nights out and taking time out now to focus on herself, not bothered about dating. She wonders how it got so serious for her, with

Chris, baby, fights. A kick from her baby knocks her out of her thought bubble, forms a temporary salve on her niggling doubts.

They eat until they're both full and push their plates back, making room for dessert.

'Eh, you make a mean lemon pie. I love it. You're the best.' Jack smiles and gets the forks.

After, Sakura pushes open the door to the bedroom on the right. New paint. *Elephant's Breath.* It's light grey really, but she loves its name. It transports her to another land, where elephants mind the babies, even hers, on their trunks and their feet, while massive buttercups tickle under your chin, delicate yellow butter.

The small wardrobe, little painted knobs, and lamp lighting the room.

'Sakura, it's beautiful! I'm going to cry, you're going to have a baby.' Jack's eyes well up.

'You only getting that now?' Sakura smiles as she puts her arm around Jack. 'Come on, mushy, let's go for a walk. I want to show you something.'

Sakura shows Jack her favourite walk, down past the trees, the path that leads to the inlet. Showing Jack makes her feel more real, more here. As if her experience of it isn't enough. Walking back up, she hears the pickup truck door bang.

'Hey,' Chris shouts to Jack.

'Hey,' she shouts back.

'There's some supper left over,' Sakura adds.

Nothing indicates anything yet. Sakura feels her breath quicken. Please let him be in a good mood.

'I brought some beers. They're in the pickup, if you fancy one, and I brought some dessert.'

'Thanks, Chris.' Sakura reaches over and kisses him on the cheek. 'I made one.' All is ok. Her breath returns to normal.

It's a nice late summer's evening. August thirteenth came and went this year, she only remembered it once, with so much going on. They decide to sit outside. Jack and Chris yak like old friends. Sakura enjoys listening. Maybe he does like her best friend. Maybe she got it wrong, that time, when they first met.

'Do you want a cuppa?' Chris asks Sakura.

Delighted, she says yes, and doesn't complain when he brings out really strong tea. They chat about the baby, horses, and University. When darkness comes in, they head inside, and Sakura shows Jack her room.

'You're so thoughtful and sweet. Look at this. Like a hotel room.' Jack reaches over and gives her a side hug.

'Goodnight, Jack.' She eases the door closed and heads into her room.

Chris is already in bed. Lying in beside him, he turns and puts his arm around her. She melts into the embrace. Why was she worried earlier? Maybe she is just too sensitive. Everything is fine. Why can't I be like Jack, chilled, ok, able to talk to Chris with ease? Maybe Chris is right. There is something wrong with me.

The next morning, Sakura is up early before everyone else, sizzling bacon and pancakes. She's heading in to work later, with only a few weeks left before she finishes up. She feels something resembling excitement.

'Ah, Sakura, this looks lovely.' Jack beams into the kitchen and grabs a piece of bacon.

'Stop it, not ready yet.' Sakura swats her hand away in jest. Chris arrives in, a little sleepy,

'Do you know how lucky you are? This amazing person making brekkie and heavily pregnant,' Jack says to Chris, smiling.

Sakura tenses, the baby kicks, and flips.

'I know I am,' Chris responds and reaches over and touches the baby bump.

Sakura relaxes, delighted Jack said this and by Chris's responses, hoping some of it sinks in.

Later, wiping the last of the crumbs away, Jack stands up to fetch her bag. Suddenly Sakura feels an ache in her stomach. No, don't go away.

Jack makes it possible for her to be more confident. She worries about what it will be now with just the two of them and baby bump.

'Come here, call me if you need me. As soon as anything happens, I'm here, can't wait to meet the baby.' They hug, and Sakura waves as the dust rises and her car leaves.

CHAPTER 34

Sakura is folding the newly washed baby clothes. Tiny, like dolls' clothes. Her heart swells and fills the size of her bump. She can imagine and can't imagine her baby in the same moment. Placing the neat pile on top of the light green chest of drawers. The cot is there, empty, the room is ready.

Her first week off work and already she's feeling everything that could be cleaned is clean, throwing out things that seem of no use, carefully asking Chris before doing so.

He has shown a strong attachment to objects that would surprise her, like random adapters to things he no longer has a use for. The house feels like his, still. She's hoping the decluttering will help make it feel like theirs. Opening the fridge, it's full, taking things out Sakura begins to make supper.

'Hey, something smells nice,' he shouts in as he hangs his coat in the backroom.

'Ah good, perfect timing. Sit down. It's just ready.'

They sit and chat. He likes supper. His plate is empty. The conversation is easy, and it continues into the sitting room. They discuss names. Since they have lost three parents, it's a big deal. They both agree, a new name, a fresh start in both their families where siblings are gone, and parents have been lost.

'Hey, I was chatting to Mom. She's said she can stay for a few days, maybe a week after the baby is born. Think she would be a great help,' Sakura says casually, not foreseeing any possible reason for unease. This child only has one grandparent.

'A week? That's a bit much. There's no need.' Chris gets up and checks his phone. His body turned away from her, he collapses onto the sofa. Suddenly the ease evaporates.

'What do you mean, there's no need? I'm having a baby. She's my mom.' Sakura sits on the couch too, turning towards him.

'Why are you acting so crazy? I am just saying I don't think there is a need, sure, you'll be here.' Chris slinks to the far end.

'I'm upset. I just told you my mom was going to stay to help after the baby is born, and you dis it straight away,' she says, shouting now. 'Why can't you ever support me? I need her here. I want her to stay.'

'She's not staying here in my house.' This time he gets up and stays up, pacing long strides into the kitchen.

Sobbing, Sakura shuffles off the couch too quickly. Her tummy aches. This is pointless.

'I can't do this, I can't do this,' holding onto her new soreness.

'Where are you going now?' Chris bellows as she goes down the corridor. 'You have the baby to think of. You can't just storm off every time. This isn't good for the baby.'

She grabs her bag and leaves into the late August night. Shutting the car door, panic rises.

Where am I going? Why is he so unreasonable? I'm going to be a mother, fuck, what I am going to do? Her world and thoughts fold in on top of her, like a domino, each one knocking the other until she sobs into the steering wheel.

Drive, just go, clear your head.

Pulling out, Sakura turns right until she reaches the seafront. The lapping waves provide little space in her mushed head. She walks along the sand, suddenly becoming self-conscious; how does this look? A heavily pregnant person walking late, oh no, someone could think she's going to hurt herself.

Quickening her pace, she returns to the safety of her car, her pounding thoughts joining her, not leaving a millisecond of a break. Recounting the whole conversation in her head, she manages to create another narrative. Maybe Chris's worried he'll be left out, although he never mentioned anything like that.

It's his calmness, his eerie calmness, stretched, body dug into the couch. She gets no say, at the edge, gesturing to add to her words. Like this might help him hear her.

I could leave, go where? I could leave. This thought provides small comfort.

Turning the engine on, the drive home is long, but it comes too quick. Head down, she lays down on the sitting room couch and grabs a blanket, the one she bought when she moved in. Tears fall on its blue colour. It's all blurry. She closes her eyes and prays for sleep.

She is woken by Chris's voice, moving her shoulder.

'What are you doing here? This is crazy. You can't go off like that. It's not safe.'

'I don't want to do this anymore.' The honest words roar out of her. 'You don't listen to me, I want my mom here when I have the baby, and if you won't let me, I'm not staying.'

Sakura feels strong, like an oak tree, roots digging into Mother Earth and beyond, the spine of her voice, her truth vibrates around the room. Most of her wants him to say no, she's not staying, so she can leave and follow her own rooted decision.

'Don't be silly. You're overreacting. Your mom can stay for a day or so. Sure, I'll be here. You get so serious about everything.'

'What are you talking about? You said *she's not staying here in my house*. That exact line you said. Now are you changing your mind? This is my house too, is it? Is it our house? No?'

'We were just talking, and you stormed off. We're having a baby, yeah. It's your home. You're living here, aren't you? I just said that she couldn't stay as you seemed to have already decided. My opinion means nothing. How about that?'

Sakura wondering had she just decided and told him. Did he feel left out? Wavering, she said, 'I want Mom to stay for two nights at least.'

'Ok, but that's it.' He reaches over. 'You need to be able to figure this stuff out for yourself. She won't always be around. Do you want a hug?' He leans in.

Walking into the washroom, Sakura splashes her face with cool water, turning to grab the towel. She is surprised to see Chris standing there. She hadn't heard him come in. Leaning in, he kisses her in silence. He pulls at her top and reaches into her breast, big now, preparing for milk.

She kisses him back, hungry for intimacy, to be close to him.

He turns her around and pulls her pants and underwear down. Removing his trousers and boxer shorts, he pushes her back down slightly and tries to find the place to enter. Like a heroin addict, prodding veins till one plump enough accepts the needle.

Deep he goes in, quick thrusts, feeling her breasts underneath.

The sound that he's finished.

After, he grabs his clothes and leaves Sakura standing naked from the waist down beside the washroom sink, bits of him running down her leg.

She falls into bed, too numb, too exhausted, to know anything. To ask what has become of her. The dream of the boats and being tethered rises. The dream of her father's face. The life of her baby kicks. This growing life, unplanned, will become the point for living.

CHAPTER 35

Two days before her due date. This morning she woke and was met with anxiety, her more constant companion. At times high, at times low, but always there. Like a rotisserie chicken, she goes over and over different instances with Chris.

They seem absurd, normal, and then awful, even horrific, all confusing. Sakura notices Chris is being extra attentive, extra offers of tea, and suppers cooked.

She keeps thanking him, making sure he knows she appreciates him, at the same time feeling slightly uncomfortable with this kindness. The washroom incident comes to her from time to time. She tries not to think about it. She has so much else to think of.

The next afternoon, Sakura feels restless, and then it starts. The dull ache, the restlessness is replaced by excitement, it's happening. Going over to her bag, she double checks she has everything she needs. Ringing Chris, he knows by her voice, she tells him not to come home yet, she will let him know how it goes. Sakura tries to keep calm.

Having read lots of books, she imagines this will be slow, very slow. Making lunch for herself and enjoying it, knowing it might be her last proper food for a while.

Next, she fills a lavender bath. It's hard to get in. The contractions are becoming more difficult to ignore. The warm water is soothing, and the smell distracts her momentarily. The rest is short. Sakura suddenly worries that she might not be able to get out. She does and decides to call Chris. He answers after two rings.

'Hey, how are you?' He sounds calm.

Sakura holds her free hand on her bump and breathes out a sigh of relief with the next light contraction.

'I think it's, I know it's happening.' Sakura is surprised by her near tears.

'Really, now? Chris voice is higher. 'Are you in labour?'

'The beginning, I think. It's happening, didn't want to ring you until I knew for sure, ooch.' Sakura puts down the phone for a moment and breathes through the next one.

'Hello.' His voice on the line, disembodied.

'Think you should come home.' Sakura not wanting to sound too insistent. Later, her misplaced anger at herself for being so concerned about him when she was giving birth. All her focus should have been on that. Not on him.

'Ok, yes, I'll just finish up here and I'll leave.' Finish things.

This is bigger than her. Never wanting to annoy or seem like she is putting upon him. But she is having his baby. The arrival of baby things slowly changes his house. Folded small clothes sit on a chair.

'We don't need that.' The line Sakura hears most.

'We do need a changing table.' Their recent trip to the baby store brought another battle to get the essentials. 'Yes, we do.' Sakura felt her face reddening, the baby leg was sticking out her belly, causing her pain. Swaying her hips, trying to move the little foot back. 'Where do you think we'll change the baby?' The swaying isn't working, the little foot hurting more.

Battling Chris about a table, too much.

'I'm getting it.' Sakura is surprised by her decisiveness. Her eyes watering, angry tears waiting.

'Fine, calm down, you get so upset about things.' Chris tells her this at least once a day.

Maybe things will be different. When the baby comes. Maybe Chris will expand, open up, change, when he sees the baby. Their family.

Their family is coming. After six in the evening, they drive to the hospital. Chris seems excited, and he helps her out and carries the bag. Minutes seem like hours and hours like minutes. Sakura is excited and scared about labour. Chris seems relaxed, not nervous.

'If a horse can do it, you can. You've fallen off enough of them. You've got this.'

This helps. She likes to believe that it's because he thinks she can do it. After a few hours, confidence is replaced by fear, Sakura goes into doubt. *Can I continue*? And then she does.

It goes and goes until the point where she lets go completely, she has no choice.

Disappearing for a moment, everything she has held is released and she feels like Sarabi in the *Lion King*, the queen of her pride land. In that moment, Chris shrinks into a tiny person, and she is so big, beating her hands against her chest, bringing her baby into the world.

It all happens before her, the circle widening, the expansion you can't stop, you go with it, the little head, it's so quiet, here where life lives beside near death. This mythical space. Later. The same circle will come back to Sakura, and she will be propelled forward into her true self. She is there and then she is brought back.

It's all happening. Nurses shouting words of encouragement and Chris doing the same. It seems slightly unnatural, lacking sincerity, copying the words of the hospital staff. Words she never heard him saying before.

'You've got this, one more push, you're doing great.'

With the emergence of the baby's head, Sakura know the big part is over. She has already witnessed this.

Another push and the baby's body slides out. Then relief and joy.

Oh my God, I did it, I did it.

And the smile is so huge it covers her whole face. Immediately she senses this sheer joy, at what she had just done, is hers alone. Her baby is handed to her. She is perfect. She can't believe how perfect she looks.

'You did great. She's so beautiful. Look at her,' Chris says, smiling as much as her. They are together again. They have done this.

'I can't believe it, I can't believe she's here, and it's a girl!' Sakura strokes her face. 'She's perfect, like a real baby.'

'Of course, it's a real baby,' Chris responds, laughing.

'Sara, it's Sara, isn't it?' Sakura looks over to Chris standing to her right.

'Yes, Sara.' The one thing they agreed about. They had gone through names before the baby was born and both agreed on Sara if it was a girl. Another thing they have done together. There is hope. It has been born in this moment, and she is holding it in her arms.

Adrenaline is pumping, and the next few hours are a haze. They move into another room, clothes changed, food eaten. Sakura keeps staring at her, exhaustion hits and they both fall asleep for a short while.

Both is now she and Sara.

Chris has gone home.

A few hours later, Sakura wakes with a start.

Where's the baby? Panic rises and then falls as quickly.

She's beside her, sleeping. Her little face cute and round, dark hair covers her little head, nose covered in gorgeous white dots. Her arms held up to her chin and her legs folded up like a frog. Used to the nine months in the small womb space, the big stretch in the real world takes time.

Sakura still can't believe she's here. Sara is her daughter. Sakura is responsible for this little person. Tears then fall, and some fall on the baby. At times she feels she can't take care of herself in relation to Chris. Maybe things will be different. They have a baby now.

Chris arrives later. Seeing him pull open the curtain around her bed gives Sakura such hope.

'How is she?' Chris looks down into the bassinet, Sakura can't see if his face reads happy.

'She's good, tiny, can't believe she's really here.' Hoping to pull Chris into how massive this is for her and should be for him. He still seems casual. Too casual for this.

Reaching in, he holds her finger. Sakura spots the smile. *You're overthinking this, he's happy. He's happy she's here.* Sakura scolds herself into action.

'I think her diaper needs to be changed.' She wants to do this together.

Chris lifts up the tiny bundle and unravels the wrap the nurses helped her with after she was born.

'Did you bring the clothes?' Sakura sits up in bed and carefully puts her legs over the side.

'Yeah.' He reaches for the bag on the floor. 'Hope these fit.'

Pulling out the little white vest. 'I'm sure it will.' Sakura lifts them into her hand.

She can't imagine ever moving beyond this point.

Their little baby lies on the bed, her little pink arms and legs scrunched up. Sakura feels so happy and sad at the same time. Sara seems so perfect. Always thinking she would have to grow to love her, she loved her immediately.

'Look at her, she's beautiful.' Sakura looks up to Chris for a reaction.

'Yeah, she is, isn't she? She takes after me.' Chris faces round and almost smiles. 'Is this the right one?' Chris pulls out a tiny diaper.

Sakura can't imagine it fitting a doll.

'Yes, that's it. Let's do it.' Sakura pulls an overexaggerated, nervous face.

Removing the previous diaper, Chris lifts Sara's little legs and places the new one underneath, careful not to touch the clamp on her umbilical cord. Excess water squeezed out of cotton balls. They will quickly be replaced with wipes when they go home. With the tabs fastened, he lifts her up. Sakura passes the vest. Chris tries to hold her with one hand and manoeuvre the vest over her head with the other. Sakura laughs and reaches over to help.

'Harder than it looks.' Chris slips her little arm in. Placing Sara back down on the bed, he buttons the vest. Lifting her up and hands her over to Sakura.

'You are lovely, so lovely.' Sakura kisses her face. Her smell is distinct, fresh, different. Sakura keeps reaching in and inhaling after each kiss. But each time she does, she loses the smell that has instantly become sacred.

'I brought you some food.' Chris reaches into another bag. Her favourite deli.

'Thank you, you know I love that place.' Sakura's whole face rounds and matches her little new baby.

'I know.' Nodding his head, reaching out, he takes the little bundle so Sakura can eat.

It's different. They are parents now.

He stays for three hours and kisses them both goodbye. He goes through the things he has to do and get organized for when they both come home. Closing down all his fingers, his thumb up. Chris starts counting.

'I've got to make sure the car seat is secure,' raising his index finger he continues, 'and then there's the job at work that I have to finish.'

Sakura can't understand why this could be important right now. Why didn't he get someone to cover? She remains quiet, not wanting to upset his enthusiastic mood. He goes through all his fingers on his right hand, only two chores relate to her and the baby.

Sakura feels secure though, because Sara is here too. She waves him goodbye, holding their baby girl. Sara, they both agree it's the perfect name. They both agree.

Then as the evening arrives, she sees other parents in for hours and wonders why did Chris have to go, and why doesn't he come back? She goes back over his reasons and compares them to her needs. They fight in her head and compete, moving between understanding then anger and fear. Sara's cry interrupts her thoughts, then she feels guilty for not paying attention.

Mom is on her way in. Sakura felt it best to wait until Chris was gone, justifying it to herself – she would need more help later when she is on her own.

She focuses on her baby as she suckles her breast, the feeling is new, and they are both trying to figure out what to do. The nurse helps.

'You are a natural,' she says. The words of encouragement help, words she clings onto, offering hope to her wilting self-esteem.

Mom rushes in in one loving swoop. Sara is a day old.

'Oh my girls, oh my God, she's gorgeous.'

The love Sakura needs is warm, is full and present.

In time, Sakura tells her the whole experience of labour and, for the first time, realizes what she went through to have Sara.

'Eli's delighted, I sent him pictures. He'll visit soon. You know how crazy his work is there.' Her mom picks up Sara's little finger, lets out a sigh, happy and sad mini tears.

'Yeah, he sent a text.' Sakura wanting to push down not seeing her brother much since Dad died. He left that day too. She feels awkward thinking about seeing him. She doesn't know Eli anymore. Those four years where she hasn't seen him at all stretch like elastic and seem like ten. She and Mom both know the visit might be a long time off. Neither mentions who they wish was here with Mom.

Grabbing her towel, Sakura heads into the shower. Mom is holding Sara, distracted by this little being. She doesn't hear Sakura's suggestions if she gets upset, this helps, or if you hold her this way. Less than twenty-four hours old and Sakura knows her little girl.

Smiling, Sakura realizes that she has it. She's wobbly on her feet, her body is leaking all over, she feels unsteady, her shoulders hurt. The warm water is beautiful. She turns it extra hot and washes her face with a hot cloth.

This moment feels like bliss. Her breasts are huge and sore. Milk hasn't yet come in. It's all so new. Her body is doing things that she has never seen it do before. Sakura convinced herself that she didn't need her mom until now. She knew Chris didn't want her there for the birth. In the end, Sakura didn't know if that was her wish also. In the end, it became her wish.

She lines her underwear with large pads as they soaked through the sheets last night. A bit embarrassed, she told the nurse, who discretely and without fuss changed them and gave her extra if needed. She feels like she is wearing a diaper. Pulling on comfy stretch pants, applying a bit of moisturizer, she feels slightly new, refreshed.

Mom stays for a little while longer.

'I could have come before now.' Mom keeps her gaze on Sara. Sakura relieved that her attention is not directly focused at her.

'I know, I just wanted to do this by myself, and with Chris I mean, by ourselves.'

'How was it?' Mom looks at her and, in this moment, Sakura knows what it was for her to have a child. For her to give birth.

'It was beyond surreal.' Sakura goes through her labour, from the moment her water broke, until Sara was born.

Her mom reaches over and takes her hand.

'You did amazing, no longer my little girl.' Mom turns her head and turns the tears away.

Sakura receives the validation she needs. Mom can't stop smiling at Sara as she half sits on the bed. Sakura feels happy Mom's here, not alone with this whole person to look after.

'Is Chris in later?' Mom holds Sara's little hand and is mesmerized at its size. 'You know you were like her as a baby, bigger though, but similar hair.' Mom continues without waiting for Sakura's answer. 'Dad held you like you were a prize. He was afraid he'd hurt you.'

Dad. There, it has been said.

Where is Chris?

Mom talks about how Dad never let her go, and never cared what other men thought about wheeling the stroller. She talks about a man Sakura wishes Chris was. But Sara is here. That's the joy she feels now. Something empty in Sakura has been filled. It doesn't matter how difficult, how unplanned, or how unsure she has been about the arrival of her child. This is meant.

'I know, right, you know that picture you have, the one of me in the spotty onesie, think I look like Sara in that one.'

Mom nods, engrossed.

'Chris was in earlier, he's got things to sort out for us going home.'

'Oh.' Mom looks at Sakura.

Sakura exaggerates his enthusiasm and caring side.

'Will I ask if I can stay? If he's not back soon?' Mom asks.

'No,' Sakura assures her when visiting hours are over for all but the parents of newborns. 'He'll come.'

After Mom leaves, Chris's absence is more obvious. Sakura pushes it away and focuses all her energy on feeding and changing Sara.

It seems to take forever, the little arms, tiny vests, so afraid to hurt her, it seems awkward and then the wail, it's massive and small all at once. Buttoning the last one of the confusing onesie, she scoops Sara up in her arms, her beautiful baby smell nuzzling her right shoulder. Little legs disappear upwards, leaving the legs of the onesie empty.

Sakura instinctively raises her right arm, holding her in place. Tears of love and disbelief fall, and she wipes them away with her free hand. This is quickly replaced by tiredness that renders every part of her unmoveable. Placing Sara beside her, ensuring the duvet is pushed way down, the heat of the hospital makes this easy.

They both sleep immediately, facing each other.

CHAPTER 36

Chris walks in, and Sakura smiles when she sees he's carrying the small empty car seat. She knew he was bringing it in. They're going home today but seeing him with this baby seat makes him seem so caring, a father. He's here for them. Why does she dissect everything between them?

'All ready?' he asks, smiling. He seems to be delighted at this step.

'Almost,' Sakura responds, 'just getting her hat.' Sara is layered up, only her cute nose and eyes peeping out. Even with the straps at the lowest level, her little body slouches down to the bottom of the seat.

They walk out together, the three of them.

Chris takes her hand and smiles, and heartwarming comments come as they walk through the corridor to the outside. This kindness from strangers carries her until they arrive home.

Chris is awkward in his kindness, he offers to make her lunch, but Sakura gets the sense that he doesn't really want to make it for her.

She accepts anyway and pushes down any weird feelings with each mouthful.

The evening and night are spent looking at Sara and smiling at her very presence. Sakura goes to the washroom, and the sound of Sara's soft cries surprise her. She hurries out and picks her up. Her little body fills up the whole space.

Chris is already up and gone out. Her mom didn't come to stay in the end.

'It's just that it's our special time,' she remembers Chris saying.

It stuck because he used the word special. Didn't seem like something he would say. When she thinks of the fight over Mom coming and him not wanting her, she has to shake it away, because the washroom comes back with it. All she wants is for Chris to find this special. So when he said it, she asked him more about his thinking, and he answered.

'I just want to enjoy this time, the three of us together. I've heard situations, where the mom stays. Then the woman can't cope after she leaves. She hasn't had that initial bonding time.'

Sakura thought that was untrue at the time but didn't challenge him. Imagining his sulky moody face if she stuck with the two nights, and Mom stayed, she would have three things to worry about. Her baby, Mom, and Chris's mood. Sakura convinced herself it was her decision.

'You know where I am if you change your mind. I've put in for time off work,' Mom said, but didn't push either. It ran in the McClean family.

Sara smells beautiful and new, changing her diaper, her little legs curling up, resisting the process. *I can't believe you are here, you are perfect, and I love you just like that.* Sakura feels that warm tingling, proud that she gave birth to her so bravely. At that moment, she scoops Sara up, puts on her favourite song and moves slowly around the kitchen. *I've got you, Babe.*

'No matter what happens, I have got you,' she whispers into her ear.

She's startled by Chris. She hasn't heard him come in. The October breeze sneaks in behind him.

'Ah, you guys are up. Did you say the nurse was calling today?' He grabs milk from the fridge. There isn't much left. She can't get out yet.

'Yes, after lunch. Do you want to hold her?'

He reaches out and smiles as he takes her in his arms. It's all ok. Sakura smiles as she goes upstairs to have a shower. She hears Chris call out,

'I'll make you tea. Do you want something to eat?'

The warm tingling continues. All is ok. We are home with our baby. The small gesture creates such hope.

The following days create their own new rhythm. Chris is off for a week. He seems busy, though, doing other things. He arrives in, and then goes out. Sakura is distracted by Mom and Jack's visit. They spend hours together and even venture on a few walks out. Pushing the stroller feels new, different, nice.

But they don't stay over. Somehow Sakura fights the need to ask.

'Let's go out,' Chris says over breakfast. Sara is seven days old.

'Yeah, sure, where were you thinking?'

'Oh, maybe the beach. We could bring the sling.'

'Yeah, fine, will be ready in an hour. Need to sort out a few things with Tye. Over the phone.' Tye normally pays her by cheque. He needs details from her for maternity payment.

It's wonderful. Chris wears the baby sling, Sara sleeps snuggled in against the lapping waves. Sakura links his arm. People smile as they pass. Afterwards, they stop at a lovely café, and after lunch, Sakura manages her first public breastfeeding. It goes fine. Chris helps, his back protecting her modesty during latch-on. On their way out, they stop to pay. Sakura feels a bit awkward, having no money. He reaches in and takes out his card.

'Thanks for lunch,' she says as they leave.

They haven't discussed money since Sara has arrived. She needed diapers, and Sakura has needed post-pregnancy things. Chris has gone in to get them. Sakura feels some shame in having little money. It's not her fault.

Tye has agreed to pay some of her salary for four months after the baby is born. When she gives her account number over the phone, he asks her,

'Is it a joint bank account, is it in both your names? Sakura?'

'No, just mine.' She goes quiet.

'Okay. I'll pay in tomorrow.'

It's more than she expected, and she can't help feeling it's above what other employers would do, having only worked there full-time less than two years.

Sakura is a bit uncomfortable telling Chris about this. Chris talks about Tye, criticizing how he does things in the stables. Sakura stays mostly quiet. Tye doesn't discuss Chris at all, only in relation to work. Sakura feels his silence about Chris and his small acts of protection towards her as unsaid knowing. Knowledge about what is really happening.

This helps, but it won't cover all the bills. So, she decides, for the moment, not to say how much it is. She will contribute, but something is telling her, saying, keep something in reserve.

It's not that she's hiding it. It's that she doesn't know what lies ahead. Chris may get careful around money again when she needs necessities. Eli has sent a cheque too, with his gift. Sakura puts it in her changing bag. There's nothing from Zoey. Chris probably hasn't told his only relative he's a father.

That night, she feels guilty. As she does a night feed, she realizes this is about Sara now.

It is her first morning, officially on her own. Chris is already gone when she wakes. She looks over. Sara is in her basket. She doesn't really remember when she put her back in. The lifting, feeding, winding, changing, it all becomes a blur. She turns over and enjoys that extra time and space, all is quiet.

Later, carrying her into the kitchen, she puts her on her little bean bag, a gift from her brother, along with the cheque she has moved to her diary. She'll wait to cash it, wait until she really needs it. He still hasn't managed to visit. Sakura's not surprised. She remembers their time in the hospital after Dad died, Eli kept wanting to leave. Sitting in the waiting area, banging the vending machine. Her mom crying, trying to get him to sit down. It didn't make sense, they knew he was dead, why did they have to wait there? Once they were told the news they already knew, Eli ran out.

He met Chris once, for an hour, over Christmas. It was brief and awkward, Eli left shortly after for the city. It felt like he didn't want to come back. Sakura is relieved, not having to worry about how Chris will be around Eli. She already has to worry about Chris and now she has a baby.

Sakura is ok with him not visiting on her own behalf also. Their few conversations feel awkward, their shared blood feigning closeness. Even when she did talk to him, he seemed distant, like he was not really listening, his head somewhere else more important.

Sakura has created a narrative that she is the messed up one, the one who couldn't deal with her dad's death. While everyone else just got on with it, why couldn't she? Her emotions bubble up, spill out and now with Chris it feels just as messy, and he is alive.

Filling the kettle with water, Sakura notices the hundred dollars folded under the coffee jar. Smiling, she realizes Chris left it for her, how thoughtful. This quickly turns to angry fear.

Why did he only leave a hundred? Why does he decide how much I need? Why didn't he leave his bank card?

A strange thought arrives and comes to the surface before she has a chance to dismiss it.

I feel like a sex worker, the money left after he leaves. Stop it, you have a baby, you are a family, this is a nice thing, why do you have to turn everything into a negative?

She shuts herself up and prepares breakfast. But the niggling doubt still remains.

She welcomes Sara's cries. After about two hours, they are both ready to leave for their first walk. It's lovely. This little person in front of her, loving the rhythm of the walking, falls back asleep. It's mild enough for a fall day, but Sakura doesn't want her to be cold. She's layered up, the final one a full white snowy winter suit, Sara's face the only part exposed.

This part will dominate Sara's first eight months of her life. Is she warm enough? Is she too warm or cold, especially at night?

The line from the nurse ringing in her ears; *babies can't retain heat.* By the time they are back at home, half the day is gone.

Sakura likes this pace, making lunch after feeding Sara. She sits down to watch her favourite show. The afternoon repeats a similar pattern. Sara is a bit unsettled. Taking out the sling, she carefully places her in. Snuggled close. Pulling clothes out of the washing machine, bending down fully to ensure Sara doesn't fall out. This hurts, a sharp reminder of her recent labour.

Sakura places the clothes in the tumble dryer, and the hum follows her back into the kitchen.

Before long, Chris is home. He takes Sara, and Sakura rests. The days and weeks follow a similar pattern, wash, rinse, repeat. Tiredness and resting when Chris comes home leave little room for anything else until it does.

Her phone beeps *we're coming* followed by multiple smiley emojis. Sakura darts her eyes around. Sara is still asleep. Unfolded clothes sit on the table, some fell off. Last night's fight lays still beside her uneaten breakfast. Chris has gone to work. Knowing Jack's text, she has about fifteen minutes.

Great, who's we? Sakura's short immediate response.

Your mom and me, of course, need anything on the way?

It will buy her a few minutes to tidy the place and make herself look less haunted. She needs some groceries and didn't want to ask Chris. Sakura asks for a few things, not too many.

See you soon x Jack's reply lands, as Sakura is already running around in circles, moving, throwing, shoving things, making less progress, returning multiple times to the airing cupboard with something else she forgot.

She knows it's ok, expected, to be all over the place and for things to be untidy with a new baby. But sometimes having things tidy, she hopes, will quieten her inner mess. That's nothing to do with Sara or being a new mom and everything to do with Chris.

She hears the car and Jacks's voice, bright and clear, unapologetic in its tone. Sakura slaps a tear back and forces the biggest smile.

'Hi, so happy to see you both.' Sakura hugs her mom first and then Jack. She smells of sweet amber. Sakura can smell her own fear and quickly pulls away.

'Thank you for coming, come on in, I think Sara might be awake.' Sakura is relieved to have something to do, the focus is off her.

'We got you a few groceries.' Her mom places multiple bags on the countertop, way more than the few things she'd asked for.

'Thank you, you didn't need to, this is way too much,' Sakura says as she leaves to check on Sara, worried that they will see her tears behind her eyes, tears that she won't let out. Why can't Chris do this? Sakura shouts at herself silently and reaches and lifts a sleeping Sara out. She makes little sounds and reshapes her body towards Sakura.

'Ah look.' Jack lowers her voice into a whisper, hunches her shoulders down, mouth open in a wide smile, and she lightly rubs Sara's rounded back. 'She's adorable, getting much bigger since I saw her last.'

Sakura brings Sara to them more often, reducing their need to come here. She can't try managing Sara, Brightwood, and Chris on her own, with visitors. Today is unexpected, no chance to make an excuse.

'Her hair is still there, dark, like yours was, Sakura.' Her mom putting the groceries away. 'I'll make you some food.' Her words are loving, caring.

'Thanks.' Sakura lets the help in and tries to block everything else out.

Since her dad died, Jack has felt sorry for Mom, especially as they got older, and she left for University. 'I just don't know how she coped, it must be lonely.' Jack's words on one of her last weekends before she left the Island. Sakura stayed silent, thinking, she didn't cope. Jack and her mom hold this gentle space between them. Familiar, present and now here for Sakura.

'How is Chris?'

Sakura is surprised by the question, then realizes she shouldn't be.

‘Yeah, fine, working, you know, busy.’ Sakura rises off the chair. ‘Do you want to hold her?’ Sakura passes Sara to her mom, and Jack takes over making brunch.

They eat, chat, and adore Sara, and tidy everything up. Suddenly Sakura feels sad, a sinkhole of loneliness emerges. She didn’t want them here, afraid they would see, feel something. They didn’t, and now she doesn’t want them to leave.

‘I put a wash on, just some of Sara’s things.’ Her mom reaches and places her hand on her arm. ‘You need anything, just call and I will see you anyways next week, when you’re in.’ She hugs her mom and pulls away before it all spills out.

The car door bangs, engine revs and they’re gone.

CHAPTER 37

It's a Saturday morning, and it's not bright, but Chris is getting up.

'Where are you going? It's still dark.' Sakura rouses herself.

'I have things to do.' He talks as he dresses. He's in a hurry to leave.

Sakura senses this. Sitting up in the bed now, Sara still asleep.

'It's a Saturday, I need a break, you never ask me what I need to do.'

'Be quiet. You'll wake the baby.' He leaves the room. Sakura hops out of bed, heart racing.

Please don't wake up, glancing over at Sara and following Chris up to the kitchen.

'What are you doing? Go back to bed.'

'You can't just go off and not talk to me. It's a Saturday, you assume it's me that is here always to look after Sara, I'm tired.' She rubs her face in agitation.

'What are you talking about? You're off every day. How could you be tired? I have things to do.' Grabbing a mug, filling the kettle, angrily standing beside it, waiting for it to boil.

'Are you serious, how could I be tired? We have a small baby, and I am feeding all night! What about what I need to do for me? You never ask.'

'Ah, I'm not doing this. You're being irrational. You're always complaining about being tired. That's what it is to have a baby.' He shakes his head and pulls on his jacket.

All Sakura's tiredness has vanished. Her heart is racing, her face is flushed, and sadness mixed with anger combines to form a miasma of panicked despair. With every new word from Chris, he stamps and stamps on her,

'I know what it is to have a baby. I'm here all the time. You come and go as you please, never asking me what I need.' Still, she tries to get him to *hear* her. 'Would it kill you to show me kindness and offer to help me?'

'I have to work, something you can't seem to get through your head. Do you think money grows on trees? I'm outta here. You need to get a grip.' Chris's face is red, eyes small and ugly in anger. He doesn't look human.

The screen door mocks her with a slam. And the kettle shrieks to the boil.

Sakura leans over on the worktop, tears fall as she tries to catch her breath. Her chest feels crushed, then the tiredness returns as she slips down onto the floor and wails.

Then she hears Sara through the baby monitor, low, persistent, deep, relentless cries.

Picking her up, Sara stops crying, but Sakura doesn't. Looking at her baby, she talks low and pleading:

'What am I going to do? You need so much of me, how I am going to cope, where can I go?' Sniffing her snots back up, wiping others on her already puke-marked pyjama top. She cries till her eyes feel puffy when she blinks.

Sara just stares at her, with big, expectant, chocolate brown eyes.

'What are we going to do for the day? I can't stay here waiting for him to come home. Let's go out.' Maybe she could visit her mom and have lunch in town. This plan gives her a little purpose.

After she feeds Sara, she places her in a bouncer and brings her into the washroom while she showers. The hot water feels great for a second, then the heaviness of everything remains.

A few hours later, they're ready to go out. She is still getting used to the baby seat. She feels nervous, fiddling with the straps. Sara starts to cry.

'Please don't, I'm doing my best.' She quickly starts the engine, hoping the drive will calm them both down. It does. Sara falls asleep as Sakura puts on her favourite music, she feels confident. *I can do this, I'm driving on my own, and we are doing okay. We don't need Chris.*

Stopping at the boardwalk, she takes out the stroller and manages to click it into place in one go. Walking along, the sadness hits her all of a sudden. *What am I doing? I can't keep leaving when Chris does something that upsets me. But I can't stay there. It's not ok. The way he behaves is not ok. Maybe I'm being unreasonable.*

The thoughts rush back and forth, one not even finishing before the next one starts. Sakura realizes that she's at the end of the boardwalk, and she hasn't even noticed her surroundings. Her confidence slips between the cracks under her feet and slides to the sea. She decides not to call into Mom. She might sense something is wrong.

Back in the car, Sakura feeds Sara and then heads for lunch, a quiet place. Afterwards, she is thinking about what else she can do. All options are anxiety-ridden. Eventually she returns home. Turning into herself, she won't say much when he comes home. She will just do her own thing. She won't be affected by Chris.

Busying herself with Sara, bending down into the bath to fill the baby tub. Her face lights up with the feel of the water against her skin. Sara loves water, and she feels like a slippery eel under Sakura's hands, her perfect silk skin.

This moment is interrupted by the sound of the screen door banging. Instantly her anxiety races from the door up the stairs and into the washroom and lands in her before she has even taken a breath. Familiar, but alien.

Even without any noise, she feels Chris at the door.

'Hey, what are you up to?' he says, smiling at Sara.

'Just giving Sara a bath.' Her response is curt, short. Lifting her onto the towel and wrapping her up quickly, she leaves the room and heads downstairs.

Sakura still takes ages, pulling her little vest over her head ever so gently and fixing her arms through the small holes. She is so relieved when she gets the button snaps in place below her vest. Cuddling her in close, easier with clothes. Sara feels chubbier now, the passing weeks noticeable in her cute features.

Feeling Chris lingering, she knows he won't apologize. It's not the same when you have to ask for one. He will just linger, acting slightly interested, slightly nicer, but she won't fall for it.

'I was back earlier, I was going to see if you wanted to do something, but you weren't here.'

'Yeah, we headed out.'

'Where did you go?' He seems keen to know.

'Just out for lunch and stuff.' She worries if he'll ask her how she afforded it.

'Do you want to head to that place for supper?' He sounds nonchalant.

'Not really, it's too late, just bathed Sara, I'm too tired.'

'Okay, come here, little lady.' Chris takes Sara in his arms.

Sakura leaves and rushes upstairs, trying to catch her tears as they fall. She slides down against the inside of the bedroom door. Sometime later, she gets up, washes her puffy eyes, and heads downstairs.

Chris comes over to her and offers a hug. It's fucked up, but she accepts by nodding, and the tears begin again.

'You're upsetting yourself too much. I was just tired this morning. I have to keep the show on the road now there are three of us.'

Head pressed against his chest.

'You can't speak to me like that. It's not ok to speak to me like that. We need you. I need you.' She muffles words.

'You're too sensitive. That's just the way I talk. I have to work, we need the money.' Sensing her about to pull away, he adds, 'Why don't we go off tomorrow for the day, that town you've been talking about visiting.'

'I don't know. You haven't even said you're sorry.'

'I try to say it.' He shrugs that one-shouldered shrug.

'Then say it,' she insists.

'We're all sorry.' He makes it sound like it's both of them.

'I've nothing to be sorry about. There is no *we* in the apology.' Sakura is getting angry.

'Ok. I'm sorry.' He finally relents and releases her from the hug. 'I'm starving.' He goes looking for food he hopes Sakura has cooked for him.

'Like I said, Chris, we went out.'

'Like I said, Sakura, we should go out for supper.'

Sakura lifts Sara out of her basket, and they head up to bed. She is exhausted, and even if her head wants to go through the day again, her body takes charge and knocks her out until she is awoken by Sara's cries. Alone she feeds her in the dark.

Chris snores beside them.

This part she fears and hates, her body a little replenished, and Sara has fallen back asleep. She lays there panicked and anxious, and wondering if she is going mad. Maybe Chris is right.

CHAPTER 38

Sakura has decided she needs to be more independent, rely on Chris less. This creates space within her. Room for the incessant thinking to push back a little.

She feels empowered, but decisions within confines are just mockery.

'Right, Sara, what colour do you think?' Holding up purple and pink cards closer to her face. Her vision is still half of what it will be. A fact that just fascinates Sakura. Her rounded chubbier face lets out a sound. 'Ah, you like blue? Great, my choice too.'

After breakfast, they head into town and pick out the paint, like the lightest bluebell she has seen in her mind's eye, drifting into fantasy where her hands run atop the flowers in a magical forest where everything is different, where she is different.

Jolted back, the store attendant is asking her for money.

Afraid the new independent feeling will be lost, she rushes home with Sara. With each paint stroke, the small washroom wall changes, a confused colour emerges, but she knows it will look different with the second coat.

After an hour, she's tired but impressed with her work. Chris will be annoyed she hasn't prepared the room. He's careful and meticulous when it comes to this work. *Why isn't he the same with me and Sara? Why don't we deserve the same attention?*

'No,' she shouts, surprised it was out loud. 'I'm not going there.' She continues placing the masking tape unevenly along the edges. Chris will comment on that too.

After she feeds Sara, she continues painting, and by late afternoon it takes some shape. Sakura is impressed with herself. Standing back to look at it from different angles. Imagining her towels, homemade soap, and little ducks there.

'Hi, let me show you what we've been working on!' Heading back upstairs. Chris follows after her when he comes home.

'Very nice.'

Sakura stares at him, waiting for him to say something else. He doesn't, so she tells him where everything will go. She turns around, and he's squatting down.

'Did you prep first? Is there is paint on the carpet?'

'I did. It's only a tiny bit. I'll get it off.' She's not going down this sinkhole. 'It's lovely, isn't it? We did a great job.' Sakura continues smiling at Sara, saying all the things she wished for him to say.

'Don't paint anything else,' is his parting shot as he walks out the door.

It's December. The first snow falls silently that night. When she awakes, Sakura can feel the brightness behind her closed eyes. Jumping up excitedly, she says,

'Look, Chris, it's snowing!' Pulling open the curtains.

He groans and turns over in their bed. Sara is beside him, slipping on the cushions on either side of her. '*Your first snow, Sara,*' she whispers to herself.

There is something about snow that lends itself to warmer, different food. Sakura is cracking eggs into the flour and mixing them into the batter. Bacon sizzles on the pan.

Chris walks in with Sara in his arms. He smells delicious, fresh, clean, just out of the shower. Sakura always comes down in her dressing gown, things to do first, change Sara, and empty the dishwasher.

Reaching over, she kisses him on the cheek, and he reacts with a surprised smile.

'Can I have a hug?' she asks. He puts his free arm around her, and Sakura nuzzles in that space under his shoulder. Chris is tall and broad.

Even in this, she feels he is elsewhere. The soapy shower gel gets closer to him than I do, she thinks to herself, and then he pulls away and releases her from the hug.

'I need coffee.' Putting Sara in her rocking chair, he turns to get a mug.

'I've made breakfast, your favourite,' she says, placing the bacon and maple syrup on the table.

'Won't be able to work today, I'll have to clear the paths.' Chris stares out.

'Great, we can walk to the woods, Sara's first snow,' Sakura adds hopefully.

'Yeah, later, when I'm finished. Thanks for breakfast.' He leaves the dishes in the sink.

Later they wrap up warm. It takes time to layer Sara and finally close her into the snowsuit. Sakura helps Chris with the sling, and Sara is placed close to his chest. The cleared path makes it easier to walk to the gate. Sakura links his arm, and he welcomes it by creating more space in the crook of his elbow.

A warm feeling rushes straight to her heart in the cold. She can't help smiling.

The forest emerges at the end of the road. Their feet mark the snow and create a trail down to the water. It's frozen and seems strange, unmoving. It's quiet. The birds are gone, bare branches dripping ice. It's beautiful and offers a clean slate for Sakura. Her thoughts are calm and hopeful.

'The road might be cleared later. We could go to the *Shack* for supper.' He is buoyant. Please let him stay like this. She squeezes his arm tighter,

'Sounds lovely. I hope they have that lovely steak on the menu.' Hope grows and spreads and dances on the snow where footprints are absent.

They enjoy their evening with food and warmth and people doting over Sara. Adoring glances to the baby and then back to them. Everyone is warm towards Chris. This is lovely and normal. *I got it wrong,* she thinks.

He helps with Sara later and makes her a cup of tea. They sit down and watch a movie together. The credits start the roll, and Chris's hand moves up between her legs. She turns to face him, and he's smiling. She knows what he wants. He kisses her and reaches his hand under her top, and comments on her fuller milk-filled breasts. Her pad falls away.

They haven't since Sara was born.

She thought he didn't fancy her anymore. She didn't even consider her own needs, her sore, changing body so soon after giving birth. Even though she's tired, she accepts any reason to be close to him. She's happy the lighting in the room is dim as her figure isn't the same as it was before and feels conscious of her baby tummy. He turns her sideways, and Sakura is now lying flat on the couch. He helps take her pants off, quickly removes his clothes, and lays down over her.

She tries to catch his eyes, and she does for a second, and then he puts his head to the side and pushes himself into her. Her head bangs again at the top of the couch with each thrust.

He groans and then comes.

Sakura doesn't. It's sore, and she just wants it to be over. After, she quickly becomes conscious of her body, pulling on her pants.

He kisses her on the cheek and walks out of the room with his clothes under his arm.

CHAPTER 39

Sakura's attempt to rely on Chris less works in part.

She keeps busy with the decoration of the washroom, looks for less help with Sara and the house, and visits Mom a lot. At times she feels almost elated. I*s that all that was needed?* Fewer rows.

Then, at times, her numbed, solitary existence feels dead and joyless, like she sacrificed her soul for her life with Chris. Is this how it's supposed to be? There may be fewer rows, but there's also the feeling that she's a single parent and alone in her relationship.

She wishes, at times, he would break up with her, making the decision for them. It's nearly time to go back to work. Chris won't support any extended leave, but he reluctantly agreed to let her go back part-time, initially.

'If Tye understands, you should.'

'Tye's not the business type. He's losing money in that place.'

'Well, it's cheaper than paying for full-time childcare.' This logic wins out.

As Mom works full-time, she gets the name of a childminder, Isobelle, through Jack's parents. She's agreed to take care of Sara three days a week. Her house is a few miles down a road off the stables. They drive out to meet her for the first time.

Sakura pulls up outside and is immediately impressed by its calm feel. Kids' toys and a swing set catch her eye in the yard on the left. They get out and Sakura helps Sara press her little finger against the bell.

'Hello, well, you must be Sara.' The woman gives her full attention and smiles directly at the baby. Sara reacts by reaching for her bright necklace. 'Hello, I'm Isobelle. Come on in.' Sakura and Sara find their new beginnings.

After returning home from shopping for a few clothes for Sara, she leaves them on the kitchen floor and forgets to put them away. When she hears Chris's pickup, she remembers, and her stomach lurches and then she scolds herself for that. *What's wrong with me? Why I am so afraid? There's nothing to be afraid of.*

Her shame crushes her fear into something resembling a hedgehog half-squashed on the highway after it's been run over by a car, an ill-judged crossing. His prickles are still in view, covered in blood, half dead.

'Hi Chris, supper's nearly ready,' she calls out from upstairs. She carries Sara down, who now sits nicely on her hip, her chubbiness making the grip easier. 'Let's look at your new clothes,' she says, talking to Sara. She will face it head-on. She is not weak. She will convince herself her fear is in her head. Pulling out a few items.

'Look, that looks great against your beautiful eyes,' Sakura says, smiling.

'What did you buy?' Chris calls out from the other room. He hasn't seen either of them yet.

'Some clothes for Sara, she's growing out of what she has.'

'She didn't need all that.' Chris walks into the kitchen. His face shows he is ready to fight.

'I got them in Costco's. There were three for two offers.'

Sakura puts them back in the bag, pushes it out of sight and gets the plates for supper.

'You can't go around spending money like that. You'd swear we were made of it.'

Trying to not rise to his insults and patronising words, she responds calmly at first.

'I'm not going around spending money. I am buying things that Sara needs.' Continuing to set the table using all of her body space, *this is not going to affect me.*

'What are you talking about? You're constantly buying things for her. She's only a baby.' He speaks louder now, his elbow and arm leaning on the lukewarm wood-burning stove.

'Her name is Sara, and yes, she is a baby, and she needs things,' Sakura responds, plating up the supper. A supper she now knows she won't enjoy. Her heart beats faster, and she worries her voice is shaking.

'You need to rein it in. You can't be going around buying things we don't need.' Chris has now sat down and started eating without her, devoid of gratitude, and not for the first time.

'A thank you would be nice.'

He pushes the chair out from under him, which makes her jump.

'This is all I fucking need, you want a thank you for everything! Do I get thanks for anything I do? It's all about you and how much you do. You go around spending money like it's growing on fuckin trees.' He points his finger at her. 'You need to get a grip, you have some serious issues, your mother must have spoilt you after your father died. You need to live in the real world. I don't know how you think it works or who you are, but you're not a princess here,' Chris spits out, filling the water up roughly, and then continues, 'can't even enjoy my fucking supper.'

The tiny residue of injustice sprouts up from within the core of Sakura as she angrily responds.

'How dare you speak to me like that, how dare you speak about my father, how dare you treat me like this! You come in when you feel like it, and if I'm lucky, you grumble a few lines at me. As for the clothes, yes, I bought them, she needs them, and I will continue to buy what she needs.'

'Well, you won't be getting any fucking money from me,' he says under his breath.

'Yes, I will. I'll take your bank card, and I will buy what I need for Sara and the house. I won't be treated like this.' She is interrupted by his loud sneering.

'You think I'll give you my bank card? You have another thing coming. Go back to your mommy, why don't you?'

She is losing, and she knows it. He won't ever hear her. With every word he is getting more and more vicious. Tears bubble up. She grabs the clothes and takes Sara, who sits nearby in her baby chair during all of this. She heads upstairs, and tears fall. She mumbles *fuck it, fuck fuck it, I can't stay here.*

Sara starts crying. Guilt for Sara erupts, and Sakura cries while holding her close. Placing her on the bed with something she has found to keep her entertained for a minute. Sakura grabs a bag, the first one she sees. Aimlessly throwing her clothes in, she can't even think about what she might need.

She needs to think of what Sara needs.

There is a panic in her now. Lifting up Sara, she drops something, reaches down to get it, and continues into Sara's room. This makes Sara cry even more. Quickly she has to think about how many vests, diapers, food, and bottles she will need. This will slow her down.

Heading downstairs, she goes outside with the first pair of shoes she finds. They look silly with the sweatpants she's wearing, and she places the bag in the car and buckles Sara in, with a baby biscuit in her hand she found on the front seat. She's not sure how long it's been there but blows on it and hands it to Sara anyway.

Back inside, she wants to be quick, opening the fridge for baby food she has already made and grabbing essential things for Sara.

'Where are you going?' Chris hasn't left the table.

'I don't know, but I'm not staying here.'

'You can't go, it's late, think about the baby,' he says, a lot calmer now.

'I am thinking about Sara. Sara, that's her name,' Sakura responds, adrenaline giving rise.

'This is crazy. Let's sit down and let you calm down.' He stands up. He is so much taller than her.

'I am not sitting down. I am leaving. You think you can speak to me like that, abuse me like that, and then expect me to take it?'

'For fucks sake, I'm not abusing you. You're watching too many of those programs.' Seeing her reaction, Chris attempts to back down. 'Okay, let's just talk about this calmly. It was just a fight. Couples fight all the time. You can't just leave.'

'I have nothing to say to you.' Picking up Sara's blanket, she heads outside.

Following her to the door, Chris asks,

'Where are you going to go? Just stay, and we can talk about it.' He seems so reasonable now.

Her mushy head just says no, and she shuts the car door and drives off. Not too fast, in case he accuses her of being reckless with the baby.

Sakura is right. It's not in her head. What's worse than fear is the feeling of going insane from not being heard, from someone else constantly saying that you are insane.

It's dark, and she needs a plan.

She thinks about going to Mom's house, then quickly dismisses that idea. She would have to explain, and she doesn't even know what's happening. Pulling in off the main road, she looks up hotels and finds a Travel Inn. It's the cheapest. She books it and goes into her overdraft.

Even this seems crazy in light of Chris's comments about money.

Pulling onto the main road, she glances back at Sara, and starts crying again. Turning on music in an attempt to distract her from her rising panic. She pulls her thoughts into her evening, stops at the store, gets some snacks.

When she gets into the room, she'll bathe Sara, thinks she may even have a bath herself later. Could this be ok, nice even? This gives her momentary relief.

After checking in, she quickly gets in the elevator, becoming suddenly uneasy about how this picture looks. Chris's thoughts ringing in her head. The key card drops and slips down under Sara's car seat outside her room. Sakura almost strains herself, reaching down to get it. Inside she unpacks the few bits she brought, trying to make it normal.

Sara looks up at her, little arms moving.

The night goes by, broken sleep, night feeds, and missed calls and texts from Chris. They start caring, then concerned, then annoyed back to caring. She sends a one-line text –

We are fine, can't talk to you right now. Too upset.

She can't afford to stay another night, she decides to call Mom. Having calmed down somewhat, she can make it appear normal, spontaneous. This will buy her another night.

Chris calls and texts the following day too. She doesn't answer. It makes her feel sad and slightly empowered. He isn't normally this bothered about them. This table will turn soon.

CHAPTER 40

She comes home. There will be many questions at Mom's. Sakura has no answers. The only available one is to go home.

Chris carries the baby seat and bag into the house. Sakura is quiet, all talked out, yet nothing resolved. He is a little nicer than normal, which is not even that nice in a normal world. He takes extra interest in Sara, while Sakura heads upstairs, crawls under her warm duvet and tries to block out the noise in her head.

The next morning he leaves his bank card.

CHAPTER 41

The day to return to the stables has arrived, and Sakura is surprised by how excited she is. Up extra early and still dark, she packs Sara's bag for the day and all her meals and bottles.

A few hours later, she drops her off at Isobelle's. After goodbyes, she leaves her baby for the first time with someone who isn't Chris or her mom. The guilt pang hits and then leaves.

She turns up the road, and the horse smells travel in through the rolled-down window. She finds a piece of herself floating in alongside the scent of hay and manure, waiting all this time for her to return. Seeing Snowy's tail swishing through the fence, tears flow which surprises her.

Tye's warm smile is the beginning of her lovely day, carrying tangled-up reins.

'Welcome back.' He walks over to where Sakura is, leaning in over the stalls, seeing who is new in the stables. She has so missed all this. A place where she can relax, feels welcome, is regarded, is at home.

'Great to be back.' Sakura means every word, she feels great in this moment.

'How is the baby? Sara, isn't it?' Tye continues to free tangled reins and glances at Sakura.

'Yes, Sara. She's great, first day with her childminder.'

'Ah good, I'm sure it'll go well.' He's not good with kids unless they're on a horse. 'Let you get settled in. I'll talk you through things in a while.'

'Okay, thank you.' His familiar sense of being is comforting to Sakura.

Tye heads back to the office, away from the stables.

*

The glow of the day follows her on the drive home with Sara in the back. Extra hugs and kisses for her. She seems to have grown in the few hours she was gone. She can't wait for Chris to come home, to tell him all about her first day back.

The screen door bangs, and she takes his glances and hello as an invitation to talk. She does, and all her excitement pours out. Chris's reaction is as she expected deep down but she always hopes it will be different.

'You had a good day, so.' He walks off. Sakura decides to hold on to the residue of excitement she has.

She calls Jack later and gets what she needs. Heard.

The following weeks create a new pattern and work gives her purpose. She enjoys her days off with Sara and sees Chris less. With a little money for her own things, she feels more independent, less reliant on him.

She still doesn't have enough for everyday household things and often finds herself having to ask. That time he gave her his bank card after she came home from the Travel Inn was a once-off event.

It's a Saturday, and Sakura has come to expect to be on her own with Sara. She makes her own plans, and today she's ok with that. Chris senses it.

'Where are you off to, so early?' he asks over dirty dishes and baby clothes not yet washed.

'Jack is home. We're off to see her and probably go for supper later.'

'What about Sara?' He raises the eyebrow again. She hates this.

'Mom is minding her.' Her voice sounds not her own.

'Think you're asking your mom to help a lot,' Chris responds.

'No, she hasn't minded her in a month since Sara went to Isobelle's. She's delighted to spend time with her.' Sakura is not going there. He will not take this from them today. 'Come on, Missy.' Sakura smiles at Sara. 'We have a busy day planned.'

Those moments where she holds her own, and he doesn't destroy it, Sakura feels pleased with herself, which is very quickly replaced by sadness. A victory where she is not destroyed by her partner, the father of her child, suddenly feels empty.

No. Sakura pulls herself back to the moment. Sakura sets off, and she realizes that Chris doesn't want to do anything with her but also doesn't want her to do anything either.

She enjoys her time with Jack, talking over food. None of the everything going on for her is discussed, but she keeps it to University and Sara.

Later she gets a call from Chris. He suggests they do something tomorrow.

The next day she meets Chris at the boardwalk. She sees him walking towards them. He is tall, wearing a warm coat, winter lingering into Spring, its tentacles holding on tight, compacted snow pushing down any new buds. Sara starts to grumble, and Sakura pushes her back and forth in her stroller. He half smiles as he comes closer and she tries to see the man she first met, who flirted with her in Tye's stables. The man who caringly put a blanket on her, the man who said, 'I love you, move in with me.'

Instead of the man who cruelly belittled her, mocked her.

The man walking towards her now.

'Hi.' He leans in and kisses Sakura on the lips. He never does this when he comes home from work.

Surprised, Sakura smiles, a little embarrassed, like she has been seen, and she starts to see the man she first met, the rest disappearing into the old creaking wood beneath her feet.

'Hey, little miss.' He smiles, leaning into Sara in her stroller. 'Where are we going?'

CHAPTER 42

Opening the stable door, a tall, elegant brown horse sticks his head up.

'Aren't you a beauty?' Sakura says as she gets close enough to put a lead rope on his head collar. But the brown horse jumps back. 'Okay, okay, let's do this slowly.' She talks calmly, lowers herself to the ground and sits away from him beside the door. She keeps talking, and after some time, he comes over and smells her hair and snorts. Getting up gradually, she rubs his neck, puts on the lead rope, and brings him outside.

Sometime later, all saddled up, they walk out of the stables onto the track, and soon they are cantering along the edge of the trees. Their joint rhythm, the flaring nostrils, hooves kicking muck into the air. Sakura's seat light in the saddle, her hair flying through the gaps in her helmet, the horse trusts her.

Her heart warms, and a knowing glow surrounds her body, moves to her face and forms a smile. She can't help it. Here everything is ok, perfectly ok. Horses she understands. Horses she's unafraid of. Other things she fears. Other people she fears. Another person she fears. Chris.

After a wash down, she thanks the brown horse. Summer has arrived and Sakura can feel the heat the day has in its promise, even though it's still early morning.

All the chores complete, Sakura drives to collect Sara, and is happy to see her crawling to her feet. She scoops her up in her arms, and today they decide to go to the beach.

Finding a spot to park, she carries Sara and the bag in her arms and feels the sand between her toes. Laying down her towel close enough to the water, Sakura holds Sara's hands and laughs at her reaction to the glittering blue.

They sit and play while Sakura stops each full hand of sand before it gets to Sara's mouth. Sakura looks at her baby and sees this beautiful person. *I can't believe you're here*. Picking her up, she makes funny faces. Sara laughs gorgeous open laughs. Her big brown eyes looking at her. Sakura lifts her closer, their faces touching, and whispers, 'I love you, and I'm sorry when I don't get it right, I'm trying my best, I will always protect you.'

Later she lifts Sara's tired sea air body into the car seat, and she falls fast asleep on their way home. Sakura puts on some music and stops at the beach hut to get takeaway coffee. It was all without Chris. Maybe she can do it on her own. They arrive home, and the smell of cooking hits her as she walks in.

'I made some supper. It's just ready.'

Sakura feels a jolt of guilt about her earlier thoughts. Here he is making supper and smiling at Sara. Here he is normal.

'I bought that nice drink that you like', he says, pulling out a glass.

'Thanks, this is lovely,' she responds. Sitting, she sees the macaroni and ready-made sauce piled high in a bowl. A tear arrives at her duct without any notice.

'You like it?' Chris looks over while bouncing Sara on his knee.

'Yeah, it's lovely, really nice, thank you.' Sakura looks down, wishing she could melt into the silver of the fork.

She can't explain why she's so upset. Why she feels so inadequate. He would just blame her, call her ungrateful, and storm off with practised gestures.

'How was the beach?' Chris's chatty mood is more unnerving than his quiet, angry self.

'It was lovely, Sara loved it.' Sakura looks back down at her fork, shushing her other voice; *you didn't mention you're earlier thoughts.* For once she's grateful for his rapid eating habits.

'I'll run the water for the bath.' He tilts the chair back, lifts Sara up and shouts back, 'Where are the clean towels?'

Later, Sakura lifts Sara into her cot, her baby-clean smell lingering in their cuddles. As she lies her down, bum up, her dark hair turning lighter, Sakura blows her one last kiss and pulls the door closed on the sounds of the gentle birds, chirping woods, moon and stars circling above her. A present from one of Mom's friends.

Sakura feels suddenly sad, the glow of the supper gesture waning, confusion coming for her. Her daughter's warm cot. The coldness of her life.

CHAPTER 43

Sakura's return to work gives her some sense of herself. The same sense she feels on a 'good day' when Chris is not around, and nothing is happening, and she is alone with Sara, being her mom. Connection, laughing, playing, they have it all between them.

It is as though she has this relationship, this special relationship, with Sara and Chris tips in and out when he wants to. Always screaming work and money and 'you're stupid' when she dares to ask for more.

Sakura struggles to avoid the invisible landmines under her feet. Wishing at times that she would just explode into a million pieces, and then immediately feels guilt and shame. What about Sara? Sakura playing both sides of the conversation in her head,

'You're a mother now.' His words circling in her head like vultures. 'You can't keep going off.'

'Well, you're a fucking father, but you don't act like it.'

It's one of those days, it's a Thursday, and she is at home with Sara, her three days of work complete. The weekend is approaching, and like almost every other weekend, she has no idea what Chris is doing, nor will she, and it won't include them, save for an hour or two on a Sunday.

Strangers catch a glimpse and remark on how hands-on he is as a father.

'Ah, you're so good with her.' The stranger smiles at Chris.

'You're lucky, you know.' The raised eye and almost finger wagging directed at Sakura by a stranger in a coffee shop one Sunday.

'I am.' Sakura wants to slap the words back in, once they come out.

Chris packs it all in for these concentrated few hours, sometimes just one hour.

Sakura wants to scream *you don't see all the rest!* Chris catches her face and looks concerned in front of the stranger.

'Are you ok?' The question he never asks in private. Get yourself together, Sakura scolds herself. She can now see the stranger looking concerned.

This cannot be happening.

On the way home, she feels herself slip down into the passenger seat, down where the lost things go and gone off bits of food.

She knows he will go out as soon as he carries Sara in. She wishes the car would crash and then almost gulps with panic, thinking her wish might come true. And wonders, maybe I am the sick one. Maybe Chris is right.

They arrive inside, and as predicted, Chris places Sara's bag with her bottle and bits down, and after a quick change, he is going out again. Sakura can't help herself,

'Where are you going?'

'What do you mean, where am I going? I've work to do.'

'It's a Sunday. Why do you always have to leave? What about Sara and me?'

Like a vampire, he smells Sakura's vulnerability and drinks while she is still alive.

'Ah, not this crap again. Is there something wrong with you? How do you think things get paid for around here? You live in cuckoo land.' A sneering smile rises to his lips.

Sakura winces.

'How can you do this to me? How can you treat me like this?'

'You need to get a grip of yourself, you need help.'

'I don't need help. I need you to be here, to step up and be a father, to be a partner!'

And then he does it. He digs in and takes the vulnerable share of Sakura's heart and tosses it out across the kitchen.

'You do need help. You have had issues since your father died. Sure, you practically killed him. You said so yourself. You are so fucked up.'

Sakura is shaking now. Her worst fear and shame about that day, about the man she loved, smeared into her face by the person who is supposed to love her. She seems to shrink. She goes in and gets Sara, who has crawled off into the dining room, picks her up, and sits on the floor. Sara pats her face and makes gurgling noises, and pretends to do peek-a-boo, moving her head from side to side.

The door slams and she jolts with the noise. Today she has no energy to leave. Instead, she gets Sara's supper. Sakura is not eating, her stomach grumbling noises of hunger and fear. It's hard to tell them apart.

She brings Sara into her room and plays there till bedtime. Closing the door shut, she sleeps on the floor beside her. The stars rotate and twinkle overhead, and for a moment, she is one of them. Free.

CHAPTER 44

'Are you ok? Sakura?' Jack asks while picking up Sara who is spouting excited noises.

Sakura bursts out crying, unable to keep it separate anymore.

Jack turns around. Sakura sees her face and crumbles even more. Gulping now. Seeing Sara in her arms. Someone else is holding her. For a moment the space gets bigger.

'What's wrong? What's wrong?' Jack asks while bouncing a wriggling Sara in her arms.

Sakura feels as though she's spilling out all over, harder to contain.

'Come here, what is it?' Jack's face changes from surprise to worry, her silk, even forehead scrunches over her eyes. Jack reaches in and hugs Sakura. Sara tries to climb back to her mama.

Jack quickly points to a toy half hiding in the corner. She runs over, says in an extra loud voice, 'What do we have over here?' and Sara is distracted for a few moments.

But Sakura can't talk. The tears are flooding her sweater as she tries to wipe them away with her sleeve. Jack gives her a tissue and finds other toys for Sara to play with. They are at Mom's house, she's out with a friend.

'I'm just struggling. Things are difficult…' she is about to say with Chris, but stops short. 'It's tough working and trying to be a mom to Sara.'

'Ah, Sakura, I had no idea. I am so sorry.' Jack reaches in and hugs her.

Sakura cries even harder. Her best friend forever and she can't even say what's wrong. As if Jack knows, she asks, softly, quietly, 'What about Chris, did you tell him how you feel?'

'Yeah, he's suggested I talk to someone, get help.' The heart falls with the deception of her own words.

'Maybe it's that, you know, postnatal depression?' Jack repeats the words she's heard but knows nothing of.

'Maybe,' she responds lowly, her heart whimpering. 'Don't say anything to my mom.'

'Ok, only if you promise me to ring your doctor and call me after.

Sakura feels better for the release of tears, but the shadow spreads. She is lying to herself and now her best friend. Anxiety lurches and causes her heart to race. She holds that fragment of hope or insanity that maybe Chris is right, maybe she does need help, maybe she is too demanding, maybe Chris will change too.

After their walk, Jack says goodbye. 'Come visit me in the new apartment.' She's working full-time now for the summer. 'Bring Sara.'

They hug, and she turns back to where her car is parked. She is praying it will last another few months. It's old, and it groans and creaks. She might have to get a loan out for a new car. But how can she do that? She probably wouldn't even get one. Chris just upgraded his pickup.

Back at home, she puts laundry away as Sara shuffles around her. Sakura pretends to catch her between putting away the vests that button under her bum and her cot sheets. Sara laughs, big belly laughs. Sakura scoops her up, blowing bubbles. This causes her to erupt in giggles, and Sakura can't help but smile. She catches the unfinished stencilling above her play area. She has lost interest. It doesn't seem to matter anymore.

*

Days after, she lifts Sara into her stroller. Resisting the buckle. Sakura always carries something in her bag, just in case. She can't find it. The panic is real. Her bag of everything. Notes, feelings jotted down when she would arrive somewhere with a sleeping Sara, having left Chris, but she always returned. If someone read them, they would agree with Chris. There is something wrong with her.

Running back to her parked car. Running too awkwardly and out of breath to look like a casual jogger with her baby. And her stroller isn't the right type. It has four wheels, and the front bar where Sara would lean and swing out of is breaking, and the hood is tricky to pull up. Chris chose it. He said it was the best of the reasonably priced ones, that day in the baby store.

She can't remember him ever really pushing it, save for their odd Sunday outing, but it always seems to be back in Sakura's hands. She sees it as she runs to the door of her car. Thank God. She grabs her bag and pushes it down too hard underneath the stroller.

'Come on, Missy, let's go shopping.' Sakura goes through the list in her head, things for Sara, things for her, and things for Chris. Although she cooks for three, it always feels like it's for one and she batch cooks Sara's meals. Chris's supper is left on a plate somewhere near the stove. Everything feels lonely.

Arriving home later, she unpacks the groceries and decides to cook a new seafood recipe. She thought Chris might like it. She knows he likes seafood, and she wants to ask him to mind Sara for the night. Jack wants to take her away for her birthday. Her mom is out of town and can't take Sara, she already asked her first. She feels nervous and then chastises herself for feeling this way.

Adding cream and finishing with parmesan cheese, the aroma fills the kitchen and escapes out the side door as Chris comes in.

'Something smells nice.'

'I cooked you something new. I hope you like it.' Sakura feels herself talking a lot. 'I went to that fish market, you know near North Bridge?'

'Ah yeah, think I heard of it. That place is probably expensive.' He's ignoring the smell, wanting the bill.

Sensing where this is going, Sakura jumps in.

'They had a special offer, it was fine, and it will do for tomorrow also. So, Jack wants to take me away for my birthday for a night next month. Can you mind Sara?'

'I don't know, I'm probably busy, that new supplier has a lot of work on. Where are you going anyway? That costs money.' More of the same. Day after day it's about money.

'It's one night, and Jack is treating me. It's not until three weeks, can you not tell them you need that Saturday off?'

'You don't get it. Are you stupid? This business doesn't work like that! It's not some silly job you do a few days a week. I'm the boss.'

Sakura sees red and snaps.

'Silly job! I work part-time to take care of our daughter. Are you serious, how dare you call me stupid! I ask for some help with Sara for one night for my birthday, and you can't even do that. She's your daughter too.' Sakura gets up and leaves the table, her face red.

She wants to slap herself. She storms to the washroom and slaps the sink instead, whispering *fuck fuck fuck* to herself. They get louder, and she bites her lip, trying to keep them in. Returning to the kitchen, shouting now.

'I am going on this one night away, and you will mind Sara.'

She stops and sees his sneer in between huge mouthfuls of food, some falls on the table. She wants to vomit.

'Well, you can go, but I won't be here.'

She's trapped and he knows it. Like a fox in a snare, its leg damaged and bloodied. Even if it does get away, it won't make it far. She leaves the room for the second time. And he's talking to her.

'Are you going to run off again?'

It's almost indiscernible with the sound of a packed mouth, but she hears it.

She lies on the washroom floor, curls into the tightest ball and resists the urge the smash her head off the tiled floor. The tiles she hates but is not allowed to change. She jolts with the bang of the screen door. He's gone. She grabs her bag and scribbles in her notebook; *I need to leave. He is destroying me.*

She doesn't see him until the following evening, having slept beside Sara on the ground in the nursery.

'When is that thing you're doing?' He says it like a breeze.

'What thing?' she responds sharply.

'Your birthday thing?'

'My night away with Jack?' She hates it when he calls everything a thing. 'I told you already, it's three weeks, the fifth.'

'I might be able to take it off.'

'Right, when will you know?'

'Late next week.' He is so clipped. He is so aware of how late that is.

'That's too late. I need to let Jack know before then.' She tries to keep her voice calm.

'What's so special about Jack? *Jack this, Jack that.*' He mimics Sakura's tone of voice.

Sakura whispers, 'Go fuck yourself.' Then out loud,

'Just forget about it. You obviously don't want to help in any way.'

'Aren't I trying to?' She senses him backing down. 'I'll let you know early next week.'

Chris didn't let her know until the day of the trip. By then it was too late. She had already cancelled with Jack, the previous week.

CHAPTER 45

'Are you ok?' her mom asks on one of her visits with Sara.

'Yeah, just tired; Sara's not sleeping great.'

'You're too skinny. You need to eat more.'

It's harder now. Her brokenness seeps through her body and head, appearing like dull skin, a pale and low-grade continuous anxious state. Sakura shakes herself, gotta try harder, she shouts to herself on the inside.

'Come on, let's go to that place you like, the place with the nice Danishes,' Sakura says, changing the subject.

Jack is on her case, too, asking if she has gone to her doctor about the baby blues. Maybe Jack has said something to Mom. Her heart races. *Stop it. You're just paranoid,* she whispers, but isn't sure if she said this to herself and looks around to see if it looks like her mom heard her.

She doesn't want to leave Mom's, but doesn't want to stay either. Her pain eating her, relentless gnawing, even her dreams are nightmares. She wants it all to stop. She gets into her car, and they keep going.

The next morning, she drops Sara at the childminder, pulls in and calls her doctor. Maybe I have postnatal depression, and Chris is right. Maybe this is what's wrong, and I can get help. Sakura is almost excited. There is an answer to all this. Crazy. She jumps ahead. She would say she is so sorry to Chris for putting him through all this, and she knows he just wants to help, and she couldn't see it.

Her doctor can see her later that day. Tye lets her finish early. No questions asked.

After sitting in the doctor's room and chatting for about seven minutes, Sakura starts to feel upset. She realizes the doctor, a nice woman in her sixties, is saying that she doesn't think she has postnatal depression, after going through the checklist and asks,

'Are there other things that might be causing you anxiety?'

Sakura says a little, that they are having relationship difficulties, then says more, that she doesn't like the way he treats her but backs up quickly by adding the stress of having a baby and sleeplessness is probably a lot to do with it. Sakura feels stupid and vulnerable. She has said too much and not enough.

And the doctor doesn't have any diagnosis for her. She almost imagines Chris's disappointment.

The doctor chats some more and hands her a card. Sakura has stopped listening. She shoves it in the bag that contains everything. The room suddenly seems tiny, and she wants to run out.

Standing up and holding the door handle, she can't even tell what her face is like, trying to make it smile or nod normally.

Finally, she leaves, and the route out the main door to her car seems like a million steps.

Practically running through the parking lot, she jumps in, her tears are ahead, spitting out of her eyes, *fuck you fuck you anyways,* clenching the steering wheel, pressing her head repeatedly against it, wishing she was bashing her skull and all that it contains.

Then, quickly glancing around to see if anyone can see her. Eventually, she calms down to a depressed, resigned state and opens her bag. Pulling out the card, it reads *Domestic Violence Shelter*. Quickly pushing it back in.

What do I need that for?

Chapter 46

Sakura passes off Jack's worries when she asks her on the phone later in the week if she has been to her doctor.

'Nothing to worry about,' she reassures her, 'normal after a having baby. The doctor suggested taking some vitamins.'

Sakura folds like a paper doll. Bits of herself disappearing. Making herself so light, almost invisible. Staying out of Chris's way, asking very little of him.

The week before Sara's first birthday, Mom and Jack wanted to have a party. Chris didn't. Sakura doesn't know anymore. So she agreed with Chris. The three of them gathered around a small cake, lit a candle, then blew it out. She promised her mom they would do a bigger party later in the month, knowing deep down it wouldn't happen.

It's a Sunday and they've headed out for a walk along the beach on the far side of the Island.

She tries to make it light, but he has found fault with almost everything she says or ignores her words completely. As though he senses her fear of him, and begins whipping her with it.

Chris declares he is hungry and stops for food at a café at the end of the beach. Sakura sits with Sara on her lap at a nearby outdoor picnic bench. She's not hungry. Chris returns with his food and sits down across from her. He asks if she wanted something, but it's that kind of asking that says *don't.*

She is grateful for the distraction when Sara looks for food, and spends time pulling things from her bag. Her eyes and attention stay here. Chris is busy eating and looking at things going on around them. Sakura then sees him, the little creature. Little white wings, speckled with pale pink uneven dots, fly to the bush nearby and then to their table.

'Look, Sara, look at the beautiful butterfly.'

Sara reaches up, dropping her biscuit, trying to catch him.

For the briefest of moments, Sakura smiles at Sara's delight and admires this free creature. She hasn't noticed Chris taking the penknife out of his pocket.

The white butterfly rises and then lands at the other end of the table. Wings gently moving. Sakura catches the steel knife at the corner of her eye and then sees it land through his wing and into his previous caterpillar body. The other wing flapping and flapping.

Pulling Sara closer to her, Sakura stands up and screams,

'What did you do? What have you done?'

Other people looking now. Her body is shaking, and Sara starts crying.

'Calm down. You're upsetting the baby.' Chris is putting the penknife away. 'Get a grip of yourself. You're making a scene.'

'You are a monster. What is wrong with you? It was just a butterfly, but you had to kill it.'

Chris stands up now and comes closer to her face,

'Get a fuckin grip. It was going to die anyway.' He walks off, leaving Sakura holding Sara beside the dying butterfly.

The drive home is silent. Sakura goes into deeper silence and, when the car stops, goes through the motions for the remainder of the day. Her body is doing what it needs to and has brought her mind to an eerie calm.

Sakura pretends to be asleep the following morning when Chris leaves for work. Getting up quietly, afraid to wake Sara, she reaches up to the top of the wardrobe and pulls down a bag bigger than her usual one. Filling it with her essentials, mostly casual comfortable clothes, clothes to blend in. She can't remember the last time she dressed up, she thinks to herself while glancing at her nice pieces. Then into the washroom, the same essentials going into the bag.

Going into the nursery, she wakes up Sara and smiles at her and then cries, her hands beginning to shake. *Come on, get it together,* Sakura whispers, chastising herself.

Placing Sara on the ground with some toys, she pulls out her travel cot, clothes and other things she might need. She doesn't know what she needs. She doesn't know yet where she is going, just in case.

Taking Sara's folded clothes does something to her. The little vest with little yellow ducks and blue ribbons around their necks. She doesn't want to take them but can't leave them behind either. This no-name land. The choosing would begin and end a part of her. Her tears drip, and wet blobs land on little ducks. Packing them in, she continues.

After Sara's breakfast, she packs her food and mentally goes through the essentials again in her head, afraid to miss anything.

Everything packed in the trunk, she carries Sara in her arms, walking the final walk, glancing at the rocking chair out on the deck, the one she sat in many times, and remembers when Chris held her. Then stops herself, shaking her head to lose her thoughts, like a horse swishing its tail in the summer heat, but the flies always come back.

Sakura locks the door and drives out and onto the main road with the one thought on loop. *Where will we go?*

Pulling onto a side lane, she feels like she's going to be sick. She doesn't have many options. Mom is the only one, really. But she doesn't want to go there. What would she say? Reaching into her bag, she pulls out the card her GP gave her and thumbs the number and name again and again. Searching the location, she is surprised where it is. Her hometown, the other side.

Sara startles her with inaudible words. Feeling like a fraud, Sakura has made her decision. At least something feels certain in the lone lane with flashing indicators.

She sees the building and small sign and drives past. Feeling more nauseous, she can't even imagine eating again. Turning around, she finds a parking space further away. Like she hasn't fully committed, allowing a change to occur last minute. Unbuckling Sara and placing the bag that contains everything on her shoulder, she walks the sidewalk and counts the steps under her feet. People pass, and no one knows.

Arriving at the door. There are lots of buzzers. She almost turns away. Then she hears the sound of a voice.

'Hello, you are very welcome.'

'I don't know why I'm here. I have nowhere else to go. I'm sorry to be wasting your time,' Sakura blurts out all at once. A woman comes out and places her hand on the small of her back, a very gentle hand, and guides them in. They go to a room towards the back on the right-hand side, all the time the woman smiling at Sara.

Chapter 47

Sitting down, Sakura suddenly feels all those things Chris said about her.

Stupid, stupid, I don't deserve to be here, she shouts silently to herself. Some must have shown on the outside, and the woman, sensing this, gently says, 'You've done the right thing. You are safe. My name is Olivia.'

'I'm Sakura and this is Sara.' She has to repeat both names like she has forgotten how to talk. Her hands shaking.

'I'm going to get you a cup of tea, and Sara can play with the toys just there in the corner. Would you like milk, sugar?'

'Just milk,' Sakura responds quietly. She can't believe this Olivia woman is making tea for her or giving her options. Why is she doing all this for her? Her head spirals downwards like slush circling the drain, a race to the bottom. *Maybe she's tricking me, maybe she's trying to take Sara away from me.* Maybe Chris has talked to them.

Rushing over, picking up her baby, when the woman comes back.

'Here's your tea, this must be so scary, we're here for you, for both of you. Aren't you only gorgeous?' she says, smiling and making silly faces at Sara, who responds. Sakura lets Sara down to play again and returns to her seat. She'd better come clean and set this woman straight.

'I feel I don't belong here. I just didn't know what else to do. My head hurts so much.' Tears fall, and she wipes them away on her already dirty sleeve.

'No one ever thinks they do,' Olivia gently responds.

'But no, I think I'm wasting your time, you see he never, you know, like hit me, you know, he just like you know, oh God, now I don't even know.' Panic replaces the tears as the tea sits on the floor beside her chair, the scum line forming on top.

The woman places her hand gently on Sakura's knee.

'Physical violence is one part of domestic abuse, but there are lots of parts, and some are hard to get your head around.'

A little tiny residue of understanding lands in her heart, and tears flow again.

'But he isn't even jealous, or you know, like stalks me. He doesn't do anything. But he has done everything to me. I just can't even explain it.' The sobbing becomes harder, and Sakura tries to quiet herself, so aware Sara is nearby.

She's used to shutting herself up, smacking herself silly from the inside until she is red raw, blistering, and bleeding. But no one can see. They see this nervous, fearful woman with a baby. But here they see. Everything.

Handing Sakura a box of tissues, the woman moves the tea to a higher place. How many undrunk teas have been moved to a higher place?

'I understand, I believe you.' Olivia's face is kind. It doesn't seem tired from all the stories she's heard. Sakura feels like the only person that Olivia is helping. She can't tell her age. Hard to know past a certain point. Maybe fifty, Sakura hazards a guess. Then realizes Olivia hasn't asked what age she is and then wonders what age she looks. *Silly naive woman, stop Sakura.* She harshly shushes her critical thoughts. That tiny residue grows huge at that moment and Sakura wails. This time she can't hold it in. Sara crawls over, and she picks her up. Tears and snot go everywhere while Sara pulls at her hair tie.

Over the following two hours, another woman came in and offered Sara some snacks. The woman said her name and Sakura immediately forgot it.

Olivia knew it was too early, too delicate, to suggest bringing Sara off to the baby room for a while. The other woman played with Sara at the end of the room while Sakura talked and talked, still not believing that she should be heard. Thinking Olivia would still say this isn't bad enough.

But Sakura heard,

'You are safe, I believe you, you did the right thing.'

These words she held onto.

'What about Chris? I should tell him, he'll say I'm crazy, oh no, what will he do?' Sakura suddenly realizes what she has done, what she is doing.

Olivia gently reminds Sakura that she is safe, she is not crazy, and she doesn't need to do anything right now. Sakura rests into someone else, someone else's safe words. Someone else will take over for a while. Suddenly she feels exhausted, sinking further into the chair, touching her forehead, sore from all the tears. She wants to close her eyes, just for a minute.

Forms are brought out, and the women chat to her, then Olivia makes an offer.

'You can stay here. Have you anything with you?'

'We can stay here?' Sakura repeats back, not trusting what she has heard.

'Yes.' Olivia smiles. 'You're both very welcome here. We'll take care of you and get you all the help you need.'

The women come and go, to fill in forms, ask questions. They are all warm and knowing. Sakura wonders, how do they know. They haven't met Chris. But they still believe her.

But she allows it in briefly, before the world out there would start clawing at her, this time she will have someone else to rest upon, to help her. *It seems a little too good to be true,* and then Sakura quickly adds, 'I don't have very much money.' The panicked look returns.

'Don't worry, you don't need any money. This is what we do. We help women like you. Everything will be ok. I know this is so much to take in.' Olivia does the talking. 'First things first.'

Women like me.

The insane woman that Chris says she is. Or the abused woman? Sakura doesn't fully yet know which woman she is. Olivia, sensing her head spin, adds, 'We help women who are experiencing domestic abuse.' And asks her again if she has anything with her.

Her bag and a few things for Sara are brought in, and they are shown to *their* room.

'When you get settled, come to the kitchen for lunch. You must be hungry. There is a play area for kids and a relaxation room.'

The corridor is dimly lit, beige carpet, women's feet wearing it thin. The colours are functional. The lamp on a small table in the middle of the corridor mocks any sense of home. There isn't enough light.

'First things first, this is your room, however long you need it.' Olivia pushes open the door, it sticks a little at the bottom, gives it an extra push, and it's released. 'See you in a while.' Olivia releases the door handle and gives a small smile.

Sakura smiles back, it's even smaller. Broken, but free. Sakura is amazed that Olivia seems to pre-empt all her questions and fears and answers them, giving her some solace. The room is nice, and bright, with a double bed, washroom, and small desk beside the wardrobe. She can't help wondering how many others have stood at this door, inwardly making the room acceptable. The room that now becomes her home.

It's mine, it's ours. Sakura twirls Sara around, whispering, 'We did it. I am going to take care of you. I am going to protect you.' Kissing her with wet, tear-filled kisses. Allowing hope in.

Unpacking her bag, Sakura puts her clothes in drawers. She didn't bring anything that required hangers and places Sara's clothes beside hers. Unfolding the travel cot, she pushes it up beside her bed, underneath and alongside the lower wall. Sakura sees a drawing. A stick woman, spiky blue hair. Big smile and big shoes. A love heart in green to the right. Unable to get off the floor. Her minute burst of energy disappears into a stick man drawn on the other side, far away from the stick woman.

CHAPTER 48

We have left, can't do this anymore.

The text is short. Sakura ignores the advice not to contact Chris directly. They said they could organize contact safely. But she couldn't do 'that to him'. She owes him a text, at least.

What do you mean you've left? Have you run off again? You need help, something's wrong with you.

After showing Olivia the responses, she gently explains that his words are abusive. Gaslighting. Shaking, Sakura is so relieved to have someone outside herself to look at this.

For so long, it was just her analysing, rationalizing, her own mind shrivelling, trying to understand his behaviour. Her tired head getting more confused, more doubtful, more anxious, more insane.

'What do I do?' Sakura asks, panicked.

'Nothing,' Olivia gently suggests. 'He can't hurt you here. You don't need to do anything right now. We will sort out all that in time. The only thing you need to do is look after yourself and Sara. Now come on, let's get you some food and then try to rest for the night.'

Sakura feels the woman's words like a warm protective blanket after days out wandering alone on a snowy mountain.

After lunch, it's late by the time she sits down, hours slip by dissecting her worries with Olivia, time taking on its own rhythm. Sakura's panic rises again. She can hear the phone vibrate. It's Chris ringing. Then the beep of messages.

Where are you? Where is Sara?

Come on, you can't do this.

Look, I'm sorry for whatever I've done.

Come home. I'll cook supper.

Sakura starts crying and hoping this time the woman doesn't see. What have I done? Maybe he is sorry. Maybe this is what it took. Maybe he will change. For a brief second, Sakura thinks about grabbing Sara, apologizing to Olivia for the fuss but that she got it wrong, and driving home. Sakura lets the moment pass but stays alone with her thoughts racing back and forth, and then the phone beeps again.

I have a right to know where my daughter is.

Where are you?

I'm calling the police. I will tell them you are INSANE.

I'm going to make sure Sara is taken away from you.

Sakura's brain flips back to panic. What will he do? Oh my God, will he take Sara away from me?

Running up to Olivia, showing her the texts, she cries,

'I'm so afraid, please help me, can he do this? He can't do this, can he? She's my baby. I feel like he's trying to kill me.' Sakura is shouting and shaking, her words high-pitched. Olivia brings Sara into the baby room and this time Sakura lets her go.

'Sit down. Sakura, you're ok, you are safe, now listen to me. He's trying to kill you. Kill the Sakura you are. Confuse and abuse you so much, that you don't know who you are anymore and look at you. He's done a brilliant job.' Olivia pulls her chair closer and grabs both her hands. 'You are safe, he can't hurt you anymore, they're all threats.'

Her words sink in, she's gone this way so many times, with other versions of Sakura.

'I could paper the wall with all the threats men have made to women after they leave, some that they will physically hurt them, destroy them, others that they will show that they are insane and take their children away from them.'

Olivia talks on and on while Sakura sobs and wails.

'They are bullies, they are abusive, they threaten you. He is trying to scare you. He is doing that. I can see you are terrified. You walking in here with your baby took so much courage, and you are going to be ok. It's going to take time a lot of time. Let's slow it down. Today was massive. Try and get some rest. Tomorrow we can talk more.'

Sakura's rigid, panicked body becomes looser, her head hurts. Everything hurts. But she knows Olivia is right. Deep down.

'Do I need to respond?'

'No, you don't need to do anything. He knows you have left, and that Sara is with you. You cannot tell him where you are for your safety and the safety of the other women. I suggest you turn your phone off. You are safe.'

For a brief moment, Sakura feels like she is floating up above her body, above the ceiling, and into the night sky.

Olivia pulls her back.

'You've been through a huge trauma. We are going to help you, you can trust us. Just for now you need to rest. Come on, let's get Sara, and I'll walk you both to your room. Do you like baths? There's some lovely lavender on the top shelf.'

'I do like baths. I mean, I did like baths.' Sakura half-smiles. She sees Olivia's ease of suggestion. Her firm but gentle ways. Petite frame, little makeup. Her hair cut above the shoulder stays in place, ashen blonde. Sakura wonders was this always her colour. She is even more surprised at her ability to consider this at this time.

Opening their bedroom door, Sakura locks it from the inside and places the key on the side table. Pulling out her phone, she turns it off and feels the full freedom of choice at that moment. Jumping up, she says, 'Sara, we are free, Sara, we are free.'

Sara starts to smile, seeing her mommy jumping up and down.

Later, Sara's bottle makes the air-sucking sound. Sara is already asleep. Her beautiful round face, skin smooth, perfect. Sakura looks at her, her heavy, sleepy weight. Her arm hangs over one side and touches her face, kissing her nose.

'You have no idea what's happening,' she whispers through kisses.

Sara is completely in her arms, and Sakura feels the weight of this. And with the full internal roar of the Mama Bear, Sakura whispers louder, 'I'm going to protect you, my beautiful little Sara,' placing her in her cot beside the teddy she remembered to pack.

Lavender drops under the steaming water. The smell hits Sakura, and she inhales deeply. Eyes closed, she takes off her clothes, feeling every layer of the day fall to the floor.

Raising her foot, the first heat hits her, and she folds into the body of water and allows it to devour and swirl into every crevasse. Submerging her head. Everything is still. Protected.

CHAPTER 49

Later. When she passes strangers in the street, pushing Sara in a donated stroller, walking in a part of the town she didn't grow up in, a part not near the boardwalk or with a view of the North Strait, they don't know her head is on fire. That she ran to a women's shelter with her baby in her arms. She pushes Sara and walks to keep from being swallowed by the past. But she wants to run back to the shelter with all her instincts and hide from everyone.

She reasons with herself. She could run into someone she knows, but most of those who know her by sight are not in this area. This is the part of town where people struggle to eke out an existence. There's little chance of seeing anyone, even her mom. Mom might pass in her car, or someone else. That thought keeps her nervous and watching each vehicle.

When it comes to talking to those she knows, over the coming days and weeks, she will say it like this to some people in her life, 'We just broke up.' And sometimes they will respond by saying relationships are difficult, especially with young children, and maybe she and Chris, they could work it out? When she will tell the same people later the truth, some will still say the same thing.

Then there are those she loves. The ones she has hidden this all from.

Now. There are the first twenty-four hours to get through. The first nightmares to get through. As her body uncoils and her emotions unfreeze, the numbness is replaced by living dread that comes for her that first night, after she has put Sara down.

'Please, not now. I'm so tired now.' The first part of the darkness is fighting sleep. Her body can't. Just like it couldn't with Chris. Her eyes closed, fear slides through the keyhole and under the door, and starts to strangle her.

Jumping up, sobbing into the darkness. This is the half-world of things over that are still happening. Things ahead that she cannot yet manage to think about.

Realizing it's still dark, she puts her hand over her mouth. *I can't wake Sara. Please don't wake up.* Praying silently. Her first moments of freedom die. Dissolve in the palms of her clammy hands. The future she has reclaimed slides away. There is a battle ahead she can't manage and might not win. Chris wins those. Ever since she met him. She can feel his hands encircle, then grip. The washroom. The times she had to please him.

Pulling the fear away from her neck, she quietly tiptoes into this washroom, the one where she is safe, if only for now, and starts to sob.

'What am I going to do?' she asks the wall. 'Shit, what have I done? What if he takes Sara?'

It doesn't answer back.

Somehow, she fights to reach the bed and tries to sleep. Sara is up in a few short hours. Her head argues with the invisible. Olivia insists Chris doesn't have the power she thinks he has. All her doubts are saved for the washroom, for the night, after Sara is slumbering.

But he saw me at my lowest. What if he? What if he?

Shush, Sakura, I have got you. You are ok. I have got you. She thinks she is trying to soothe herself. Her arms move from between her legs and cross in front of her heart.

Then, for a brief moment, Dad's smell hits her nose. As if she were with him only yesterday. He is here. She opens her eyes, and all has gone into the darkness.

I've got you. You are okay. I have got you. Him, it was him.

'Dad, I haven't told anyone about this yet.' Fear held at bay under her tight fist, walking back towards her bed. 'How do I tell them?' She glances in and sees her baby asleep. 'Will they make me go back to him? Am I crazy, Dad?' Her free hand pinches her lips, and she wipes away the tears she knows are coming.

Sara is lying on her belly, her head facing the side. Even in this dark light, she can see her perfect skin. Gently placing her hand above her back. Just to touch her almost. Sakura doesn't want to wake her.

'Dad, please, help me.' The way he did the pond. The way he did the special project. The way he confessed to Mom he feared his children growing away from him. Did he know then his heart was not going to let his first grandchild touch his face?

There is no answer. The wall is the wall again.

Lying back in bed, waiting for the night to end.

Monsters recede into the shadows only when they are pierced by the rising sun.

CHAPTER 50

The first morning at the shelter, a vacation from physical fear. The beginning of freedom. The white butterfly stirs. Still feeling impaled. Not dead, not lifeless, not yet capable of flight.

Not knowing what time she should leave her room. Eventually, deciding that eight-thirty is respectable enough, Sakura carries Sara in her arms as she tries to remember the way back into reception.

'Good morning.' Olivia approaches. 'Did you sleep ok?'

'Yes, well, yes, ok thank you,' Sakura says. She still needs to say nothing and by saying nothing she is still lying. About walls that don't answer and dads that don't answer. About monsters.

'Come on, let's get you breakfast.' Olivia, smiling at Sara who coos back, and reaches out to touch the soft-lined face and ready smile. 'Your mom might let me hold you. She looks tired.'

The food seems to mock her.

'There are tasks ahead. You need to eat for energy. Look at Sara tucking into her croissant! How about one for Mom? Didn't Mom do a brave thing, Sara?' Olivia speaks to the child, but her eyes are on Sakura's face. Sakura nods. They watch Sara eat and Olivia says, 'I'll leave you to it.' She knows that saying more will push.

Delighted and sad, watching Sara pull chunks off a pastry and put them in her mouth. All of this is happening to her, none of which she will remember. But her little body will hold all of this.

Sakura wants to eat, to drink a hot coffee, to sit and be with Sara. But bits of her are falling away. She feels like she is hurtling into some reality she can't prevent.

Sara is beginning to mewl for the juice, reaching out her stubby hands for the weaning mug just out of reach. What is wrong with her? Is she sick? Is she missing home and Dad? Sakura immediately lifts her out of the highchair and kisses her chubby cheeks. Folds her beautiful baby girl into her chest. Trying to hold her and shield against the oncoming vehicle, a giant pickup, trying to steer out of its way. But the crash is already happening. Everyone around her must see. But she cannot see everyone around her. It is only the nightmare-made day. Then, the voice, the voice again.

Dad's. Dad's voice,

'I've got you, I love you.'

As if he is here. As if he were alive today.

'I've got you, I love you,' Sakura whispers, and hands Sara the juice mug and can't help smiling when Sara plays with her hair, pulling strands long hidden.

It passes. There are two other women with children at the far side of the room. Sakura half waves awkwardly. The shared knowing looks. They know it's too early to come close and too soon. They raise their hands and smile.

Sakura's arms drop like dead weight in the middle of the room. No one hears the ricochet of her fear in all directions. Sakura's ears ring with it all the same. Coffee, try to sip a little coffee. Hot and black, it burns her tongue. She pours some milk in, and it slides down her throat. Something in her warms up. She picks at the rest of Sara's pastry. Sara is now on her lap, watching their new world, smiling at it. Almost as if in answer to Sara's smile, Sakura sees a smiley young woman with colourful clothes approach through the glass door of the hallway. Sakura can't imagine smiling again, her face feels permanently frozen in pain.

'Would you like to play with some toys?' this woman who can smile says, grinning at Sara. 'Come with me, please. If you're finished?'

Sakura nods. Feels the dread come. It's time for the work to begin. Should she have gone to Mom's? Should she phone Jack? No. This has to come from her.

They follow the woman out, and Sakura's stomach starts to lurch and swirl, knowing or not knowing what's coming. They go into a smaller room than yesterday. That big room must be where you go first, Sakura thinks as she walks in and notices the limp, almost dead flowers in the pale blue vase on a small table to the right.

These rooms will become her security maze, each having its own exit in what looks like a dead end. It must be designed by the architect to mitigate the threat of entry from abusive partners. For now, she doesn't know, can't know anything, but she doesn't want to begin. Through rooms of dead ends, ways out appear.

'Take a seat.' Olivia smiles, pointing at the chair. Sakura likes the smaller room. Fears are more contained. The doors and walls try to line up with the square boxes in her head. 'How are you today?'

'I'm okay, I think.' As she says this, Sakura's tears just appear. She wipes some away. She isn't even embarrassed anymore. 'I'm scared I don't know what to do. I haven't turned on my phone. The thought of it is making me sick.'

'I think you're wise.' Olivia lowers her voice, softer reassuring tones. 'You're safe. He can't hurt you anymore.'

'He could call my mom. Oh God. I haven't even told her.'

'Are you close to your mom? Sakura?'

'Kind of at times, yes, not really.' Sakura looks around for Dad. What will he think? Will he forgive her for telling the truth of their lives after his death? Spirits understand. Don't they?

He is not giving any answer. Olivia is watching her.

'Should I not have come? She lives in town. I just didn't think she would understand. I don't even understand. Oh God, you probably think I'm wasting your time.'

'Sakura, let me stop you there.' Olivia catches her mid-spiral by reaching out and gently places one hand one on Sakura's forearm. 'You're so welcome here. We're here for you. Women exactly like you. Women don't often feel safe or comfortable staying with family.'

Then she senses Sakura's discomfort with being touched. It makes the feelings unmanageable. With the practice of a woman who has done this so many times with other women, she pulls back, but not the loving concern. She speaks firmly.

'Please hear me. When I say you have earned your place here, I can see your fear, your confusion, your exhaustion. Many women have sat where you are, and they are ok. In time they see what has happened to them. They see the truth.'

'What's the truth, please?' Sakura's eyes fill with tears. This is the word she has been longing to hear, to have told to her.

'They are warrior women. You are a warrior woman. The courage it took to come here was huge.'

All of a sudden, the missing breath is found. It resurges, finding her lungs. Sakura knows that Olivia, without knowing her, knows the truth of what she has lived.

'Now, we have a few practical issues to take care of.' Olivia sits up taller and reaches for leaflets on a small table to her left.

Then it begins. The toil of getting away from imprisonment. Olivia goes through legal things concerning Sara, access, financial support, and her job. Sakura sinks into the details. But she is a warrior woman. She is a mom to Sara. She is Dad's child. He is with her. Mom couldn't be told. Can't yet be told. Olivia explained this to her, alleviating her guilt, and hopefully, Dad has heard too, how hard it is to involve family. It's like your whole history disintegrates. Just like his did at the waterfront, over a decade ago.

'You need to get ahead of these things, have everything in place. As he will likely throw all sorts of accusations your way, deflect from why you and Sara are here, right now.' Olivia has sensed the rise in Sakura and knows no matter how hard, she has to be told the hard things.

'Oh shit. I don't think I can face this.' This is the fight she has been fearing. The one she can't win. There is so much to this. Too much to this.

Seeing the fear rising in Sakura, the woman reassures her.

'It's okay, we will help you with it all. I've made an appointment with the legal aid office for this afternoon. Our support worker will go with you.'

'Already?' Then it has begun. The monster has found the day. It was supposed to stay behind the sun.

'Already.' Olivia, used to moving women on into the field of their battles, slips on Sakura's armour. Legal aid. Support worker. Meals. Care for Sara. Sara's childminder. She will wonder where her charge is. The phone sits in her bag. Not yet switched on. So many people to face.

'I know.' Olivia breaks in again, opening the chain of panic. 'But it does get done. Let's make your list. You've got this, Sakura. I saw it in you the moment you walked into reception.'

They go through everything in Sakura's head. It feels a little lighter. She knows what to do now. Just for this first morning. It will be full again by four p.m. The not-yet-formed questions gather like little cells marching, growing, joining to create a supercell.

As she finishes her paperwork with Sakura, Olivia looks up from it and smiles.

'Should I turn my phone on?' Sakura asks, bewildered.

'Time enough. Why don't you spend a while in the yard, it's small but has lovely trees and the fresh air will do you good. Sara will be ok for another short while. You need to take care of yourself. We are all here to help you.' Olivia rearranges the chairs.

Even though Sakura has only been here one night, she can't imagine being able to make any decision now without Olivia. How did I do it before? Sakura's brain flicks back to yesterday morning, packing their bag with Sara, all on their own. Now that she has help, her body lets go in exhaustion.

'Why don't we look in on Sara?' Olivia suggests. 'Before you head out.'

'Could you promise me if she cries someone will come for me?'

'Sure.'

Sakura walks with her to see Sara taking her nap on a beanbag, with an array of toys.

Sitting outside, she takes out her phone. Tye, she never contacted him, panic surges like a hot iron up through her body, forcing herself in an upright position. She'll have to see whatever Chris has said or done. Turning it on, whispering to herself, 'Whatever is here, I am ok. Whatever he says, I am ok.'

The light comes on, the excruciating wait, until. Nothing. There is nothing, no messages, or calls. This worries her more. This makes her so afraid.

Chris is playing the waiting game.

Her text to Tye is short. She knows she can keep it simple with him.

Can't make work.

His reply is instant.

Are you ok, Sakura? Chris came by today looking for you.

He doesn't even mention being left short-handed without explanation. She remembers how he walked away when she tried to tell him about her and Chris. Then the baby coming. He never said a word. He won't now. So she must trust him on some deep level. But there is nothing she can say right now that will not threaten her sanity. So she answers,

Sorry for no notice. Please do not tell Chris.

Just as quick back, *Agreed. Promise.*

He will win. Then the sound comes. Of Sara, and with Sara, Olivia. Just like she promised.

This is a place where people do what they can and help those who need it.

Sara immediately nuzzles into her mom. Olivia walks them back to their room.

'Take your time, lunch will be ready shortly.' Olivia stops short at their door.

'Thank you.' Sakura turns her head to the side, trying to manoeuvre Sara on her hip.

'You're going to be ok.' Olivia rubs Sara's arms and turns. Sakura, glad of this, bites her lower lip and can't get into the room quick enough, to unclench her teeth and release the tears. Sara sits on her lap, touching her wet, salty pain.

The afternoon brings a deluge of facts. Proof needed. Papers needed. Certificates needed. Statements needed. The support worker is not Olivia, but that's because she works with the facts and gathering them, and so does the legal aid office. It's an impersonal horrible meeting where no one is unkind, but no one has time to comfort. There is no feeling of endless time. There is a clock and an hour. But at the end, the two professionals say to her,

'You'll get there. You've done well already. For someone who's been through so much you are strong.'

In that water, dragged out onto the pier, trying to revive Dad. She learned to face the unbearable and she never liked to hide from it. She grew up then. Even with Jack in her life, childhood was gone.

'Thanks.' This is all she can say to these people who are not to be her friends, but they are her team.

After the Legal Aid office, the support worker drops her off to reception and heads straight out, to another woman, on another case. A conveyor belt of women in crisis. How can anyone form a relationship without fear? How will she? The man she loved most died in front of her. The man who was supposed to love her most goes inside her head and is in there still.

Sakura has a little time before she has to get Sara. Walking into their room, it looks different during the day, when she is here alone. She hadn't noticed the collection of small stones in a basket on the windowsill behind her bed. Picking a deep purple one, she rolls it in her hand, feeling the cold against her skin. Its solid form brings her back into her body.

CHAPTER 51

The day passes. The night comes. The next day passes. How can those she loves not reach out to her? How can they not sense or know? She's been distant from everyone. To keep them away, from knowing. The only text has been from Tye. Has she really pushed everyone so far away?

More meetings. Then Olivia asks, when the day of talking and management is almost done and she is bone tired,

'Are you worried Chris is doing nothing obvious?'

'Yes,' she admits. 'I'm afraid he's planning something.'

'So why don't you consider doing something?'

'What?'

'Phone someone? Maybe your mom? If that's too difficult, one of your close friends?'

It's such a simple thing. A thing anyone would do. But anyone else is not Sakura and anyone else is not her mother.

'If it's because it's too difficult, why not try someone more neutral then? I told you it's often hard to go to family for women at first.' Olivia reads minds because she has seen so many of them confused and dulled like Sakura's.

Sakura nods, there's too much history. Then she sees Dad, in her mind, at the kitchen table, with the fishing tackle, getting ready for the last day of his life. She's in the corridor again, hearing him fear that he's losing her to horses. Then she sees Tye, who gave her no pressure. Who offered no solutions. An older male figure offering support without intrusions. They have always had horses in common. They also have the fact they don't talk a lot and especially they don't talk about other people's business. His text the only one. *Agreed. Promise.*

'I can see you're at least ready to think about it.' Olivia presses the back of Sakura's hand. 'I know it's tough.'

Sara's in the baby room. Sakura makes the first of many calls.

'Hello? Tye, it's Sakura.'

'Oh hi.' Tye's tone says he didn't expect to hear from her. 'Hmm, how are you?'

'I'm ok thanks. Thank you for your text.' Her heart is racing. He's her employer. She'll need work. 'I'm just ringing to say that I won't be in work at all this week. Maybe even next.'

'Sakura, okay.' His voice has lowered, and he sounds kind. 'No problem. I hope everything's okay.' Sakura feels this is a statement rather than a question. She is glad of that.

'Yeah, I am. Or I will be.' The heart races again. 'Uhm, myself and Chris. We broke up.'

Saying it aloud for the first time feels weird. Break up doesn't give justice to what is happening. They didn't just break up. Like 'normal' breakups. Hurting people. Putting Sara first. Insisting on providing for them, for Sara financially. No, this is different. They are staying in a shelter. They are homeless. She was abused. She is abused. Those words finally put sense on what's happened. Those words simultaneously fit and feel fraudulent.

'Eh.' Tye sighs. 'Uhm, I'm sorry to hear that.'

Sakura breaks his awkward words.

'It's okay. I just wanted you to know. I don't like letting you down, Tye.'

'Don't worry. It's fine. You just take care of yourself...' Then a pause on the phone, so she wonders is he still there. 'Sakura, if you need anything, just ask.'

'Thank you so much.' Her employer thinking of her over himself and the inconvenience. She was right to try him first. She was right to trust him the way she did after Dad died.

'Take your time, don't worry about things here. I've got it covered.' His kindness. Too much. *I don't deserve this.*

'Thanks.' Sakura's voice breaks. She wants to end the call. 'Okay, bye.' Holding the phone in her hand, wanting to fill the silence but knowing she can't without falling apart.

'Your job is safe.' He puts down the phone. Sakura tucks her body into her knees. Tears mark her blue pants. She doesn't care.

Tye texts her back later that day. He wants to pay her wages for the next four weeks, and then they can talk.

Thank you, thank you. This is all she can write. Tye is near the same age as Chris, plus a few years, but has always felt more adult, more stable. Offering practical support. Not asking anything in return. Seeing her. After realizing this, tears fall. The kindness of others is coming in.

The rest of the calls are business. Tye was all she needed to know if she was going to able to support herself. Mom, Jack, Eli, the few she knows, they are all familiar with her not being in touch a great deal. The baby. The job. The house move, to live with Chris. These were all reasons to let go of the fact that she seemed to be the only one who could not leave that pier.

Mom, busying herself with life, didn't comment on not being asked to stay over when Sara was born. It was Sakura's choice, but Sakura was being held in a snare. Might Mom have noticed more? Is this why she cannot speak to her yet?

She thinks of the days she had to come home to Mom in bed, having been all day at school. They got past it. But it has left Sakura with a sense that she had to shoulder everything, keep trouble away from Mom. Mom and Eli lost Dad. But they didn't have to watch him die. All three of them have lives that moved on. Hers is in a shelter. She has taken refuge. Things will change. People know now. She has support now. Smiling, she runs back to get Sara. She is pushing up, like the lupins, through the dark and sticking their heads into the light, hoping nobody will chop them off. But still, she has begun to reclaim and it's the first step of fighting back. For her life.

CHAPTER 52

Walking out the door of the shelter for the second time, the first was a brief walk, this feels different. Sakura feels naked. It's only been two days, but it feels like part of her has been there forever. With the woman's advice ringing in her ears, she places Sara in the car seat, checking around more than once to make sure Chris is not behind them.

He wouldn't even know this place, she thinks as she tries to calm herself. Tye's money should arrive later in her account. She can get some gas, seeing the dial below red. She's doing basic math, thinking she will make it to Mom's and back. It's time to tell her.

'Well done.' Olivia put a hand on her shoulder after Sakura had sent the text to Mom. *Coming to see you. I have something important to tell you.*

Walking in through the porch door, holding Sara in her arms, she remembers Jack and herself running, giggling. Dad was still alive then. Mom's voice jolts her.

'Are you alright? Your message sounded serious.' She's come to the hallway, unable to wait and let Sakura through.

'We're ok. Can we sit down and talk?' They need to go to the kitchen. Sara is reaching out to her grandmother, excited, sensing the tension maybe.

'Yes, come on in.' Mom's eyes are full of fear. 'Please, is Sara okay? Is Chris okay?' Her name isn't on Mom's lips.

Sakura realizes she has had to be too strong. Sakura meets the first of many questions about Chris. Yes, she thinks to herself, he is okay. I'm not. How did this happen to them? How did the daughter end up being the mother in all of this?

An exhausting hour later, Sakura gets up,

'I need to go to the washroom.' But it's more than that. She needs fresh air.

Looking into the mirror. 'Olivia warned you of this, Sakura,' she whispers to herself. She tiptoes out and into her old room. In the kitchen, she can hear Mom playing with Sara, as if nothing is really happening. She sticks her head out of her old bedroom window. She can't even look at her room.

Walking back up to the kitchen, Mom is holding Sara now, who has begun to call out for her mom. Her face is white with shock.

'I don't understand. Why didn't you call me? You could stay here, what are you staying *there* for? You need to think of Sara!'

'I told you. Chris can easily come here. We need to be safe for now, Mom.' *There* is her sanctuary, her saviour, her safety rope, her everything.

'You can't be safe here? In your own home? With your own mom? Why, Sakura?' The questions are phrased as if this is happening to Mom, not her. Just like the pier, where she was the one watching Dad, where she was the one living Dad's death when Eli and Mom were on vacation, that first Christmas. Olivia had warned of this. Family reactions can be more about what they will suffer, than the victim.

'Because of this!' Sakura shouts back. 'I knew you would react like this!'

'But he seems so good to you, Sakura.' Mom sits down, bewildered.

'You don't understand. You don't understand what he is doing to me.'

'But Sara, he's her father.' She can't get past her own shock.

'And I am thinking of Sara. All of it is for Sara.'

Sara is looking up at them both, her smile has vanished, and her lower lip starts to tremble. Sakura hates that she is losing a steady world. But she needs a safe one. Not like the one Sakura has occupied since she lost her father.

Mom and she calm down, as Sakura strokes her daughter's head, and hands her a little snack to keep her diverted. The voices above Sara quieten.

'Help me understand,' Mom pleads.

It would be so much better if she could accept, the way Sakura has had to. After raking through her almost normalized experiences, picking them out of the closet of her brain, like clothes, all there, hung, waiting to be worn, a fashion show.

He did this. He said this. He demanded this. With each reveal and more examples, she wonders if she should talk about the washroom. Even she can't talk about the washroom.

Sakura feels that day in August, shouting, trying to wake Dad up. None of it landing.

Mom attempts to rationalize, talking to herself more than Sakura. Asking for help from the daughter who now so desperately needs it. Sakura feels naked, cold and exposed. For a moment, she imagines walking back to her dad on the pier, lying down beside him, taking his hand, and dying with him. This thought pulls her sideways away from the earth and sky and into the abyss. For a moment, she feels calm.

It's only then she realizes Mom has raised her voice again and is almost shouting. And Sara. Sara's cry shocks her and she comes to with that sense of strangers stamping on her chest.

'Sakura, what are you doing staring into space? Please, please talk. Please.' Mom's calling.

The CPR that failed Dad working for her. Taking Sara. 'I have to go.'

This is no longer the time and place for her and her daughter. They are the ones who need to move on, from death and dislocation, from abuse, from just surviving.

'I have to get out of here, you don't understand anything.' She picks up the change bag for the other shoulder. They need a better life.

'Please don't go, please don't go,' Mom pleads, crying now. 'I won't say anything else, I promise, just please stay.'

Sakura knows she won't be able to keep that promise. She's also too reactive now, will retaliate, and scream. *You weren't the one who watched Dad die! You made it all about you. Crawling into bed. Not getting us ready for school. Eli was old enough to leave. I had to stay with you. I only had Jack. I only had Snowy. I only had Tye. Then I only had Chris*!

'I have to go,' Sakura responds. The screen door bangs behind them.

On the drive back the red gas light winks. The fear she will break down expands. The fear that Chris might be on these roads, delivering feed, or just looking for her.

Returning to the shelter, she feels distraught. She knew it would happen exactly as it had, but hoped it would be different. Something about it feels similar to the days after her dad died.

Her feelings were lost, screaming, everyone asking how she was, but no one listening.

'How did it go?' Olivia meets her on the way to her room. 'Was it ok? Are you ok?'

This word ok, how many times has she been asked it over the years since Dad died? How few have gone past the first inquiry to help when it really mattered? It really matters now. Sakura knows, even after this short space of time, that Olivia will understand. Validate her feelings. No longer going insane alone.

'I met my mom, and it was just…' Sakura's voice disappears.

Olivia waits, she doesn't fill in the silence with meaningless comfort and useless words. She has the patience, and the experience, to hold quiet.

'I should have known, I did know. She doesn't get it. I just thought she would at least hear me.' Sakura chews her top lip. Annoyed her tears are always there, waiting. Annoyed at herself.

Olivia calls someone from the baby room. Sara is once again led away from her mom, once again Sakura has to deal with a choice she should never have had to make. Isobelle the babyminder has texted twice. Sakura can't answer in case Chris goes to her. Nothing about telling people will be easy. Nothing will be easy ever again.

'Come on. Have a seat.' Olivia's calm voice is a salve, instantly reassuring Sakura. They walk along the corridor into the room they went into when Sara and she first arrived. 'What happened?' Olivia looks at her with genuine care.

Sakura wonders why she does this, and how she can do it day after day. Sakura imagines herself to be far less caring. Except when it comes to horses and Sara. Even with Jack, she couldn't hold that closeness she loved. She loved the hugs. But Jack had two parents and normal problems. Eli did what children do, he survived by playing hockey. She just hardened when she felt isolated, or left behind, or left out. Then she is cross with herself for this false judgment. She has had to survive,

'Every time I tell someone how I really feel, it makes them fall apart. So when I have to tell people things, really important things, I can't manage it. Horses understand. People don't.'

'What happened, Sakura?' Olivia holds her hand and brings her into the present moment.

Sakura talks through the whole encounter. Feeling exhausted, letting out a deep sigh, she slumps into the chair.

'I handled it really badly. I shouted in front of Sara. Then I had to run to the washroom and stick my head out of my bedroom window to get fresh air. I'm not a child now. I'm a mother.'

'It's your mothering instinct that has made you move on, Sakura. You have survived.'

'How come you get it, Olivia?'

'I get you're the only one in your shoes. Your mother hasn't experienced what you've experienced.'

Sakura sits back up.

'Many don't understand domestic abuse, especially coercive control.'

Wanting to immerse herself in Olivia's wisdom, something she feels so lacking in.

'Do you not realize you're already wise, Sakura?' Olivia asks. She does this so well, asking the questions that lead to insight.

All of a sudden, her chest expands. Her breath reaches her. As she talks, Sakura feels extra space in the room. As though she has gained access to a hidden truth. Another dimension. The conversation brings awareness and understanding. She feels very sane.

This three-dimensional sense, this awareness of creation, will save her. No longer her and him, or her and her mom. Her, him or her, and awareness.

Olivia explains that her mom didn't experience what she experienced. That she is the only one who can know how it feels. Her repeating it somehow releases the burden of guilt over her reactions, the sense she has made error after error. She sees the space she created even in a limited life. Pushing Sara into the world. Learning how to care for her without any real support. This is what the wild animal does. She has done it too. She has honoured her own, knowing in her actions and her daughter is the living proof of her willingness to live on and to protect those who live with her. So she can answer, in full,

'I believe you, Olivia.'

Olivia's words become her sanctuary. The basis of truth. And then the wild fairy Jack loved, the knowing she had from when she was young, the respect she saw in her father's eyes for her, the way Snowy let her into his world, and Tye trusted her even with the hardest horses, it all comes into the sense that one man tried to take all this strength and intuition away from her. Because it threatened him. Because he would never have chosen her if she had not been different, strong, and vulnerable with this difference and this unique strength.

It happened to me. It happened to me. It fucking happened to me. Sakura chants silently. Out loud she says, 'Thank you, Olivia.'

'I'm only saying what I see, Sakura, and I see you are ready for lunch.'

'Am I? I don't know.' There is so much more going on.

'You're doing the work of a lifetime in a few days. You need to keep fuelled.'

'You might be right.'

After a big lunch, she's surprised. She was hungry.

CHAPTER 53

It's not a straight line. The discovery of her inner strength, the knowing of her true nature. Then the human collapses under the long list of details and issues to tackle.

For the first few days, she can only keep it to the collection of rooms – the washroom, the meeting rooms, the baby room, and the dining room. It's great that the others seeking refuge here seem to understand. Maybe they were like this themselves when they first arrived. No one pushes her to connect. Everyone here is going through their own war.

Sakura takes Sara out again to the small yard at the back of the building. She has begun to discover new places and rooms within the shelter. A TV room. A small library. A tea room for those who want to be in a smaller space with one or two others. These rooms are slowly revealed to her.

After the legal aid office, after the visit to her mom, after a walk with Sara in the donated stroller, she feels she can't yet be in the outside world. But they need fresh air. She gets Sara's jacket, as late Fall is biting at Winter. Her little hat. Sakura smiles. She looks so cute.

Sakura opens the door to the outside.

Holding hands, they walk onto the grass, and seeing the swing, Sara goes straight for it. Pushing high with giggles and again and again and again. In the laughing and the moment, her chest expands again, with relief. Sakura realizes she doesn't have to go home or see Chris tonight. The thought takes shape and is a salve to the wound. She is away from him.

'When we go back in, I'll check for messages,' she tells Sara out loud, in mid-swing.

She hasn't turned her phone on after coming home from her mom's. Sara doesn't ask about her dad. She is so young and he was away so much. Sakura is her world.

The phone takes time to power up. Her stomach lurches and she almost loses her will. But then it will only have to happen later. She's relieved it is quiet. Mom has sent a text, and there is one missed call from her. *Sakura, sorry. I love you.*

'You know where the shelter is, Mom,' Sakura says out loud. At the moment she can't carry anyone forward but herself.

The legal aid person has decided to come to the shelter as there are a few women needing advice. Sakura is relieved as she's still happy not to leave. One outing to the office was enough. It will be easier to manage the details in a safe environment.

The family law lawyer goes through the basic first steps. He has a pile of files and Sakura knows there is a queue, so she understands the reason for their functionality over compassion. He is the only man she's seen in the shelter so far. The firm this man represents will act for her.

'The first step is to inform Chris that you have left the family home…' The thin man starts talking before Sakura sits down. His hair sits mostly flat on his head, but a few strands free themselves from the earlier grooming attempt and flop aimlessly to the right, then left.

'I think he knows this already,' Sakura ventures, then reddens, as the lawyer continues.

'…due to domestic abuse. And we will have to organize access. He's legally entitled at present.'

'He was controlling yes…' Sakura thinks it seems a little strong, *domestic abuse*. Is that what she is a victim of? The truth is landing like fireflies at dusk. Some flash, others don't. She has not talked about the sofa time and the washroom time. It's as if she can't allow herself to see it all at once.

'From the finances to the parenting, he's controlling, and he has sent you a text message indicating he will take Sara and that you are insane. This is the beginning, Sakura.' The lawyer stops processing and writing and stares straight at Sakura.

He warns her that Chris could play dirty. That is why she needs to do all she can on her side, to get ahead of it. His eerie silence when she turned on her phone comes back to her.

What is he doing? Shut up, shut up, Sakura shouts at herself. She can't help it. She can't wait to get back to the room.

Later, Sara is asleep in her cot, and Sakura picks up her phone and turns it on for the third time since she got here. The beeps are instant and numerous. There are five missed calls and two texts:

How are you? How is Sara?

I miss you.

Sakura folds, her held breath released. Crumpling to the ground beside her bed, tears fall and fall, and she tries to silence the gulps.

'I miss you too,' she whispers. Her hands grab the phone to text this back, but something reaches and stops her. She pulls herself off the floor and into bed with all her clothes still on and falls asleep.

CHAPTER 54

The days that follow have a simple routine. Essential grounding. She has missed calls from her mom. She keeps her at bay, *I'll call in a few days, just need some space* – the holding-off text.

At this stage, it's like she is drowning alongside Dad. The rescuers hurt, and the threats are all-consuming.

The family law lawyer has let her know he hasn't heard anything back. But then, one day when she thinks it might be okay, there is a message to the lawyer at his office. Her heart drops. Her stomach feels like a stone.

Chris is looking to see Sara.

It has taken seven days and eight nights. The waiting is over, but for a moment she wishes she had one more day, just one more day of refuge. The texts have stopped. He's communicating with her legal aid lawyer now. He is insisting on seeing his daughter tomorrow.

She tells Olivia who, for the first time, does not smile.

He can't do anything to you. Repeating this mantra in her head.

It's been over a week since she left this dust road behind. Driving up to the house alone, against Olivia's advice, Sakura thought bringing someone with her was too heavy. The horror and normalcy struggle to find their place with each other. Her stomach is lurching, no breakfast this morning.

The front of the house appears, and then she sees him. Chris walks out. She recognizes his features, but nothing else is really familiar, really known. His heart was clawed out a long time ago and replaced by some artificial replica. He fooled everyone.

'Drop and go, quick.' This is Olivia's advice since she couldn't dissuade her from her decision.

The fantasy of happy co-parenting looms large in Sakura's mind. But co-parenting and abuse are not happy bed partners.

'Hey.' He sounds so casual.

'Hi, here's her bag.' She hands Bunny to him. 'She's sleeping with this teddy.'

'Ok, how are you?' Waiting for the bullet, surprised by the soldier's kindness. It is hard to see the enemy in plain clothes.

'I'm ok.' Sakura stops herself before telling him more. Handing over Sara, she walks away to get back into her car.

'I'll collect her back at two pm tomorrow.' She hasn't looked at him once.

'Yeah, fine.' He's so offhand, but she knows he hasn't taken his eyes off her. He is waiting for a chink.

Sakura jumps into the driver's seat. She feels the tears racing to her eyes. He can't see this. Through the rearview, she watches him, watching her. Sara is reaching up to touch his face. She didn't object at all to her dad. From the time she was born, she knew long absences. He's a friendly face, coming and going.

Once her former home is no longer in the mirror, Sakura roars and screams. The tears fall hard on the steering wheel. At times she can't see ahead, praying she won't rear-end someone. Pulling in, she cries so hard she feels she is breaking apart.

'How can I survive this?' she pleads to herself.

All tears come to a stop. Sakura wipes the last away, her face red. What now? Twenty hours alone. All she thought about was dropping Sara off. She hadn't thought past that. She welcomes and dreads alone time.

Arriving back at the shelter, the reception worker goes to get Olivia.

'I know why you told me not to go alone now.'

'Did he say anything?'

'No. He only asked how I was.' He isn't going to put a foot wrong now others are involved.

'Good. Sakura, I just want to let you know a counsellor is available in the afternoon.'

'It's ok. I talk to you, Olivia.' Telling, talking to someone else is exhausting and scary.

What if, deep down, this is all my fault? Sakura's fears surface.

Sensing her fear, Olivia adds,

'And you can keep on talking to me. This counsellor has worked with women in DV situations for years.'

'DV?'

'Domestic violence.' Olivia lowers her voice, knowing it's so hard to hear, and that it's still a fragile stage where Sakura doubts. 'It would be good for you to process what has happened, and what is happening to you.'

'I don't know what to feel.'

'Have lunch. It will give you energy.'

'Can I take it to my room?' She suddenly can't speak to another soul.

'Absolutely.'

After lunch, Sakura is grateful someone else made her food, sitting alone in her room. These basic tasks are overwhelming right now. Yesterday she was shown the laundry room. Sara's little vest and pants dry on the airer in her room. Looking at the pink bow, she tries to remember where she got them. It was Mom's friend, yes that's right, she thinks. Then remembers the day Chris was with her, Sara only a few weeks old. They went to a café. She remembers trying to feed Sara and Chris placed the wrap around her. He was smiling. It was a good day.

Feeling the nausea return, Sakura pulls herself out of remembering. And then pulls herself back in when she thinks of that following day. She remembers Chris roaring at her over firewood not being in the right basket. Anger and relief arrive simultaneously. Relief that she is not insane and here for no reason. Then angry that he did that to her.

'How fucking dare you? How fucking dare you!' The words become louder, Sakura catches herself afraid someone might hear. Yes. Olivia is right. She has to talk to someone.

Knocking on the door, she hears the counsellor say come in. Another room she hasn't seen before. The shelter seems to go on and on in rooms off corridors. She hears other women in other rooms and watches them bond with each other, discussing their lives. She sees Sara playing with the other babies. She hears the staff. But the only one she has been able to talk to freely so far is Olivia. Olivia can't be there all the time.

'Hello, Sakura, I'm so pleased to meet you,' the counsellor offers.

Sakura can only nod.

The light sneaks in the half-closed curtains. Two chairs at right angles to each other, a worn cushion with a dent on the empty one. Sakura wonders how many women have sat in that chair she will sit in now. Tissues on the small table. Sakura doesn't intend on needing them. Sakura can't be sure of anything anymore.

'Will you take a seat?'

Pinching her fingers together, she notices the counsellor's boots, elegant and they look warm. Her dress has small bright flowers. A scarf draped over one shoulder falls and lands at the fold of her lap. Her fitted jacket is casual but smart. No rings. Looped small earrings. Maybe she is meeting someone more important after this.

An hour passes. An hour in which the things she could not say are said. For the first part, Sakura could barely speak. Then, when the counsellor says,

'Begin, if you can, with the first thing that comes to mind.'

The visit to Mom comes out. Behind it a whole history of grief is waiting. There aren't many tissues left in the box for the next person.

The counsellor makes her feel like she is important enough to be listened to.

'Thank you, yes, see you next week.' Sakura closes the door behind her. Who knew that room could hold so much? But outside, bereft of tissues and assurance, the fear rises up. Sara is still with Chris. Now. How is he treating her? Racing back to her room, grabbing her coat and hat, she needs to get out straight away. Nature is calling her. The Recreation room has maps of trails she saw earlier, and she grabs one.

Walking across the street she was afraid to walk down with Sara last week, she has the objective of getting away from everything and everyone.

Following the road for about three kilometres, she sees the outline of the woods on her right. The cars go past, and she wishes each one was the last, still checking to see if they belong to people on the other side of town who would spot her, maybe pass on to her mom that she has been seen. She is aching for silence.

'I think I know this place,' she says aloud to herself. She then vaguely remembers driving by with her mom a few years ago, just before Jack left for University. She slips in to the trees, and the hum of cars fades. Breathing in deeply, the air is cold as it enters her lungs, clearing everything at that moment. Sakura recounts her session with the counsellor. She heard herself talk. She heard herself being listened to. The counsellor embedded and solidified everything Olivia said in her first few hours at the shelter. That hour is the beginning of many hours to come, and this wood will be the centre of her emerging clarity.

For now, her head is buzzing.

'How could I not know that? It seems so simple,' Sakura questions while flicking the branches, causing the snowflakes to disperse and fall gracefully to their spot. 'How could I not know what it was?'

She will learn the terms and live the understanding the first counselling session has given her about coercive control and gaslighting. She will develop an understanding of what has happened to her, a frame of reference to pull her in from the depths of despair.

Chris yanked the already frayed cord to unravel everything. The cord began to fray on a pier end, years before. Dad's loss drowns her again. Memories of Chris's cruelty. Seen now with the emergence of a different mindset, Sakura starts running through the woods and lets out a roar and then another and then another. Disrupting unmarked snow. Soon out of breath, she stops and pants, holding her hands close to her knees. Tears drip onto the mushy snow, barely leaving a mark. She stays that way another hour and feels the past envelope her as she sheds out the tears of evidence. Then, a calm descends.

Standing back up straight, Sakura breathes in the stillness of the woods.

'You're going to be ok, you're going to be ok.'

The whispers she almost missed. The ones first heard that night at the shelter. Sakura feels her dad's words permeate the solid frozen woodland. Weightlessly they float and gently land in her heart. Her hand automatically raises to her chest.

'Please don't go, please stay,' she whispers back to him.

Her whisper remains in the clearing, held in this place amongst hibernating red foxes and bodies of little birds that didn't make it.

'Will I survive?' she asks the space he has left in her life. The question she has been asking since the beginning of the grief. She is doing this alone, so far. No Mom. No Jack. No Eli. There is only Sara. She sees her face, and the fear of what the day is holding for her little daughter penetrates, but then there is a peace. Sara is Chris's flesh and blood. Sakura was his puppet.

Sakura continues her walk through the path, winding by trees, tall and wide. Arriving back onto the road, she returns to the shelter, her shelter. Happy not to see anyone, sneaking inside, Sakura fills the bath and rests in steaming lavender.

For this bath, she uses the lavender oil she has in Sara's change bag, bought with the hidden money from Eli. She decided to cash the cheque that first week in the shelter. Her secret account kept her in small things for herself. Not having a joint account means Chris cannot follow transactions to find her location. His meanness is now her chief blessing. Her account is now a rescue fund. But she lived month to month. There is so little left. How long will that money last? Where will she live after the shelter?

The water takes all planning away. Suddenly she is just herself. She stays still until the water cools so much she must move to get warm. She rises.

The faded lavender smell lingers in the washroom. Grabbing the towel, inhaling, wishing she could return to the earlier calm. The more she sniffs, the more the smell disappears. She grabs the bottle, it's empty. Tossing it aside, now she remembers the sink, holding onto it. Him behind her.

Laying on the floor, hands tucked in between her legs.

'Please help me, somebody, please help me.'

CHAPTER 55

The next morning Sakura wakes alone. Fear spreads all over. She can almost taste it. The energy of the woods is gone. She tries to rise out of it, but Sara is not there. There is no need to mother, and no need to move herself. *Two pm, she'll be back with me at two pm.*

In time she will learn to shush and hold herself. The woods will always be there waiting for her return. The sobbing that never seems to stop finally does. She is still in bed. But her limbs can move now. The phone on the bedside locker, on silent, lights up.

'Sara,' her first thought. She grabs the phone.

She has missed several calls from Jack. Mom must have told her. *Please Sakura, you have to let me know you are ok.* That word again, she hears it once a day from someone. Ok is a miracle at this point. She goes to dial Jack, but her stomach lurches. Not yet out of bed, having slept so deeply, the anticipated conversation exhausts Sakura. Texting is easier.

Are you home this weekend?

Straight away another text comes.

Yes! I planned it immediately I heard. Are you ok? I love you.

Sakura sends a love heart emoji in response. That's all she can manage. The rest will have to wait.

Sakura thinks of her old hugs. That gives her warmth, then the flush of secrets, things to hide from Jack, comes through. Jack knows the Chris of barbeques. She doesn't know how he was at the bar, at the birthday event. Jack bats guys away who follow her like puppies. Jack has never been on a leash and had it yanked.

Let's meet up and talk then.

It's too painful for Sakura to think that those closest to her, those she loves, may not understand, and right now she needs everyone to understand. Because she just might not believe it herself.

It's two o'clock. Sakura stands down the street, away from the shelter, outside a convenience store, a public place, waiting for Chris to arrive. Her heart feels lost in her body. Fear rises up in her chest, her throat, her mouth. 'Everything's ok,' not believing her silent chant.

The sound of his engine turns the corner before the pickup does. It seems big and out of place in town. Moving her hands between her pockets and into a fold. The opening of his door and the unbuckling of the car seat is endless. Slow motion time. Finally, he takes out Sara, a half-asleep Sara.

'She napped the whole journey,' he informs her.

'Her change bag?' Sakura lifts her to her arms. Being this close to Chris feels strangely intimate yet miles apart. Passing their child between them. Again, she cannot look at him at all. But she can feel his eyes on her constantly.

As he drives away, without another word, she sees the top of the stroller in the trunk. She has the donated one at the shelter. But it's ok. This is ok. Utter relief and foolish feelings flood her for being so afraid. Back inside the big door of the shelter. Olivia and another worker hover at Reception. Their jurisdiction ends at the door. But they are present, just in case. Sakura knows Chris is too clever to cause trouble. He does not appear angry. He doesn't give anything away at all.

Safe.

'We're going to the room.' Sakura cannot release her half-sleeping child, she can't get enough of the smell and sight of her.

'No problem.' Olivia's assurance follows her down the hall.

Later that week a second visit is set up. Chris never had time when Sara lived with him. Now he has given over two days and nights to his daughter, in seven days. Sakura gets her ready. If this beautiful being is what they made, how is it that part of what made her is so ugly?

Smiling at Sara, twenty-four hours the last time felt like an eternity and not long enough. She will have the woods and the counselling session to help her.

The following day, she waits outside the convenience store. Again, the pickup's engine sound is heard before the truck is seen and her heart races. This time Chris hands the change bag to her and passes a hundred dollars directly into her hand. Sakura almost breaks when his fingers touch her palm.

'I'll give more next week.' He slips back his hand and then reaches back to touch hers again. He can sense the feeling in her. He always could. This is what he relies on. 'Please, can we talk, maybe later? It doesn't have to be like this.'

Sakura pulls her hand back. 'I've got to go.' Turning, she walks away.

Back inside, she wonders what he meant. Her heart starts racing. Maybe he is sorry, really sorry this time. Perhaps he realizes what he has done. Maybe. With these thoughts, Sakura feels like she is already betraying Olivia and her place. These secret, bad thoughts. This time Olivia is at Reception with another worker, and she just nods to them, taking Sara down the hall to the room.

She has already decided to call him later. Just to hear what he has to say, Sakura convinces herself. We have a child together. We will have to talk at some point. She is half convincing herself. The gentle truth held in the woods and in the counselling sessions vanishes.

That night she is anxious to get Sara to bed. Her hand is shaking as she picks up the phone. He answers after two rings. Sakura remembers the times when it would ring out. She would be begging him. Please come home. Please help me.

'Hi.' He sounds surprised she has called.

'Hi. You wanted to talk?' Sakura says.

'Yeah.' He seems a bit uncertain. 'I just want to talk about what is happening. Are you ok?'

'Not really.' Sakura suddenly feels dirty listening to his voice. 'What did you want to say?'

There is a pause she can't fill. She has to wait to hear him.

'Just think this has got out of hand.' Chris's words are slow and deliberate.

'What do you mean, got out of hand?' Sakura is getting angry now. She has enough perspective to know the sense of his voice reeling her in, not committing himself to anything, just waiting for the right moment to tell her what he knows, and she must believe.

'I mean, I miss you. I miss both of you.' His voice almost normal, almost feeling now. Almost. Sakura melts immediately at the possibility. This might all get fixed, he might have learned.

'You hurt me, you hurt us.' Sakura walks around the room holding the phone back and then close to her ear. She has to move while she speaks. She has to feel she is moving, or the fear will rise, and the past will live again. Then it does.

'I know, I'm sorry,' he begins, but then he says, 'you hurt me too.' The sound of his familiar indignation. 'It's difficult having a baby. It's normal to feel overwhelmed.

You just got overwhelmed.' His reasonable tone, his reach for a pushback, enrages Sakura. No, he's not doing this again.

'I'm not overwhelmed because of Sara. It's because of you.' Sakura's ear and face feel hot. Her eyes hold angry tears.

But she must not say more than she should. She must keep it factual. That's what the counsellor advises. Don't try to prove. Don't try to get him to agree. For once the space of silence has Chris scrambling, not her.

'I just mean, Sakura, it's a lot. It's normal for couples to fight. Why did you have to go *there*? Everyone is asking. You're making me sound like a monster.' Chris's voice is breaking.

'Who is everyone?'

'Isobelle. Your mom phoned too. I even missed a call from Jack, Sakura.'

'Did you talk to them?' Her heart races.

'Your mom. She said what you told her.'

Mom, trying to find things out because she's not reaching out. Sakura suddenly feels guilty. Did she get it all wrong?

'I know you're not a monster, but you hurt me so much. I had nowhere else to go. I had to leave.' Sakura doesn't fully believe her words, seeing her mom and her best friend in front of her.

'But you could have stayed with your mom for a few days until we got sorted. Not making it seem much bigger than it is!'

'Is that what she says?'

'She doesn't understand why you just left. She says you won't talk to her. Like I said, you're making this bigger!'

Sakura feels annoyance burn now, the beginnings of the fight back.

'But it is big. This is massive. I've realized a lot of things here. Things that are not normal.'

'What do you mean? What are you telling them? They'll try to fill your head with all sorts. Sure, you know you have issues from what happened with your dad.'

'Is that what Mom and you discussed?'

'No. I knew that when I met you. The first time you told me, but it was obvious before.'

'This has nothing to do with my dad!' Sakura shouts down the phone. 'You lost your parents. You should realise, Chris!'

'Look, you're at it again, losing it. See?' He sounds so calm, so reasonable. His tone says no wonder he and Mom had to confer, to figure out the mess that is Sakura, who shuts everyone out.

Sakura can't believe she is here again.

The counsellor and Olivia's words break free from his entangling of her. Their phrases trying to land in the confusion. He will convince. But he doesn't want change. He will offer it. Gaslighting you. Coercing you into seeing things from his perspective. The one where he controls your life.

'I'm going. I am not doing this.'

'Hold on, please don't go. I didn't mean that.' He feels her slipping away and he tries to reel her in. 'I just meant that they don't know us. The people you're talking to now. They don't know you like I know you. I love you. I miss you, please come home, Sakura.'

Sakura melts in an instant. She so badly wants to hear the words, yet doesn't want to hear them.

'We could go away, maybe to that place you mentioned. We could go for a long weekend. We can figure this out, for Sara's sake.' His voice is soft now. Like the time he took her to his family home and talked about losing his parents to death and cutting ties with his sister.

Cutting the ties. Sakura imagines packing her bags in silence, carrying a sleeping Sara to the car, and driving home in the dark. She could never go near this part of town again. And then what? Sakura is jolted out of her thoughts.

'I have to go, Chris.'

'Okay, goodnight.' He returns to being matter-of-fact. Like her hanging up is not important.

Sakura hits the red button on her phone.

CHAPTER 56

She sees Jack walking towards her. They arranged to meet on the boardwalk not packed with people, just local weekenders. Sakura feels she needs the whole outdoors. A coffee shop would be too small, too intense. She imagined pretending to drink, playing with her cup, to avoid Jack's gaze and questions. She is only trying to figure out the answers here. The boardwalk also has space to hide her tears.

In winter, everything looks duller, as though all the light and brightness of the landscape has been pulled under the surface and the sky held down lower on puppet strings. Tears can hide in muffled neck warmers and the ends of sleeves. They immediately start to run down her face as she sees Jack quickening her pace towards her. Sakura frantically wipes, pushes, and moves them away, but they spread. Her face scrunched like an old, wrinkled apple. Her breath caught in gulping sounds. Sakura tries to quieten her cries. But they burst out, a high tide dancing with a spring storm. All she can do is stop and hold her face in her hands.

Jack running now. Sakura can feel her arms all around her. The hug she wished for from Mom. The hugs that got her through so much over so many years when she was too young to know how many more of them she needed and never got.

'I'm here, I'm here, I'm so sorry,' Jack whispers. Their tears mix as their embrace continues. A few walkers pass, pretending not to see. The high tide washes, and they wade through the water, mud, and floating debris of the past. 'I had no idea, Sakura. I feel like an idiot, a bad friend. How could I not know?' Jack shakes her head.

'You're neither of those things. I didn't even know myself. I'm still figuring it out,' Sakura manages to say through muffled tears. Jack believes her. Jack believes. They go through Sakura's last two weeks, every hour accounted for.

'I thought you were happy. I know you struggled after Sara was born, but you know I thought that was normal new baby stuff.' There won't have to be any trying now. Jack knows Sakura.

'I struggled because he kept putting me down, saying horrible things', Sakura responds with the first things that come to her. It's been so long since she could do that naturally, without second-guessing herself.

'Why didn't you just tell me!' Jack starts to cry now too. 'I'm your best friend. I've known you since...' They look out at the place where her dad died. They look back beyond that. They go back to the very beginning. Sisters by choice.

'I couldn't.' Sakura's the calm one now. She has been living with doubt for so long that she knows how to address Jack's. 'If I said it out loud, I would have to believe it myself. That moment I found myself driving to the shelter. I just couldn't do it anymore. I knew if I stayed, I would be like that butterfly under the knife.' This is a story she hasn't told yet. The counsellor knows about the sofa and the washroom. Olivia knows the things he has said. But Jack is the first one to hear about this.

'What butterfly? What knife? Did he hurt you? Has he hurt you? The fucker, I'll kill him!' shouts Jack. Jack who was in school the day the first butterfly got trapped at the window. Later she told her Ms. McLeod had let it out.

'No, he hasn't hurt me like that. Not in the way that you mean.' Sakura tells her of the incident with the butterfly. The truth seeps out like crude oil leaking from fractures in the seafloor. She can see Jack's struggle to grasp it all.

'I cannot believe that I didn't know this,' she repeats. 'What kind of friend am I? Why didn't I pick up the signals?'

'I wasn't giving them. He was good when you were around.'

There are many incidents, many moments, she could share. Stored up in her brain, catalogued like library books. With Jack knowing her, she doesn't have to explain the setting or situation, like she does at the shelter. She will just find the right index card, and a story of isolated horror will emerge. Stories she tried to file or archive, or to change them with explanations of how she was confused. That she had picked up the wrong meaning of. But now is the time to revive a white butterfly. It's the first and most important story she will tell. Jack is horrified. Sakura can see her seeing what she saw, being powerless to prevent it, a baby close by, their baby. Sakura, who watched a father die, watching a thing of such beauty not just die randomly, but be killed purposefully.

'Why didn't you just leave? I'm sorry. I mean, I wish I had done something. He's a dead man when I'm around him again.' Jack's voice is cold.

'No,' Sakura insists. 'He's already dead. His heart died a long time ago. The things he cares about. I'm not one of them.'

'I hate the thoughts of someone hurting you. You're the brightest light, and it breaks my heart to see you like this. You love all living things. Do you remember the pond? You showed me to respect all life, Sakura. I just work on paper, you work with horses. You're a mom. No wonder I've been so useless. You always knew more than me, even before your dad died. I haven't been there for you. I was so young when you lost him. I didn't know how to help a lot of the time.'

'You couldn't have done anything about Dad, and you couldn't do anything about Chris. You're here now, that's what matters. And you may not know more than me about some things, but right now I need you, Jack, I am so scared.' Sakura's eyes well up now.

'What are you scared of?' Jack, thinking she is missing something. 'You got away from him. You have the right help.'

'I'm scared of everything,' responds Sakura, her voice lower. She suddenly feels exhausted, leaning into Jack's linked arms. *Please carry me*, she whispers silently.

'I know you don't want to stay with your mom.' Jack sounds sad saying this. She loves Sakura's mom. 'But why don't you stay with me tonight? I don't have to go back till after the weekend.'

There it is. Jack's life is in a different place, a city off the Island. She's just visiting this one, the one that Sakura has to live in.

'Thanks, Jack.' Sakura sighs, taking on the mantle of motherhood and huge choices again. 'But I'm worried Chris might turn up at yours. Or Mom's. They're so close to each other.' It's hard to think of Mom being only a few minutes away by car and a walk they did so many times.

'Would he do that?' Jack asks.

But this is why Sakura has to take everything slowly. There's so much to adjust to. There is in every move, every conversation, a probability to face. Sakura tries to rationalize her fears, sensing Jack thinks she is paranoid, but then Jack hasn't lived the past decade of loss and fear.

'I just feel safer at the shelter, I have support there, and Sara is back in the morning. I have to be back anyways.' She's a friend who can walk with Sakura but can't fully carry.

'Okay, I just hate the thought of you staying there. I'm trying to get my head around everything. Listen, I'm here for you.' Jack grabs Sakura's hands and jolts her gently. 'You are going to be ok, you hear me. He can't hurt you anymore.'

They've walked the whole length of the boardwalk, and all that can be said is said. Jack pulls Sakura into a hug, freeing held hands.

'I better go back, meeting my support worker shortly.' Sakura pulls up the mental list of endless appointments.

'Come on, I'll walk you back.' Jack is not ready to let go of her just yet.

'Ok, it's this way.' Sakura knows she can't protest.

They step off the boardwalk and crisscross through streets until they arrive outside the shelter.

'I never knew this was here!' Jack exclaims.

'I didn't either until…'

Jack reluctantly releases Sakura. She waves as she follows the sidewalk up towards the door and steps inside. 'See you tomorrow!' she shouts after her.

Sakura meets Jack the following afternoon, with Sara. They talk some more, mostly coded. Jack is great with Sara, taking time to play with her.

'Hey!' She's bought a ball for Sara to play throw and catches it in funny poses. Someday Jack will be a good mother. She has so much fun in her. It's not the same with her daughter about. They can't talk as freely and also Sakura senses that Jack has more questions.

Sometimes they feel like judgment. Not of what she has said about Chris, but why she got with him in the first place. Jack's long-held thoughts release.

'Do you think you rushed into it?' She's rolling the ball to Sara and saying this. 'I mean, you didn't know him that well when you moved in, you said so yourself.'

Sakura feels sick and doesn't answer. As if her head hasn't gone through all these things in loops like a drunk merry-go-round.

Again she reaches for the words of the women of the shelter.

'Sakura, you'll experience huge vulnerability post-breakup. Remember, you will be sensitive to every comment.'

Sakura sees her choices, her state of mind then and now, gives way to others. Gives others without experience the same permission to question. Even strangers sometimes. She holds her response inside herself, leaving the space, like she did with Chris on the phone. Jack walks backward away from her self-placed land mine.

The counsellor's words come to Sakura's mind.

Chris knew what he was doing. He reeled her in. He saw the vulnerability she is only now seeing in herself. The idea that she was groomed makes her feel sicker. She normally associates those words with children and the darkest of humans. If she tries to say this to Jack, she knows there will be more questions.

'I gotta go.' Sakura gets up. 'Get Sara sorted. She needs to go for her nap.' She puts Sara's toys in her bag.

'I didn't mean to upset, I'm sorry,' says Jack picking up a fallen teddy. The one she told Chris Sara was sleeping with. Sara is still holding the ball Jack gave her. 'Sorry, Sakura. My bad. I never had to live what you lived. Sharing a room with Mina was as big a trauma as I had to deal with.' Jack stumbles, looking for a way back.

'It's ok. I'm tired, talk tomorrow.'

'Yes ok, I'll see you tomorrow.'

It was supposed to be a three-day weekend. It was supposed to be fun tomorrow too. After all this opening up, a chance to be young again, pick earrings maybe.

Remember things that aren't so awful. But Jack left the island Sakura still lives on.

Sakura doesn't see Jack the next day. She says Sara is sick and would better leave it until another time. Her phone rings. It's Jack. Sakura doesn't answer. She lies on the floor, crying, huddling her legs to her chest that night. *It would be easier if he had just hit me*, Sakura thinks. The invisible violence swipes the punch to the face, the swollen dripping forced inside. *Nobody understands, nobody understands, not even Jack.*

*S*he tried, but Sakura can see her pull a puzzled face like she is supposed to understand but doesn't. A modern University-going woman, feminist, fighting for equality. But Sakura feels her slight inherent prejudice against her own sex. *What did I do to cause this?* The question felt upon every word she didn't ask.

Olivia's first response on her first-day lands like gentle, refreshing snow. 'I believe you.'

CHAPTER 57

Texts from Chris go unanswered. She can't trust her mind yet to deal with him with confidence. The few encounters she's had dropping off Sara, the one phone conversation she's had. This keeps her unsure even of herself. Every conversation with anyone from her past has left her feeling like she has done something wrong in leaving, leaving her feeling doubt. She has to wait for a clearer vision. So far, that only comes in the shelter, which she only leaves when she has to.

There has been one text from Eli. *Mom told me. Sounds like she crowded you. I won't call. I know you need space. But I will do anything. Not the best talker. Sorry, we lost touch. My bad. You need help, you have it. Call you tomorrow.*

Sakura knows the call won't come and is relieved when it doesn't. A part of her feels he is a hero to her again. But talking with Jack and Mom has led her to realize the past will come up, and she cannot talk about Dad as well as this. There are moments she still feels he is with her, she heard his voice in the first week. Now she is listening to the counsellor, Olivia, and her lawyer. She talks with the workers about Sara. She has brief words in passing with the other women staying and smiles at the children. But she cannot speak of what has happened, not yet.

Here, no one pushes. Here everyone is going through the same thing.

Sakura is gathering strength. The day comes when she needs it.

*

That day starts with Olivia's knock on her door close to lunchtime. Sakura immediately feels sick. She had been looking forward to lunch. She is sleeping better, she is smiling a little, she is eating well. Sara is content and so is she.

'This arrived for you. Remember, whatever it is, together we can handle it.' Olivia places the package in her hands. Sakura holds the brown envelope, large, formal, unruly.

Opening it while Olivia distracts Sara with some toys. Sakura scan reads, trying to get to the key points layered with legal jargon.

'What?' Sakura reads. 'Full custody, unstable mother? What the fuck, full custody of Sara, he doesn't even mind her!' The first two visitation requests were the last two. He hasn't bothered to take Sara since.

Sakura can't catch her breath. Olivia runs over, leaving Sara on the floor.

'Listen to me, look at me.' Olivia puts an arm around her. 'You're going to be ok.' There's that word again, the one everyone uses all the time.

'This is not okay,' Sakura whispers now. They're both aware of Sara watching them.

'I've seen this so many times. This is their way of threatening you. They try to take away the thing or person most dear to you.' Olivia points to Sara. 'You're that little girl's mother and have been since she was born over a year ago. You're a wonderful mother. We're going to fight this, you hear me?'

Sara has calmed now and is back to scrunching up the face of a teddy, talking to it.

'I can't lose her, I can't lose Sara, please, please help me.' Sakura feels her legs go and presses against Olivia, a closeness she would never seek normally. 'Am I a bad mother?' Sakura falls into the older woman, who has seen all of this before and devoted her life to helping women through it, who tries to stop her shakes with steadying hands and a soothing voice.

'Come on, let's bring Sara down to the activity room, and I'll make you tea.' Olivia has a firm grip of her hand. 'The lawyer's in later this week. He'll go through everything.'

Sakura just keeps thinking less than forty-eight hours ago, Chris had texted her wanting her to come home.

'He hasn't asked to see Sara in a week. Why does he want her all the time?'

'Why do you think, Sakura?'

Holding Sara in her arms, holding her close, afraid to think of even a day without her, Chris was often gone before she woke and home after she slept. Then Sakura sees it. His revenge when he doesn't get his own way. She knows then, absolutely knows, that he will *always* try to destroy her. This is not relief. This is horror.

She has chosen to love and make a family with a destroyer. Silently calling herself awful names as they walk up the corridor. Berating herself. *How did you fall for it, all those texts?*

'I'm so stupid, what's wrong with me? I actually felt sorry for him, I thought he was sorry!'

She finally admits to Olivia that she has been in contact, and that she has considered going back.

Olivia grips the hand she's holding, and speaks slowly.

'Do you honestly think you are the first woman to say this? Or wish this? This is so common, Sakura. So natural. It generally takes most women seven or more attempts to leave an abusive partner for good. This is the damage they do. You're not to be blamed.'

Sara is taken out of her arms by the staff. Sara might be taken out of her arms forever.

An hour later, Sakura feels slightly calmer, the woman's words reassure her.

'Sakura, you've been Sara's primary carer since she was born. What reason would the courts have to change that?' She has seen this all before. Olivia pulls Sakura away from the fear and into the facts. The fact is, Chris always gave excuses why he couldn't mind Sara when they were together.

'He doesn't even want her, Olivia! He doesn't know that she needs a cuddle for a few minutes before she goes to sleep,' Sakura's tears run in all directions, 'and that she needs me to hold her hand over the cot just as she cuddles her teddy.'

'You see?' Olivia smiles. 'You see how well you know your own child?'

'She needs me. She won't know that I haven't abandoned her if he wins.' Panic rises again. She wants to leap on Snowy and gallop away, to be back at work with creatures she understands, to be back before the time she met Chris at the stables. If she hadn't worked there, if she had gone to University like Mom wanted and Jack thought, they wouldn't be in this situation. But she wouldn't have Sara.

'Why do you think he'll win a custody battle? Sakura?' Olivia gently prompts.

Sakura raises her head, the head of a girl that was once a wild fairy, with a dream childhood full of Friday pizza and earring shopping and *Timbars*, a cool big brother, a great best friend, and a mom who cut her hair and told her stories about Ikigai, the Japanese art of a meaningful life.

The meaning of her life, she states out loud for the first time, because this is what has happened. She has no support from Mom. Her best friend and brother are gone from the Island. Her boss and job are the only true support she has, and they are practical. She has no father.

'Because I lose everyone in the end.' Sakura cries even harder, starts gulping, and tries to suppress her wailing sounds, surprised at how it feels. The exact same as the moment when her dad died. Fear and grief both scream, looking for something to swallow them up whole. Swallow her up whole. She's a snake eating its own tail.

'Sakura, you have a long road ahead of you. This is horrific that Chris did this to you, is doing this to you, I am so sorry that you are going through this.' Olivia holds her in the truth of the moment.

'This is hell, but this is not history repeating itself, Sakura. He wants you to spiral, to be devasted. He wants to have this effect on you. Many men applying for full custody are not interested in their children's needs. They're interested in hurting the woman. Many drop their application.'

Sakura stills, feels her eyes dry and the skin red and puffy around them.

'What if he doesn't?'

'You're a wonderful mother, don't ever forget that any instability in your life is down to his abuse of you. I see how you are with Sara. That first day you arrived, you managed to bring her things and little for yourself. You were so scared. I see the way you play and how you are with that little girl, despite what is happening to you.'

The woman's words don't land well. This praise makes her uncomfortable.

She knows something she cannot say because it is something too awful to be voiced. If she loses her child she will not have the courage to live at all. She lost her father to death. She cannot lose her daughter to a man who has not been a true father. Sara is all she has and, worse, she is all Sara has. All the people who could help are not here. Strangers assist instead. Experienced, available, and insightful strangers. But the people who love her are not here.

That night, Sakura wakes, and she immediately remembers the brown envelope. Fear gallops around her body like a wild horse dashing and kicking dust with every turn. Racing to the washroom, her stomach unwinds the little that she has eaten, and she makes it just in time. Sakura tries to remember Olivia's words of earlier. But she is running ahead of an erupting volcano, Sara in her arms. Chris is a monstrous mountain of lava running down, destroying everything in its path.

The voice of before, the washroom voice, Dad in this voice, says,

'Go and look at her. Don't let yourself imagine. Go and see her.'

Sakura walks out of the washroom and puts Sara's teddy back close to her small chubby hand.

'Please don't take her away from me,' she whispers while blowing a gentle kiss. The need in the whisper stirs the child. Sara moves and turns restlessly. Please go back to sleep, please, Sakura begs silently.

Sara wakes to cry, fearful energy dancing between her and her mom. A mom who may not get to be. Sakura picks her up, and they both cry.

The soothing of Sara makes her realize. Sakura can't comfort herself right now, and this little person needs her. She sits in the chair cradling her child. Afraid to put her down. Afraid to have her out of reach. Sara seems to need this too. Finally, she makes the noises of sleep. Sakura carries her to bed.

Sitting in her bed, the dark night wraps around them. Sakura prays for the morning.

CHAPTER 58

Later that week, the legal aid lawyer responds. Snatching up the letter left under her door, her hands shake ripping the envelope. Anxious to devour its contents. Dreading its contents. He sets out their defence and asks her for evidence and documents: *Sara's routine. How you are the primary carer.*

Sakura's head is spinning. She begged Chris to be more involved. Now he is cutting her at the knees. Reading on, nausea spreads so far it feels as though vomit will leak out her fingernails.

Your plans for housing. His note of caution screaming. *He could argue he is better placed to provide a stable home.*

She doesn't have time to process all the threats and imperatives. She has to drop Sara off for access. Now that he has put his cards on the table, he has demanded access. His job means he can't do it every day, thankfully. But he requests times that will make it hard for her to return to work. How long will Tye keep the job for her?

She drives out to Chris's in her little car, worth a fraction of his. The words of the letter circle like vultures. She tries to change their shape, lessen their impact. Nothing works. Arriving at the turn off to his road, she shakes herself. *Act normal.* Sakura doesn't speak. Still unable to accept the help of someone from the shelter to come with her for access drop-offs. Thinking it's too much. Still, at times, thinking of Chris.

She never looks at him directly, but she can still sense his face, smirking, sneering.

It's so hard to pass Sara into his arms. She must. And she must turn and go as quickly as she arrived.

She can't get into her car fast enough. Hands shaking, she tries to put the key in the ignition and fumbles. He watches with their daughter in his arms. Not moving an inch, not engaging with Sara, just looking at her. The screams come before she's safely on the main road.

'You bastard, you fucking bastard, how fucking dare you? I'm never going to be free from you.'

Tears follow. Sakura is afraid she might crash; the roads are icy. Pulling over, she slows her breathing down. It's time to let the people she loves in. Anything at all at this point. Mom or Jack?

Jack is more likely to come through. Jack is trying her best to show support and at the same time Sakura doubts. She doesn't understand coercive control and Sakura is really never sure which part she will get. So she rings Jack, but Jack can't hear her through the crying. Eventually, she manages to tell her.

'I can't believe he wants the child he barely takes care of. Sara is a pawn to him, Sakura.'

'Yes.' Sakura is surprised at how supported she feels.

'Look, are you sure legal aid is enough? He's loaded. I can offer money for a good lawyer.'

'Oh my God. Thank you. I think we have someone really experienced. I can't be sure. I'll run it by the shelter support worker when I get back.' Jack's support makes her support herself.

'I know your mom hasn't been coping with this. But I know she wants to help.'

'Please, don't go there right now.' Sakura hasn't seen her since the first time. She knows Mom is still hurting that Sakura didn't come to her, before going to the shelter. Maybe she even feels shame her daughter and granddaughter are there.

Right now, Sakura can only help two people, herself and Sara.

As if Jack is following this train of thought, she adds,

'Do you remember the song and dance he made about minding Sara for that one night?' Jack's outrage soothes Sakura. But then it comes.

'I wish you had let us all in sooner. We might all have helped you get away earlier. If only you had said something.' This jump between understanding what's happening to Sakura and blaming Sakura for the situation she's in causes her emotional whiplash.

'I couldn't say anything, because I didn't know what was happening and I didn't plan on having a daughter, Jack.' Trust eroding. 'But I have one now.'

'God, so sorry. I'm still learning how to be a grown up and you have to live with nothing but.' Jack is quick to apologize. But it will happen again because she doesn't really understand, few do and she's a talker.

'Thanks.' Sakura was always the listener in the friendship.

'You shouldn't have to thank me. I'm supposed to be your best friend.'

'Are you? Jack?' Sakura can't help asking.

'I always will be. Not there all the time. But I'll be there anytime you need me to be.' This is the first of crossing the bridge, just like the one to the Island.

Heading back to the shelter, she has to pass the road to the stables. She can't wait for the day it's safe to return. Suddenly Sakura feels taller. It's exhausting trying to get people to understand when she is still trying to understand herself, but she is doing it. Her breakup is happening to her. Her fight is happening to her.

As if she knows it, a text from Mom comes through. Not saying she feels shut out. Just stating. *Thinking of you.*

Maybe one day she will have the ability to understand it all. But Sakura can't give that to her. The bonds are so tight around her own mind, she can't translate too much for others.

But she is ready to take on the world and Chris to keep Sara. The worst thing that could happen is him gaining custody. He will only do to Sara what he did to Sakura, and possibly his sister, the one he never sees, and she never met. It's not like her and Eli, where the grief was so great it separated them out. He is angry at his sister. He is angry at all women.

'Fuck you, fuck you!' she shouts. 'You won't do this to Sara. You won't do this to me!'

A session with her counsellor later solidifies her fears into courage.

'He chose you for your strength and your courage. But he also knew you had dealt with so much you were not seeing all that you were.'

The idea that Chris saw her coming makes her feel sick. He saw her vulnerability, her caring, sensitive side, her grief.

'How could I have not seen this?' Sakura questions herself, in the session, and again and again after it.

'He didn't let you.' The counsellor reminds her of the tactics and mindset of abusers.

It wasn't her fault. It was never her fault. Later Sakura replays their early relationship like a movie in her head. The gestures, kindness, and romance, and then she remembers his negative comment about Jack, who he thought was all about herself.

It was nothing really, but back then it made Sakura feel uneasy. Fast-forwarding the movie in her mind to the night he held her and comforted her when she was upset by her dad, and then he used to cut her in ribbons with the same information. Sakura wants to scream. Instead, she asks,

'Was it all a part of his plan? Did he fake being caring?'

After her sessions with her counsellor, Sakura doesn't bother walking the long road. She just gets in her car and drives to the woods that now have become her sanctuary. No one sees her here. She witnesses herself. This is what she does now.

Between the trees and sunken hollows, everything is held in winter's breath. She feels she can be held here too. Thoughts loop and get lost. One catches.

'Why did he do this to me?' Going back over the session she just had, she remembers something that was said. Because he could. Abusers themselves are dark. They attract bright, empathic people. At some point, they need to quench the victim's light to be able to stay in their own darkness.

Sakura feels like her body is going to break, and bits of her fall off. Falling to the frozen snow, her knees barely dent the ground underneath.

'Why me, why me?' she screams. This time she doesn't care if anyone hears. Then she thinks of her Sara and cries more for wishing she'd never met Chris. Sara is here because he is her father. Fuck fuck fuck. Sakura lowers and almost kisses the ground with her forehead. A silly laugh arrives as she thinks she must look like she is doing some yoga move.

Jack loves yoga and dragged her to a class before. Before all this. After her dad died, Sakura thought nothing else like that could ever happen. She never again would feel so bereft. Lying here on the frozen snow, she realizes how wrong she was. This is far worse. It was horrific what happened to her dad. Still, she could understand it but never accept it. Because it was an awful unavoidable event.

What Chris has done to her, is doing to her, feels like she is on fire, but nobody can see the flames. Chris sets the invisible match while rubbing his hands together in dark delight. Because it was an awful, deliberate destruction.

'Get up, get up, Sakura.' The voice arrives again. Jumping up quickly, she suddenly realizes how cold she is. 'Dad.' Sakura's face softens. She feels his presence all at once and then all gone.

Arriving back at the shelter, she sees missed calls from Mom. She didn't reply to the last text because she had to get to counselling and after counselling the woods and surviving. She doesn't bring her phone to the woods. But it's time. So she dials.

'How are you?' Mom picks up at the first ring.

'I can't say.' She hasn't spoken to her since that day.

'How is Sara?'

'With Chris.'

'Can we meet?'

'Ok.' That word again.

They agree to meet in the morning, before Sara comes home. There is a choice now, stay in the room, or go out and be with others.

That evening Sakura has a little supper and makes polite chat with two other women staying at the shelter. She can see marks on one of the women's faces. Sakura makes her excuses and leaves. All her marks are on the inside.

Sakura knows at some level she belongs here yet feels like a fraud. Back in her room, away from people but never away from herself. Seeing Sara's blanket half folded over her cot, she picks it up and immediately smells her baby and cries into it, then stops. She only has one blanket with her. Wiping her eyes, she smells it again, but it's not as strong, and sniffs the blanket, again and again, wishing to get back to that first inhale. Time for a lavender bath.

Lying in the water, Sakura wonders how the hours will ever pass. Then they do. That night she kisses Sara goodnight in her mind, and she turns to sleep, thinking she won't. But somehow, she does.

Walking into the café, Sara sees Mom in the corner. It is quiet, too early for bustle and noise. Sakura inhales deeply. *Just listen,* she says to herself.

'Hi, Mom.' *Don't say anything you don't want to.*

'Sakura.' Her mom stands up and pulls her in for a hug. She doesn't have a chance to say no, she isn't sure if she wants to. Sitting down, the young girl takes their order, two coffees.

'Do you want something else? Please let me get something, breakfast?' Mom asks.

'I'm ok, thanks.' Sakura lets the silence fall.

'Well, thank you for meeting me, I'm…' Mom starts to cry. Stopping mid-flow, continues, 'I'm sorry about what I said to you, I shouldn't have, I was just so shocked. You are my daughter, and I love you so much, and Sara.' Mom swallows down hard.

The young girl arrives with the coffee. Sakura bites her own lower lip, raises her hand, and tries to stop her own tears that have already escaped.

'Ah, Sakura, I am so sorry.' Mom reaches across and grabs her hand, almost knocking the sweeteners over.

'It's ok, Mom.' Sakura eventually gets the words out. Used tissues lie on the inside of the table near the undrunk coffee.

'Are you ok? Is Sara ok?' her mom asks. That word again. 'What's happening?

'He's looking for full custody.' The words are barely out, Sakura's hands shake and tears drop between them. There are too many to control.

'What do you mean, full custody? Ah Sakura, I'm sorry, you know Carol's husband is a lawyer. Maybe we can ask him for advice?' Reaching over she grabs her hand.

'Jack offered to pay for one.' Sakura doesn't pull away.

'So will I. I'll do anything!' Mom starts to be a mom.

'I have legal aid. My support worker says they all do this to get revenge. It rarely works. I don't know, I can't lose her.' Sakura pulls her hand back to soak the wayward tears.

'Here.' Mom pulls a fresh tissue out and hands it to Sakura. The custody application solidifies both her mom's and Jack's support.

'I will do everything I can to support you. Please let me help you with this.'

'Thanks, I have a lawyer with the shelter.' Sakura lowers her voice and whispers over the word *shelter*. 'But he seems busy, I don't know…' She trails into disillusionment.

'I'm going to ask Carol. We need someone good, to fight this!'

'Okay maybe that would help, I just don't want you…'

Mom stops her, anticipating her next words.

'I want to help, that's that.' Mom reaches back over, grabs her hand, and sternly states, 'It's going to be ok. We'll see to it.' Mom waves at the girl clearing a table nearby. They order two more coffees.

Sakura feels a weight lift from her chest. Jack yesterday. Mom today. Eli's text. Tye's financial support and patience. People are there. People are coming back to her. It's not just her and Sara. There's the shelter. There's a counsellor and there's Olivia. There are women at the shelter who understand. There is hope. Then, just as with Jack, when she feels like she won't have to explain, Mom begins.

'I just wish I knew what you were going through.' Mom asserting herself in their newfound confidence.

'I didn't even know. I'm still trying to figure it out. I have great help at the shelter.'

Mom goes quiet like she just said a bad word, and she's ten years old again.

'I still don't understand why you both can't stay with me.'

'We've been through this.' Sakura feels her face flush, betrayed by the moments of understanding before. 'I don't feel safe there. Chris could turn up at any time, and I can't deal with it.' Sakura's voice trails off, not wanting to hurt, but having to state it.

'He won't do anything to you at my house. Did he hit you, Sakura? Tell me.' Like this is the big reveal her mom needs to get behind her. The unacceptable acceptable reason.

'No, he didn't hit me, he did…' Sakura doesn't even bother finishing her sentence. Her stomach starts to turn. 'I have to go.' Sakura pushes the chair back.

'Please don't go yet, just sit for another minute.' Mom panics, grabbing Sakura's arm.

Sakura sits back down, knowing she will have to push the chair back shortly. Her pain misunderstood. Her not being seen.

'I don't want to talk about this anymore, this isn't helping, I have people who get it, who understand, the people at the shelter. Do you know what they say, Mom? They say you don't need a bruise to be abused.'

'Ok, I'm so sorry.' The word held so much when Mom said it first, and Sakura wanted to believe she really meant it. Now it just seems a word to hold her. 'Why don't you and Sara come and visit Sunday? We don't have to talk about anything, please, I can cook supper. Maybe I can ask Eli home for the weekend?'

'I don't think so, Mom. He and I have seen each other so little. I don't want to deal with any more reactions. Every day at the moment is a battle for me.'

'I understand, just the three of us then.'

'Only if you don't bring up anything. I mean it, I know you're trying to help, but this is not helping. Just before Sara was born, I said I wanted you to be with me for a week. Chris put a stop to it for reasons I won't go into now. Now I need you, Mom.' Sakura pulls her hand back. 'Help me with Sara. Help me without any questions.' Sakura is surprised by her own words. The support of the counsellor, Olivia, and women at the shelter, keeps the devastation of Mom's lack of understanding slightly at bay from her.

'Got it.' Mom nods but her face shows she's still coming to terms with the instruction. The next time Sakura pushes the chair back, she leaves.

That Sunday, they go to her mom's for lunch where there is enough food ready to feed an army. She remembers the times she had to eat the corner of a stranger's pasta bake for supper. Mom collapsed in grief in the bedroom. Trying to feed herself, dress herself, and even educate herself.

This is a mother taking care of her daughter and granddaughter, holding her dam of questions. Sakura enjoys somebody helping with Sara and eats lots. This once she is hungry. Just like the time Olivia encouraged her to have lunch after she dropped Sara to Chris that first time.

This is a day when he can be forgotten about. Each time he comes into Sakura's mind, she turns it to here and now, with her mom, with her child, with a moment to be savoured.

CHAPTER 59

Pulling on the black pants and top she found in her old room, together with a jacket her mom insisted on buying. Sakura takes out her rarely used makeup bag.

She can hear Sara giggling. Sara is with Mom today. They spent the night before at home. Things are calmer since she and Sara called for lunch that Sunday. But she's always ready to run, waiting for her mom to let her down. Her old home. The one before everything happened. She smiles at the sound of her child and then immediately removes it.

I could lose you today. Leaning over the sink, she feels her insides might emerge. *No, stop it. You are not going to lose her.* Sakura schools herself with silent shouts in front of the washroom mirror. She emerges cold, but ready, ready for what's ahead.

'Setting off already?' Mom has taken the day off work. She's in lounge clothes. Sara is not even dressed. They look like it's a day off instead of a day to determine the future.

'I don't want to leave anything to chance.'

She leaves Mom's house earlier than needed. This is the reason she agreed to stay over, in her old room, where she once cried herself to sleep countless nights. She wants Sara to be with family. In case something goes wrong. Olivia will meet her outside the courthouse.

Sakura is early and waits across the road. Terrified she might see him, his face, his sneering. The courthouse is tucked in along the road with bigger houses and across from the sailing school. How many times did she and Jack pass that school on the way to something happy?

Never did she think she would have to do something like this.

Olivia is also early. Sakura was never so relieved to see a friendly face, and together they go in through the side entrance.

'This is a bit easier than going in the front way.' Olivia opens the door to a small room. Sakura feels her hands shake, and even her face feels funny like she can't control the lower part of her mouth. She wonders for a moment if there is something seriously wrong with her. Olivia, the woman who was there on the first night, and has been since, takes her hand.

'You're going to be ok.' Those words again. 'All you have to do is tell the truth.'

Sakura nods. But it's never that easy. Especially when you have been told and taught what to think. Olivia's words, and all the words of exchange between her and Olivia after, bounce and slide off the small table they are sitting at, to the left of the room. It's a time when she cannot think of anything but what is going to happen.

A knock on the door, her lawyer, Diane Dawson, from Dawson and Coleman Family Law, has arrived. A virtual stranger who has Sakura's life story, and Sakura's future relies on her actions today.

It's Sakura's second time meeting her since she accepted Mom's help. She seems like a giant even though she's not much taller than her. Bright blouse, skirt, shiny boots, and a smart jacket. Dark hair pulled back into a low ponytail. Olivia understood the change in representation.

'She's one of the best for a reason. Our guys have a huge caseload.'

Diane has confidence, a voice that carries, that seems loud but probably isn't.

'Okay.' She starts. 'Let's outline the change in application.'

That word again. New words after it. Another impossible learning curve. Sakura feels herself shrink, a little child waiting to be rescued.

After what seems like a lot of legal talk, Sakura realises that Chris has changed his application from full custody to equal custody before the hearing.

'What do you mean he's changed the application? Can that even happen?' Sakura suddenly jumps up, standing, and realises she is shouting. Her anxiety makes her sound hysterical. Her words are high and then almost unheard.

'He can do whatever he wants since he took the application, but this is a good thing.' Diane takes this in her stride. This is her job. Dealing with hysterical people about to have their children's future decided in alien environments. 'Having gone through the situation, and Sara's routine, and your role as her primary carer, it's no wonder he changed his application. His own representation would have been hard-pressed to get what he wanted.'

Diane explains that she surmises that he will likely get access, not equal custody. She thinks Sakura can follow but Sakura is lost in the before. She's been terrified of losing Sara for weeks. Thinking the worst thoughts of herself as a mother, solidified by every horrible thing he has said about her. Thinking that she wouldn't be able to live if she lost Sara. Thinking of ways to die and then the guilt for thinking it.

'What's the point of all this if it's what he has now?'

Sakura can see the lawyer looking at her in that way. *Look, here's another hysterical woman, not a surprise that we are here. Isn't that what you're thinking? Do you know how little I slept since this application arrived?*

Sakura jumps in and voices the words for her. 'Have you ever had to think of not having your daughter in your life anymore because her father has more possessions and property to offer her? I can't even get back to work to give her anything she needs until this is done.'

Olivia rises, to put hands on Sakura's shoulders, to calm her down.

'We can talk about that later. Right now, we need to get through this. We're also going through the maintenance application we submitted. You'll need the financial support fixed. We'll be in court shortly. You need to be able to talk. I'm going to get you a drink. I'll be right back.'

Even she thinks I'm insane, Sakura thinks to herself.

Diane returns with a glass of water for her.

'Okay, what do I need to do?' Sakura asks, trying to calm down. Afraid now they believe all the things Chris has said. Things he has said in the brown envelope. Bad mother.

She thinks of the things he said on their first day, noticing, complimenting, flirting. *You are special, Sakura.* She doesn't know how she got here. She can feel the tears before they arrive and does everything to swallow them down large. One sneaks out, and she turns her head. It rolls down and kisses her ear.

I can't cry today. Sakura scolds herself silently. The layered mascara seldom worn stays in place for now.

'Sorry,' is all she can say.

'I don't blame you. Better you did it here than in there.' Diane goes through the process and what will happen. There is noise and urgency outside, it seems the judge has called their case. Even Diane jumps up.

'We have to go in. Are you ready now?' Diane pats down her skirt and pulls her file close.

Olivia, drink in hand, holds the door open.

Then it happens. She hears the lies. There are so many and they are so blatant she finds it hard to stand. They all originate from him.

Sakura sees Chris already seated and catches a glimpse of his pants and tie. She doesn't recognise them. Did he keep them for these special occasions?

His back is straight, his broad legs spread wide. Then she sees it. The curve of his outer lip, the sneer. Even in here, he continues to abuse her. This mantle will be picked up by someone else shortly. Chris, handsome, successful, propertied, will find another woman to work on.

It all happens so quickly, although, at times, it feels like slow motion.

The lawyers stand tall, talk straight. The judge nods. Some words she recognises, most she doesn't.

Legal jargon mixes with his name. Chris stands up, fixes his shirt, walks slowly from his seat and takes the few steps to his left. Pulls the blue swivel chair out and slowly sits down. Half smile in the judge's direction. He doesn't seem nervous at all. He almost looks like he's enjoying this.

Sakura hates this about him now and hates her own sense of sensitivity and anxiousness. After swearing to tell the truth, he lies, twists, and distorts the truth. He brings the wild pack of hungry animals to lunge at her throat.

'I didn't know what was happening, why she left, everything was fine.'

'Everything was fine?' His barrister leads him in question.

'Well, we have a young baby, she seemed to struggle adjusting, you know, after the baby was born.' His face manufactures concern.

'What do you mean by struggle?' The barrister is well paid and well prepared. It's clear they have worked out every word of this together. Don't blame her. Shame her. Act considerate. Get revenge.

'She was upset a lot. I didn't think she was coping very well. I did everything I could to support Sakura. But it wasn't enough. I suggested she see a doctor, thinking she might have postnatal depression.'

Sakura feels her heart scream. I asked for my mom to stay for a week after Sara was born. You told me that I had to learn how to manage by myself. The reaction of the barrister and the calm of the court situation makes her want to shout out, '*What's wrong with all of you?*'

She knows what is happening, what is going to continue to happen. Dissection. Dysmorphia. Discard. Of her. She tries not to gulp as the tears leave. Holding her head down. An attempt to minimise the attacks. Trying to let them wash over her with each disgusting lie. Instead, they smash against her insides. *Who believes you?* The question rises in her. *I believe you.* The answer she barely heard after Dad died.

She had thought of letting Eli come today. He had texted to say he would. But he hasn't come home since all this happened, and she can't help feeling that he was relieved when she texted back to say, 'no need', he'd only be waiting around outside. It would not have gone well to have him see this and what if he began to question if Sakura was all that Chris said? It's been so long she doesn't know anymore. The battering of her capabilities ends with his concern over how this is affecting Sara.

'I just want to protect my daughter and make sure she's ok.' Chris looks down and pauses.

'I'm sure this is upsetting for you,' his barrister offers.

'Yes, it's very upsetting.' His hand rises to his face to wipe the tear that never arrives.

Sakura used to be unnerved and curious about his steady hand in every situation. Never appearing upset or scared or emotional. Even after Sara was born. He acted like he did every other day. Ice.

Sakura sees his dance of pretence.

Chris returns to the day she left. He came home from work and found them both gone, no word left, and discovered she had run away to a shelter and made up a pack of lies only later. He only wants what's best for Sara and will do anything to protect her and wants Sakura to get help. He picks two instances and changes them entirely, focusing on Sakura's out-of-control behaviour after each, never mentioning his abuse at the beginning of both incidents. The ones that made her react. The constant thumbscrew he would keep turning until she reacted.

The time she wanted to go away with Jack and very reasonably he said he was busy and couldn't mind Sara.

'She flipped out acting crazy, and then left anyway. I just couldn't take time off. I was trying to manage everything. Money was tight.' He sounds so reasonable.

He forgot to mention, it was booked for ages and he had promised to mind Sara. Just one night. She would have to let Jack down. She had paid for the night away. Money never seemed to be an issue when it came to his nights out or upgrading the pickup. He would claim it was needed for his business.

He even brings up the day she realised she had to leave for good. The day he stuck a knife through the butterfly. He recounted other people looking as Sakura was making a scene. She was upsetting the baby. He was simply trying to help a butterfly, and Sakura overreacted as usual. Chris glances at Sakura and raises his lip ever so slightly. No one else notices.

He could have taken a gun and shot her through the chest right there in the courtroom. The impact on the inside feels the same. Sakura no longer turns her head sideways to avoid the mascara run. She drips all over the place, and Olivia, who she has forgotten is even present, along with her own lawyer, grabs her hand and passes her a tissue. But the black remains underneath her red eyes. Her lawyer listens, taking notes, impassive.

Sakura is called to the stand. Her feet seem not to know what to do. Walking alone with everyone watching, Chris watching.

She is asked questions. She is shaking so much that her words come out quickly, then slowly, with little coherence. The Judge even asks her if she needs a minute. She shakes her head and tries to continue. Key lines she has gone through have vanished.

She keeps saying Sara's name over and over again. She does manage to say she is afraid of Chris. She went to the shelter because she was afraid of what he might do.

The cross-examination solidifies everything Chris has said earlier. She is asked if she was so afraid, why didn't she seek an emergency protection order. Is there any police report? Does she have any evidence? Any bruising?

No, no, no, no.

His lawyer surmises, here is an unstable woman terrified of losing her child because of her own behaviour. Willing to do anything to paint his client in a bad light to detract from the truth. Here is a woman not in a position to care full-time for her child emotionally, financially, or physically. Here is a woman who needs help to deal with the issues that arose before she met Chris.

His client is willing to reduce working hours to care for his child, has a suitable home and financial means to do so. He is even willing to share access. But it must be seen that what has happened to Chris is that he has been manipulated and then has had to still find his way to today when his daughter has been taken out of his life without warning.

Sakura's lawyer jumps up and tries to counteract all that has been said. Maintenance is discussed. Since that first day Chris slipped money in her hand after dropping off Sara, he has promised more the following week. No more has arrived. They have lived on Tye's month advance and his patient holding open of her job.

'Would Sakura's former employer advance her salary, and hold her position if she was unstable?' The lawyer puts it in such economic terms. 'Here is a woman who is willing to work for her daughter's future and create one, who has not received anything but a hundred dollar bill, who is living in emergency accommodation with a preschool child. What is unstable about her? If she was so unstable why has a petition not been filed for her removal from her mother's care? There is no evidence, this is why. But there is a doctor's report. There is a psychological report. There is the shelter report. They all state that this woman's first priority is her child. It is there in the evidence that this is how it will remain.'

Sakura struggles to walk to her seat. Her head is down and she's gulping back tears. Olivia holds her hand so tight it starts to hurt, but Sakura doesn't care.

They leave. They wait. They return. Sakura doesn't care. Her life has been shredded by accusation and lies. Her mothering questioned. Her finances held up. She might as well be naked.

In summary, the Judge decides that Sakura will have full custody of Sara as there was no Child Protection Report to indicate the child was in danger. Olivia breathes a sigh of relief. Sakura holds her breath.

Chris will be granted access, slightly more than he currently has. Provided that Sakura finds suitable accommodation in the next three months. Maintenance is decided. Chris looks angry when he hears the amount. It is the first time Sakura can look at him fully since she left him. She knows that he is most angry about the money.

A walk back into the small room to discuss. Diane thinks this is great news. Sakura shakes her head. Her body feels ravaged. She didn't lose Sara, her worst fear. They abused her instead. Why does no one else think this is wrong, insane? Diane goes through the practical details and leaves the way she came in. She dismisses Sakura's horror at what has happened. 'This is how court is, don't take it personally.' Diane gathers her papers and smooths her already perfect skirt down. *But it is personal, to me.* Sakura wants to scream and scream.

Olivia takes Sakura's arm and they leave the courthouse. Outside they sit in her car.

'I can't believe what just happened. I know I should be happier that I didn't lose Sara or that he didn't get equal access. I just can't understand how that is allowed to happen. Did you hear what they said about me? Is that what people think? Is it true? Am I unstable?' She shakes her head.

'No.' Olivia puts her hands on the dashboard. 'None of this is true. Courts can be brutal. This is what they do. We've been petitioning for different courts for domestic abuse. The system is horrific for victims.'

For the first time, she sounds as weary as Sakura. How many times has she listened to this?

'But you heard what he said, what Chris said about me? Does he really believe that? I feel like I'm losing my mind.' She can't fight others' battles. Today she can only fight her own.

'Chris will say whatever he wants to say. I know you can't imagine this now, but what he believes doesn't matter, and someday his opinion of you won't matter at all. You've been through an ordeal. We will support you.'

Olivia swings into action. 'Come on, let's get back and make some food. You need to eat.'

But Sakura doesn't want to eat. Lunch won't solve this.

'Why did his lawyer say all that about me? It was awful. Like I was lying about everything Chris did to me. You know all the courage it took me to turn up at the shelter. How could he say all that stuff? That I was a really unfit mother.'

'That's their job. They defend their clients. It's awful, they re-traumatise victims in the process. As I said, we've been fighting to change this. I can see what it does to women, what it's doing to you. You know the truth. You know what happened to you. I believe you. I believe you, Sakura.' The words of their first encounter, a few weeks and a lifetime ago, are repeated.

The car feels hot now. Olivia puts the window down. The breeze is a welcome addition to break up the layers of pain. Olivia's words melt into Sakura, and she folds and cries and cries. Olivia reaches over and holds her hand. Sakura knows it's clammy but doesn't care. Her body was exhausted, and her mind praying for it all to stop.

'Come on, let's go, we can talk more later, now food and rest, you're going to be ok.'

'I'm going to put that phrase on a t-shirt,' she mumbles through tears. 'Everyone keeps saying it to me.' Sakura holds onto Olivia's words like a baby blanket. At that moment, she is so grateful for her and then panics, thinking, *if something happens to her, what would I do?*

The woman who is the chief figure, the biggest source of strength to get her through, just pats her hand and says, 'I'm not going anywhere,' and smiles.

Sakura wonders how she knew what she was thinking.

After food, Sakura feels the adrenaline fade as she drives to pick up Sara. The hug feels extra special, Sara's delight at seeing her. They look into each other's eyes, and for a second, Sakura's heart beats differently. Different to all the crazy beats today. Beats of love, and they share that truth.

Babies don't break gazes. They break their gaze only when something else catches their attention. Sara's head swings around to Marie, her nana, who is smiling so big a smile, delighted with the outcome.

'Thanks for helping me find the lawyer.' She pictures the woman on her next file, her next case, leaving this little world of three generations to their future. One that has three generations now.

'You've always been strong,' Mom suddenly offers.

Sakura doesn't go into any of the rest. She knows there would be no point.

Afterwards, Sakura realises she shouldn't have been so shocked by Chris's lies. And yet she will continue to be shocked time and time again. Even today, she thought before she got here, she wished maybe he would see her and see the mother of his child, the woman now in a shelter because of what he has done, and stop all this and breakdown and cry. Beg for forgiveness. She will realise that her frame of reference for people and life is one filled with deep empathy, sensitivity, care and compassion, and Chris's is not. He lacks empathy, the ability to love and show kindness. Instead, his frame of reference is of darkness and hangs in darkness. Any opportunity to expand this he takes and takes with twisted joy. Sakura sees evil as the maleficent force, living in people she has never seen. People incarnated with heavy chains in federal jails with life sentences for cruel deeds. Later she realises that evil threads delicate webs, so fine you almost can't see the people who have learnt to smile and fake emotions. Sometimes it's hard to spot them apart from other people. Its tiny, like a seed, a gut feeling, a niggling, almost nothing. Like the time Chris first met Jack, his comment while manoeuvring the wheel of his pickup with one hand. Nothing and everything. For those who get caught in their web, if you are lucky enough to make it out alive, the sticky web will take much to undo. There is a trail of brokenness. There is much to recover.

That night Sakura falls asleep at the same time as Sara and wakes up to Sara's morning sounds. No lying on the washroom floor to grieve, no need for a lifesaving lavender bath.

The following week, Sakura's session with her counsellor helps her process what happened in court. She feels held, heard, and validated. Why is this space so tiny and the whole world filled with the opposite?

Should it not be that victims of abuse should be heard and validated in large courtrooms out there, not in tiny rooms where the people here already know? She realises that Chris has done a good job in trying to get her to doubt her own mind, her thoughts, her ability as a mother. And that she did great to survive and mind her baby to the best of her ability.

The counsellor again describes the abuser's tactics. She will hear it over and over again, and some days she hears it so loud, and others she whispers,

'Why me? Did I do something to deserve this? Did I show weakness in me that he knew he could do that to me?' The soft *no* answer turns into a firm *no* later.

CHAPTER 60

Despite winning, Sakura still feels lost. Everything has changed now. Even with the people she has known all her life.

The evening after her court case, when she was with Mom, the phone rang. It was Eli. She's seen Eli once since Sara was born and that was before all of this. He was awkward and sweet, holding Sara. All arms, both looked uncomfortable. She was happy when he left after a few hours, catching up with friends.

'Hey.' He sounded so weird, removed, and a bit afraid.

'Hey.' She smiled as she spoke.

'Well, result,' he joked in true Eli style. She knows he doesn't know what's it like, the court process, having a child, everything.

'Yeah, result.' She gave him the tone that told him it was ok.

'I should have been there for you, Sakura. I'm your big brother.'

It was years since he had said that.

'None of us knew how to handle things,' Sakura quoted her counsellor to him. 'We'll get there. You have to come and see your niece.'

'I should have come before, Sakura.' He sounded so melancholy. 'Is now the right time?'

The big brother asks the little sister, who has become the older one now.

'Wait until I'm organized. Sara and I want to see you. I'll let you know when we're ready.'

'You need help, you call,' Eli urged suddenly. Sakura can't help feeling that it's something he says as a way to end the conversation.

'I will.' But she knows that she can't just yet.

It's been six weeks since she had left Chris and two weeks since the court date.

'I can't just come back to work, Tye.' She calls him the day after the custody hearing. 'I have to find somewhere for us to live.'

'No, I get that.'

'I understand if you can't keep me on.'

'When you come back, you'll be ready. We miss you here. I give Snowy a carrot now and then, and tell him it's from you.'

She smiles to think of a routine a decade old happening.

'I'll continue paying you,' he says, abruptly, like he is the one who should be embarrassed.

'Even after the agreed time?' A gift she accepts but feels undeserving of.

'I'm not good at this talk. I just know what's right.' It's clear he wants to hang up now. She thinks of Chris dropping bedding, wants to say something. But he's gone.

Another breath, another sigh of relief comes when Olivia seeks her out. She calls her into the small room to the front after breakfast. The one where all this began. It is a conversation she dreaded, every night feeling so safe in the room, with the washroom. She has bought candles and baskets to hold their things. It's becoming home.

'Look.' Olivia smiles. 'I have some news. There are small townhouses belonging to the shelter and funded by the Municipal Government that might become available.' Hope. Sakura is waiting for the catch. This room, where Olivia wants to chat but her smiling face says its ok, good even. But Sakura is always waiting for the other shoe to drop. So much bad has happened.

For two weeks she and Sara take a breath on the days when Chris doesn't have access. They can just spend the days being together. Sakura doesn't have to make lists and files. It's all about waiting now. The forest has her daughter. She can visit the boardwalk. It almost feels normal until she has to return to the shelter, and this is when she sees Olivia is right. Life moves on and so must she. The apartments on the Island are out of her reach unless she moves rurally, and for now, she needs to be where the support is, and where she can reach help quickly.

Then one day, as suddenly as she came, the next step comes.

'A house, a lovely two-bed townhouse right by Green Water Street, has become available. There's a childcare facility, two streets over, and they accept our reduced cost payment.' Olivia is beaming. 'I know you mentioned your work with the horses before and how much you love it. This would help you go back to work.' Sara never returned to Isobelle, her first childminder.

All of a sudden Sakura feels the wave of fear again, another change.

'You would still have us and your counselling sessions every week,' Olivia advises. Sakura sighs with relief, she couldn't lose Olivia, this place too. The link and support will be there always. Excitement starts to push through fear. Life beyond here.

Sakura can't quite believe it. She had started to panic after the court date that she might have to move back in with Mom in order to keep Sara, as she couldn't afford anything by herself.

'I can't believe it, for us? That's amazing. Are you sure it's ok if we stay there? Like…'

Olivia interrupts her. 'Yes! This is for you and Sara to help you get your life back on your own track.'

For the first time in years, Sakura feels something she doesn't quite recognize – hope and freedom.

'Thank you, thank you for everything you have done for Sara and me. I don't know where I would be.' Shining tears spill down her face. Sara's lower lip goes as she watches her mom.

'No, no, don't worry.' Sakura bends down to the stroller to show her daughter a real smile. She has more of those.

'You're welcome. That is what we do.' When Sakura looks up she can see Olivia is also tearing up. Some people in the world just care, and they would help even if it wasn't work. 'What happened to you will change and shape your life to come. You are bright, kind, and caring. Lean into all that love and become the person you are, free of Chris!'

Sakura can't let the kind words about her in. Not yet.

But she can stand up again, and she can show in her face that this means everything.

'When can we move? What happens now?' Sakura's excitement is palpable. What once were walls and doors slamming are now options, choices she can make. She didn't choose for her dad to die, or for Chris to abuse her. It feels as though she has been contained by fear where no joy can enter. Dad, he comes to mind. She hasn't heard his voice, but she knows, just knows, he is there.

'The keys will be available at the end of the week.' Olivia who spends so much of her life dealing with threats and violence, must love days like this that prove her work worthwhile. 'Maybe it will get you through tomorrow.'

Tomorrow is access day. If Sakura thought the ones before the hearing were endurances, the ones after show open hostility. Chris hates to lose. The first access after the court hearing was traumatic.

Driving out with Sara buckled in her car seat, Sakura's stomach started to heave just as she left the main road up to Chris's house. Driving in, all familiar yet unfamiliar. There was another offer from a resource worker with the shelter to go with her to his house. Sakura declined. 'I've done this before, and I'll have to do it again.'

Now wishing she hadn't. The car skids a fraction on ice on a road made for pickups. Her winter tyres need replacing. The door swings open, and she spots the chair she painted inside.

'Get out quickly,' she whispers to herself. 'He's going to be pissed.'

Opening the back door of her car, she lifts Sara out and her bag. She stands and turns. Chris is closer than she realises. Right behind her. His face angry. She feels trapped in the place, this place in the country surrounded by snow that just won't leave.

Sara makes a noise, and Sakura kisses her, not wanting to let her go but also needing a break. *Please, don't take it all out on her.*

'Did you bring her rain gear?' Chris snaps as he takes her.

'No.' Sakura looks away and hands the bag over. She can't let go of Sara.

'I told you to bring it.' He is clipped and expecting answers.

Sakura hadn't checked her phone and starts panicking. Always feeling she has done something wrong when she is with Chris. She doesn't want to answer his direct question but feels she has to.

'I didn't know you asked for it.' She feels her lower face shake, putting a tremor in her voice.

'Of course I did.' He is keeping his voice low. 'You're lying. What's wrong with you?'

The tiny bit of herself speaks up, quivering and uneven,

'I'm not lying, I am not doing this. Especially in front of Sara.' She turns away.

'That's it. Walk away! I can't even talk to you. There is something seriously wrong with you.' He feels like a monster. Growing tall, taller than his house. Booming voice. His face distorted.

Sara is in her arms throughout. She doesn't want to let her go. Almost sensing her stepping back, Chris reaches over and lifts Sara out of her arms, smiling at her.

'Hey Sara, come on with Daddy now.' Night and day.

Sakura walks faster as she can feel her tears ahead. Jumping into the car, impatient to start the engine. Driving out, 'What the fuck, what the fuck!' she screams at herself. 'How dare he? Why couldn't you say something, stand up for yourself! Fuck!' At that moment, Sakura wishes for a truck to slide off its path and career into her car, killing her instantly. It would be an accident. Then shame and guilt land.

'Stop, stop it! What about Sara?'

Sakura pulls in, her hands sore from hitting the steering wheel. Looking down at her feet, she has managed to drag mud into her car.

That's what I am, dirt. Sakura feels the lash of her internal dialogue on all sides. *I can't even stand up for myself. I let him do that to me. There must be something wrong with me. Jack wouldn't put up with that.*

This comparison collapses her completely. She has never left the pier. The trauma waits for her at every challenge, in every threat from a person. She can ride a partially broken horse, deal with the most difficult horses, and love her daughter, but she cannot forget. Part of her is still watching her father die. It surfaces each time. Little Sakura lies at the footrest, curled into a ball.

'I am never going to be ok.' That word again.

Today, Sakura beats herself up, alone, on the side of the road. It takes her almost half of the access break to recover from the drop-off. She doesn't want to talk to anyone who will ask her anything.

Her eyes dry up only when she is totally dehydrated and hoarse. Her body weak, she knows she just has to get back to the shelter. A receptionist buzzes through and Olivia comes out and immediately invites her into the room.

'You like chamomile?' Handing her a warm cup of tea.

'Yes, thanks. He didn't act like that on the previous visits.' Sakura's voice resigned.

'I thought you liked chamomile. What happened? You look upset.'

Sakura spills out all her anger and shame, mostly at herself. Olivia reaches across.

'This is because he has lost, Sakura. I want you to hear the way you are talking about yourself. Chris knows exactly what buttons to press, and he does. He goes for your wounds and sticks the knife in, and he will *continue* to do this always, for as long as he can.'

Sakura feels hopeless. Slumping into the chair, pulling at her worn-out grey pullover, using the sleeve to wipe her face. Olivia pushes over the tissue box.

'You'll get stronger. Remember, it's only been a few weeks. Leaving was the first step. Many women experience post-separation abuse and leaving an abusive relationship is often the most dangerous time for women. We'll help you have tools to protect yourself and create your own boundaries so he can't hurt you again or at least limit his impact on you.'

'I just go to pieces when he snipes and shouts. I'm so afraid, even though I know he's wrong, I feel wrong!'

'I've been thinking of this. I wonder if you should be changing the access point. If you don't want someone from here to go with you, this is another option.'

'I didn't even know I had a right to. I felt I should do the driving. To make sure she gets there safely.' Sakura shakes her head.

'You have custody, the full care of your daughter, access points should suit Sara and your needs best.' Olivia spreads her hands on the table. 'I think you should consider access here or at your new home for both drop off and collection. You're too vulnerable out there, no one around, no protection.'

'Can I do that? He'll get mad. I don't want him to take it out on Sara.'

Sakura feels fear and strength at the same time. Realizing she has the *right* to protect herself and to set boundaries.

'What can he do?' Olivia presses.

'I guess nothing really.'

'That's right. He's had one failed court ruling. He won't risk his reputation or his business. This is the Island, Sakura. You work in his field, with horses.'

'I don't want any more trouble.'

'The court order is in place in relation to access. You don't have to drive out there. You just let him know that the arrangement has changed in relation to dropping off Sara. He'll have no choice if he wants to spend the time with his daughter that he fought for court.'

'What if he says something awful back?' Sakura asks worried.

'He might. You can choose to respond or not respond. The key thing is you have choices now, and he doesn't want that. He doesn't want you to be free, to be happy.

He'll constantly try and pull you back and pull you down.' Olivia takes her hand. 'When you start to see this clearly and the pattern, someday you won't care what he says. Most likely, he'll go away. It's awful to say, but probably he will abuse someone else. You can protect yourself from him physically, psychologically, and emotionally.'

'There will be days he'll still manage to get in, to affect me.' Sakura slumps.

'To abuse you,' Olivia corrects her. 'But we'll be here to help you through.'

Sakura picks up her chamomile tea, now cool. Her anger shifts, allowing the pain to surface.

'How could he do this to me? I thought he loved me. I'm the mother of his child.' Tears fall, and some land in her cup. She can feel a wave of fear, from below and beyond. She cannot stop or control it. From her lower stomach, it enters her centre. Her heart feels like it will burst. No longer able to hold her tea, she tries to put it down on a table but misses. It drops and breaks and smashes into three big pieces. A light yellow colour runs on the tiles and stains the side of the chair.

'I'm so sorry, I'm sorry.' Sakura throws herself on the floor and tries to collect the jagged pieces. One smaller piece embeds itself in her knee. She barely feels it.

'It's okay, it's just a cup, it's all going to be okay.' Picking her up, Olivia sees the blood through her pants. 'You've cut yourself, come here, let's get that cleaned up.'

Afterwards, she sits directly across from Sakura.

'You are incredible, you are smart and beautiful. You have been through so much. You can't see what I see, but I hope one day you will.'

Sakura plays with her band-aid under her pants, unable to look at the woman. Thinking to herself: Those words are not for me.

CHAPTER 61

The silver shape in her hand. The key. Sakura doesn't even have to try and be happy.

'Thank you, thank you. It's not enough, but it's all I have… someday.' Her face scrunches up, and light fills all the lines.

Olivia. The woman who talked to her on the day she arrived, and followed her through every twist and turn, who now hands her the key to the door of freedom, interrupts her.

'You live your best life. This is all the thanks I need, and I have no doubt that you will.'

'How many people have you helped, Olivia?' Sakura whispers.

'Too many. I want a world where no one needs refuge from someone they love. But until then I experience women like you, pulling through, and it gives me the energy to keep going.' Olivia shows a side of herself Sakura has not seen. She is a rock of strength and a witness to too much. So, Sakura sees, days like today are important.

Another wave is coming. Sakura can feel it before arrival. Different, small. Tickles her tummy in a similar way to the butterflies she felt when Sara was the size of a bell pepper, making her presence known. The wave continues upwards and enters her heart. Sakura takes a breath and instinctively raises her hand. Her chest fills with something vaguely familiar yet almost unknown. Hope. Her whole body smiles. At that moment she is dancing.

'Sakura,' Olivia says very softly, 'in this new stage, take all the help you can get. We are here for the times Chris affects you and for how he has affected you. But there are others. Please try to remember, no matter how much you love them, they will not be able to understand all you have been through.'

Sakura knows what she means. It's time to let family, friends, her employer back in. Not just for her sake, but for the daughter she will raise now on her own. But it's no longer time to be judged, questioned, or to put up with misunderstanding. There are times when their ideas have set her back, their solutions have caused harm to her. It's still hard to understand why they can't understand her. With anyone else, outside her family and Jack, she can state her case and be heard. Because she stood in a courtroom being annihilated and still won. What she feels, thinks, understands, she will never dismiss again.

This is what the past two years have done for her. To survive Chris, raise a daughter, hold a job, fight a system, and deal with questions from the most loving people, who could not understand. They have shown her that she is not a child on a pier watching Dad die in front of her, getting herself ready for school, losing her close ties with her grieving brother and mom.

She is the woman who came to terms and now sets her own.

'I am starting to know how to do that now, Olivia.'

'You will continue to. I know you, Sakura. You had it in your eyes the very first night.'

But the terms just keep on coming.

They wave to Olivia as her Mom pulls up outside their new home. For the past few days Sakura has had to keep Olivia's advice in mind and stay true to herself, but take the help she needs.

'I don't understand why you won't move in with me,' Mom kept saying when she first told her she was leaving the shelter. The housing is known as being for women from the shelter. Mom still struggles with the public face of the breakup. She feels Sakura has all she needs now. But it will be a long haul. That is the problem, she doesn't understand any of this.

'This is what's best for us, Mom. Sara and I are a family the way you and Dad were with me and Eli.' Sakura kept strong during that first conversation. She didn't reveal that she still can't yet trust her fully. With help from the team, she kept the focus off the shelter support in getting the house. And kept the focus on Sara having her own room and their own space. The one place she doesn't have to second guess her instincts and defend her position is in the shelter, with the staff there, and with her counsellor.

'I'll grab that.' Mom leans into the trunk and lifts a box.

'Thanks. Look, Sara, that's our door!' Sakura lifts her out and lets her press the buzzer over and over.

People who have known her all her life are trying. They can't understand like the trained professionals and support. But they are doing as much as they can. Sakura is the only one who knows where the new lines are and she's still drawing them. Like when she had to recover some of her belongings from Chris. Jack had offered to help with this.

'Let me do something for you. Please. I feel like I've done nothing since you told me what was really going on,' Jack had pleaded with her down the phone.

But Sakura didn't know how Jack would react. She thinks of the times before the court case when she offered to pay for a lawyer but couldn't understand how Sakura allowed it to happen to her. Then the times when they socialized, Jack never sensed the change in her. The night of her party, when Sakura and Chris were at the bar and he was abusing her with two male strangers for her pregnancy weight, Jack and Chris had a brief exchange. Sakura remembers them both laughing. She couldn't take it if Jack laughed or tried to keep social norms around Chris.

'If it was the other way around, how would you react to her?' Olivia asked her when Jack and the friendship came up.

'I would have just known,' Sakura said simply. Because it was the simple truth. From the time of the mouse dead on the path, to the time after her dad died, to the time of now, Sakura has never had to doubt Jack's love, but she has always been wiser. The one who gave Jack's life the emotional depth she didn't have, sharing a room, sandwiched in the middle of two sisters.

'My friend didn't know what had happened. Still, I felt betrayed. But I know she didn't fully understand domestic abuse and how he tried to alienate me by joking with her. Then he'd say how self-absorbed she was. So I was full of doubt.'

'That's the way it works.' Olivia gave Sakura space before saying. 'He used your vulnerability to gain a foothold. Then he dismantled your self-belief and questioned your support system. But you'll get it back, Sakura, because you're supporting yourself, we are supporting you. Your family and friends may not ever understand the true extent of what you have gone through.' She repeated what she had warned of all along.

'I know.' Sakura sighed. 'But it doesn't mean they don't have a place in mine and Sara's life.'

'Yes, and it's the place you want them to have. The one that makes you feel safe.' Olivia smiled. because she knows Sakura knows her own position now. 'This is why I recommend you take someone from here with you when you go to collect the things you left behind.' Sakura remembers Olivia's clear advice.

So much thinking has to go into every single encounter with Jack and Mom. So all that history is brought to bear. 'I know you want to help. I really do,' is all Sakura said to Jack, she knew she wanted to help, but Sakura was worried she might say something to Chris, or worse, he might act all friendly towards her, and she might just respond.

The support worker knows about appearances not being the entire reality, and can read for coded messages fed through innocent remarks, for gaslighting. They're seasoned in what these abusers are like. That day a support worker came with her. Sakura didn't have much and was glad of this. Sara's highchair was the biggest thing. Folded, it fitted into the trunk. Chris hid some things and then lied about them when she asked.

'The linen I bought for us, where is it, Chris?' She had chosen this, although Mom had paid. It wasn't good that it had been bought for here but it would save on cost. Chris didn't like it. So a packet of it was still unopened. This was a life being built from scratch. It would be financially and practically easier to move in with Mom. Emotionally it would take away all progress.

'I don't know. Maybe I put it in the trash. It was cheap stuff.' Chris threw out the bait.

Sakura found it buried behind the water heater in the linen closet. Some of it is unopened.

'Do you want this stroller?' Chris offers her when he sees her carrying the packet of unopened bed linen. The used linen she is going to leave behind.

The stroller he had chosen, the assistant cooing over Chris. Sakura ignored and feeling powerless.

'It's okay.' That word again. 'I have one now. She's getting too old for it anyway.' Putting on steel armour, she got all that she could and left, not allowing herself to go anywhere emotionally.

Sitting into the passenger seat of the support worker's car that day, clutching the small album, the one thing she really wanted. Pictures of Sara after she was born. Their moments together. It was underneath all Sara's clothes. Chris missed it. Driving away with the support worker, for the first time she didn't fall apart and scream.

Now at her new home with Sara, Sakura notices this part of town looks different from how she remembers growing up with Jack. They lived in a neighbourhood, not exactly close by, but within walking distance. Rose Avenue and Cedar Lane are quieter. It's busier here, with cars passing, and a small store at the end of the street.

'You'll be close by!' Mom becoming more comfortable with her decision.

Sakura has mostly managed not to discuss anything to do with Chris and focuses their relationship on Sara. It hasn't stopped Mom trying.

'Ah, it's lovely Sakura, you'll be here for visits and outings. You'll be able to drop in on me again.' She plans an intimate future, smiling, taking Sara upstairs.

'This is your room,' Mom says to Sara, pointing to the smaller of the two rooms. Sakura doesn't say anything, knowing that Sara has always been beside her and is not ready for this to change.

'Come on, let me show you the yard, Mom.' Sakura opens the screen door, revealing a small, cute space. Winter is pushing back, finally releasing its foothold to spring.

'I was thinking I could get a small swing for Sara, you know the single-seat one? Think it would fit in that space?' Sakura already knows her mom is going to do this.

'That would be lovely, especially in the summer. Would you like that, Sara?' Mom holds her up, tickling and smiling. Sara bursts out laughing. She loves being outside and is more relaxed. Inside the house, Sakura and Mom are both trying, both tense and working on it.

'Eli could help put it together when he's home.' Mom trying to put them all together again, happy families in a family where nothing has been happy since the pier.

'Yes, great,' Sakura ventures, knowing the void. She hasn't seen Eli since there was the conversation, limited but both trying. He sent a short text a few weeks after. For some reason, when Sakura was in her room at the shelter, and Sara asleep, her mind would go to her brother.

Ever since Dad died, Eli vanished into hockey and girls and then University. She didn't know how to be with him. Dad's loss occupied the space between them. Before Dad died, she was the younger sister protected by her older brother. Reluctantly going to family things together, but she could tell he secretly enjoyed it. They talked about hockey and boys' things she loved being around but not involved in.

Dad's presence filled her first few weeks at the shelter, and after the court case, it vanished. As if he had done his last parenting from spirit. The black hold his death had on her life has eased. Chris to survive, Sara to raise. Eli is too removed to occupy the space where a male member of the family might be. Now there is no one to hold that space, and he has floated off, she doesn't even know if she wants to try to catch him.

'Mom.' Sakura smiles. 'Can you take Sara now, please? Let me sort things here on my own.'

'Okay, we'll head off and let you get unpacked.' Mom, once Sakura has the presence of mind to instruct her, can react. Sakura kisses Sara goodbye. She loves seeing how her mother is with her and feels grateful that this part is easy. 'See you later!' she shouts, making a funny face as they leave.

For the first time, she is alone in her new home. The one where everything will change for the better.

Sakura walks around the house again, going into every room on her own. She can't quite believe it. The nights she would lie, Chris sleeping beside her, thinking, where will I go, how will I manage? She would go through the list, her mom, Jack, Eli, Tye, and dismiss them all one after another. She didn't have enough money for rent. Then she would turn over and try not to hate the rising snore from beside her, in such a deep sleep, oblivious to her pain. Her list never included this possibility. A house attached to a shelter. Attached to vital support and people who understood the kind of support needed. She didn't even know that *this* existed. Then something Olivia said comes back. 'As soon as you live without the pressure and stress of managing abuse, you will find yourself coming alive. Again.'

Laughing, she runs down the stairs and jumps, hitting the kitchen ceiling she leaps so high.

'We did it,' she whispers.

You did it. The silent, loud voice returns, for the first time since she won. Sakura thinks then of the day before the boat trip. Him at the table with his tackle, confessing his insecurity to Mom. Knowing he was losing his place as Dad, the day before he did.

Smiling, she whispers, 'Thank you, Dad.'

The hours without Sara mean she can work fast. On the kitchen table, Mom has left an envelope. Inside is a card and she has given her a voucher for the *Home Depot* store. Her little beat-up car outside. The chance to shop for new things without a child in tow. 'Thanks, Mom.'

Going from aisle to aisle, she feels excited that she can draw this new life for herself and Sara into existence. The freedom. No voice saying that won't work there, you can't paint that. No ever-critical eye. The house has utensils, cutlery, all the essentials. What can she get? The extras! Passing the throws and cushions. The bright purple catches her eye. That will look lovely on the couch. Smiling, she grabs it and adds it to her few bits.

Chris would have commented on the colour. This comparison would happen frequently, then sometimes, then seldom. Then this would catch Sakura by surprise. The silent, invisible vocal partner, the one who encourages her, has taken over from Chris. And at that moment, Sakura pushes on a little too fast with her shopping cart. Her energy is uncontained in her body. Giddy excitement. *I can choose*. Grabbing bright colours. She is to paint the room to the front of the house. Sakura imagines adding toys and books and making it a play area for Sara.

The shopping trip, on top of unpacking most of the boxes, on top of negotiating with Mom, Eli, and Jack to stay true to her needs, on top of having to visit Chris with a support worker, on top of saying goodbye to the safest house she has ever known since the house she lived in before Dad died, makes her realize she's done too much.

She drives, afraid she will panic at being entirely alone for the first time with Sara, with no one to call if she has anxiety. There is security for the row of houses, just a phone call way, so the abusers have to think twice about entering the complex.

'I'm doing this alone,' she whispers.

'Because you always did. You've shown you can.' The inside voice answers.

Arriving back, pulling up outside. The lack of dread of seeing her front door creates its own space. Where fear constantly lived, it takes time to fill that void. At times Sakura feels lost without it. Right now, she's happy to leave it empty. Maybe a little joy.

Spreading Mom's unused bed linen over her new bed, she pats it down to remove the last crease. Walking to the door, she turns back. Her bed, Sara's cot. *Just us now.* In an instant, her face loses its light and sadness creeps in and steals a tear. Sakura doesn't try to push it away.

Walking into the washroom, admiring the wooden panels and curved bath. She decides this is her favourite space. The tall trees occasionally bang off the window. She doesn't have time for a bath today but imagines lying there, opening the window, hearing the trees in a lavender-infused oasis.

She remembers her first nights in the shelter. Olivia's insistence on her having a bath. And how she wanted to be sucked down the drain, out through the pipes and disappear. Sakura pulls herself back into her new house and recognizes at that moment every feeling passes as she imagines lying in a similar body of water with joy.

Having collected Sara from Mom's, they sit down for their first meal together. Pasta. Sara banging plastic cups in her highchair. It's the first time Sakura has cooked since she left Chris. Coaxing Sara to eat the last few spoonfuls, she looks at the clock and realizes that the normal anxiety of waiting for Chris to return home is absent. Scooping Sara out of her chair.

'Let's go for ice cream. Yes, ice cream!' Sakura smiles, copying Sara's sounds.

It's still bright as winter lets go of its grip. Into the small store on the corner, Sakura gets the ice creams and continues on further to the park. 'You've been here twice today, Sara!' Such a long day. So much has happened in it. Sara lives in the moment. This is the one right now.

They eat and play, and Sara doesn't object when Sakura points to the stroller. They return back to the house, their house. Again, the front door doesn't make Sakura want to run away. She has already, in a day, created a home inside.

That night Sakura begins their new bedtime ritual of bath, story, and cuddles. Sara resists letting go. She finally settles. Sakura returns downstairs and takes in their new space. Looking at her yard, seeing it for the first time in this dark light. Walking back to the front of the house, she tidies Sara's toys.

Standing up, she glances out the window, which leads onto the street. She sees a pickup truck. Dropping the toys, she runs closer for a better look. Then it's gone.

It can't be his. It's not his. These words loop multiple times. Finally, the point arrives. Even if it is his, what can he do? He can't do anything. Not fully convinced. Her eyes are drawn to the window for the rest of her first night. Holding her phone, thumbing numbers for emergency services, and the shelter itself.

This is the second step; housing. First, get away from abuse. Second, build a life after it.

'Remember the calls from here are given priority with services,' Olivia said as a mantra over the days between getting the news and moving out. 'Besides, you'll need to give Chris your address for legal correspondence, and access dates.'

For a few days, Sakura thought it would be avoidable. Of course, it had to happen. She informed Chris of their new address and, with the help of the support staff from the shelter, set boundaries on how he would have to collect and drop Sara home during his access time. She'll never return to his house.

At the time of setting her terms, it felt as terrifying as the court date. What might he say back? To Sakura's surprise, he accepted it without argument. The surge of power at that point brought Sakura to a tall standing position as she punched the air.

For now, on her first night, still trained to watch windows and doors, still alert to signs, Sakura has to remind herself that her first full day of freedom has gone so well. She has negotiated everything. Tomorrow, she'll take Sara to daycare to see if she'll settle. If it goes well, she can return to things she knew before that she loved.

Chapter 62

The following day Sakura walks Sara down to her new childcare facility. They stay in it together for an hour. She loves it.

'This might work,' she says to herself on her way home to their new house. Another day of sorting ahead.

The next day Sara's tears at the door pull and yank at Sakura's already bruised heart. She eagerly goes to collect her at midday, by which time Sara doesn't want to leave. Having fun with a sand tray.

Sakura shakes her head at the thought she has just sat in guilt and shame for three hours. It's been this way all along. Everything is always her fault. Then she sees that it's just an adjustment. When is she going to learn to praise herself?

The first day back at work. Her hands guide the steering wheel around the last turn to Tye's. Wearing her black pants and boots, Sakura places her hand on her belly, trying to soothe her fear.

'Thank you for all your support.' She rehearses in the mirror. 'I will make my absence up to you.' There you go again Sakura, blaming yourself. It's so hard to accept help without strings attached. She hasn't seen Tye since before all this. And worries about bumping into Chris.

'You've got this,' she shouts out loud. An attempt to drown out all other hysterical voices.

Closing her car door, the smells and sounds both welcome and haunt her. Tye must have known. He's moved someone to the nearest stable and opened the half door. She sees Snowy and immediately melts. The carrot in her bag for him. Then she can see Chris walking over to her that day. The day he asked her out. His flirting, his smiles.

Sakura's body starts to wobble, dizzy. She promised she wouldn't cry today. *How could I be so stupid? I believed him.* Her thoughts are interrupted by Tye's voice. Roughly wiping her tears. She turns around.

'Hey, Sakura, good to see you. Tye looks away at the sight of her smudged face, his sleeves rolled up, his peak cap holding his dark sweaty hair in place. Sakura is grateful for the big open space around them.

'Thanks, it's good to be here.' Her body says different, and she feels like one of the runaway horses, she has to hold her legs to prevent herself from running.

'Are you ok?' That word again. Tye stands waiting for her to answer. The open space shrinks into a dot.

'Yeah, well, you know, getting there.' Sakura feels her eyes burn and turns away, rubbing her boots together, shifting from one foot to another.

'You know, I'm here for you if you need anything.' Tye moves to walk and gently places his right hand on her left shoulder as he passes.

'Tye, I just want to thank you.' She starts the rehearsed speech.

'No need. You're someone I value. The horses do too.' Tye makes the necessary polite conversation. She is grateful for his discretion and diversion. The safe topic is horses for both of them.

Onto horses. Sakura still feels his hand on her shoulder. It remains all day, loyal.

She's glad when he leaves and, after greeting Snowy, Sakura goes to meet the bay mare. Tye had quickly gone through the jobs, including exercising this mare. Tall, elegant, strong-limbed, hooves scraping the ground. Leading her out of the stable, Sakura places her foot into the stirrup and lifts up and into the saddle. Her face beams. Everything disappears up here.

They soon break into a gentle trot. Taking it easy. Her body has been out of the saddle for some time. Sakura sees the gate towards the edge of the forest, and they both can't help themselves. Sakura sits back as the mare falls into a canter. Sakura imagines her arms outstretched, the wind caught between her fingers. Her body raises up and meets a part of herself, long lost and almost forgotten. They dance like old lovers. Suddenly Sakura is a child again. Linking arms with Jack going home to their Friday evenings, her dad standing at the BBQ. Complete, together, happy.

She hadn't planned on galloping today, but she gives the cue to the mare who responds, together with the rise past the trees. Hooves in unison, kicking up dirt. The horse holds her head high, letting out sporadic snorts. White foam seeps past the bit. Sakura feels like she's galloping for the first time. Her grief and Chris's abuse held her down. An anchored sea buoy.

Now free to float and drift.

Returning to the stables, Sakura washes the mare down and prepares the rest of the stables. Her first day over. On her way out, Tye stops her with a rundown of the day and lets her know that their supplier of bedding has changed. His name isn't mentioned. Tye walks away. Sakura punches the air in silent yes and drives off. Joni Mitchell, *You Can Close Your Eyes,* roars.

After collecting Sara, they go home and share a bath. Washing the horse smells away. Sara giggles as she splashes, trying to catch her floating toys.

That night, after Sara settles for sleep, Sakura unpacks the last of her boxes. Hearing Sara crying, she goes upstairs. Fear travels along. What's wrong? Is she sick? Picking her up, she checks for temperature.

Feeling none, she tries to soothe her with cuddles. This doesn't work. Pacifier in her mouth, Sakura puts her back into her cot. But the wails continue. Sakura stands outside her door, praying for her to stop. *Please go back to sleep.* In and out, in and out. An hour passes. Sakura feels the night creeping up and strangling her in darkness. Both crying now. Sakura has lost any sense of what to do.

Another hour later, Sara eventually falls asleep. Sakura's hand cramps, gripping the side of the cot. Afraid to move. Guessing time's passing, she eventually releases and moves slowly sideways out, stepping carefully on each floorboard, not familiar enough yet to know which ones creak.

Safely in the hallway, Sakura inhales completely. Just as she steps away, the cries start again. Placing her hand over her mouth, Sakura presses in, hurting herself. 'Please help me,' she shouts into her palm. It's not this moment that terrifies her but the moments and hours and days of this alone into the future. There's no one else here to care.

Sakura goes back into the room, repeats the soothing, and places back Sara into her cot.

At midnight, she eventually settles. Sakura drags heavy feet downstairs and sees the half-empty box. She realizes she hasn't eaten anything. She was meant to cook herself supper when Sara went to bed. Lying on the couch, she falls asleep, angry. Angry that she wasn't calmer. That she isn't a better mother. Angry that she is doing all of this alone.

The night passes, and daylight floods in. Sakura wakes up cold. The blanket slipped off during the night. Rising to the kitchen, she forgives herself with the smell and taste of her first coffee. She hears Sara not long after and is grateful that she slept long enough for her to swallow the last mouthful. Upstairs, Sakura pulls the curtains, greets Sara with exaggerated noises, and moves to erase her guilt.

Sara giggles and is raised into stretched arms. Daylight swoops in and replaces the night. They begin again.

CHAPTER 63

Jack is home for the weekend. Sakura feels slightly nervous. In their last conversation, Sakura felt she said too much. Court had just happened, and she was so upset. They meet at the top of the boardwalk.

'Hi.' Jack waves from a distance. Somewhere, long ago, before all events, below her feet their names were etched into the ground. Full tide, the waves washing their initials away. Bringing them back to the sea. Sakura waves back. Jack's clothes fit perfectly. A ring on her index finger. It suits her. Hair just past her ear, pulled into a short ponytail. She still has the student look. The look of someone wanting to change into something they are not quite sure of yet.

Sakura suddenly becomes self-conscious. Becoming aware of the well-worn seven-year-old jeans that still fit her. Jack was with her when she bought them. Her extra effort to wash away the horse smells and to apply a little makeup seems to melt into insignificance. Sakura leans in for a hug Jack offers. The hugs that got her through a death. This one is full of things unsaid, but there is love.

'Your hair is longer, you look lovely.' Jack releases the hug.

Sakura smiles but doesn't believe her compliment. Chris complimented her before. Later he turned them inside out. Ugly hideous parts of Sakura. Parts she wants to cut off.

'Is Sara with Chris?' Jack walks alongside, glancing out to sea.

'She's with Mom.' It's easier not to have to see him. 'Sara is going next weekend. I hate the thought of it. The thought of handing Sara over to him. Everything.' Sakura's words drift off and land on foam buildings with each wave ripple.

But he didn't get full custody, not even near that, she remembered Jack said at the time. Jack reaches for her arm and pulls her in for another hug.

There's a new café Jack wants to try out. They walk past their favourite stores. As children, hours spent picking out earrings. Today they just pass with not even a glance.

Having heard all the evidence and the age of the child, access will remain as is, summer access to be added to order as discussed. Sakura remembers the matter-of-fact voice of the judge. Clear and concise. Cold even. Then something whispered to the clerk.

The judge went on to other minor matters. Sakura zoned out. This was the part that her ears were alert to. She hadn't lost Sara. Sakura knew deep down that she wouldn't. She lost herself. She tries to bring herself back to today. The boardwalk, her best friend, the life she's working towards.

Jack looks at Sakura, trying to reassure her. But she's gone. Back in there. Back in court. She would revisit that room many times again and go over the words. Still shocked at its horror. Seemingly only obvious to her. Jack's voice pulls her back, back from the blindfolded statue holding the scales of justice, through the splintered wooden chairs waiting for licks of paint, to two best friends trying to do what they have always done. The concern in Jack's life right now is the right blend of coffee.

'Thinks it's over here, yes, that's the one, *Café Cocoa*?' Moving closer, Sakura smells her strawberry shower gel. The type that stays on long after the water has left. Today she got a minute in the shower before she dropped Sara off at her mom's.

Jack doesn't get the process of recovering from an abusive relationship and it feels pointless trying to explain it and how devastated she felt by the way she was treated in court. She tells Jack the questions she was asked:

'Do you think you contributed to the conflict?'

'Are you not just oversensitive, with what happened when you were a child?'

'Do you think you provide a stable home for Sara?'

In any day of leisure, this will come for her. The mind can't rest yet. Sakura travels down the wormhole of hell. Chris was abusive and, somehow, they made him sound like the victim. It felt so unfair, unjust.

'You got the result you went in for.' Sakura remembers Jack tried to pull her back to the positives. 'A friend of my roommate in University is a lawyer. She says this is how the legal system is. It's nothing personal.'

That's what Diane Dawson had said, the solicitor her mother paid for, swinging ponytail, clever cross-examination, all in a day's work.

But it was personal, Sakura wanted to scream again at the top of her voice. She didn't then and after court when Chris said it. It would have just added to his legal team's assertion that she wasn't mentally fit. An assertion that has landed alongside Chris's history with her. The nights where she had done nothing wrong but sat, blamed, for everything.

The impact is made smaller by her sessions with her counsellor. Then something else will happen and it will grow and almost take over her whole body. Legal people, who are supposed to be trained, are allowed to dismantle. How can they do this? And she hears the answer again. Everyone has a right to a defence.

'Come on.' Jack opens the door to the new café. Little boats shake. Nautical cushions stacked high in a wooden crate. All this remembering is going on inside. Jack assumed Sakura was comforted by her superficial, third-hand advice from a member of the legal profession her roommate knows. It's all she can do to follow her inside.

'There's a table.' Jack walks ahead, smiling at the waitress. Sakura lowers herself into the seat. Glad someone else is making decisions. Sakura feels like the small wooden table, where they're seated. Unchanged. The marks on the top and along the legs, a natural distressed look. She never left this place and Jack's presence is a sharp reminder of this.

Sakura sees Jack's change in clothes and looks. She's annoyed by her opinions. But then she sees that she is just on another side of a canyon.

Her life has diverged so much, and the experience of two years amounts to decades. Sakura's shell is falling, falling. Her change is deeply layered and doesn't look like much. Her old jeans, scant makeup, and hair needing a trim carry sameness. At times she wants to scream, *what is happening, what is happening to me?* Then at others, a petal floats to the surface, a white form reflecting against the sun, catching subliminal colours only she can see.

'Can't wait to see your new place, how are you? Really?' Jack reaches for the menu, giving Sakura a chance to respond.

'I'm ok.' That word everyone uses. Even her. Sakura pauses for a moment, wondering if that's true. She's ruminated mentally for the entire walk. She's run through court. She's dealt with her annoyance over Jack's opinions and silver lining things that have only just begun to be normal. But you know what? Today, her anxiety is small. It's attaching lightly to every cell of her body, making it possible to do normal things but always prepared that something bad could happen at any moment.

'Haven't seen you in ages, I miss you.' Jack's face gets smaller. Sakura can picture her. Eight years old. Sakura wanting to check out the new boats docked, on their long way home from school. Jack would pull her back. Later after school. Later never came most days.

'I know.' Sakura glances away. She isn't sure if she misses her now. Their time together can go wonderfully. She can feel her life-long friend right there, side by side. Her aloneness vanishes. Then at others, she feels she is being hit by mini stones, they all hurt small at first then big, and everywhere at once. After these encounters, Sakura wants to run and run and never see her again. She misses the old Jack. In that moment she realises that she misses the old Sakura. Before everything – it used to be before her dad died, now it's before Chris and before her dad died. And wonders if there will be any more befores. This thought causes Sakura's anxiety to lurch and choke all her cells at once. *I can't go through any more things that will become another before.*

'Are you ok?' Jack's worried face is all she can see.

'I'm fine, be back in a minute.'

In the restroom, Sakura tries to bring to mind some of the breathing exercises the counsellor spoke about. They seem pointless and her breath seems to be only a reminder of her out-of-control body and mind. Resting her hands apart on the washbasin, Sakura lowers her head and whispers,

'Nothing else is going to happen to you, I promise.' Dad doesn't use this voice. This is her voice. The one of later.

Sitting back down. Sakura talks first.

'I'm ok, I'm still dealing with everything that happened. That is happening.'

'I know, of course, I'm sorry that I'm not always here for you.' Jack's voice cracks a little.

'You are, you have been, as best you can. It's a lot if you haven't lived it.' Sakura jumps in, reaches across and grabs her hand. An act that surprises her. She realizes it's not Jack's fault that she doesn't fully understand what has happened to her. But she knows if she needed her in the middle of the night she would be there.

'It's just that so much has already happened to you, and I just…' Jack can't continue. Her tears fall.

'I'm ok, I'm going to be ok.' Sakura sits up straighter and reaches over to be closer to Jack. The roles have reversed. Sakura now comforting Jack. She just wished it was something to do with Jack herself. Instead, she's comforting Jack because of her.

'You've always been here for me, Jack.' Sakura squeezes her hand for extra effect. 'Remember when you drove to Cedar Bay to collect me to rescue me from that awful date? You had just got your licence and you weren't supposed to be driving on your own.'

Jack smiles. 'You were wearing those high boots and you were trying to run.'

They both laugh. The café seems different. Lighter.

'Come on, let's order, after we can walk over to our house. Can't wait to show you.'

For a moment, Sakura's cells feel free. Movement. And something else enters. It's different. Giddy. Light. She has felt it a few times before in fleeting moments since she left Chris. It feels slightly scary. If she allows it in completely what would happen when fears need to return? Would her whole body just collapse?

Sakura scans her mind. Is there anything she needs to worry about today? Right now? It's a soft no. She allows the giddy, different thing to enter a little but keeps space.

After lunch, Jack and Sakura walk with the ease of old times together, down and across a few streets, and arrive at the house.

'Ah, it's lovely, Sakura. Remember we used to say what would it be like to live right in town? We could go to Tim's all the time?' Jack's body turns sideways, laughing, her hair falling out of the ponytail.

'I know, and now me and Sara are here. You could never imagine things the way they are.' Sakura smiles back and catches Jack's hair tie before it falls as it holds onto its last strands.

Sakura shows Jack around her house, and they sip tea in the yard. Blankets cover their shoulders. The month of May tries to assert itself with bursts of sunshine, but the heavy prints of winter are hard to erase.

Later on, they collect Sara and spend the evening together. Sakura appreciates Jack's attention to Sara, but she doesn't get why certain things don't work with babies. Like that Sara doesn't always sleep through the night or why she seems to scream for no reason.

Little and big boots line the wall inside the front door. Jack lies across their floor, pulling silly faces and pretending to be a train. The red soles of her woolly socks face the backyard, light parts appearing where they've worn thin. Sara loves this and shouts, 'Again, again, again!

Jack leaves before bedtime. Holding Sara in her arms, Jack hugs them both. 'Love you and you.' Jack does one last silly face. Sara laughs. 'You're doing great.' Jack's head turns sideways and she smiles and walks off.

'We are,' Sakura responds in almost a whisper.

CHAPTER 64

The first few access visits from their new house go without incident. The two hours leading up to his arrival to collect Sara, and the two hours waiting for him to drop her home, create a familiar sense of dread. Her body leaves and travels to the land of what-ifs. What if he does this? What if he does that? The release of energy when there isn't any.

Sara arrives into her arms. Sakura brushes away anything that might have arrived with her on her return home. Sara is often tired, upset, and confused. Sakura works hard not to let it chip away and chisel permanent etchings on her heart.

You're not a good mother, she doesn't want to be with you, she wants to be with Chris, the voice of before says, and Sakura sometimes can't fail to listen.

Sessions with her counsellor have helped her unpack this label that was never hers and never is and never will be. During one particular session, Sakura realized that Chris plucked her insecurities, like a hyena plucking the entrails of a lion's fresh kill.

Sakura felt her mom's distance after her dad's death. That apartness, that sense of abandonment. She needed them and they were both gone. To feel that she was not a good mother after all she knew and needed as a child would dismantle the very thing she's holding onto. Her.

Chris moved and slid into Sakura, whispering,

'Come here, I love you. Come here, you are nothing. I will destroy you completely.'

The counsellor spoke about the abuser's own insecurities and that they need to take victims apart because that's what gives them strength. Dark strength.

Evil. Sakura's horror and anger that she just happened to be the person there at that time. Tomorrow there will probably be someone else. They need people to feed on, to fuel their darkness.

It was never about me.

Most Sundays after an access handover, Sakura sits on the floor just inside the front door, Sara on her lap. Bag to one side. One boot on, one off. Her child's tears and hand-hitting frustration will eventually melt into an embrace. Their hearts hear each other's beats.

So long as Sakura is able to stay with this long enough for it to happen. Some days she isn't able to, she breaks too soon. Sara's continuous cries and lashing out are too much. Sakura gets off the floor, cross. Crying Sara follows her into the next room, still hitting out. Sakura shouts at her to stop it.

She doesn't. An hour later they are both on the kitchen floor, both crying, both embracing. Both hear each other's heartbeats. Those evenings Sakura works hard to erase the etching that now rips into her flesh.

You are an awful mother, the voice of before says.

Sara is fast asleep. Sakura paces the house and eventually falls exhausted, whispering, 'You are doing your best. You are a…' The words refuse to come out. Her dried tears form even shapes on her pillow.

It's Friday. Sakura has Sara ready, her bag packed. Waiting. She's always ready too early.

Sakura sits with Sara in the front room, trying to distract and play while having a view of the sidewalk. She sees his pickup arrive. Before she met Chris, she never noticed how many there were on the Island, but now she sees them everywhere. And wonders if every man she sees driving them pretends to be nice and turns out horrible like Chris.

'Come on, Sara. Dad is here.'

Sakura wonders if her daughter notices the insincerity in her voice. Sakura closes the door behind her and walks across the street, to where Chris has parked. She hands the bag without looking. Kissing Sara.

'Bye, bye, see you Sunday.'

'Did you put her wellies in?' Chris asks while lifting Sara into his arms. He seems angry.

'Yes, they're in the bag.' Sakura can feel her hands start to shake. She turns to walk away, still not sure if she needs permission to leave this conversation. Always worried he will take her back to court.

I can't even talk to her. I was just asking her something about Sara and she can't even manage that, she imagines him saying on the stand.

'You didn't the last time.' Chris stands up, having buckled Sara in. 'Did you say something to Tye? Did you talk about me to him?'

Sakura can feel the words at the back of her head and feels she has to turn around. It would be rude if she just walked away and didn't answer. But this is now. Turning around, he has stretched to his full height. Hand pressed against the top of the door. Like he is holding it shut. Sakura's head tries to race through all the conversations she had with Tye. Did she do something wrong?

'I don't know what you're talking about.' Sakura takes a step back.

'Yes, you do, you're lying, you think people are going to believe you?' Chris's face is snarled and crunched. Parts of his knuckles turn white. 'You better be careful what you are going around saying.'

'Are you threatening me?' Sakura is surprised at her own words. Glad she has said nothing so far, that he can't claim she is losing it.

'I'm just saying you better be careful. Telling people lies about me.'

'I have no idea what you're talking about, don't you dare stand there and tell me who I can and can't speak to.'

'Look at you, just trying to talk to you and you losing it again, you're so fucking messed up.' Sakura can see Sara's face underneath his outstretched arm. Her whole being wants to push him aside, open the door, and take her daughter into her arms. She knows she can't. Olivia's words, which lay dormant, rise and arrive. *You don't have to engage with him.*

'Leave and if you ever threaten me again, I will report you to the police.' Sakura turns and crosses over the street, thankful there is no car to pause her leaving.

Chris's shouting continues. 'You won't get away with this.'

His last words as she shuts the front door and quickly locks it from the inside. Holding her left hand over her right to stop it from shaking. She waits there until she hears the roar of his pickup disappear. Sara's face in the window, staring out at her, is the last thing she sees. Why did she rise to his bait?

Sakura stands aimlessly in the kitchen, going over the words in her head. Punching the air, shouting, 'Go fuck yourself, you can't hurt me anymore!' Wondering where she got the words to defend herself. His last line surfaces and plays with her all day long.

You won't get away with this. Ruining her time alone. Time she has planned lots of nice things for her to do. Now she spends her time imagining what will he do. Will Sara be ok? What could he have meant? Spending hours in his head, trying to decipher how dark will his darkness get. Remembering the moment he held Sara as a baby. A gentle hold, a caring hold. To dissuade her from thinking he would ever do her any real physical harm.

Sakura worries about Sara. What is he like with her? His anger. She can't allow herself to go there. She feels she'll be sick. Picking up the phone.

'Hi, it's Sakura, hmmm, I'm sorry to be calling you again, I just need to…' Her voice trails into shame.

'It's ok, what happened?' Olivia's voice calm and empathic.

'Sara just went with Chris, he was so horrible to me, so awful.' Sakura's voice chokes with tears. 'I reacted in front of my daughter.'

'Come on over. I can't really hear you. We can talk about it then.' Olivia gives permission to Sakura to return to her safe place.

Sitting back in the familiar chair, once strange and unknown. Now a place she knows where her panic will start to gently fall back. A place where she feels held, heard, understood. A place for her.

'He just started. I was so unprepared for it.'

'It's ok, you're safe now.' Olivia places her tea on the table. She doesn't even ask now. She just makes it for her and brings it in.

'I felt I couldn't walk away until he did. Now I'm angry at myself for not walking away sooner. Why did I feel I had to stand there and wait for him to threaten me on the sidewalk?'

Olivia sits up, her hand reaches out in front of her. Sakura notices she looks lovely but is too distraught to pass comment.

'Please don't blame yourself. You did walk away again. You did stand up for yourself. You said you were going to call the police if he did it again.'

'Will it always be like this? Will I always have to be prepared for what he might say or do? And what did he mean when he said, I was not going to get away with this?'

Sakura's pacing slows a little. Picking up the tea. Glad for the warmth in her hand. Sipping a little, she feels herself sinking into the chair. The hours and hours of her life trying to recover from Chris.

'I don't know what he meant by that.' Olivia presses her fingers together. She doesn't show tiredness at repeating all these words to all these women. 'What I will tell you is that men like Chris threaten, intimidate, most of it is just talk. Still, women are hurt and murdered by abusive partners. I would suggest going to the police and reporting it anyway. It'll be logged and, if he does it again, you can take court action to protect yourself.'

'No, no.' Sakura is surprised at her own force. 'I've already been in court, and remember what they said about me?'

'Okay, think about it, know you can always go to the police. From what you have told me about Chris, and from what I know about you, he seems too keen on trying to destroy you psychologically and emotionally. Maybe he will try to slander you and disrupt your relationship with Tye. You mentioned that you have a good working relationship.'

'Yes, Tye has been there for me, I don't want to drag him into all of this. He's already found a new supplier. My job is the one thing… what if he destroys that?' Sakura feels she has left her body, arches then throws her head back. It hits the rear of the chair a little harder than she'd expected. Invisible attacks sink into her flesh, no one can see that's she bleeding out. It's all on the inside.

But Olivia sees. She leans forward and tries to pull Sakura out mid-spiral.

'You could spend hours thinking about what he meant by his sentence. And that's what he wants. Your time without Sara is spent thinking about him. You said earlier, you wondered why you felt you had to stand there and wait for him to threaten you. Maybe next time you walk away before he gets the chance. All you have to do is hand Sara over safely. You can leave. And not engage at all.'

'You mean not speak at all?' Sakura sits up in the chair very tall. 'What would he do?'

'It doesn't matter what he does. What matters is what you do.'

Sakura lets the words *what I do* dance and float. For the first time, she realizes that she can choose what to do, to speak or not to speak, and to whom she speaks. Even if she thinks it's rude not to speak. Even to an abuser.

'I never imagined I had a choice. It feels scary and powerful to imagine this. Thanks, Olivia, for your support, for all of your support.' Sakura's body leaves the panicked stage and moves into an unfamiliar space. She moves her arm to make sure it's still there.

'No need, that's what we're here for.' Olivia looks pleased Sakura is well again.

'I know, but you do way more. Thanks.'

'You're welcome. Go off. Enjoy some you time.' Olivia reaches for her empty cup and presses her other hand into the side to help herself up out of the chair.

'Thanks, I'll try.' Walking down the steps, the potential freedom, if she chooses to take it, feels lighter, lighter than air. And terrifying.

The next day, Sakura sits in her usual spot. The minutes seem to crawl like sloths. No hurry. Then she hears it before she sees it. His pickup. *I can choose. I can choose. I can choose.* Whispering to herself out the door. Standing on the sidewalk closest to her house. He parked on her side today. She waits. Her arms are lost. She folds them. She can see his rear and back as he is unbuckling Sara from her safety harness. Walking the few steps closer to them.

'Hello, Sara.' Sakura unfolds her arms, smiles exaggeratedly, and looks straight at her daughter.

Sara wriggles and makes her way to her mother. Sakura reaches as far as needed but she can still smell his smell. She manages to lift Sakura without making any physical contact. His smell lingers and infects her being. Missing that which was once so familiar, so hers. Now frightening and necessarily distant.

Chris mumbles something about her clothes in the bag. His head turned, sensing his anger without any visual.

Sakura simply responds, 'Right.'

Turns and walks straight inside. Her legs heavy and woozy. She has to tell them to move quicker.

Behind the door, she whispers to Sara, 'I did it.' Sakura's heart beating fast, elated at this small triumph, and then deflated that this seems like a win at all.

I can choose what words, how many, maybe none. I can choose. As though she has discovered this secret weapon. She holds.

CHAPTER 65

Sara is settled. Bedtime was easy this evening. A gentle flow between times. Bath, ducks squirting water. Storytime. Sakura making funny noises. Cuddles and Sara slips off to sleep. Sakura feels at ease and realizes the best bedtimes with Sara are always when Sakura herself is not being dismantled by stress outside herself. Immediately she is pulled towards guilt, a magnetic force, for all the times bedtime doesn't go well. For all the times it's uneasy.

No! Sakura shouts to herself, *don't go there, you are doing your best.*

Sakura has been thinking about it for a while. She sits down and pulls out her laptop. Her mom had given it to her the year she finished school. Before she met Chris. Her mom's not-so-subtle way of saying then: University. It's worn on the sides and a bit battered looking. But it still works. She types *equine University courses* in the search engine, can feel her heart rise and the flutters travel everywhere. *We're just looking,* she reminds herself.

Since she has gone back to working in Tye's, Sakura realizes this is her place. Her passion. Now unbridled. There was fantasy talk with Chris about her going back to University after Sara was born.

'Of course, I'll support you.' Sakura remembers his body turning away from her, pretending to load the dishwasher, as he finished the conversation with, 'Once I can organize work, and we get help with childcare.'

She probably knew then that he would never organize work and she would have to sort out childcare. But in that moment, she stayed in the false hope of empty promises. It didn't happen. She realizes if she had stayed it never would.

Sakura suddenly realizes that all her pain, her decision to leave, is giving rise to a long-hidden Sakura. Making space for her own identity. Excitement replaces the flutters.

'You can do anything,' she whispers, smiling. 'Okay, one thing at a time.'

Then she lets out a loud laugh at herself, scrolling through the course choices. Her time spent working with Tye has focused her search. Initially, she had thought of Equine Science. Then what she wants catches her eye: *Two-Year Certified Equine Therapy Programme*.

Reading through the modules, she loves them all, especially the energy balancing technique. Sakura has noticed the last few weeks Tye has returned to asking her to work with the newer horses that arrive. They're often giddy, and unpredictable. Instinctively, she can feel their grief, their hurt, and seems to know what to do. At times Sakura feels silly, *What would I know*? Waiting for Tye to leave so she can be alone with the horse.

Tye has shown his surprise when, sometime later, Sakura returns from the edge of the woods with a horse that didn't want to saddle up. 'I knew you could do it. But not so quickly.'

The way he puts things makes her feel at ease. He doesn't draw attention to her skill and doesn't detract from it. He sees her as trustworthy and capable. Things she is only learning she is herself.

The cost. Sakura scrolls down quickly. She sinks back. It's expensive. Too expensive for her. Sitting back up, checking the date for applications, maybe it's already too late. June 30th. Two weeks. She still has time. Her head is circling options. How can I get the money to do it? The course includes face-to-face lectures, one weekend day a month in University. She would need her mom's help with Sara.

Broken sleep, dreaming of horses running. Then Sakura is trying to catch up. Then she jumps to a class. The lecturer asks her who she is and why she's here. Waking up, her neck and in between her breasts pooled in perspiration.

The following day, she's off. Pushing Sara in her stroller, they walk towards the shelter. Olivia might be able to offer her some direction. Sakura can see Sara's chubby little legs, moving up and down, hitting the footrest. Her purple-dotted shorts show her dimpled knees. Her sun hat is still on. It's early and the sun is already announcing its big arrival. Sakura feels it in her throat. This little person and she is fully responsible. She has lived in survival mode, she just didn't see it. The looking forward triggers the same trauma she's lived with since the pier. A terrifying beautiful weight. But then, at times, it feels like a world of prospects, a time of her own choosing, makes her so light like she could twirl it on her index finger, a circus clown. The leaden feeling returns in nightmares, in moments of panic. The fear feels so heavy, it doubles her over, hands and knees on the floor. She feels she can't get up.

She has to move forward. Instinctively, Sakura reaches down while pushing the stroller and gently rubs Sara's cheek. Sara turns and half looks up. They both smile.

'I'm sorry, I'm sorry for everything,' she whispers to herself, to Sara, and to all of her past. It's time to plan and make a future that they deserve. Arriving at the door, the bell she first pressed. Terrified. Now one of comfort and safety.

'How lovely to see you both.' Olivia's face is round and full of recognition for theirs. The sun sneaks in and dances dazzling lights in the hallway, gone once the door is closed. Sakura is delighted that her visit here today for once has nothing to do with Chris. It is for her. Her only. 'Look at you, gorgeous girl, getting so big.' Big smiles at Sara's level.

Sakura explains that she's looking for information about financial support for University.

'I've seen this course I think I would really like.'

'Ah that's wonderful, Sakura, I knew by your face that you were here for different reasons. You appeared lighter walking in!'

Sara stays with them while they chat. No tears today. They go through all the options.

'There's a fund supported by the Provincial Government to access University. We can look into that.' Olivia reaches for her phone to find the contact numbers. 'And I think there might be support available from the WF, the Women's Foundation.'

They would all amount to some help. She would have to get the rest. Before she goes, she uses the printer. Holding her application, Sakura feels she's holding a ticket. The ticket she bought. Her lifeboat, which she captains. The light twirling on her own index finger sensation.

'Come on, Sara, let's do something fun.' They walk through the streets and follow the sidewalk toward the Yacht Club. 'Look at all the boats.' Sara sits up, pointing, trying to repeat her mom's words.

Everywhere else is still gently waking. Down here life is busy. Releasing ropes. Navigating their way out of the harbour towards the sea. Baseball hats and life jackets reflect against the sun. The rise of ache from her feet stops at her heart. Even before her head has even thought of him. He's there, her dad. Pushing it down, *not today*.

Sakura forces the ache down back through her feet, down through the earth and into the sea. Allowing one thought. I would love to tell him about this course. He would be excited.

They continue walking and stop at a bench. Letting Sara out, her walking coming into its own in the last few weeks. She runs, chasing the birds. Although she's walking for a while, running is more uncertain. Wobbly. Sakura is close behind. Even though the edge of the water is at least ten feet away. She knows those little legs can go fast, a speed that surprises Sakura.

Afterwards, they walk over to a new coffee shop that has opened close to the harbour. Its blue and nautical theme is fresh and not overdone. Lifting Sara out, the young girls help with the highchair. Ordering croissants and coffee, Sakura takes the first sip and lets the smell hit her as she catches a glimpse of the sea from the corner of the window.

Sara pulling chunks. Looking at her face, her hair past her ear. Different lengths, not quite long enough to tie up, she has tried only to see, a few seconds later, Sara's hair standing on end. The electricity giving rise. Laughing, Sara joins in. Sakura wishes she could capture her changing features. It's only when she looks at pictures, she sees how small she was at one, two, and twelve months old. Then she thinks of how she was, and Chris, and she can't look anymore. Sakura knows that, as she takes her phone to capture this moment, she will look back one day and every year after that when her phone reminds her, and realize how small she is now. Sakura will berate herself for having unrealistic expectations of a child. But so much is up to her now and it's hard to see straight.

These are the moments when she can relax and just be with her daughter, having fun, making memories.

They finish and the white table is covered in flaky pastry. Sakura tries to gather it into one pile. But it refuses to conform, drifting back to where it wants. Lifting Sara into her arms, Sakura wipes her face and pushes their noses together. Then moves her back with big eyes, exaggerated moves, then back in touching her nose again. Sara giggles and her soft small hands reach for Sakura's face.

CHAPTER 66

Having completed the application, Sakura brings it to work. She needs a reference. Feeling nervous, but not sure why. This is a good thing. Maybe he'll think she'll want to leave. Shushing her thoughts. She sees him across the yard. He turns and waves.

'Hi.' Sakura waves back. She never really looked properly at Tye before. She was only a kid when she started, and he seemed to be very grown-up. Not loud but quietly always there. Walking towards him, she asks, 'Do you have a minute?' She tries to hide the envelope behind her back.

Suddenly, Tye looks huge in the yard. She hates having to ask for something again. From him. Tye finishes tightening the girth on top of the saddle.

'Yeah, sure.' He looks up and, for a moment, Sakura sees his eyes. Piercing. He has been here the whole time. Kind. Too much. She looks away. 'Let's go inside.'

They walk towards his makeshift office. More like a large stable, with chairs and a dusty table. Sakura has probably only sat down once in this room. It feels too strange. She keeps standing.

'I'd like to talk to you about something.' She pauses and then continues. 'I'm thinking about going back to University, to do a course about horses.' Sakura finally looks up. He's smiling,

'That's awesome. Here, take a seat.' Tye pulls the chair out and tries to dust it down with his dusty hand. 'Where are you thinking of going?'

'It's in Bordon, the *Certified Equine Therapy Program*.' Sakura sits up on the edge of the chair, not fully committing to a long conversation. 'It's a two-year course, Tye.'

'Ah, I've heard good things about that course.' Tye sits opposite Sakura, the desk between them.

'I was hoping you could write me a reference?' Sakura pulls open the envelope.

'Yes, of course, whatever you need.' Tye is eager to talk. He never sits in a chair unless it's for lunch or damn paperwork. 'If you don't mind me asking, have you your funds organized? I know those courses can be costly.' Tye wants to help, looking at her, then moving his eyes away around the small office. Lifting his grimy hands, he places them on the dusty table.

'I have some of it sorted. Thinking of taking out a loan for the rest.' Sakura looks down at her boots, then back up.

'I'll give it to you.' Tye looks straight at her.

'No, I couldn't, you've done enough already.' Sakura's body starts to squirm.

'Look, Sakura, I've seen you with the horses. You're able to connect with them. Especially those who are in pain for whatever reason. How about this, I fund the balance of what you don't have sorted. And I can take it off your wages an hour a week, it's two years, right?'

'That wouldn't cover it,' Sakura interrupts him.

'Sakura, you're already helping with other horses, this course will help me also. You have something special. You need to explore this.' Tye is tilting almost on top of the table now. His hand moves back and forth over the table. Disturbing dust with each stroke. 'If I'm honest, I thought you would have left before now, moved onto a bigger place. But I know that you…' His voice trails off, he looks down. 'That you've had a tough year.'

Sakura hangs on the word 'special.' Her. Special. She has felt unworthy for so long. Even Chris used to put down her work here at Tye's stables. She knew she could connect to the horses but was afraid that people would see it was because of her own brokenness.

'That's settled. I'll write a cheque. When do you need it for?'

'Once I'm accepted, I only have to put a deposit with the application.'

'Do you need that?' Tye looks down, fumbling with papers on his desk.

'No, no, I have that covered.'

She doesn't, but it's only 100 dollars. The arrival of maintenance will cover what she doesn't have.

'That's fine. I'll have the reference ready by end of the week, if that's okay.' Tye pushes his lips together and nods.

'That's great, thank you, thank you.' Closing the door behind her, she jumps and whispers, 'Yes!' punching the air with her right hand.

Sakura runs to the stables and takes out Snowy first. Always waiting patiently for her, Snowy knows Sakura. He sets a knowing pace. Afterwards, Sakura washes him down and lets him cool off. Sakura moves into the far stable and takes out a horse she has been working with. He's new and giddy. Sakura feels their energies match. They travel down the track and decide its time to venture near the water.

'It's okay, you got this,' she reassures the horse as his feet seep into the sand.

They canter along the edge, gently lapping waves kissing hooves, spray, and foam left behind. Today, Sakura feels the full expanse of the sea. Endless possibilities.

CHAPTER 67

Sakura has the weekend to herself. Sara is with Chris. Things feel calm. Having spent the morning tidying up, she decides to take the longer trail route through her forest. Hers since the shelter, after counselling sessions. Her place. Big enough to take all her thoughts, her pain, her ideas, her now emerging joy.

Short pants, a top, and a light sweater, the summer sun sneaks through the tall trees and its light creates shards along her path. Legs losing their winter pale colour. Hair pulled back, covered by a baseball hat. A small bag. Water and snacks. Today Sakura is just here. Seeing the colours, the crackle of the branches, and the crunch of the leaves under her feet.

The birds fill the forest, their own music, a private call only they understand.

Afterwards, she passes the road near her mom's and decides to call in. She would normally ring or text. A boundary she has put in place. Thankfully her mom accepted with ease.

But today she doesn't let her know in advance. Driving up towards the house, she sees it. The big, black pickup.

It can't be. Sakura's breath gets fast. Her mouth dry. The summer sun feels extra sticky. What is he doing here? Her head goes to the darkest place. Are they working together to take Sara away from her?

She doesn't want to go in, but she can't just leave. She tries to turn her car. Her panic making her moves jumpy. Missing the in-park slot. The car conks out.

'Fuck it!' she shouts, angrily starting it back up. Then she hears the front door open. Chris walks out, Sara in his arms. Her mom smiling, waving, handing him what looks like leftover food. Sakura pulls the car up on the sidewalk and pretends to be looking for something. She waits to hear the roar of his pickup leave. How could she do this? Getting out, she walks quickly up to the front door. Her mom answers the knock.

'Hi Sakura, what are you doing here? Didn't think you were coming today.' Her face looks caught out.

'What was he doing here?' Praying there is some practical explanation.

'Come on inside.' Mom is non-committal, moving away from the door.

'Just tell me, tell me what he was doing here?' Sakura follows her mom in, the forest walk leaving a trail behind.

'Sit down, I'll make you a cuppa.' Mom moves towards the sink and starts to fill the kettle.

'I don't want tea.' Sakura feeling her face redden. Tears just waiting. 'Has he been here before, is this a regular thing?' Sakura's mouth opens, then closes, afraid she might vomit.

'He asked if he could call in today. I feel he's lonely and maybe not managing on his own when he has Sara. They had lunch. Sara played outside for a while, and they left. It's not a big deal.'

Mom stands beside the kettle, its sound getting louder. She looks smaller, her shoulders hunched, trying to hide her shame.

Sakura's blood runs cold.

'Not a big deal, are you kidding me? How could you do this to me? After everything, everything he did to me.'

'It just seemed like…' Her mom doesn't get to finish. Sakura cuts her off.

'This is why there are access dates and things in place, Mom. For my sake. I don't believe this, so all that talk of *I'm here for you*, was all bullshit?'

Sakura feels her whole body slip away. Holding onto the workshop to feel something. Something solid. Real.

'Sakura please calm down, there…'

'Don't you dare tell me to calm down! I walk here to my mum, my family house, to say hello. You're here with my abusive ex and my daughter.' Sakura suddenly feels all alone, quickly running through the people she can trust, Olivia, the counsellor, maybe Tye. So few and no one she loves and has history with. 'How many times, is this a regular thing?'

All this time, God. Her feet feel like ice, slipping, stuck, sinking deeper. Frozen.

'It's only been two or three times. I just felt bad for him, I guess. He has no one and Sara is my granddaughter, I never meant to hurt you.'

Her mom flips the button off on the kettle and moves to the table and sits down, her face paler.

'He has no one? He doesn't deserve anyone. Do you remember? I fled with my daughter and stayed in a shelter. I thought you were *my* mom, I'm such a fool.'

Sakura feels the weight of her mother's betrayal. All her earlier hope mushed into lead. Holding her down.

'Please, Sakura, I am your mom. I think breakups are difficult on everyone.'

Mom looks like a stranger. Her words alien. Who is this person? Sakura thinks she might hate her.

'Breakups are difficult on everyone. Oh God, I can't even talk to you anymore. You just don't get it.' Sakura throws her hand in the air and turns around. 'Maybe you don't want to get it. Maybe you don't believe me. You know, I don't give a fuck. I have people, people in the shelter, who get it and believe me.'

Sakura continues walking towards the front door.

'I do believe you, please don't go.'

'You can't believe me and allow him in your home at the same time. If you really trusted in me, you wouldn't ever let him cross that threshold. You don't see what he's doing, how he's manipulating you. You allowed him into my world, the home I grew up in.'

'I thought I was helping!' Mom bleats out. 'He is Sara's father after all.'

'Oh God, don't I know that?' Sakura turns to show her anger, show her face, use her voice. 'And because of that, you should be there for me and your granddaughter. Instead, you invite the monster in for tea.'

Her hand is on the screen door, half open, ready to leave, to get away.

'Let's come back inside and calm down.'

Her mom waves her hand toward the hallway.

Sakura ignores her gesture.

'Tell me, why did you keep it from me? Why hide it?'

Sakura's questions cause her mother's head to bow. She waits for an answer she doesn't get.

'You know what, it doesn't even matter. I know this is your house and who you invite in is your choice. But let me be clear – if you have him here, you will not have me or Sara in your life. Ever. I wanted to die many times because of what he did to me. Now I'm just starting to see some hope, and choosing to live, and whatever this is,' Sakura moves her hands in big circles, 'will have no part in my life.'

'Please come back, please don't go.' Mom follows her out.

But Sakura keeps walking. Getting into her car, she turns the engine on and drives away from her childhood home.

Arriving back at her house, Sakura runs in. Afraid she will break off in little bits if she lets herself go in the street.

The door just shuts. Her boots drop muck and scatter at her feet. I was having such a nice day. Fuck.

She lets out an anguished cry. 'Why all this? Why can't she just be my mother? I have no one.' She's falling sideways on the floor, the tears turn smaller, resigned pain. Resigned.

Sometime later, Sakura takes herself off the floor. Like a puppet, one limb at a time. Still, the muck lies there. She'll have to clean it up at some point. The release leaves her feeling heavy. So heavy. Chains shackle her heart and the links spread to every part.

I could have just not called, and I wouldn't know. I would still be happy right now, enjoying the afterglow of my walk.

A voice adds gently, *You would have found out at some point. The pain would have been the same. Worse because it would have gone on for longer.*

She drags herself around life that weekend. Calls from her mom go unanswered. Clears them from her phone. She doesn't have to see the red reminder of what she missed, what she is missing.

Mom comes to the door, knocks on it several times, even tries speaking through it. Her voice full of urgency. What is happening to her daughter? Sakura lies still on the floor, watching the pine knots. Knotted in pain. Crying without end.

What is happening is her daughter is falling apart, betrayed by the woman who gave her life. Sara is the only thing that keeps Sakura going.

Sara arrives home on Sunday. Sakura doesn't even look at Chris. Not wanting to know if he sees her face, smacked red with betrayal. Him at the centre. Not wanting to see his sneer. She might die on the spot in a twisted form. Quick, get safely inside.

She places Sara and her small bag down. Her heart beats fast. The move from pain to anxiety. A frequent dance. Neither one brings joy. She just wants someone to talk to. The days after Dad died she remembers walking to Jack's house and Mina being told to let them talk in the bedroom. That's what she wants. But she needs to talk now, not just eat *Timbars* and go for walks. She needs the best friend in an equal and adult-to-adult relationship.

Sakura is never sure when Jack will get it. She just doesn't know. She thinks of the laughter she and Chris shared at the few social events they were at together, and that weekend she stayed. She thinks of how Chris slagged her off once the door was shut. Also, Jack likes Sakura's mom, and could think she was just trying to help. And despite all that Chris has done or not done, people, including Jack, don't fully understand coercive control. No wonder Eli steers clear of the Island. He's not coming home to the mess and the emotional mayhem. He's still damaged from the death of his father. Now he has to avoid a mother who still tries to turn everything into happy. A sister who has been abused. A niece he doesn't know.

He never came to put up the swing. The intention is there, with them all, to make it okay. But they think that involves doing the things that make Sakura unsafe. Still this message of *Sure, do it for the child. Can you not put your feelings aside for the sake of the child?* runs under everything. Jack might be appalled at Mom, or she might just try to explain it with her third party advice. A friend of a roommate had a mother who tried to ignore realities and make everything happy once and managed it with Friday pizza and cakes, and lemonade. Those things that made Mom her mom won't work on Chris and make him support her daughter. She paid the lawyer fees to help Sakura. But she still can't absorb the evidence.

Her world of Ikigai, best friends in Japan, husbands in graves and sons absent with full leave, with daughters in supported accommodation and granddaughters seeing fathers who were lukewarm even in the days they shared a roof, it's all too much.

Sakura can hear Jack, *Your mom meant no harm.*

She just can't risk it, she's too vulnerable. And can't defend herself against someone else, someone who is supposed to understand. It's also Sakura's inability to know who she can really trust, including herself, and how to recover when people don't understand.

Every time she thinks she has turned a corner; the corner presents for turning. These are her feelings. They will change. But when?

She will have someone to talk to on Tuesday at ten o'clock. Sakura counts the hours.

Arriving outside the door of her therapist's room. She's nearly there. Someone will hear her, hold her in her pain. Understand. She thought about calling Jack all weekend. But still afraid she would sense gentle words of justification for her mother's actions. Sakura doesn't want to see both sides. She wants someone, anyone, to see her side. To see her.

Her session is everything she expected it would be. This time someone is here to validate her experience of utter betrayal and abandonment. *That must have been so awful for you.* The therapist's line reaches across and delicately holds Sakura's pain. The line gives full permission for Sakura to fold further into grief. When she arises out of the fold, they talk and go through every detail. Anger at her mom's justification of her actions. Sakura realizes that her experience of what happened is real and all her feelings are real. Her sense of betrayal is real.

While that carries its own loneliness, being heard and validated creates a fine thread of silken strength, holds fast through all threats. Over time this will grow so strong, that nothing can break its hold.

Then they move gently into the space of what is. Her dad dying when she was just a girl. Her mom's way of coping. *We need to let go and move on.* The line her mom said years ago after she ran out of Ms. Macleod's class. The line that stood a foot in front of her, chastising her every tear that followed. Sakura was doing grief wrong. Everyone else was getting on with it. Why couldn't she? The therapist gently moves back to the incident of Saturday. Her mom inviting Chris in. Just then Sakura sees it. So much so her back jolts to an upright position, a gesture that surprises Sakura.

She's doing the same thing. It's not happening. Chris isn't abusive. Let's all get on with it and pretend this is not real.

The therapist holds the moment of clarity.

Sakura sees this and for a moment she has entered into the world where only they speak this secret language. They speak the truth. Immediately Sakura sees her whole life rotate and, from this standpoint, it looks very different. Sakura's thoughts are running. Grabbing the large invisible jigsaw pieces, she puts them in place.

Maybe it's not that her mom doesn't believe her. It's that she can't believe her own mind.

She didn't believe that Dad was dead. Now she doesn't believe her daughter is really being abused. She can pretend none of this is real.

It's all to do with her. It's all to do with the world she has painted for herself, where everything can be fixed.

But she's trying to fix it in the wrong place, with Chris, for Sara. Not because of and for Sakura. She paid for a lawyer and gained trust. But she can't believe the worst truth. Her daughter was being hurt. Her daughter was being dismantled. Her daughter needed someone to notice how far this was going and how far back the vulnerability ran and began.

Sakura's body feels so light that she has to pull it down. Afraid she might float off. No longer a mouse running, hiding. Waiting to be caught. They are the ones that are terrified. The therapist gently brings her back to the room. And they stay long enough for the sadness to surface.

She didn't just lose her dad on the pier. She lost her mom as well. She lost her brother Eli too. Sakura has been an orphan since that day.

Walking out, Sakura holds this knowledge like another dimension. Creates space between what's really happening and the old mantra: *There's something wrong with you.* At times Sakura will hold this with such certainty and will feel like Sedna, the Goddess of the Sea. At others, she will collapse into the spinning darkness. Holding on to the self-spun Rihendi thread. The one that will let her find her way to light again, with the evidence of events, the strength of her own initiative, and the depth of her own mother love.

CHAPTER 68

The letter arrives. Sakura holds it, feeling its content. Guessing its words and travelling off to where her life would go. Where it would bring her. Pulling herself back, Sakura rips the lip of the envelope and reads the important line,

You are accepted onto the 2-year Certified Equine Therapy Programme.

Starting in the fall. A list of books and things to do. Accept the course place. Sakura moves back and forth, kissing the letter. Allowing the smile to spread all over. Her toes are dancing. Lifting up Sara who has walked over.

'Look, Mama is going to University, your mama is going to do things that make you proud.'

Sara tries to take the letter out of her hand and starts putting the part she can reach into her mouth.

'Oh no, we need to keep this, this is important. Come on, let's go celebrate.' The possibility of what could become enlarges Sakura's day. Everything looks bigger. Different.

The first call is to Tye.

'Hi, it's Sakura.'

'Oh hi. How are you?' Tye's voice sounds pleased.

'Just wanted to tell you I got accepted onto the course.' Sakura's smile travels.

'Congrats, I'm delighted for you, you'll do great.' Short on words, high on support.

'Thank you. Just thought you'd be happy to know, and your reference really helped.' *Everything you have done for me has helped.* She can't say that part, the part he already knows.

'It was nothing really, just the truth. Actually, that couple from Breggs have asked for you to work with their horses,' he ventures.

'Really? Can't believe that, no, sure, how I can help?' Sakura goes quieter, to listen. 'Are you sure I can take that on, Tye?' She pulls her talent down. A habit that will be hard to shift.

'You know you can help, we'll talk about it next week.' Tye says it like it is. 'And I'll have that cheque ready for you in the morning.'

'Okay, thanks.' Sakura goes quiet, hating this part, owing somebody. 'Talk then.' She ends the call, relieved the end part was brief.

Other realities set in. She won't get to tell her mom about the course. Or to ask her for help to mind Sakura when she has to be at lectures. It's been a month since what happened and apart from a few texts she hasn't been in contact with her.

Guilt-consumed, Mom misses Sara and wants to see her. Sakura can't allow any of it yet.

The next session with her counsellor will be later this week. It'll help her examine this and figure out something that keeps Sakura's boundaries in place. She hasn't told Jack either. Not wanting to tell her she applied at all in case she wasn't accepted. Not wanting to discuss why she and Mom aren't seeing each other for now. It may be that her mom has already told Jack. But it's not likely. Mom won't want to intrude anymore. She'd be putting too much at risk.

Another reason Sakura holds back is it seems a lot smaller and less of a big deal compared to Jack's degree and continuation into the Postgraduate course in the fall.

She'd tell her the next time they see each other or talk. Not big enough for a specific call. Sakura shrivels her excitement. Still, a little smile sneaks back up. She looks in the mirror, the one where she's beginning to like the woman looking back, and states, 'It's a big deal to me.'

CHAPTER 69

July. The sun is out early, meeting the blue fully melted water, the not-long-ago frozen mountains. Sakura takes her backpack down and fills it with towels and sunscreen. Sara follows and empties the contents while Sakura slips out to the yard to retrieve her spotted play shovel and watering can.

'You helping Mama?' she asks, smiling at the little girl, bigger now. Wearing a princess swimsuit, her diaper tags sneak out the sides.

Sara wants to play with a watering can. Some persuasion and a dried fruit bar later, Sakura buckles her into the car seat and they travel along the coast road to a smaller beach. Pulling in at a coffee hut alongside the road.

'Why not? Today is a special day.' Sakura jumps out. 'I'll be back in a minute.' Waving and making funny faces. Sara responds every time. Wide-open smile, revealing bits of the nearly eaten bar on her teeth that have emerged. Sakura loves that she doesn't care.

Fresh cinnamon roll and coffee in hand, they continue their journey. Sakura puts on the radio. She can't believe it when one of her favourite songs is playing: *Anything is Possible* by Dante Bowe. It's the local Christian radio. Sakura loves the songs but not the talk around them. God to her is her little self-whispering *I love you. We got this*. It's not something external. It's internal, that, when heard, makes the external massive.

Sakura moves and sings along, shouting out the lyrics.

'We've already won, Sara, you hear that?' Rolling down the window, Sakura stretches out her arm fully, whispering, 'Anything is possible.'

They find a spot close to the steps down. Lifting Sara, she manages the bag and all the toys. Sara throws a few more things in. Sakura fast forwards and thinks of the steps back up afterwards.

'We'll manage it,' she whispers to herself.

Shaking the picnic blanket, Sakura lets it land and they dive into the centre, giggling. Sara moves quickly off the blanket with her bucket and spade. Together they make little lopsided sandcastles and collect water from the waves nearby. Back and forth.

Then she lifts Sara up and they walk into the water. It reaches above Sakura's knees, and she lowers Sara in. Little legs kicking furiously, Sakura can feel it under the water. Her little face a mixture of shock and delight. Sakura's wide beaming face.

This is beautiful. You are beautiful. She can feel Sara pulling, trying to unravel the hold and release her into the water fully. *I can't let you go*. Sakura distracts her with swooping moves back and forth.

Sara giggles. Her dark hair is wet, her eyes seeing everything, fully trusting the person holding her.

They walk back to shallow water, where Sara can sit, and her legs let the sand and water seep in between her toes. Sakura allows the grains to run through her hands. Digging back in deep to reach more cold beneath layers. They stay here until they tire themselves out.

Returning to the blanket, Sakura takes out the snacks which they eat with bits of sand. One more dip into the blue and then they rinse off under the cool tap and move to the part no one likes. Sakura peels off Sara's swimsuit and diaper, now full like a balloon, wobbling her walk.

Then she runs off laughing, free, naked. Sakura catches her and wraps the large towel around her, revealing only her face. A little later, Sara dressed, Sakura puts on her own clothes while trying to stop Sara from running fully clothed back into the water. Back up the steps, bag heavier now.

They travel home. These are the moments she has fought for.

Sara's head is tilted to one side, held by her car seat. Asleep. Her chubby hand holding the side. Seeing this in the car mirror, Sakura melts into tears she can't explain.

Supper later outside, the kitchen and the yard become one. Afterwards, they lie in the hammock together. Sakura pretending to swing too far and let Sara fall out is met with loud, and giggling smiles. The pace slows and Sara eventually rests her head on Sakura's chest.

They both fall asleep. Held in a hammock cocoon.

Chapter 70

It didn't arrive the day it was supposed to. There are twenty dollars in her bank account. She has so little gas left and not enough food in. It isn't the first time it's happened either.

Since the court order was put in place, Chris is to pay maintenance every Monday. While she is looking at her bank account on her phone, Sara is running up to her, trying to pull her down to the floor to play.

'Not now, Mama has something she needs to do.' Sakura feels her hands shaking, and anger and fear arrive simultaneously, whispering, 'Fucking bastard, what am I going to do? What if it doesn't arrive tomorrow?' Then Sakura takes that perilous sordid journey into his head. *He knows what he's doing. He's doing it on purpose. He doesn't even care about Sara. He just wants to hurt me.* Pulling her head out of the sewer, she goes through the list of people she could ask for help. No is the answer she arrives at each time. Then she thinks about the shelter. *No, they*'ve *done too much already. I can't.* Sakura feels helpless. Feels she can't even ask the people she should ask for help.

She'll wait until tomorrow and, if it doesn't arrive then, Sakura will contact her lawyer. But how will she pay her? That was once off, her mom helping. If it doesn't arrive tomorrow, she won't have enough gas to drive home from work. Pulling herself back from panic. It will, trying to reassure herself but not really believing it.

Sakura stands up and looks through her cupboards, pulling things out from the back. They'll make do. These moments, strangely, allow her to surrender after the initial panic. Mentally listing what they do have: a roof over their head, clothes, water, some food. It allows her creativity to come out. They didn't need to travel to the play centre today as they had planned. Today this will be their play centre. Canned food, noodles, and brownie mix. Reaching down to Sara.

'I'm sorry, I know you wanted to show me something earlier, Mama was distracted. I'm here now. Look what I've found.' Handing the packet to Sara. 'Let's bake some brownies.'

They add the little ingredients required to make the brownies, they're missing vanilla essence, but it's just them. No one will notice. Sara loves standing on a chair, mixing and sticking her fingers in. Helping her with one hand, Sakura pours the mixture into the cases, most of it dribbling over the sides. Once they're cooked, the smell of baking immediately gives Sakura a sense of home.

Sara doesn't understand that they have to cool. Sakura tries to show her by pushing her lips together.

'Look, Sara, blow, this will cool them down.'

Not convinced, Sara still tries to reach in. They decide to bring them outside and let them cool under the morning sun. Full of promise but not yet delivered. Sara is distracted by a bug she spots. Then, all at once, they're cool. They sit at their table and share.

Sara with her beaker cup. Sakura's steaming coffee. Grateful she has some in and enough milk to add.

The following morning, Sakura's panic resumes. Dropping Sara to childcare, kissing her goodbye, thankful they provide her food while she's there. Calculating that she will make it out to Tye's but not back. There's a gas station at the junction beyond the stables.

Her morning is filled with increased anxiety, wondering how she'll explain this. An idea pops into her head. I'll tell him I forgot my wallet and I can ask him to spot me twenty dollars until tomorrow.

This reasonable excuse calms Sakura a little but not fully. She always has a sense that Tye knows a lot more than he lets on. As though he can read between the words.

Lunchtime arrives, Sakura eats a defrosted bagel she retrieved from the freezer earlier this morning, layered with peanut butter. She'll check her balance after she exercises one of the new horses.

Typing in her passcode, it circles, waiting to display her accounts. Yes, it arrived. Sakura lets out a relieved sigh and melts into calm. She hasn't fully allowed herself to go to the next stage of panic.

What if it didn't arrive the next day or the day after? What if it never arrived and she had to go back to court? University, everything would disappear. Seeing the slight increase in her bank balance allows all her dreams to settle again. Sakura pulls them down, like a string attached to the moon. They arrive and take their place alongside her with what is real and possible.

Later she collects Sara, having filled her car up with gas. They stop at the boardwalk and get the special ice cream and Sakura watches Sara run ahead, trying to catch her shadow. Bits of white run down her face and onto her top. Today they taste extra nice.

Every day brings fresh challenges. Still, when she looks back, it's better than crisis. It's better to have the fear of survival than the threat she wouldn't. That realization brings her to her next challenge.

Tomorrow she has arranged to meet Mom.

Sakura has agreed to coffee. Now that she's here, she's kicking herself. This is the merry-go-round she keeps boarding, in the hope she will be seen, her voice will be heard, her opinions and experiences will matter.

Sakura picks the venue. It won't be the same this time. It'll be different. She'll be clear about what she wants, pretty sure her mom won't be able to deliver. Expecting to leave for the last time. But it's never the last time for them, it seems.

Sakura is already seated. Her mom arrives and she sees her wave and walk towards the table. Sakura hates her for everything she doesn't see. For everything she can't see. The words of her therapist create context. Anger turns to sadness. *Why can't she just get it?*

'Hi Sakura, you look lovely, your hair…' her mom's voice is quiet, soft, unsure, then trails off.

Sakura's face is stony, hurt, and stops her words. It says you lost the right to talk about me, or aspects of me. She is already tired of the conversation and pretends to look at the menu, she already knows she's just getting coffee. No appetite.

'Mom, do you know what you want?'

'Why don't you get something, my treat, I'd like to, please?' Mom unravels her silky scarf.

'No thanks, I'm not hungry. I've already eaten, just getting coffee,' Sakura lies. She's planning something nice once this is over. 'To be honest, I'm not sure what there is to say.'

Sakura looks at Mom, then away.

'Please, I think we need to talk.' Mom regresses. It feels uncomfortable. She's the child. Her pleading voice. 'I want to say I'm sorry. I didn't realize it would upset you so much, I mean I should have thought that it would. I was just trying to keep everyone, everything together.'

'But you can't,' Sakura jumps in, 'you can't keep everyone together. It's not your job. It's my relationship. It was my relationship.'

Sakura realizes she could let it all out, everything about her dad and how she felt abandoned but feels it would just bounce back, unheard, and then justified. She also doesn't want to hurt her mom.

'I know, I know, I'm sorry. I've made excuses to Chris. He hasn't been back since.'

'You're still making excuses? Maybe you should have told the truth. That you realized it was wrong, Mom?' Sakura points out quietly.

The girl arrives at their table to take their order.

Sakura wonders how many serious, awful conversations she has had to interrupt. The unknowing half-time referee. Faces flushed or pale, twisted in one emotion or another. Sweaty palms. Fast hearts. One begging the other to hear. Confusion, resignation.

Is there ever real understanding, a meeting of hearts? True listening? Sakura wonders. Then thinks, not today.

'Coffee please.' Sakura goes first.

Her mom orders the same.

'What I said that day still stands.' Sakura sits taller and looks straight at her. 'If he's over at your house again, I can't be a part of it. I have to protect myself and Sara.'

'You don't need to protect Sara from me.' It's a question statement. Her mom looks hurt. She's the one who has done the hurting.

Sakura doesn't respond. Thinking she really does but couldn't possibly explain, that knowing again none of it would be understood.

'I was trying to do my best.' Her mom looks down. Sakura's silence has forced her to hear her own words and see her role in seeing herself as a victim in all of this.

'Mom, this is the way it has to be.' Sakura begs silently that she doesn't cry.

'I know, he won't be over again.'

The line Sakura waited to hear. For a second, she travels to the future conversation and watches her mom flail and try to say it to Chris, that he cannot come over anymore, without being too clear. Chris trying to hide his anger while getting a jab in at Sakura at the same time.

Sakura knows how this will play out and her knowing she will receive the brunt of his anger at a later stage will be right. She's learning to read ahead, ready herself, watch the patterns, and place herself where the protection is needed. For herself and for Sara.

'How is Sara? I miss her,' her mother chimes.

'She's good. Talking more.' Not responding to the last part. Missing Sara is her own doing.

'Can I see her? I'd love to see her.' Her mom looks pleading and conflicted at the same time.

'Yes, of course you can see her. I have to be clear about minding her and keeping Chris away, even if you don't fully understand it…'

'I know, I know,' her mom cuts her short. 'How about Sunday, you could both come over, I could make lunch?'

'Ok, thanks.' Sakura decides not to mention University. Too much over one coffee. 'I've got to go now, collect Sara.' She drinks a mouthful of coffee and stands up.

'See you Sunday.' Her mom stands up too.

'Yes, see you Sunday.'

They hug awkwardly. Sakura leaves.

Sunday arrives and Sakura is surprised that she's excited to go to her mom's. The familiar family home. The smells. Her mom's cooking. Paying attention to all the details. How she takes care of Sara, her every need. Each time it happens, Sakura is yanked from the warm home and thrown out into the cold. Then, having taken time to realise, what she needs is often not there. To reach a truce and to freely walk back into the warmth and hope she isn't cast aside again.

Carrying Sara in her arms. Bag in hand. Some goodies she brought. Things she knows her mom likes. The scented candle from *Light Moon*. The place they would wander together. Her mom holding her hand. Things glistening and shining over her little head. Smells of oil and calming music, leaving the kickstand of boots at the door as they enter little haven.

Sakura leaves her childhood, tugged by Sara's hand on her face, reaching over to try to grab the little butterfly as they near the front door.

Hugs and hellos. Her mom reaches for Sara and wants to show her something special she got just for her. Sakura can see her mom is making her favourite dish. It used to be pizza.

Smells of bread and seafood fill the kitchen and spread out onto the patio yard where her mom helps Sara pull the wrapping off. Revealing a little wheelbarrow and little garden tools. Sara immediately starts to dig. Sakura is surprised at how easy it is to forget everything that went before, until she imagines Chris walking through *her* home and eating out of her dishes and what he might have said. She's yanked out of her own horror imagining.

'Lunch is ready,' her mom calls.

Sakura parks her rising hurt and thinks of her session with the therapist. And knows deep down that if her mom knew different, she would do different.

They gather outside and eat their fill. Followed by dessert. Home-baked cake and fresh fruits. Her mom has gone to extra effort.

'Thank you, you went to a lot of trouble. Thank you.'

Her mom reaches over and gently places her hand on Sakura and removes it just as soon, before Sakura can break the moment of intimacy.

They play with Sara as she fills up small buckets of water and tips them into the wheelbarrow. Laughing at her little wobbles, most of it is gone before she manages to pour it in. Sakura has brought spare clothes but knows that her mom has some if she hadn't.

To her surprise, Sakura finds herself telling her mom about her University course. And is more surprised at her mom's excitement. Having minimized it into something so small in her own head, she might not even get through it. It's raised up, enlarged to its full size as her mom takes out her laptop and Sakura downloads the brochure and shows her all the modules.

'Why didn't you tell me before? This is wonderful.' Her mom reaches over her shoulder, scanning the details.

Sakura doesn't answer. Her mom moves on to her next question.

'When does it start? How often do you need to go off-island to the University?' Before Sakura has a chance to answer, she continues, 'I can help with Sara. And what about money?'

'This is something I have to do without your financial help.' It would feel like opportunity balloons held down by mini-lead weights. Only stopping her when she has hopes to fly. 'Thanks, I've got it sorted. There's a grant and I've got other things lined up.'

Changing the emphasis on Tye's help, with more of a slant as an investment on his behalf with the horses that need specific help, traumatized horses, makes it look less like a handout which Sakura knows it is. Later she will turn this around.

'Sakura.' Her mother flushes. 'I am so proud of you.'

'Thank you.' Sakura can hold it. Because she is proud of herself.

After the second helping of dessert, they leave. Arms heavier than when they arrived. New toys and leftover food wrapped up. Sakura will appreciate it tomorrow, not having to think about what to cook for the two of them.

CHAPTER 71

Sara's bag is packed. She wouldn't get a chance to do it later.

'Are you excited? Dad's collecting you later.' Chris is due.

'Dada, Dada.' Sara pulls at Teddy's leg sticking out of the bag.

For some reason, Sakura decides to check her phone.

Got caught up, delayed, won't be able to collect Sara at the usual time. Might be in the morning. Will update later. Chris

Sakura takes Sara's hand, opening the back-sliding patio doors and outside into the air. Her heart feels like it's up in her throat, her stomach wanting to vomit the beat out. *What the fuck*? Going through the words again in her head. *When will he tell me, am I just to wait?* Completely vague.

Knowing this will happen doesn't lessen its impact when it does. Just makes her curse her instinct. Sakura had planned to travel with her mom up to the University campus this weekend and check everything out. Letting the tap run, she needs time in her own messy head.

Sara runs over and immediately starts to fill her plastic ice cream cones.

It's like he knew I was doing something, planning something with my life. Then the familiar gallop into fear. What if he does it again and again and stops taking Sara altogether? I won't be able to do my coursework or go to University. And Sara, she won't understand why.

It runs and runs until her head is sore, everything feels silly. Everything seems difficult. Even how to mind Sara at this moment. Her first call. To someone who will understand,

'Hello, hi. It's Sakura, I was just wondering if I could chat to Olivia?' Sakura likes that she can ask for help and hates the words as they come out. Why does this get too much, so much? Why does *he* get to me so much?

'Hi Sakura, Olivia's not here right now, but I'm free to chat, my name is Cassie and I'm one of the support workers here at the shelter. Would you like to tell me what's been happening?'

'Okay thanks, well, hmm, my ex hasn't turned up for access to collect my daughter, he gave a vague excuse, just thrown me a curve ball.' Sakura misses Olivia's voice. She knows Cassie is qualified, but will she care as much?

'Of course, that's totally understandable, when was he due to collect your daughter? Sorry, I don't know her name.' Clearly, things have moved on. Sakura is annoyed that she's not Olivia. Upset that she has to tell a stranger. Again. A stranger who understands and cuts through and sees the truth in a few short sentences.

'Oh, it's Sara. My daughter's name is Sara.' Sakura jumps in, easing over the awkwardness of their lack of familiarity. 'This came in only a few hours ago, it's just that I'm going to University in the fall and I'm relying on Chris my ex to take her every second weekend. If he's starting to do this now, maybe he'll stop turning up at all.' Sakura hears her words and sits on the floor.

She can hear Sara running around the other room, words heavy now, filling the space with fear where hope once was.

'If there's a court order in place…' Cassie stresses.

'There is,' Sakura states.

'Then he's in breach if he doesn't turn up without a valid excuse,' Cassie outlines. 'By the way, that's great about University, well done!' She's warm, just like Olivia. These women have women's backs. 'And look, don't worry about that, that's a few months away, let's focus on this weekend. Do you have help or something else to do if he doesn't show?'

'Very little.' Sakura shakes her head as it dawns on her that she and Sara are the bits that fall between the cracks. This support person, this organization, holds her where the family courts and government organizations don't. 'What can I do?'

They go through what her options are and plan a response. Sakura is reminded that he's breaking a court order with no clear reason why. This gives Sakura some focus. Getting off the phone, she drafts what she'll send.

Hi Chris,

This is court-ordered access. Please provide a clear reason for the delay and when you will be able to collect Sara. She is expecting you at the agreed time.

Sending does little to decrease her anxiety. The constant checking, waiting for a response. Having decided that it's too late for today, Sakura explains to Sara that her dad couldn't collect her. Not yet two years old, she doesn't understand and runs off shouting *Dada, Dada.*

That night, restlessness fills the house, like the cooked fish smell that won't leave despite lighting a scented candle.

The next morning, they are up early, eating breakfast. The hundredth time to check and still nothing. Sakura will have to call her mother shortly. And imagines her gentle excusing of his behaviour. Her lack of calling it out, her silence. The most shocking part, imagining her aloneness in her almost exploding head. *Thank God I have the woman in the shelter. She gets it.*

It arrives, in between half-poured orange juice.

I said I got delayed, don't threaten me with the court order. I will let you know when I know.

Sakura spills the juice, and it leaks between the crack on her table and onto the floor. Shit. Reaching down to stop Sara walking into it. What the fuck? Sakura's head runs angry.

She won't wait for him to decide. Calling her mom, she lets her know that Sara isn't going to Chris this weekend. She doesn't go into any detail. Her mom doesn't ask. She suggests they all go to the University. Sakura thinks the drive will be too long for Sara. Her mom's excitement in her voice is palpable.

'Let's stay overnight, there's a lovely town, a half-hour drive from there.'

Silence follows. Sakura knows she doesn't have enough money to do that.

'I'll pay, I want to pay, we didn't get to go anywhere this year. It's my present to you.'

Sakura can't remember them going anywhere any year for the longest time. Sakura keeps this quiet. 'I can't, Mom, you've done and given us so much already.'

'No, I want to, I insist.'

Sakura gives in, torn between that piece of accepting her help and feeling so guilty that she can't do these things herself.

'I'll look right now and book something, it'll be lovely.'

'Okay thanks, we'll be over in an hour. Can you check if they have a travel cot? Thanks, Mom.'

Sakura feels relieved that she's not waiting by her phone. Empowering herself. She won't wait anymore for Chris to decide. *He can choose to behave however he feels like. But I can also decide how to react.* Sakura's thoughts punch her into action.

'Sara, we're going on a little vacation with Nana, let's go get your jammies.'

Upstairs they pack the essentials. It always takes longer than Sakura expects.

Arriving at the house, they pack the car and click the car seat into place. Her mom's car is bigger and newer. Leaving her phone behind, Sakura decides she doesn't need it. Free from waiting to see what might come.

The journey up is easy. Much talk of University and what it might be like when Sakura starts in four weeks' time.

Stopping for lunch, Sara provides constant distraction, allowing Sakura not to move back into a panic over Chris's message and access and what might happen. Arriving at the University, Sakura moves into hope.

I can do this with or without his help. Looking around, the lecture rooms, the space. The possibilities. After, they check into the hotel her mom has booked. It's lovely, with two adjoining rooms and a small pool. She didn't want to ask her mom but packed bathing suits just in case. Seeing Sara so excited in the water was so worth it.

Her mom insists on Sakura checking out the therapy room.

'I didn't get you anything proper for your birthday. This is for you.' Mom hands her an envelope. Her voice is low but full of intent. Her whole being big with the look of anticipating joy on another's face.

Sakura thinks back to her birthday, a non-event, they weren't talking at that time.

'I'll check it out, they might be booked out.'

Sakura rings and there's a facial slot in an hour. 'Thank you, Mom.'

Her mother cuts her short. 'No more thank you's. Just go off and enjoy yourself. Sara and I have plans.'

She leaves them giggling, hiding under the duvet.

The facial provides an unexpected journey into calm. She didn't realize how stressed she was. Tears sneak down her face. Sakura hopes the therapist doesn't notice. She tells Sakura how lovely her skin is and how beautiful her eyes are.

In the mirror afterwards, she looks at her reflection. The last few months have given little reason for her to notice herself. Today her face looks glowing, her face stands out. Sakura notices her eyes and remembers the first time Chris commented on them. Shuddering with these thoughts.

'These are my eyes,' Sakura lowers her voice and whispers. 'You are beautiful.'

Arriving back, Mom pulls up outside their house and pops the trunk.

'Thank you, I… we had a lovely time.' Sakura, holding her bag.

Mom has already reached over. Sakura lets the hug in. She wants to stay there forever but is afraid she might be caught out again and breaks the hug.

'Me too, it was lovely, you better get sleepy head inside.' Mom opens the passenger door. Sakura lifts Sara up, heavy arms and legs fall where they go. Sakura carries Sara and their bags inside.

After supper, Sakura fills the bath and decides to hop in and join Sara. For a moment they are sea creatures blowing bubbles. Hands turn to mermaids. They swim in the sea. Sara floats up to her belly. Sakura remembers the day she was born. Complete with the most perfect features she had ever seen. All growing inside her. All there waiting to be born. She can't believe how big she is and how little she is all at once. Jammies and stories read; Sara goes to sleep easy.

Logging into her email. There it is, the one she dreaded and expected. Chris had emailed saying he was free later Saturday to collect Sara. Followed by another one later that evening.

Stop playing these games. I called to collect Sara when I said I could, and no one was there. Don't think you will get away with this.

Sakura remains calm and doesn't respond. Turns off her phone and decides, with delight, *you don't get to intimidate me anymore.*

The next day Sakura calls the shelter and gets back in touch with her first lawyer, having finished with her other lawyer, Diane, after court. Her mom paid the bill and didn't think she would need another one.

He suggests writing a strong letter reminding Chris of the court order and if there are any more threats they would be forced to take further action. Sakura really hopes there are no more surprises from Chris. She really doesn't want to go back to court.

Jack is home the following weekend. Their hug is close, familiar. Sakura notices that when she's ok, her friendship with Jack is ok.

'How are you?' Jack holds her back to look at her. 'You look great.' Her eyes scrunch, almost in surprise.

'Thanks, I'm good. I think.' Sakura is fearful of holding onto the positive feeling, lest it disappears. Fear and sadness are her more common companions. But her smile is too big and doesn't go unnoticed by Jack.

'What's that, a smile?' Jack teases her. 'Are you seeing someone?'

'No, gosh no.' The thought shocks Sakura. 'I'm just disentangling myself from Chris, don't need anyone. Just me.'

'What is it then?' Jack pushes, years of friendship making things invisible to others visible to Jack.

'Okay, well, I applied to go to University, and I got in.' Sakura tries to make her excitement smaller. It seems too much.

'Ah Sakura, that's great, what's the course, when do you start? Why didn't you tell me?' Jack has so many questions.

Sakura isn't sure which one to answer first. And decides to get lost in the first two and to distract from the last one. Why didn't I tell her? Too big for today. Sakura is surprised by Jack's enthusiasm. Then feels guilty for doubting her friend's loyalty and ability to share in her dreams.

'I'm so happy for you, I can help with whatever you need, mind Sara, assignments, whatever you need. How long did you say it was?' Jack walks side by side with Sakura now, along the familiar boardwalk.

'It's two years. Mom is going to mind Sara.'

'Things ok there?' Sakura can feel Jack's eyes on her.

'Yeah, they're better.' Sakura doesn't want to bring anything heavy on her hopeful mood.

Jack talks about equine science programs she's heard of that Sakura could consider after. She nods along. Not mentioning her own plans. They seem a bit silly now. Deep down, when she's walking in the woods alone, inhaling all its ancient knowledge, she knows it's real. Later, it will become very real.

'So, have you been there yet to visit?'

Sakura loves Jack's excitement.

'Yeah, Mom and Sara actually came with me, long story but Chris didn't show up for access.' Sakura is suddenly pulled back into bitter disappointment and pain.

'What, what do you mean he didn't show up?' Jack's voice raises loud above the waves. They reach the top of the boardwalk and sit down on the faded steel bench. Jack's hands cover someone's memorial mark etched into the bench.

Sakura tells her what happened and is surprised at the feelings it raises now.

'What weekend was that?'

Sakura is puzzled by her question. Then Jack pulls out her phone.

'I'm sorry. I wasn't sure whether to show you or not.' She shows her a picture tagged on her social media account. 'A friend of a friend shared it.'

There's Chris with someone else. It's obvious they're together. Even in the light glare on the phone, she can see it. Away at a festival. Date stamp, the day he was caught up.

Sakura's surprised by the kick that immediately winds her seeing that picture. Making her excuses for leaving Jack, Sakura runs to the outdoor restroom. She had built up another narrative in her head as to why he didn't turn up that day. She didn't allow herself to go there. Wiping away the tears as quickly as they arrived, knowing they'll leave their red tell-tale smudge on her face.

Jack will probably not understand why. Maybe she will. Sakura doesn't know anymore. To fully understand coercive control is often beyond reach, even to her. Especially to those on the outside. The cycle – love bombing, abused, then discarded. Sakura knows it well and feels the last part with all the kick intended.

Sakura struggles to understand her level of woundedness, sitting on the loo, cursing her tears. *He hurt you so much, why does it feel like an utter betrayal?* No point in trying to stop them. Unwinding the tissue in the dispenser, the harsh paper adds to the already rough sense of injustice in all this.

Then she hears Jack's voice. 'Sakura, are you in here?'

Nowhere to hide. Emerging from the washroom. Sakura's face is a mess. Erupting again. Jack reaches in and catches her.

'I'm sorry, I shouldn't have shown you.'

They return to the bench. Talking through it, Sakura tries to be less angry with herself for being so upset. She could see Jack's slight confusion. She thought she would be delighted he had moved on after he treated her so badly.

On her way home alone afterwards, Sakura goes through it all in her head once more. And comes back to the same point again and again.

How could he do that to me? Everything he did to hurt and abuse me. All the cruel things he did to me. He gets to just move on and so soon.

Realizing it wasn't that she wanted Chris but wanted some acknowledgment that this happened to her.

He gets off scot-free. *How many more things to do with Chris will I have to recover from?* Sakura doesn't even care how she looks now. Angry at the sense of injustice and then the question she almost shouted at herself not to ask. What if he treats her differently? *Was there something about me, that allowed him to abuse me?*

Little Sakura baulks at these questions, knowing deep down the answers will come later.

CHAPTER 72

The day has arrived, September sixth. Still over twenty degrees. Their winters often trample over spring, but the compensation is their summers travel into fall. Sakura loves the gentle heat without the intensity of July. Her mom collected Sara earlier that morning.

It will take Sakura two hours to drive to campus. It's off the Island. All the excitement of her earlier week disappears as she travels with fear and doubt.

What if I can't do it? It's so long since I was in school. Then the biggest what if. If not this, then what? For now, filling her backpack with a notepad, pencils, and pens. The book she ordered, the main textbook. Lunch and snacks for the day. There's a canteen, but she needs to keep costs down.

The road out of Bridgetown is surprisingly rugged as she spots the small sign to the equine University. Arriving early, Sakura parks up, hating the idea of walking in late. Everyone is staring. At least that's how it feels. The main University campus is big, imposing. Sakura finds it intimidating. Taking her time, Sakura finds the right room.

The doors all look the same. Inside a tiered setting. It's a small lecture hall. Sakura feels like she's entered another world, a world seemingly out of grasp, now here, firmly anchored. She sits next to a girl who says her name is Kaya. Sakura hopes she might make friends with a common interest. Sakura had no one up to this, but for Tye, to share her passion for horses with. Chris did at first, then appeared disinterested, judgemental. She realized afterwards that he was jealous.

Kaya is petite, with short fair hair. Chatty, curious, kind. Sakura hadn't realized they needed a second textbook. She thought it was optional, having planned to buy it after she got paid before next month's class. Kaya offers to share hers. Sakura immediately likes her.

The lecturer, passionate but maybe a bit tired, goes through the plan. Instruction is set out over the two years in two modules. Classroom and hands-on instruction happen here or at another campus an hour away. The rest of the manuals and textbooks, apart from those on the initial list, are handed out. Sakura is relieved, seeing the second list, thinking she would have finished the course before she could have had a chance to buy one each month. They're handed the list of instructions.

Sakura and Kaya chat excitedly about which ones are their favourites. They all relate to horses. Sakura feels giddy.

Taking notes and listening to new ideas and information takes her up to lunchtime. They finish their first day with small group work and leave with their project title for the next month. They will do research and take it up the next time.

Driving home, Sakura becomes aware of the space created in her body, head, and heart for something other than being a mom and recovering from Chris. Something that is hers. Just hers.

Two months later, Sakura sits down to complete her case study. Settling Sara in bed finally after eight-thirty this evening. She seems unsettled. Having started work on it in October, Sakura has spent time on each section, hoping she was answering what was asked. There's still some tidying up to do before submission tomorrow at University.

Pulling her chair over to the table, Sakura takes out her laptop and starts to work. Afraid it won't be good enough.

Sakura is overthinking elements of the study, second-guessing herself. Just as she decides what will go in the mid-section, Sakura is disturbed by a high-pitched cry. Sara. Running upstairs. *That cry sounded different*. Sakura turns on the small light.

Sara is standing up in her cot, holding onto the sides. Tears streaming. Sakura lifts her up. Checking for temperature. Sara wriggles, upset. Unzipping her grow bag, Sara vomits all at once on top of Sakura. One bit lands in her mouth. Straight to the washroom. Sakura tries to spit it out. Sara roars in between each retch. Holding her over the toilet. Not sure there is any point. Pretty sure most of it has landed in her room.

It's ok, Sara, Mama's here. Sakura lifts her into the bath and strips her down, wiping away the vomit. The bits in her hair forming clumps are harder to remove. The smell causes Sakura to retch. Offering her a drink, Sakura puts Sara in a clean sleep suit and places her in bed. The smell in her room makes her gag. The bath filled with sheets and clothes.

Sakura returns upstairs with wipes and spray. Stripping what's left of the cot. Hands and knees, wiping up the heap that landed on the floor and sprayed on the wardrobe, chest of drawers, and wall. Sara starts to cry again. Removing the gloves, Sakura lies beside her with reassuring hugs. When Sakura hears the deeper breathing, she peels herself away, uncurls her arms, and finishes off the cleaning.

An hour later downstairs. Sakura panics about tomorrow. She can't leave Sara if she's sick. Sitting back down, she returns to her assignment. Just get it done. Angry at herself.

I should have done this earlier in the week.

But you were working, you're doing your best.

The self-dialogue accompanies her work, judging her every move. Halfway through, Sara cries again. Sakura looks at her phone. Eleven o clock. Carrying her just in time to the washroom. She has no clean sheets for her bed. The spare set is in the wash basket.

Sara cries and vomits. Nothing much comes out.

Sakura feels guilty for thinking about her assignment. Lifting her back into bed. She looks so vulnerable. Face pale. Her full weight in her arms. No holding on. She can't.

Lying down beside her.

'I love you, I'm sorry that you're sick. I'm here.' A little later, downstairs, Sakura finishes her case study. It's not perfect but it'll do. It's late.

Heading back upstairs, climbing into bed. She'll call her mom in the morning. Falling asleep, quickly woken to cries. They seem to be in her dream. Realizing it's Sara, she tries to wake herself up. Turning on the light. She sees the vomit on the bed. Back up, back undressing. Cleaning, wiping.

Sakura places a towel on the wet patch and swops sides with Sara. Return to sleep. Loneliness adds tears to her sore head. Finally asleep, the towel twists. Wet sneaks up the back of her pyjamas.

Woken by Sara, she seems brighter. Sakura feels her body heavy; her eyes refuse to open. She begs to go back to sleep just for a minute. Sara is on top of her. 'Mama, Mama.'

Wake up. Stepping over wet clothes and towels.

She stumbles downstairs. Feeling like she's been hit by a freight train, Sakura turns on the TV. Sits Sara up with a beaker cup and blanket. Struggling to find the cups, the coffee does little to help.

An hour later she chats to her mom. She insists on taking Sara.

'You said yourself, she seems much better. You can't miss University.'

Arriving at University, it's hard to concentrate. Getting a burst of energy at lunchtime, helped by the endless coffees. Sakura gets through and returns home, and they're both asleep by eight.

The laundry will wait for another day.

CHAPTER 73

Arriving at her therapy session. Sakura builds up things she needs to talk about from the week previous. Sometimes they get discussed, sometimes something else comes in. What totally surprises Sakura is when she has tears. But always when she leaves after crying it's with extra space around herself.

Today it's the thing she mentions only in passing. A frame of reference. Her dad's death. It came up, Sakura remembering what Chris said. How kind he was at first. How understanding. Then his finishing blow, 'You practically killed him.'

Her therapist gently leads her back to that day. The day he died. Sakura talks about the facts, and what happened. Twisting, turning in her seat. Eyes looking at her. Caring, trusting, and non-judgmental. Encouraging her to keep going.

Sakura talks about how she felt it was her fault. She was with him on the boat. Maybe if she had done something different, maybe he would still be alive. Maybe her mom and Eli think that too. Then the question that she never fully allowed herself to go into. Did she think it was her fault? After talking around what-if details, the maybes, arriving at the biggest no.

Why was I there? Sakura's thought surprises her. *I was just a kid.* Realizing she didn't do anything wrong. It wasn't her fault. The therapist repeating that line: It wasn't your fault. Sakura returns to that day, her little girl, screaming, hitting her daddy to wake up.

Rolling her head into her hands. Catching her tears, shouting inwardly *but why was I there, why did it have to happen? If we didn't go on the boat that day....* Sakura never let herself really go there. Now all the whys are thrown and scattered, lying between their feet.

No one tried to shush her or stop her crying. Traveling into the waves, feeling the smash and toss at every curve. Thinking before if she ever went there, she would die. Die and lay at the bottom with bits of brightly coloured sea glass.

Surfacing now, barely whispering, 'I miss him'. The therapist caught it. Her response stays with her and gives her permission in future days of grief waves. Of course, you do. Miss him.

The puzzle pieces float. Start to join themselves together. In front of her eyes.

They continue talking about what it was like after her dad died and how abnormal she felt. And the sad realization that her mom was not there for her.

Alone in her grief and being the only one to witness it. Sakura hid with horses, their long legs and tails, their huge bodies, and wise eyes, providing safety. Until Chris arrived. Reaching in, taking her hand. I've got you. False promises. Her little girl desperately wanted to believe. She went with him. *I love you* turned into *I hate you and everything you are*.

She didn't realize that she hated everything about herself from that day on the pier onwards. Chris saw this. Pretending. When he had her, he turned and stamped all over her again and again.

He'll do it again and again to someone else.

She's not a special victim.

She was an opportune moment. He took what he wanted from her when he arrived that day at the stables. He tried to mould her and then he tried to ruin her when she couldn't be moulded. Sara was her link to sanity. Now she has found the link to herself.

Leaving the therapist's room, Sakura feels like she has time-travelled to the hidden darkness of her life. Her heart is beating a different beat.

Finding that little girl of eight years old, kicking dust on her school walks, stopping to examine every bee and flower. She picks her up, the mother in her reaching for the child in her, *I have got you. We are going to be ok. We will be afraid again. We will have to dig deep and reach for the courageous warrior within when pain arrives. We will lean into exciting new adventures. We will discover what we are supposed to do. I have a feeling you already know what that is.*

Sakura smiles to herself and doesn't care who is watching. She tells the child and the woman she is *We will recover from this. We already have.*

Chapter 74

The screen door bangs, wobbling the picture.

'Don't stay out too long, supper's nearly ready.'

But Sara is already immersed in the sand and sprinkled water.

Sakura reaches up and straightens the picture. Then unhooks and lifts it down. Beside it hangs her framed certificate. Her mother insisted.

They looked lovely that day, nearly three years ago. Her dress had small blue flowers. Her mother's smile. Pride. After two years of trying every way to pull it all together. Trying to meet assignment deadlines, missing class due to Sara being sick or Chris not turning up for access. Completing her work experience with the help of Tye.

She did it and was so surprised when she saw her final marks.

The timer goes off and interrupts her daydreaming. Taking out the garlic bread, annoyed she hadn't used the oven glove. She does it every time, thinking it's not going to be that hot. It's always hotter. Hopping it from one hand to the other, dropping it quickly onto the table while shouting:

'Sara, supper's ready.'

'Not yet, Mama,' Sara shouts back.

'Come on, you can go back out after you've finished!'

'Just this thing to do.' Sara persists.

Sakura sees Sara trying to take her hair out of her face, only to add sand. Now the wisps just hang down heavier, annoying her even more.

Sakura smiles. These moments. Full of her. Her little girl. Knowing to let her finish. Sara's world is right now. It will seem less important later. Even a few minutes later, after supper is over.

Sara, arriving in, covered in sand. Sakura returns with her daughter to the outside tap and washes the grains away. Taller than the tap now. When they moved in, Sara could barely reach it. Her long dark hair getting in the way, splashed by the cool water.

'Where's your hair band? You're always taking them off.'

Sara looks up to Sakura with a funny scrunched-up face.

'I didn't take it off, it fell off at camp today!' she answers with such indignation.

'Ok, all done.' That word ok again. This time, in this place, it truly is.

Sitting down, Sakura grates the cheese and sprinkles it over the pasta.

'What was the best part of your day?' Sakura begins their evening ritual.

'Mmm.' Sara looks up and away, holding a fork with pasta in one hand, waving it around as she thinks back. 'Going to the playground after camp.'

'Yeah, that was fun, wasn't it?' Sakura reaches over and gently places her hand on Sara's head.

'What was yours, Mama?' The fork now back near the table and lands in her mouth

'I think the best part of my day is here right now, eating with you, talking with you.'

'Can I go outside after, once I'm finished eating?' Sara has already moved on.

'Okay, for a little while. You need to come in then and have a bath.'

They're interrupted by the doorbell. Sakura gets up and Sara follows close behind.

'Hi, Tim. Didn't expect to see you here at this time, is that it?' Sakura glances down at the small envelope in his hand.

'Yes, they came in later, all done. I was passing and thought you would want them as soon as possible.' Tim's tall frame looks awkward. A salesman for sure. But a man of his word. 'It's all yours.'

'Thank you. Oh my God! I can't believe this is really it. Thank you for all your help.'

'No worries, you must be excited.' Tim lowers his head and talks to Sara half behind her mom. Sara doesn't answer. Dancing on one foot. 'Best of luck with it all.'

Sakura remembers the first time she met Tim, opening the door to his office just off Hatton Street. Sakura was hanging around outside. Afraid to go in. *T & F Realtor* sign above the door. The last two letters a little faded. The many times folded brochure in her hand.

'Come on in.' Reaching out, he shook her hand firmly and looked straight at her. But not in a way that made her uncomfortable. He treated her like anyone else. Like she had money to buy.

He made it happen. So did she.

Sakura closes the door and walks back into the kitchen.

'Can you believe it, Sara? This is it!' Sakura opens the envelope and tilts it slightly; two keys fall out.

'What is it? Mama?'

Sakura whips up Sara and twirls her around in an excited frenzy. Sara, delighted whenever this happens, lets her head go back free falling. Sakura reaches over and tickles her into an upright position.

'Is it the place with all the trees and stables?'

They come to the ground together.

'Yes, that's the place. Our place.' Sakura pulls the folder from their wood-stained bookshelf, opens it, and places it alongside the now-cold pasta.

Sara hops into her spot on her mother's lap. Safe in between folded elbows.

Sakura's face is different. Open creases, rounded cheeks. The smile that stays.

Sara's wriggly bum on her knees matches the wriggles in her tummy. If they could be released, they would float right out of her body, into the sky and pull all the light into one spot. The creative place where anything can be possible.

She picks up the keys, feeling them in her hands, making sure they're real. The jagged form of the zig zag presses into her hand, leaving a mark that fades quickly on release.

'Is this it, Mama?' Sara pulls the picture out.

'Yes, this is it, I can't believe we got here. Can't believe we did it.' Tears fall and form little blobs on the page.

'Mama, are you crying? You're messing the picture. Are you sad?'

'Ah Sara, they're my happy tears.' Sakura pulls her even closer.

'You're squeezing me, Mama!' Sara pushes her elbows out.

Sakura laughs, releasing Sara.

'I'm sorry, I'm just so happy. Don't worry about the picture. We don't need it anymore. We have the real thing.'

Sara hops off, takes her cold pasta bowl outside, and eats the rest of it with grains of sand. Sakura doesn't even try and stop her. Looking at her from the opened doors, standing pressed up against its frame. Her little girl.

Changing into her big little girl. Four and three-quarter years old.

'I'm four,' she can hear her saying, holding her thumb down, delighted she can count her age. Brown hair down her back. Strays float to the front of her face.

Sakura smiles, seeing Sara a little annoyed, fully concentrating on not spilling the pasta into the sand tray, pushing her hair back behind her ear. Little bits of sauce are now stuck to the strands. The dress she picked out this morning, covered in the day's adventures. Her legs longer, leaner, pushing away from the chubbiness. Growing into her own.

We've done ok. Better than ok. That word, the yardstick of all this history. Now it has been superseded, Sakura comforts and acknowledges herself.

These moments where time wraps around and holds everything in. Sakura feels every blade of grass growing, every bird singing, every wing flap in her small backyard. Water trickling into sand. Her daughter's mind and body engrossed in what she's doing.

Sara looks up and, seeing her, jumps up.

'Come on, Mama, let me show you.'

Reaching out, Sakura takes her sticky wet hand, and her play becomes their play.

CHAPTER 75

Pulling the boxes across the floor. Stacking them high. Sakura takes the lid off the marker, holds it in her mouth and writes *Sara's winter clothes and books.*

Having gathered things over the years, the move-out takes much longer than the move-in. Sakura remembers that day.

The one she wandered from room to room, knowing this was her first independent home. Moving now to her next.

Picking up Sara's picture animal book, its cover is worn, missing the tiger's tail. The first night that week they read it. Sara pointed and made elephant sounds together. After, Sakura placed a sleepy Sara in her cot. She lay on the floor and held her hand firm on the wood, begging her heart to slow down. Watching the window for a black pickup. She felt her heart break and the bits of it fall. Caught in the knots of the wood.

It was a feeling, she has learned they all pass.

Now she's alive to herself. Invest in the good thoughts, acknowledge the bad, but keep moving, and pull yourself up.

Pulling herself forward years, Sakura knows she's the same in person, her hands the same, her face the same but altogether different. Today she holds her beating heart and knows its strength amidst doubt and fear. Knowing it beats alongside her intuition. Holding strong. It reveals its truth. Her truth.

'Hello, Sakura, are you here?'

'Hi Mom, I'm here, come on in.' Sakura stretches her neck out from her seating position and straightens her cramped legs.

'You've been busy, I've brought some coffee. Take a break.'

Sakura stands up, slowly allowing her body to rebalance.

'Thank you, you've read my mind.'

Her mom's loose linen pale pink top draws attention to her brown hair, just above the shoulder. There's more space around her. Since that day after Sakura arrived at her house and saw Chris's pickup outside. That day her call to the door sounded different, urgent. She came over because she knew her daughter was losing her grip on life.

They hadn't seen each other in so long. Too long. Then they had the coffee and then they had the Sunday lunch.

That night, over three years ago now, Sakura and Sara went home, Mom knocked on the door shortly after Sara went to bed. Sakura opened the door to her mom, she could see she had been crying. The reapplication of makeup that wouldn't cover the red marks blotched under her eye.

'What happened?' Sakura remembers asking, 'Is Eli okay?'

They had talked about him a little, but it wasn't okay. She knew he was a long arm's length brother. Didn't have too much to say. But he was her only sibling. Remember those few close moments with him before her dad died. He was her bigger only brother. Maybe someday he would come close enough to reach.

'Eli's fine.' The words that helped to relax into whatever had caused her mom to arrive late, upset.

Sitting down, Sakura brought her mom herbal tea, hoping it would help bring calm. Just as Olivia had brought to her in the shelter.

'Take your time,' she felt the need to say. She was so tired and needed her bed for work in the morning.

It was strange to see her mom so unravelled. She was familiar with her mom's deafness when it came to her and the upset that denial brought. But this was different.

Even though Sakura wanted things to change between them, there was some familiarity and predictability with their pattern.

Sakura would try to explain. Try to get her mom to see her, hear her.

It would bounce back to denial.

Sakura would be upset. Leave and retreat, further away from her mom.

Maybe it was because of this. She had been the one to see her mother devastated, unable to get out of bed. Maybe it was something serious. Was she sick? The thing she forgot to ask and then panicked, waiting for the answer.

'No.'

'Then what's wrong?'

Her mom tried to take a sip of the tea and explained that she had started seeing a therapist. Something Sakura said in the row that day outside her home had stuck.

'I saw what I was. I see what I still am.' After the initial few sessions, her mom explained that they started talking about Dad and what happened after he died.

Even saying that, as her mother placed the tea down, some of it spilt. Shaking tears came.

Sakura instinctively sat beside her and put her arm around her shoulder. Mom carried on.

'I'm sorry I was so devasted after your dad died. I couldn't see you, couldn't see you in your grief, I pretended you were too young to be affected. But I knew.'

'It's okay, it's okay.' Sakura grabbed the tissues.

Her mom's hands didn't manage to catch them all.

'You were just a child who needed her mother. I'm sorry. I'm so sorry.'

Her mom turned around, and Sakura embraced her. Feeling her arms, her smell. Sakura was surprised by her own sudden dismantling. Her mom's tears. An ancient call to grief. Long-buried. Long waiting for their release. Sakura's body started to shake. The gulping howling follows.

For a brief second, Sakura wanted to pull away. Then she gave in. Her eight-year-old and her adult self merged. They allowed the tears until they stopped. No longer need for words.

Afterwards, Mom and she sat, Sakura's hand in hers. Vulnerability held its sacred space. Mom apologized for not understanding what happened to her with Chris. She couldn't hear that her daughter was hurt by someone. She couldn't bear it. Pretending it wasn't real. Explaining that she was just starting to understand and had a long way to go with the help of her therapist.

Sakura remembering the line,

'I hope it's not too late, I haven't lost you?' Her mom's pleading naked voice, free of advice.

'You haven't lost me, I'm here, right here, I've been waiting for this.' Sakura stumbled, their hands held tighter.

'I know, I know,' her mom jumped in.

Later. There were many more conversations. They heard each other. Openness and vulnerability delicately threaded a new, different bond.

One Friday, Eli came home for the weekend. Mom made pizza.

They played with Sara in the yard.

'Tomorrow I'll come over and build your swing,' Eli promised.

A faint whisper in Sakura's ear. I am here. Then it was gone, like the filled-in pond.

Now they're at another beginning. The truck arrives. The two men make it look so easy. Sakura and her mom spent the morning perspiring.

Sakura collects Sara from summer camp and together they walk upstairs for the last time. Checking under the beds for anything missed.

'Thank you, house, thank you for holding us.' Sakura picks up Sara, too big for her hip. Her legs wrap around her waist. Arms around her neck.

'Do you want to say anything?'

'I'm going to miss my room, the way my bed faces that way.' Sara leans back pointing towards the window.

'But you're always in my bed.' Sakura reaches in and tickles, causing Sara to wriggle and laugh.

'And my swings, I'll miss my swing.' Sara suddenly becomes sad.

'We're bringing the swing. The guys are going to take it apart and put it back together in our new house.'

Sakura walks through the house once more. Placing her hands on the wall.

Thank you for allowing me to grieve, to recover, to learn, to love, to hear, thank you. I'm ready to go.

Within a few days, it will be filled with another woman and her family, building a new life from the wreckage.

Driving out, leaving the town behind. Sakura glances at the worn brochure on the passenger seat.

Log-style cottage features 2 bedrooms, kitchen, living room with wood stove and heat pump, full bath, and large mudroom inside, as well as a large storage shed, and screened-in porch. Stables, 6 acres.

She saw it first in the window of Tim's realtor's office over eight months ago.

The red spruce and red oak that surrounded the cottage grabbed Sakura and she couldn't let go. She could see the one closest to the house holding Sara on the swing they would make.

After University began, Sakura started to see more horses arrive. Tye asking if she could help. Hearing the stories of others at University, Sakura didn't really feel she was doing anything special. She thought most people could see what she saw; their pain; their fear of whatever trauma has made everyone afraid or why they're not succeeding perhaps as they once did.

Her course cemented her knowledge further and gave her the confidence to believe she could do more. Diving in. Opening up possibilities others may have dismissed. Courses followed on courses. Sakura quietly completed an Aura-Soma Colour Healing Course, pushing the door open to everything.

This healing harmonizes body, mind, and spirit by using the vibrational energies of colour, crystals, natural aromas, and lights.

A horse arrived at Tye's after a road traffic accident. The horse lorry it was travelling in crashed. Recovering from his minor injuries without much fuss, the owner expected him to do well at a big race some months later. The horse had spooked, didn't want to be handled by anyone. Arriving at his stable, he settled for the night.

Early next morning, Sakura saw him, snorting head sticking out the door. Taking him into the smaller arena to the back. Even on the walk, she could feel his fear. Releasing the rope, Sakura took out the small bottle from her jacket, applied a few drops of blue to her left hand and gently rubbed palms together.

Standing on his left side, Sakura closed her eyes and began to see the horse's fear. Using the colour, Sakura raised her right hand above the middle of his back, while lowering her other hand a few inches below his belly.

Sakura felt her whole body tingle.

Immediately she could see the horse's back begin to tremor.

His eyes softened, his gut made gurgling noises and his head dropped slightly. Sakura could feel the horse release the shock of the accident.

After a few more sessions the owner reported a remarkable turnaround and improvement in the horse's temperament. He was back racing after a few weeks with great results.

Tye insisted that she charge her own fee for her work. Only asking for a minimal fee for the use of the stables during their stay.

Over the few years of this work that has become her passion and full expression, Sakura had enough for her five percent deposit. Part of her plan to buy a small holding and set up her own business. A plan never said out loud or even quietly to herself.

But the arrival of each cheque from her one-to-one work with horses creates its own vision. When she found her holding, her mom became guarantor on her mortgage. The precarious and unfamiliar type of work spooked the bank.

Deep down, Sakura knew she would never have to rely on that guarantee.

Her original work in Tye's stables eased out.

CHAPTER 76

'We're here, Sara.' Sakura pulls up outside the cabin. 'You see, it's not that far, fifteen minutes from Nana.'

Sara unbuckles herself, having just gotten the knack a few weeks back.

'I did it myself, Mama.' Jumping up and down between the car seats, beaming.

'You did. You're so smart. Will we go in?'

'Yes.' The loud response is followed by more jumping.

Her mom's car wheels sound over the gravel lane and pull in behind hers. Jumping out, box in hand.

'It's more beautiful than I remember.' Closing her door shut with her foot.

'It is, isn't it?' her mom replies.

She unlocks the door to the screen porch and then the main door that lets them into their house.

The off-white units contrast with the wooden walls and floors. The wood-burning stove angled in the corner beside the window.

Sakura loves the feel of the wood under her feet and all around her. Later she will decide which bits to paint, and Sara will help. Brush strokes every which way. The living space near the kitchen will hold a table. Their table.

Sakura can visualize opening the door out to the porch with her morning coffee. Seeing the trees that surround her cabin bow with her in reverence and morning ritual.

She's pulled back by Sara's hand, grasping at hers.

'Come on, Mama, let's find my room.' The smaller of the two. Sara decides where her toys and teddies will go.

Pointing at the empty spaces, imagining them filled. Neither of them mentioning that after the initial two hours in her own bed, Sara walks out into her mom's room, standing beside her head. Sakura knowingly pulls her in. Arms under and above. Full cuddle until someone breaks and turns over.

In the mornings Sara always wakes Sakura with a smile, knowing she has snuck in and stayed all night. Every night.

'Let's check the washroom.' Sakura gestures to the door, Sara following.

The bath is how she remembers. Perfect for soaking her aching limbs. Releasing the day, watching the horse smells disappear into lavender. She couldn't believe it when she first saw the brochure, thinking she would have to relinquish one of the must-haves. She didn't have to. It had everything she wanted. Created, carved, waiting for herself and Sara. Waiting for the horses to arrive. Waiting to be helped.

The removal truck arrives and late into the evening they are surrounded by boxes. Her mum fills the fridge with essentials. Following a heated-up meal her mum bought, shared and washed down with local apple juice, she leaves.

'Get some rest, chat tomorrow.' Her mom reaches over and kisses her. 'See you, little miss.'

'Bye, Nana.' Sara runs over and gives her a hug.

'I'm so proud of you, Sakura, look what you've created. You should be so proud of yourself.'

Her mom's support now real and steady. After she called over that night to open up about going to therapy, Sakura could see a change in her mom. Last year she finally made that trip to Japan to visit her friend, Kana. She's painting again, her Ikagi.

Sakura, still seated at the table the removal guys put together and just in time, gestures her right hand to her heart and then out to her mother.

*

Finding the linen box, Sakura is relieved that she marked them all on at least two sides. They make the bed in Sakura's room. Late May still needing extra warmth. Sakura shakes out the cover and manages to pull the duvet in, all the while Sara trying to get inside. This would normally annoy Sakura, especially with being so tired, but she just lets it be, knowing she'll be asleep soon.

It takes her a while to settle and then, all at once, her body feels the tiredness.

Stepping over the boxes, Sakura gently walks out the back door which creaks on opening. Not noticing it earlier with all the coming and going. The cabin will reveal all its quirks and ways over the coming weeks, months, and years. Later, it would push its back wall out, extending to allow more room. More feet. More creaks.

Walking towards the trees that surround the cabin, Sakura looks up and then stands under their huge branches. Allowing them to hold her. They've been here before. Seen people come and go. They have witnessed it all.

Whispering a silent prayer, she heads toward the stables. Opening the door of one. They need a little fixing up.

Tye had said he would help during his first trip out. Alongside Mom, he was one of the first people she showed the cabin to. He would know if it was suitable for the horses and the work she planned.

During University, she noticed that her wages started to go back up, the way they were before they had agreed to take out a certain amount to cover her fees. Sakura insisted that he deduct it again. She would only accept his help on this condition. Tye did what she asked.

Sakura didn't want to be dependent on anyone. Least of all a man. She could do this on her own. Having observed the increased footfall through Tye's stables since she started doing more individual work with horses, she was happy to give something back to him after all his support.

Tye's stables being a ten-minute drive away will benefit them both. Someone is already booked in. Arriving in two weeks with their chestnut showjumper. The stables need to be ready by then.

Releasing the mental list, Sakura returns to the cabin. Filling the bath, she steps in for her first soak. She's tired but this is essential. The water feels delicious and washes away the grime of unpacking. Unable to find her pyjamas, Sakura slips into a sweatshirt, folds back the duvet and hops in. Cuddling up beside her little hot water bottle. Sara.

CHAPTER 77

The following morning, Sakura wakes first. The birds making their presence known in the many nests outside her window. Looking over at Sara. Her long hair across the pillow, some of it caught. Gently releasing it without waking her, Sakura places her hand on Sara's. Wanting the last of chubbiness to remain.

Their first day is much like the day before. Unpacking, moving. Things finding new homes. After lunch, they walk out of their cabin, onto the side road and follow it until it meets Route 1 into the small town.

It takes them ten minutes to arrive at Fort Jackson. One main street holds most of the nine stores or cafes.

'This is where your school is, Sara.' Picking her up so she can see it in the distance.

'My big school.' Proudly announcing.

Sakura booked her name in after Christmas. Putting everything in motion should the sale go ahead. She would start in the fall. Sakura knows she's ready. But part of her knows that schoolyard is where the wrangling of life really starts. Not wanting anyone to upset or hurt her, while also knowing that Sara pulls her up on things all the time. She has no real worries. Just the worries of every mom not wanting their child to go.

They sit in the local café and order hot chocolate and buns. Sara runs over to the corner with the books. A little boy is there, and Sakura can hear them chatting. Looking over. A smiling woman, his mom perhaps, sitting at a nearby table.

Sakura raises her hand in a slight wave and smiles back. Their drinks arrive. Sakura walks over to get her, but

Sara is engrossed, chatting, and pulling out books with her new friend. His mom comes over and they start talking. Within minutes they realise they are both new to the town. Both are mothering solo.

Her name is Aria. Sakura learns too that she is an artist and next month plans to host her work in the local gallery during Festival Week. Sakura suggests getting their drinks and buns. Bringing them over to Aria's table. They sit down together. Within an hour they are firm friends.

Red big unruly hair, bright yellow top. Aria's energy is electric and vibrant. Something Sakura intuitively knows has taken some time to harness.

When she stands up to call her boy Leo over, her back is straight and tall, and Sakura sees the lioness emerge. The Roar. Loud and clear.

Walking the same path home. They continue with unpacking. Sara runs in and out, wanting to tell Sakura every new thing she discovers. Sakura tells her not to go near the stables alone.

'Mama must be with you.' Sakura looks at Sara, waiting for the sign that she has been heard.

Not getting it, Sakura repeats herself.

'Okay, Mama.' Sara runs off.

Not getting much done, Sakura is relieved she will be dropping Sara to summer camp tomorrow. Her mom is collecting her after. This will give Sakura much needed time to properly unpack.

Tye is also arriving tomorrow with two builders to take a look at the stables and fix what needs fixing. And to make sure the paddocks are secure. Sakura's doubt creeps in. The voice grates a low angst. *What have you done, is this too much?*

'No.' Sakura is surprised that she said it so loud. Pushing through. Shushing her fear. 'We've got this.'

Chris is due to collect Sara at the end of the week for overnight access. As predicted, he has eased out of their lives.

When it happened the second and third time, Sakura thought about returning to court. The paperwork was almost done. Then, last minute, she just decided not to go through with it. Realizing she can't force him to be a different person. To be a good father. To turn up. What she has to do is hold Sara when she's confused and disappointed.

Trying to explain that it's never about you. It's always about them.

Recalling the third time and the big tears. Sitting in her bed.

'You're perfect the way you are, you deserve the greatest love. Sometimes people and parents are not able to do that. That's on them. There's nothing you could have done or not done to change this. It's not your responsibility. Your only job is to be you.'

Sara's tears come all at once. Sakura immediately pulls her in, wishing she could take this part of her story away, to take away her pain. And also knowing, in that moment, that it's precisely this that makes this her story. And her only part is to hold in love.

Holding her out from the hug, Sakura's hands firm but gentle.

'I love you. You make my heart go boom bada boom!' Sakura sings the line to their song and releases one hand. Moving it from her heart to Sara's. Her little face immediately softens and despite not wanting to smile, she does.

Sakura pulls her back in and whispers,

'I hear that you're sad and big mad. I am always here for you.'

*

That Friday Sakura is almost surprised when Chris arrives to collect Sara. They meet outside the gas station in town. He knows their address, but she doesn't want the angry roar of his pickup near their home.

Getting out, Sara runs over. Handing him her overnight bag, she says goodbye to Sara, turns and walks away. Over the years, the ballooning fear at every access and subsequent dismantling has shrunk. It's a little niggle at best.

Reminding herself that he has nothing on her. Nothing to fear.

She remembers the first time she felt no fear. The moment after Sara's third birthday. Her moment to integrate all bits of herself. Her moment to say no. No more. Chris was dropping Sara home and, not unusually, he was in a mood. She could read it from across the street. Handing the bag over, Sara ran ahead. Turning to walk away. He called after her.

'The wellies you sent out are too small and gave her blisters.'

Hearing the words, Sakura kept walking and said one word, 'Right.' Sakura's heart raced. Trying to stop the smile that got bigger on her face.

A victory only she witnessed. She could almost hear the shuffle of his brain.

Sara pushed the door open, Sakura right behind. Not turning around. A mumbled word.

With a kick of the kerb, he was gone.

CHAPTER 78

Jack is calling over for a visit. Home from Toronto for the weekend, having continued working there after University. She had been out to see the cabin before they signed contracts.

Sakura hears her car come off the small road. It's easy to hear someone coming. Two neighbours are on either side. To the right is a much bigger cabin. To the left and back is one similar in size to theirs, hard to see with all the trees. Over time she will get to know her neighbours. At a distance at first. The winter will bring them closer together. Out with their mini snow ploughs.

The Tremblays from the big cabin will always plough her short lane. Thanks, said in cakes, often chocolate, and offering to help a friend of a friend's horse. The cakes Sara will make with her in white, calm, short winter days.

Jack gets out and runs over.

'Oh my God, it's beautiful, Sakura, I can't believe it's yours.'

Jack hasn't changed over the years. Her figure and hair are similar. Lighter maybe. Blonde streaks. Her nails are done. Always looking so clean, together, neat.

Sakura is in her jodhpurs, having helped Tye out earlier with a horse. The easing out that will never fully ease. And she doesn't care.

'I know, can't believe it either. Come on, let me show you around.'

Walking around the cabin. Things beginning to say home. Walking into Sara's room. Jack notices the bunting she got her last summer.

‘Ah, that looks lovely there. I bet Sara decided where it would go.’ Jack laughs, reaching up and touching the last triangle.

‘Of course.’ Sakura laughs too, knowing Sara is her own person. Knows her own mind. A mind that pulls Sakura’s insecurities into full focus, that questions everything, having learnt not to cower behind fear. This is largely down to Sakura’s openness. Everything in the open can be held.

Pushing the door out into the yard and paddocks, they walk side by side.

‘Sakura, it’s amazing you did all this, with everything going on and raising Sara.’

Reaching in, linking arms. Jack seems smaller beside her. Sakura wants to quell the fears she can feel seeping into her through their mixed limbs.

‘I did, but not without help from you, from Mom, from Tye, from everyone.’

‘Yes, but you did it.’ Jack jumps in. ‘Look at me, working in a big city, rent takes most of my wages. You have your own home. It’s not that I don’t like my job. It’s just that at times you know…’ Her voice trails off.

Sakura knows. Sakura stops walking. Turns and faces Jack.

‘You are the smartest person I know. Acing your post-grad, getting that special recognition award. I was so proud of you that day with your cap and gown, you are amazing. You have your own cabin to find, and you will. Meanwhile, when you want to get away from the hustle of the city, we’ll be here.’

Jack smiles. ‘Only if you don’t make me get on a horse.’

Returning to linking arms.

‘You might have to muck out the stables though.’ Sakura playfully shoves her to one side.

Inside, Sakura makes lunch. Together they sit. Sakura takes out the picture of the horse arriving next week.

'He's a beauty, look at you, Sakura, the horse whisperer.'

Sakura gives her that look. Forehead creased. Head tilted.

'Come on, one more thing I want to show you.'

Sakura takes her down to the big tree furthest from the cabin.

'See, here is my mark,' Sakura points to an etching, shoulder high on the old bark, 'and this is Sara's.'

'Cute, of course, it's a butterfly.' Jack runs her hand over both.

'You decide what your mark will be and make it.' Handing her the metal pick, Sakura walks away. 'Meet you back inside.'

At her car door, Sakura hugs Jack goodbye. She will be back home in two weeks for the folk music summer festival. Letting her go with ease. No longer angry for her lack of understanding. She hasn't lived what Sakura has lived. She has had her heart broken. But it hasn't been pummelled. Something Sakura once resented. Seeping into the old line. Taking up residence. *Why me*?

This, Sakura came to realize, was her greatest asset. Helping horses.

CHAPTER 79

Flying High arrived. Settling into his stable they managed to fix up in time. Sakura delighted how professional it looks, having spent the previous few days cleaning out the last of the dirt. Holding the anxiety of expectations at bay.

Sakura waves goodbye to the owner. His horse truck turns, raising a trail of dust as it leaves the lane.

Her mom is keeping Sara for the night. Giving her space to focus on her first client. Sakura and *Flying High* alone. Tye will be over later.

The owner filled Sakura in. Here, he is just a horse. Away from his intense training schedule and broken ambitions. His sporting calendar stopped short two months ago, after a miss at a high-stakes competition. Balking at the water jumps, throwing his rider off. Since then, he's missed other jumps. The owner tried many things and ended up here at her small cabin.

Opening the gate to the small arena, Sakura leads the horse in. Huge limbs, glossy coat reflecting the early summer sun. Horseshoes clip clop on the pavement and then disappear into the soft ground of the arena. Here it's just the two of them. Her ritual allows the horse to relax. Snorting sounds as his head moves up and down, running with ease in circles.

Placing her hand on his muzzle. Flying High jolts back. Just then Sakura sees his fear. His trauma. Over the next few hours, they work together. Take breaks together. As the day surrenders into the night. Standing in the middle of the arena, Sakura waits. Closing her eyes. Seeing the centre of everything. Body tingling in all directions. Then she hears it. Her face softens, rounded into love.

Nostrils exhaling and inhaling. Sakura feels his breath on her right shoulder. Nuzzling. Turning around, she lays her cheek on his.

Over the following days, Sakura uses everything she knows. Saying goodbye to Flying High, she waits to hear. A week later, she receives an email.

Whatever you did worked. I can't thank you enough. I have to say I was sceptical about bringing Flying High to you at first. But it worked. He just won The Royal Summer Fair. Thank you.

Yes! Sakura punches the air. Almost hitting the ceiling fan. Dancing around, arms and legs moving in every direction. Sara arrives in from outside. Her face surprised at Mama dancing alone in the kitchen.

'Come on, let's dance.' Taking Sara's hand they twirl, laughing until they both end up in a heap on the floor. Getting up, Sakura remembers to feed the horses. Two arrived earlier in the week.

'We'd better go.' Pulling Sara's hand and helping her off the floor.

'Okay, let's go feed Apple and Pear.' Looking up at Sakura, waiting for a reaction.

'That's not their names,' Sakura says in exaggerated tones.

'Yes, it is.' Sara laughs and giggles, repeating Apple and Pear all the way out to the stables.

Filling the hay bales and their water trays. Sara stands back. Happy to stay at a safe distance. Pulling at the bucket of things. Sakura moves around each horse, brushing down the day's work.

Bolting the doors, she washes her hands under the nearby tap. It's cold and knowing this doesn't change her pulling hands back each time. Picking up an old cloth, Sakura dries her hands, then scoops Sara up in her arms.

Walking into the evening sun. Sara pulls away in a sudden jolt.

'Look, Mama, it's a white butterfly.' Sara turns Sakura's head with both hands.

'I see it, I see it.'

Flapping wings. Fly high. Gone

Acknowledgements

White Butterfly is only possible thanks to Suzanne Power who held a light where darkness lies.

And to Mark Turner who through his hard work, belief, and humor brought *White Butterfly* home.

Thank you to my family and friends for their ongoing support.